The
Shop Girl's
Soldier

KAREN DICKSON

**SIMON &
SCHUSTER**

London · New York · Sydney · Toronto · New Delhi

A CBS COMPANY

First published in Great Britain by Simon & Schuster UK Ltd, 2020
A CBS COMPANY

Copyright © Karen Dickson, 2020

The right of Karen Dickson to be identified as author
of this work has been asserted in accordance with the
Copyright, Designs and Patents Act, 1988.

1 3 5 7 9 10 8 6 4 2

Simon & Schuster UK Ltd
1st Floor
222 Gray's Inn Road
London WC1X 8HB

Simon & Schuster Australia, Sydney
Simon & Schuster India, New Delhi

www.simonandschuster.co.uk
www.simonandschuster.com.au
www.simonandschuster.co.in

A CIP catalogue record for this book
is available from the British Library

Paperback ISBN: 978-1-4711-8549-6
eBook ISBN: 978-1-4711-8550-2

Typeset in Bembo by M Rules
Printed and bound by CPI Group (UK) Ltd, Croydon, CR0 4YY

MIX
Paper from
responsible sources
FSC® C020471

For my husband, John, with love

And
Stuart Martin Ralph (1965-2018)

I miss you, my friend.

PART ONE

CHAPTER ONE

1905

'Jack, wait!' Ellie-May Bramhall scrambled up the slippery steps from the beach. One hand held up the hem of her dirty pinafore, the other clutched a glass bottle, caked in mud and slime. Her nostrils were filled with the stench of damp and rot, her ears with the haunting cry of seagulls wheeling overhead and the rush and hiss of the surf on the shingle beach beyond the rotting wooden groynes.

She saw Jack's lips move in reply, but his words were whipped away by the chill wind blowing off the English Channel.

She shivered. Thick mud oozed between her frozen toes and splattered her skinny calves. She reached the top of the steps, almost slipping on the carpet of slimy moss, and crouched down to inspect the motley collection of flotsam and jetsam left behind by the outgoing tide. Apart from her mud-caked bottle, there were a couple of buttons, a china plate miraculously intact, and a selection of tin household items.

'Not bad for an afternoon's work.' Jack strolled towards her, salt water sloshing from the tin pail he swung by the handle, splashing onto legs that were as thin as a bird's. 'If we catch Mister Rag 'n' Bone in a good mood it'll be pie and mash for Ma and me tonight.'

In anticipation of the meal, Jack's stomach rumbled loudly. He grinned and rubbed his belly.

'Did you skip dinner again, Jack?' Ellie-May scowled, her small, freckled nose crinkling.

'Ma didn't have anything in the house,' her friend replied with a shrug, as if it were no big deal. He sloshed the briny water over the assorted objects, and Ellie-May rubbed at them with her half-frozen fingers, ridding them of the thick, glutinous tidal mud.

'Why didn't you come round ours for some bread and dripping?' she chided him sternly, as she rinsed her hands and feet and padded over to where she'd left her shoes and stockings. 'You know you're always welcome.'

'Ma said I'm not to make a nuisance of myself.'

'Oh, Jack. Don't be silly. You're never a nuisance. Mum loves having you around.' She grinned. At ten, she was already tall for her age, skinny, with pale, freckled skin and hair the colour of the freshly dug-up carrots her Dad grew on his allotment. Her eyes were the shade of a forest glade, flecked with yellow, and fringed by pale blonde lashes.

Older than Ellie-May by three weeks, Jack stood an inch

taller. He had never known his father, but his unruly mop of dark hair and dark, almost black eyes, hinted at some exotic ancestry. Rumours about Jack's parentage abounded. With her fancy way of talking, Verity Pickup had always been something of an outcast, and local gossip had it that she had been disowned by her wealthy family after allowing herself to be seduced by an Irish gypsy who'd scarpered as soon as she got in the family way.

Jack ran a hand through his thick hair, flashing Ellie-May a sheepish grin. 'Your Mum's got a heart of gold, all right,' Jack grinned. 'I don't like to take advantage of her kind nature, that's all.' The truth was – and he would never admit it to himself, never mind to Ellie-May – he was ashamed of the permanently distressed state in which he and his mother lived. He loved his ma with all his heart, and he'd flatten anyone who dared to say a word against her, but he knew his ma's child-rearing methods bordered on neglect, and being so often in Eileen Bramhall's warm, cosy kitchen only served to highlight what was missing in his own home.

'Right,' he said, pushing his thoughts aside and turning his attention to their trove of treasure. Seemingly oblivious to the chill of the sea breeze, Jack whipped off his too-small jumper and used it to wrap up the items.

He dried his hands on his ragged shorts and straightened up, his gaze sweeping the horizon, savouring the salty tang of the sea air on his lips. He loved it here, down by the shore. Southampton was a busy port and he loved to watch the ships: the dredgers and fishing trawlers, the cargo ships with hulls low in the grey waters, the sailing ships and sturdy little tugboats, each puffing clouds of black smoke from their funnels.

Ellie-May smoothed down her pinafore and they set off along the harbour front, the soles of her shoes crunching bits of shingle. Jack was barefoot as usual. Even in winter he went barefoot, his toes alternately blue with cold or red and swollen with chilblains. Eileen had given Jack a pair of shoes last winter which Ellie-May's brother, Bert, had outgrown. She'd been livid a few days later when, spotting Jack hobbling barefoot across the frozen yard to the privy, she discovered his feckless mother had pawned them. With a temper to match her flame-red hair, Eileen Bramhall had marched straight next-door to give Verity Pickup what for. The whole street had heard the exchange.

The water was grey and choppy. Ahead of them was the bustle and noise of the docks; huge cranes silhouetted against a pewter sky, hulking dark warehouses, the smell of ozone, fish and tar filling their senses.

Jack grabbed hold of Ellie-May's hand and hurried her across the street, dodging a tram and a horse-drawn cart laden with bolts of cloth, before darting down a narrow stinking alley inhabited by mangy cats and ragged-looking children. Jumping over stagnant puddles, Jack led Ellie-May further into the labyrinth. A woman's laugh sounded from an upstairs window, a harsh, mirthless sound that set Ellie-May's hair on end. The hollow-eyed urchins watched them lethargically from the doorways of dilapidated tenement buildings, rows of washing dangling above their heads. The air was heavy with the greasy odour of stale cooking and urine.

They turned a sharp corner and came to an abrupt halt. Their way was barred by a wooden gate behind which a dog snarled viciously. Without a second's hesitation, Jack pushed the gate open, sending the dog into a frenzy. A large creature of indeterminable breed with short, black fur, balding in places, it foamed at the mouth as it strained against its chain.

'You'll be all right as long as you stay out of his reach,' Jack reassured Ellie-May in a low voice. Terrified she would be torn limb from limb by the ferocious beast, Ellie-May flattened herself against the brick wall, well out of the way of the frightful jaws, clinging tightly to Jack's hand. The yard was piled high with orange crates and battered tea chests. In a corner, a moth-eaten piebald pony cropped dispassionately at a bundle of damp hay.

The door of the ramshackle dwelling burst open and a man emerged, blinking in the murky light. He was short in stature and very thin, with facial features that reminded Ellie-May of a weasel. Greasy grey hair fell over his shoulders in lank strands. She huddled closer to Jack. She was terrified of Mister Rag 'n' Bone, always had been, ever since she'd first heard his gruff tones echoing down their street. Whenever she heard him coming, she would run indoors until he'd moved on.

'Quiet, Brutus!' he snarled at the dog. Brutus gave one last, throaty growl and fell silent, but continued to stare at the children with bloodshot eyes, his body quivering. 'You again,' Mister Rag 'n' Bone grunted. He ran long, nicotine-stained fingers through his greasy hair. 'All right, sunshine, what rubbish are you offloading this time?'

'It's not rubbish, mister,' Jack contradicted him confidently. 'It's good stuff, honest.'

Mister Rag 'n' Bone sucked on his yellow teeth, and nodded. 'All right, then. Let's have a look.'

Keeping a wary eye on the dog, Jack inched forward, and unwrapped his bundle. The rag 'n' bone man glanced at the items in Jack's outstretched hands with disinterest. 'That it?' he growled, his thin lips twisting into a derisive sneer. 'You enjoy wasting my time, sunshine?'

'No, sir,' Jack squeaked. He cleared his throat, determined not to let the rag 'n' bone man see his desperation. 'What about this plate, sir,' he said, his voice firmer now. He met the man's rodent-like stare. 'Look.' He held it to the light. 'There isn't a chip or a crack to be seen. It must be worth something.'

Ellie-May held her breath and crossed her fingers tightly, trying not to be intimidated by Mister Rag 'n' Bone's fearsome stare, and praying that they had caught him in a charitable mood. If he paid Jack a few pennies her friend wouldn't go to bed hungry. She hated it when Jack went without meals. Her mum did what she could, slipping Jack a slice of bread and dripping every so often, or inviting him in for a bowl of mutton stew, but what with eight mouths of her own to feed, Eileen never had much to spare.

The old rag 'n' bone man sighed deeply. 'All right, then. Come on.' He indicated the dark doorway with a toss of his head. 'You'd better come inside.' He glanced up at the surrounding tenement buildings and tapped his nose with a dirty forefinger. 'Don't want people nosy-poking my business.' Ellie-May exhaled in relief and flashed Jack a triumphant smile.

Mister Rag 'n Bone cleared his throat, and spat a glob of phlegm across the yard. 'I must be going bleedin' soft in my old age,' he grumbled as they followed him indoors.

A single oil lamp cut through the gloom, revealing a windowless room crammed with bric-a-brac and items of mismatched furniture in various stages of disrepair. Ellie-May wrinkled her nose at the fetid air, hovering in the doorway as the rag 'n' bone man squeezed his way over to a scuffed chest of drawers in one corner of the room. The wood was swollen with damp and it took him several attempts to get the drawer open and remove the battered tin box from within.

'Here.' He groped his way back through the maze of furniture to drop a handful of coins into Jack's cupped hands. 'Don't say I'm not a generous old sod. Now, be off with you,' he said gruffly, 'before I change my mind.'

'Thank you, mister.' Terrified the old man would have second thoughts, Jack gripped Ellie-May's hand and dragged her outside. The dog barked again, rattling its chain as it lunged at them. Ellie-May shrunk against Jack as they edged their way along the fence. They practically fell out of the gate, slamming it shut and collapsing against it, shaking with relief.

'There's enough here for a decent supper,' Jack told Ellie-May, his dark eyes shining with delight. 'Come on, we'll stop at the pie shop on the way home.'

With the tantalising aroma of meat gravy filling their nostrils, they rounded the corner into Church Street. The sun had come out, bathing the grim terraced row in soft yellow light.

Imagining biting into the soft pastry crust, the thick, meaty juices running down his chin, it took Jack a few seconds to register the commotion going on outside his front door. But eventually the sight stopped him in his tracks.

'Jack ...!' Ellie-May crashed into him, her protest dying on her lips as she took in the scene unfolding outside Jack's house, halfway up the street. Her mother, Eileen, was standing with her arms around Verity, who was loudly berating a burly, bald-headed man loading furniture onto a waiting cart.

Ellie-May gasped, recognising the sticks of cheap furniture as coming from Jack's home, the door of which a thickset man was in the process of boarding up. The sound of his hammer echoed down the street. Children who had moments before been engaged in games of hopscotch and tag, stood pressed against the soot-stained terraced walls, faces solemn. Their mothers stood in huddled groups, arms akimbo, watching with a mixture of embarrassment and pity.

'Ma!' Jack dropped the pies and ran, all thoughts of supper forgotten in his desire to protect his mother. The pies lay in the gutter, gravy staining the torn paper bag. Ellie-May gave it a brief glance, then hurried after Jack.

'Please!' Verity screamed, straining against Eileen's embrace. 'Have some pity. Just give me a few more days. I'll get the money somehow, I promise. Have some mercy, I beg you.'

'Sorry, love.' The bailiff at least had the grace to look embarrassed, noticing Ellie-May as she hovered nearby, unsure about what to do. 'It's out of our hands.'

'Ma, it's all right, Ma,' Jack said, his voice soft and gentle, as if he were talking to a frightened child.

'What will become of us?' Verity cried. Her knees gave way and she would have fallen, had Eileen and Jack not held her up.

'You not got any relatives who'll take you in?' the bailiff enquired, his hooded gaze raking the assembled group of onlookers. 'Friends?'

'They can stay with us,' Eileen spoke up. 'Come on, Verity, love.' She gave the hysterical woman a gentle shake. 'You can stay at ours tonight. Jack can go in with the boys and you can come in with me. My Sid won't mind bunking down in the kitchen.' The bailiff gave her a grateful nod. This was the worst part of his job, throwing powerless women and children out into the street.

Between Jack and Eileen, they managed to bustle Verity into the house. Like its neighbours, number 12 Church Street was a two-up two-down terraced house. They shared a privy with four other families.

Once Eileen got Verity settled at the kitchen table, she sent Ellie-May out into the yard to fill the kettle from the communal tap. When she returned moments later, Verity was hunched over the table, her head in her hands. She had ceased wailing, but her thin shoulders shook with silent sobs. Jack knelt on the floor beside her. He met Ellie-May's frightened gaze, his expression grim. His friend hovered in the doorway, her heart thumping.

'What's happened?' she croaked. Tears burned behind her eyes.

'We've been evicted,' Jack spat angrily.

'Drink this, Verity, love.' Eileen set a mug of strong beef tea in front of Jack's mother. Her fingers twitched in acknowledgment but she didn't look up.

'Come on, Ma,' Jack whispered encouragingly. 'It's good for the shock.'

Verity slowly raised her head, her red-rimmed eyes staring at her son as if she'd never laid eyes on him before. She had been a pretty girl once, with blue eyes and wheat-blonde hair, but years of poverty had taken its toll. Now her thinning blonde hair hung in a greasy plait down her back. Years of poor diet had ruined her teeth. Despair had etched deep lines into her face. Long, thin fingers, nails bitten to the quick, snaked around the mug. She lifted it to thin, chapped lips.

'That's it, Ma,' Jack encouraged her. 'Drink up. We'll sort something out, I promise.'

'It's the workhouse for us, Jack.' Verity swallowed a mouthful of tea, wincing as it scalded her throat. She glanced up at her neighbour. Eileen was slathering butter on thick slices of bread. 'You've always been so kind to us, Eileen,' she said, fresh tears welling. 'You're the only one in the street who's ever given me the time of day. I'll miss you.'

Eileen set the plate of bread and butter in front of Jack, who eyed it hungrily.

'Go on, lad, tuck in.' Jack took a slice, biting into it greedily. Ellie-May crept closer and crouched beside her friend, an unfamiliar ache in her chest.

'Like I said, you're welcome to stay here tonight, Verity.' Eileen pulled out a chair and sat down opposite the woman who had been her next-door neighbour for ten years. She took Verity's hand. 'Things will look better in the morning.'

Verity shook her head, a look of steely determination in her eyes. The rest of her tea remained untouched, tendrils of steam curling upwards. 'No, we'll go now,' she said dully. 'No point delaying the inevitable.'

'It's a long walk, Verity, love,' Eileen cautioned her. 'You might not make it before they shut the gates for the night.'

The pain in Ellie-May's chest grew more intense. Jack was going to the workhouse? It must be a mistake, a cruel joke. Jack couldn't go away. She wouldn't be able to bear it. She let out a sob. Eileen reached over and stroked her red hair, her own heart heavy. It would break Ellie-May's heart to lose Jack. They'd been inseparable since they were old enough to toddle into each other's houses.

'Can't Jack stay with us, Mum?' Ellie-May implored, a tear trickling down her pale, freckled cheek. 'Our Bert will be off to sea in a few weeks. Jack can go in with Arthur, can't he?'

'He'd be welcome to stay, Verity,' Eileen offered. 'Just until you're sorted out.'

Verity shook her head. 'Thank you, but I can't be parted from him.' Pulling herself together with noticeable effort, she gave Jack what she hoped was an encouraging smile. She'd let him down, she knew that, and she knew it was selfish of her to insist he went with her, but she couldn't manage without him. She needed him. 'We'll look after each other, won't we, Jack? Just like we've always done.'

Eileen pursed her lips, but held her tongue. Now was not the time to remind Verity that it was usually Jack who did the looking after, rather than the other way around.

'Come on, Jack.' Verity pushed her chair back. 'We've a long walk ahead of us. Thank you for your hospitality, Eileen, but we'd better get going.' Jack got to his feet, his head hanging in shame. His heart felt too large for his chest.

Eileen sighed, and got up, flinging a plump arm around Verity's drooping shoulders.

'I hope things get better for you, lass, I really do,' she said with feeling. For all her faults as a mother, Eileen was very fond of Verity. She certainly wouldn't wish her in the work-house. Heck, she wouldn't wish that fate on her worst enemy.

'Don't go, Jack,' Ellie-May whispered. They were standing on the front step. Many of the neighbours had gone indoors, respecting Verity's privacy in what they realized was a dreadfully shaming moment. Only the children, making the most of the late afternoon sunshine, still lingered, pausing in their play to watch the goings-on.

'I've got to, El,' Jack said, his voice low and thick with the shame of it all. His cheeks burned. He knew his ma found managing her money difficult, she always had. Why couldn't the landlord be patient? He'd be able to get a proper job in eighteen months' time when he turned twelve. Then he'd be able to pay back every penny of rent they owed. Hot tears burned his eyes. He blinked them back. He wasn't about to cry in front of the bailiffs.

'We'll be back, El. I promise. Soon as I'm old enough to work, me and Ma will be back.'

Ellie-May nodded, desperate to believe him, yet her heart felt leaden. 'I'm frightened for you.' The threat of the dreaded workhouse hung over Southampton's impoverished streets like an ever-present shadow. An accident at work, an unexpected bill, a sudden death, and you could find yourself incarcerated within its grim, grey walls before you could say 'Jack Robinson'.

'I'll be fine, El,' Jack promised with his trademark grin. 'You know me.' His gaze swivelled towards his mother. She had started to cry again, her face pressed against Eileen's ample bosom. 'It's Ma I worry about,' Jack whispered to Ellie-May. 'She's never been very strong. I don't know how she'll survive the workhouse.'

'Hey, missus.' Both Jack and Ellie-May turned as the older of the two bailiffs approached Verity, cap in hand, his expression benevolent. Verity raised her head, blinking back the tears. She wiped the mucus from her nose with the back of her hand, a flicker of hope flaring in her eyes, only to be immediately snuffed out as the bailiff shook his head.

'We're going near to St Mary's Road,' he said, his grey eyes kind. 'You're welcome to ride along, save your legs.'

Verity glanced over at Jack, searching for guidance. He shrugged. He would never admit it, but he was terrified of the prospect of going to the workhouse. If it wasn't for his Ma he'd take Eileen up on her offer. The prospect of leaving Ellie-May behind fair broke his heart. But his ma would never cope without him. He'd always looked out for her. He wasn't about to stop now.

CHAPTER TWO

Ellie-May lay in the bed she shared with her sister, Nora. She could hear the twins, Jess and Bea, snoring softly in the other bed. Being high summer, it was still light, the last of the sun's rays moving slowly across the room. She heard whispered voices overhead. Bert and Arthur in their attic room. Perishing cold in winter, it would be as hot as Hades up there now. No wonder her brothers had trouble sleeping.

Bert was the eldest. At fifteen and ten months, he would be off to sea as soon as he reached his sixteenth birthday. Jess and Bea, the fourteen-year-old twins, were going into service come September. Both had secured places as scullery maids in two of the grand houses in Southampton's prosperous Regent's Park area.

Much as Ellie-May was dreading the imminent departure of three of her beloved siblings, she doubted their loss would compare with the misery she was experiencing right now. She missed Jack so much there was a physical ache in the pit of her stomach.

Dry-eyed, she stared up at the ceiling. Her pillow was damp from crying, but now she had no more tears to shed. Beside her, seven-year-old Nora snuffled softly, and rolled over, her strawberry-blonde hair fanning the pillow, her pixie face peaceful in repose.

Voices drifted up from the street below, people taking advantage of the pleasant summer evening. The stairs creaked. The bedroom door, already slightly ajar, opened further and Eileen peered around it, her benign expression changing to a frown when she saw Ellie-May still awake.

'Go to sleep, Ellie-May,' she whispered, crossing the room to her daughters' bed. She placed a cool hand on her hot forehead. 'Don't worry about Jack. He's a big lad. He can take care of himself.'

'But I miss him so much, Mum,' Ellie-May whispered back hoarsely. Her throat hurt from crying.

'I know you do, sweetheart, but unless Verity's fortunes change, it'll be a long time before Jack's able to escape the workhouse. You've got to try and forget about him, love.'

'I'll never forget Jack,' Ellie-May declared in horror. 'Not as long as I live.' She closed her eyes and turned her face away. Sighing, Eileen leaned over to kiss her feverish forehead.

'Goodnight, love. Go to sleep now.'

Ellie-May could hear her mother and father talking in their room across the landing, their voices too low for her to catch the words. She heard the creak of their bed, the twang of the springs. Then the house fell silent.

Watching the shadows creep across the ceiling, her eyes

grew heavy, and she finally fell asleep, wondering if Jack was missing her as much as she was missing him.

Jack was wide awake and thinking of El. He couldn't remember a day they hadn't been together, and it was a wrench knowing he was unlikely to see her again for a long time. He was also consumed by a crippling, nauseating worry for his mother. He stared up at the ceiling, listening to the snorts, grunts and occasional coughs of the other eleven boys, and wondered how anyone was meant to get any sleep.

He tugged on the thin blanket and rolled onto his side. A pale moon lit the long room. There were twelve beds, six along each wall. The barred windows were too high to see out of, though Jack doubted the view would be worth seeing anyway.

They had arrived at the workhouse at quarter to six that evening, just before the wrought-iron gates were closed for the night. The two-storey, purpose-built redbrick building was as unwelcoming as it looked, and Jack's stomach lurched as he passed between the gates clutching his mother's trembling hand. As he forced himself to cross the threshold into the bleak concrete yard, he was unable to shake the feeling he was walking into Hell itself. There wasn't a blade of grass or tree to be seen.

Before allowing them access, the weary-faced gatekeeper had summoned the warder, a thin, stern-faced fellow in an ill-fitting black coat, whose curt, 'You'll address me as Mr Jakes,' was his only greeting. Jack squeezed his mother's hand. She looked terrified, and, despite his own misgivings, his heart went out to her. He gave her an encouraging smile as they crossed the bare yard and slowly climbed the steps to the front entrance, the huge doors clanging shut behind them with frightening finality.

The warden delivered them to a well-furnished office where they were greeted cordially by a pompous-looking man.

'Jeremiah Fisher, custodian of this establishment,' the man introduced himself. His voice was curiously high-pitched. Almost as wide as he was tall, he had a florid complexion, and looked as if he was turning prematurely bald, a condition he attempted to disguise by combing strands of well-oiled mouse-brown hair across his shiny pink pate.

'Please, sit down.' He gestured at two straight-back chairs placed at angles in front of a large leather-topped desk before settling himself heavily into his own chair. It was upholstered in red leather and creaked noisily as he made himself comfortable. He folded his plump hands together and beamed at Verity and Jack across the desk, his ill-fitting jacket gaping over his round belly.

'Now, it is my pleasure to welcome you both.' Mr Fisher placed his hands on the desk and leaned forward. It was hot and stuffy in the office, for, despite the summer warmth, the fire was lit and his face gleamed with perspiration. Jack squirmed, feeling the prickle of sweat down his spine as Mr Fisher's small, blue eyes settled on him, his plump lips parting to reveal a set of small, white teeth.

'Let me be clear,' he said. 'You are not prisoners here. You are free to leave at any time, Mrs Pickup, although you would have to leave Jack here, unless you were able to prove you were able to care for him adequately.'

Jack shot his mother a quick glance. Her face was very white. She nodded in resignation.

'I haven't anywhere else to go.'

Mr Fisher nodded dispassionately. He'd seen it all before.

He spent the next half hour explaining the many rules and regulations and preaching over St Mary's benevolence to the largely undeserving poor, all the while laboriously copying down their details in a large leather-bound ledger. Whether by some prearranged signal or because he had been loitering out in the corridor the entire time and heard his superior's customary final question, the door opened and Mr Jakes entered, jangling a large bunch of keys like a jailor.

In spite of Mr Fisher's assertion to the contrary, jailor was exactly what he was, Jack mused a short time later as they were hustled down one grim corridor after another. Doors were locked, movement restricted, husbands and wives separated, brothers and sisters parted, and, as they were about to realize, mothers torn from their children.

'You get an hour visit every Sunday afternoon,' Mr Jakes informed Jack imperiously as they were met at the entrance to the women's quarters by his sour-faced wife, Jenny.

'Don't separate me from my son,' Verity pleaded, as she was dragged unceremoniously down the corridor. 'Please, he's all I've got.'

'Ma!' Jack called after her in anguish.

'That's enough,' Mr Jakes told him sternly, maintaining a firm grip on Jack's arm. 'If you behave and don't give me any trouble, you'll see her on Sunday.'

Jakes led Jack to a storeroom where he was kitted out in a pair of grey trousers and a shirt, before a sullen-faced inmate about a year or so older than Jack marched him to the boys' quarters. They arrived just in time for evening prayers. Jack knelt on the hard floor with about thirty other boys ranging in age from seven to twelve, the vicar's monotonous voice wafting over his head, determined that he and Verity would leave St Mary's at the first available opportunity.

Verity sank to her knees, shaking uncontrollably. Her hair had come loose from its bun and hung in a wild mess around her blotchy face. She had been forcibly stripped of her clothes by Jenny and another, equally miserable female warder whose name she hadn't bothered to remember, and dressed in the rough homespun skirt, blouse and cap worn by all the female inmates. When she had first entered the huge refectory, the sight of the rows and rows of spiritless, hollow-eyed women seated at the long wooden tables, had set her teeth on edge. The words 'GOD IS GOOD' and 'GOD IS JUST', painted high on the brick walls did little to assuage her fear, and she had given into the panic she had been fighting to keep at bay ever since the bailiffs first knocked on her door.

It had taken three of them to subdue her, the sharp sting of Jenny's fleshy palm connecting with her cheek finally shocking her into submissive silence. They had left her in the corner, weeping quietly, attracting little interest from her fellow inmates as Jenny led them in a lengthy prayer and dismissed them to bed.

'Come on, love.' The voice was kind. Verity glanced up at the old crone peering down at her. It took her a while to realize that she wasn't that old, not really. Perhaps only in her late thirties, but lack of hope and despair had robbed her of her youth. 'You'll get used to it,' the woman said, her tone friendly as she helped Verity to her feet. 'I'm Ruby, by the way. Ruby King.'

Verity hiccoughed. 'Verity Pickup.'

'Pleased to meet you, Verity. Come on, the dormitory's this way.'

As they made their way slowly down yet another draughty corridor and up a narrow flight of stairs, Ruby filled Verity in on her own situation. Her husband had been killed in an accident two years previously and, with five little ones to feed, and an elderly mother-in-law to care for, daily existence had grown ever more precarious until, when the last stick of furniture had been pawned, they were finally evicted by a landlord who had, according to Ruby, been as patient as was humanly possible.

'God bless him,' Ruby whispered. She had then made the heart-breaking decision to throw herself on the mercy of the parish.

'My Terry is in the boys' quarters,' she said. 'He's twelve. The others are all under ten so they're in the children's section. I had little Mark with me, but he turned five in April so now he's there too.' She forced a smile. 'At least I get to see them all on Sunday.' She laid her thin arm across Verity's shoulders. 'You'll see your boy then too. That's something to look forward to, isn't it?'

Apart from a quick nod of the head and a whispered 'hello', Jack had no time at all to get acquainted with his fellow inmates as they were herded single file towards the dormitories. He was allocated a bed at the far end of the long room. The metal-frame bed was covered with a thin blanket and the pillow was stained from years of use. Each boy stood in silence beside his bed while Jakes intoned yet another lengthy prayer, then it was into bed and lights out.

'Straight to sleep now,' Jakes barked from the doorway, the thin light from the corridor casting a halo of light across the bare floorboards. 'You know the rules, but for the benefit of our new boy, anyone caught talking after lights out will go without meals tomorrow. Goodnight, God bless.'

Now Jack lay on his side. His tummy rumbled. Apart from the bread and butter Eileen had given him earlier that afternoon, he'd had nothing since, and he was starving. According to the lengthy itinerary explained by Jeremiah Fisher, Jack would have to endure an hour's physical exercise before breakfast. He suppressed a groan. He was dreading the day ahead. Used to coming and going as he pleased, the thought of being locked up and supervised twenty-four hours a day filled him with dread. He would be starting a new school, too. He knew how the other pupils viewed workhouse kids – at best with pity, at worst with scorn and derision.

But what about his ma? How would she cope, being cooped up all day? She wasn't used to hard work. Much as he loved her, he wasn't blind to her faults, and laziness was one of them. He wondered how she was coping. He doubted either of them would get much sleep.

He forced himself to look on the bright side. As soon as he was old enough he'd get a job and he'd be able to look after his ma, and El. Neither of them would have to worry about a penny. He'd take care of them, or his name wasn't Jack Pickup.

Suddenly, his bravado evaporated, and he began to cry the hot, bitter tears he'd been holding at bay ever since he'd arrived. Not wanting to be heard by his fellow inmates, he buried his face in his pillow, and eventually cried himself to sleep.

CHAPTER THREE

Ellie-May sat on the front step watching Nora and her little friends playing hopscotch on the cobbles. It was a warm evening in late August. The summer holidays were drawing to a close and she was wondering how she would manage at school without Jack by her side. She had never had to worry about bullies before. No one would dare take on Jack Pickup. He was the kindest, gentlest boy, but if anyone dared to pick on his El, he'd give them what-for.

She sighed. She missed him so much. It was as though she had lost a part of herself. She moped around the house, getting on Eileen's nerves.

'For pity's sake, Ellie-May!' Eileen had cried not ten minutes ago, shooing her daughter out into the sunshine. 'You'll trip over that bottom lip if you're not careful. Cheer up, girl!'

So here she sat, the summer sun warm on her face, the heat of the smooth stone step warming her bottom. The street teemed with children. Their mothers stood gossiping in small groups on the pavement, enjoying a brief respite from the endless household chores before their husbands arrived home demanding their supper.

A family of five had moved into Jack's old house. Eileen had been around to welcome them with a pot of tea and a plate of her light, fluffy scones. To her chagrin, Ellie-May had to admit that the Norris family were lovely, and they had quickly slotted into life on Church Street.

Their two children, Davy and Harriet, or Hattie as she was called, aged four and two respectively, were soon absorbed into seven-year-old Nora's friendship group, and Rose Norris could often be found in Eileen's kitchen enjoying a cup of tea and a chat. Tony Norris worked down at Cameron's Shipyard in Millbank Street with Sid, and the two men would often pop in to the Belvedere Arms on a Friday evening for a swift half on the way home from work.

They were coming up the road now, her dad and Tony. Tony Norris was big-boned and ruddy, with a mop of yellow hair, whereas Sid was shorter and slighter with thinning, mouse-brown hair and round spectacles that lent a somewhat owl-like air to his appearance.

'Dad!' Ellie-May jumped to her feet and ran to meet him.

'Hello, sweetheart.' He swung her round. Slapping Tony on his broad back, Sid bade his neighbour a fond farewell and they parted, each to his own front door.

Hanging his cap and jacket on the peg in the tiny porch, Sid passed through the seldom-used front room with its polished dresser, large mirror over the empty fireplace, and the ever-pervading smell of beeswax polish, into the kitchen where Eileen stood at the range, stirring a pot of stew and dumplings. The back door was open to the breeze and the smell from the privy reminded Sid that it was their turn to clean it out. He'd have a stern word with Jess later about letting her duties slide.

'Good day?' Eileen turned from the stove, her round face flushed from heat of the range.

'Not bad. My shoulder's been playing up again so the foreman's talking about putting me on lighter duties for a bit, just until it's properly healed.'

'And so he should,' Eileen remarked, using a tea towel to lift the supper plates out of the warmer. 'That was a nasty fall you had, and on company time too. It was wrong of management to insist you went back to work so soon. You should have taken another week off, in my opinion.'

'Yes, well, don't go on, love. What's done is done.' He sat down at the table, which was laid for supper, and bent down to untie his boot laces.

'I'll rub some of that salve on it later,' Eileen said. She laid her hand on Sid's arm, her tone softening. 'That'll ease the stiffness a bit.'

'That'll be a help, love. Thanks.' Sid gave her hand an affectionate squeeze and sat back in his chair, his gaze following his wife as she bustled about the kitchen, his eyes filled with adoration.

Eighteen years they'd been married that spring, and he still felt the same way about his Eileen now as he had the first time he'd laid eyes on her standing on the quayside almost twenty years ago. She'd been a bonnie lass of sixteen then, her striking red hair streaming down her back, her pale skin almost translucent in the pale winter light, her emerald-green coat matching perfectly the colour of her eyes. She had been waiting for a friend, she'd told him when he had finally plucked up the courage to talk to her. Thirty-five bitterly cold minutes later they both realized Eileen had been stood up so he'd offered to buy her a cup of tea. To his surprise, she had accepted, and they were married fifteen months later.

'Did you see our Ellie-May?' Eileen asked, placing the warmed plates on the table.

'I did. Still moping, is she?'

Eileen sighed. 'I'm at my wits end with the child. She's taken Jack's leaving very hard.'

'They were always together,' said Sid with a chuckle. 'Two for the price of one, we used to say, do you remember? You never got one without the other. No wonder it's knocked her for six. They were friends to the exclusion of all others. It'll probably do our Ellie-May good to mix with other kids a bit more.'

'Well, she'll be back at school soon,' Eileen removed her apron and hung it over the back of a chair. Peering into the mirror on the wall, she fluffed up her hair, dampened by the steam. 'Concentrating on her schoolwork will take her mind off Jack.' She set the pot of stew and dumplings in the centre of the table and went to the door to call her brood in for their supper.

*

The following Sunday at church, Ellie-May gazed down at the shiny tips of her black shoes, letting the vicar's monotone voice flow in one ear and out the other. As usual, the church of St Peter on Northam Street was packed. Ellie-May's family occupied an entire pew. Bored, she risked a sideways glance. Her mother sat beside her, prim and proper in her Sunday frock and hat, her white-gloved hands folded piously in her lap. Sid sat at her other side, uncomfortable and hot in his suit, his scalp glistening in the shafts of multi-coloured light streaming in through the stained-glass windows. The twins, Bea and Jess, both wearing new dresses, sat soberly on Sid's other side. Bea's dress was pink lawn, Jess's blue. The only way strangers could distinguish between them was down to their preference for wearing different colours, Bea preferring bright feminine colours while Jess favoured more earthy hues. This would be their last service in St Peter's. Now fourteen, they would be leaving for their new positions that very afternoon. Nora sat beside Jess, trying desperately hard not to fidget lest she feel the cruel pinch of her elder sister's fingers. A pinch from Jess had been known to leave a bruise that could last for a week.

Bert, lanky and spotty, languished at the end of the pew. The eldest, and the only one of the six children not to have inherited Eileen's fiery-red hair, his mouse-brown locks were plastered neatly across his head. Disinterested in the sermon, his gaze was fixed on his favourite of the stained-glass windows. Set to the left of the altar, it depicted the disciples' boat being tossed about on a stormy sea. He closed his eyes and daydreamed about his own imminent adventures on the high seas.

Eleven-year-old Arthur was serving as altar boy. Clothed in angelic-white, he sat solemn and watchful near the altar, his unwavering gaze fixed on the vicar lest he miss his cue, his short-cropped red hair as stiff and straight as a wire brush.

Ellie-May's stomach contracted painfully every time she thought of her sisters' imminent departure. It would be strange, her and Nora having the whole front bedroom to themselves. She wouldn't have to complain about the twins' stockings draped across the floor, or listen to the them giggling and whispering under the covers at night, sharing secrets Ellie-May was too young to share.

In three weeks' time, when Bert joined his ship, there would only be the three of them − Ellie-May, Arthur and Nora − at home with Mum and Dad. Why did everyone have to leave? she wondered, her green-eyed gaze raking the sea of worshippers as the congregation rose to sing one of her mum's favourite hymns.

She'd lost Jack, and now she was losing Jess, Bea and Bert. She had never been very close to her older sisters. Being twins they hadn't needed anyone else, and anyway, Ellie-May had always had Jack. She wondered what he was doing. Was he as miserable as she was, or had he forgotten her already? She'd asked Mum if she could write to Jack, and Eileen had bought her some writing paper and a stamp. With great excitement, Ellie-May had written her letter and taken it to the post office. Despite Eileen's warning not to get her hopes up, she had been eagerly awaiting a reply ever since.

'You really do need to stop moping, Ellie-May,' Eileen said, her voice laced with exasperation as they emerged into the September sunshine. Birds warbled in the surrounding trees. Children, released from the restraints of church, chased each other amongst the centuries-old gravestones.

'Remember Jack with fondness,' she went on gently, ushering her brood towards the gate, glancing around for Sid who came hurrying down the path after them. 'I know it's hard, but clinging onto the hope that he'll come back is only making it worse for yourself, love. It'll be a good couple of years before Jack is old enough to leave the workhouse. You need to try and forget about him. It'll be easier that way.'

Pouting, Ellie-May sullenly dragged her feet as she followed along behind her family, unshed tears burning her eyelids. No matter what anyone said, Jack would come back, he'd promised. She would never forget him. How could she? He was part of her. *I'll never forget you, Jack,* she vowed under her breath. *I promise, I'll never forget you, as long as I live.*

Verity lay on her thin, lumpy mattress, staring listlessly up at the patch of pale blue sky, the only bit of the outside world that was visible through the high windows of the infirmary. The brightness hurt her eyes. She squeezed them shut. Even though her skin was bathed in sweat, and her eyes glittered feverishly, her teeth were chattering. She felt chilled to the bone. She was vaguely aware of the early morning hustle and bustle. The daily routine of the infirmary never changed. She exhaled a long, shuddering breath, claw-like fingers clutching at the bedclothes in agitation, a slow smile spreading across her face as his image swam into her mind. Seamus Pickup. The handsome Irish gypsy-boy to whom she had willingly given her heart and her innocence. Then one crisp autumn morning, he was gone, the still-smouldering campfire the only sign that he'd ever been there at all.

She opened her eyes as Seamus's dark, olive features dissolved to reveal Ruby's pale blue eyes regarding her anxiously. She was perched on the edge of the narrow bed.

'Try and eat something, Verity, love,' Ruby coaxed softly, leaning forward and lifting a spoon of watery porridge to her friend's parched, cracked lips. Verity turned her face away.

'You need to build your strength up, love,' Ruby tried again. It frightened her how quickly Verity had changed in the few weeks she had been in the infirmary. Her hair was now brittle and coarse. Her skin was dry and chapped. An ugly sore had erupted on her upper lip, and there were dark shadows beneath her eyes.

'I'm not hungry,' she croaked. Her throat hurt and her cracked lips made talking difficult.

Still clutching the bowl, Ruby forced herself to sound cheerful. 'At least you'll get to see Jack later,' she said in a tone that belied her anxiety. 'That'll cheer you up.'

Verity didn't answer. Ruby let out another sigh and got to her feet. 'I must go or I'll be late for chapel. I'm on duty again tomorrow. I'll see you then.' She leaned over and kissed Verity's hot, dry cheek. 'Perhaps you'll feel brighter then.'

Across the yard from the infirmary, Jeremiah Fisher was just tucking his freshly starched napkin into the collar of his shirt. He rubbed his hands together in delightful anticipation of the hearty breakfast set before him. Bacon, eggs, fried tomatoes, mushrooms and four rounds of toast, dripping with melted butter. Oh, how he loved Sunday mornings.

He picked up his knife and fork and had just opened his mouth to accept a forkful of bacon and mushrooms when there came a knock at his office door. He scowled, his mouth closing with a snap of annoyance. He glared at the door, and set his cutlery down. 'Yes?' he barked.

The door opened to admit a sheepish-looking Jakes.

'Yes, Jakes,' Mr Fisher growled irritably. 'What is it?'

'I'm sorry to disturb your breakfast, Mister Fisher, sir,' Jakes said in a tone that implied he felt no such remorse. He twisted his thin hands together, his beady gaze alighting on the heaped plate of food, the aroma of which was fair causing him to water at the mouth. Lumpy porridge and weak tea – that's what the staff got for breakfast, seven days a week, Sunday or no Sunday.

'Well,' Fisher grumbled, shoving a rasher of crispy bacon into his mouth and talking with his mouth full. 'Now you have interrupted my breakfast, would you mind divulging the reason?'

'Ah, yes.' With difficulty, Jakes dragged his hungry gaze

from his employer's breakfast and indicated, with a nod of his head, somewhere beyond the office walls. 'A gentleman to see you, sir. Says it's urgent.'

'A gentleman?' Fisher tugged the napkin from his neck and mopped at his lips. 'At this hour? On a Sunday? Does he have an appointment?'

'No, sir. But he was insistent I bring him to you immediately.' Fisher leaned back in his chair, a perplexed frown puckering his brow. 'He is a very grand gentleman, sir,' Jakes added, lowering his voice. 'Arrived in a very fine carriage.'

Fisher's' frown deepened. 'Oh, Lordy,' he sighed. 'Let's hope it isn't some God-bothering do-gooder come to ruin my day.' With one last, lingering glance at his rapidly cooling breakfast, he sighed. 'All right. Show him in.'

The words were barely out of his mouth before a tall, elegantly-dressed gentleman with slightly rounded shoulders, a grey goatee beard and mane of silver hair, strode purposefully passed Jakes, glaring at Jeremiah down his long nose.

'Lord Farquharson,' he barked without preamble. 'I'm here to collect my daughter.'

'Your daughter, Your Lordship?' Fisher blinked in surprise. He gave a high-pitched giggle. 'Surely, sir, you're mistaken? This is a refuge for paupers and orphans. No lady of breeding would ever ...'

Lord Farquharson cut him off with a wave of his ivory-tipped cane. 'She was taken in by yourselves just over two months ago. Verity Farquharson, or Pickup, as I believe she calls herself these days.' This last was said with a shudder of disgust, a wave of revulsion rippling across his distinguished features.

'Mrs Pickup?' Fisher blinked again. His visitor snorted derisively, his beady gaze never leaving Jeremiah as the agitated custodian chewed on his bottom lip, reaching for his ledger with clumsy fingers. He licked his index finger and began to flick through the entries for July. 'Ah, yes, Verity Pickup, and her son, Jack.' He looked up, the creases on his brow deepening. 'You'll be taking the boy, too, I presume.'

'No.' Lord Farquharson leaned on his cane, his expression determined. 'No, the boy is to remain in your care.'

There was a lengthy pause as Fisher and Jakes exchanged glances. 'I see.' Fisher leaned back in his chair, motioning for Lord Farquharson to be seated, and trying to ignore the ominous rumbling of his belly. He moved his breakfast aside, and folded his hands together on the desk.

'Your Lordship, surely if Mrs Pickup is your daughter, it should follow that her son is . . .' The words died on his lips as Lord Farquharson leaned towards him, the expression on his face leaving Jeremiah in no doubt that Jack would be remaining at St Mary's.

'The boy is no concern of mine,' Lord Farquharson said, in a tone that brooked no argument. He sat back in his seat. 'I'm not an unkind man, Mr Fisher. I am happy to make a generous donation in support of the charitable work you do.'

'That's most kind, Your Lordship, sir,' Fisher simpered. He motioned to Jakes, hovering by the door. 'Will you fetch Mrs Pickup from the dormitory, Mr Jakes, please.'

'Pardon me, Mister Fisher, sir, but Mrs Pickup,' Jakes stressed the word, finding a measure of sadistic pleasure in the way Lord Farquharson's cheeks coloured slightly, 'has been a patient in the infirmary for some weeks.'

'Well, fetch her from there, then,' Fisher snapped in irritation. He flashed Lord Farquharson an apologetic smile. 'I'm sure it's nothing serious.'

'I have my informants,' Lord Farquharson replied. 'I am fully aware of my daughter's condition.' Fisher was about to enquire about which of his staff were so indiscreet as to discuss an inmate's business with an outsider, but the expression on his Lordship's face brought him up short. 'I trust whatever passes between us in this room is confidential?'

'Of course, sir,' Fisher replied with an emphatic nod.

'Good. As I said, I am willing to be extremely generous in my bequest to your good work here.' The sum he mentioned caused Jeremiah's brows to shoot up in astonishment. He licked his lips. A sum like that would go a good way to keeping the wolf away from the door.

'There is, however, a condition attached, which I would expect you to adhere to.'

Fisher's round head bobbed up and down vigorously.

'Anything, Your Lordship, it goes without saying.'

Lord Farquharson knitted his fingers together, a painful expression on his face. 'My daughter has always been difficult, rebellious even. She suffers an imbalance of the brain. She is unstable and will require constant care, which I am willing to provide for her, on the condition she cuts all ties with the boy. I must insist on that.'

'Will she, Your Lordship? He is her son, after all. It follows that there must be an attachment.'

'She will do what I tell her,' Lord Farquharson said sternly. 'Unless she wants to rot in this place for ever. However, if the boy were to one day come looking for her ...' He let the words hang in the air. 'Perhaps if he thought his mother was dead ... ?'

Fisher baulked. 'You're asking me to lie to the boy, Your Lordship?'

Lord Farquharson shrugged his narrow shoulders. 'It will be for the best, don't you agree?'

Fisher hesitated as his moral conscience warred against the part of him that was already planning on how his Lordship's money might be spent. Finally, he let his shoulders drop, assuaging his conscience with the comforting thought that the benefit of all the inmates far outweighed the distress of one little boy.

'Very well.' He leaned back in his chair, not bothering to disguise his distaste. 'The boy will be informed of his mother's passing as soon as you leave.'

CHAPTER FOUR

Verity watched the clouds drifting past the window. She wrinkled her nose. The air in the infirmary was fetid. The beds around her were filled with women too ill or too weak to work. All night long her sleep was disturbed by wheezing, rattling chests, laboured breathing, and pitiful sobbing.

Turning her head painfully to the left, Verity squinted against the light. Matron sat at her desk, scratching something in her ledger, her usual scowl etched on her thin face. She glanced up in surprise as the door swung open.

'Mister Jakes?' Matron sat back in her chair and removed her glasses. Jakes said something too low for Verity to hear and they both turned to look directly at her. Her stomach knotted anxiously, her fingers clutching at the bedclothes in agitation as Matron began to walk steadily towards her.

'Verity, dear.' The endearment sounded strange on Matron's lips, and Verity pushed herself against the pillows, willing them to leave her alone. She gripped the bedclothes even tighter, her knuckles whitening as she tugged them up to her chin. 'There's no need to be afraid, dear.' Matron's fingers tore the bedclothes free of Verity's grip, exposing her emaciated frame, the oozing bedsores on her wasted thighs. 'You're going home.'

'Home?' Verity whispered, her fevered brain immediately conjuring up her house in Church Street. 'We're going home?'

'Your father has come for you,' Matron said briskly. 'Come along. Get dressed. We don't want to keep His Lordship waiting now, do we?'

'My father?' Too weak to protest, Verity was quickly manhandled into a plain cotton dress. Matron helped her into a pair of clogs, and tugged a brush through her tangled hair, causing Verity to wince with pain. Her brain was struggling to process what was happening to her. Her father had come for her? Had he relented at last? Was he now prepared to offer her and Jack a home after all these years? She managed a smile. Her lips cracked and she tasted blood.

'My father has come to take us home?' she said with such childlike wonder that even Jakes felt a twinge of sympathy for her as he escorted her to the office. 'Jack will be so excited,' she gabbled. 'He's never met his grandfather before. Oh, praise God. I knew he would relent eventually. I knew he cared, and he'll love Jack. I know he will.'

Jakes let her babble on. The wretch would find out the truth soon enough. It wasn't up to him to enlighten her.

*

'Father?' Verity stood in the doorway of Jeremiah Fisher's office. Lord Farquharson stared at his daughter. It was the first time he had laid eyes on her in ten years, and he was visibly shocked. He could scarcely believe this creature was his beautiful Verity. In the shapeless frock and cap, her lips scabbed and oozing, she could be mistaken for one of the dock-dollies that plied their trade down by the wharfs. 'Father?' Verity said again, more uncertainly this time.

Lord Farquharson swallowed down his revulsion. 'Bring her a coat, something warm,' he snapped at Jakes. 'For goodness sake, man, jump to it.' Jakes did as he was bid, returning a few minutes later with a heavy black coat which he draped around Verity's thin shoulders. 'Is she contagious?' he asked Jeremiah. He had not yet shown Verity any affection, but merely regarded her as he would some beggar on his doorstep.

'I don't believe so, Your Lordship.'

'Father, please.' Verity's voice trembled.

'Help her to my carriage.'

His gaze rested on Verity's face. She had wanted for nothing, and how had she repaid him? By throwing herself at some gypsy like a wanton trollop. He would never forgive her. Yet even in his implacable anger, his conscience could not allow him to leave her to rot away in the workhouse. No, it would be a discreet sanatorium for his Verity, somewhere she could rest and live out her days in relative comfort.

'Have you sent someone to fetch Jack?' Verity asked, as Jakes made to lead her away. 'Father?' She gave a nervous smile. Her father ignored her. He shook Jeremiah's hand and gave a curt nod. Jeremiah followed them down the chilly corridor, Verity's protestations growing more panicked by the minute.

'I'm not going without Jack.' She squirmed in Jakes's grasp, twisting her head this way and that, her thin, reedy voice bouncing off the walls as she called for her son.

It took all three of them to bundle her into the waiting carriage. She fought like a wildcat, screaming now for Jack, tears streaming down her hollow cheeks. Fisher swallowed, a sick feeling in the pit of his stomach, as finally, Verity was overcome. The door was slammed shut and the order given to drive on. Fisher's last glimpse of Verity Pickup was of her slumped against the carriage door, weeping copiously, under the watchful gazes of her father and a nurse.

'I'm covered in scratches,' Jakes grumbled. He swore under his breath. 'I'm glad to see the last of her, the little wildcat.'

'Have a heart, Jakes,' Fisher admonished him. 'The woman has, for all intents and purposes, just lost her son.' He laid his hand on Jake's arm. 'Before you return to your duties, there is a matter I need to speak to you about.'

In low tones, Fisher explained Lord Farquharson's request. Jakes whistled through his teeth. 'That's a bit harsh, isn't it, sir?'

Fisher shrugged wearily. 'I must beg your discretion, Jakes. There will be a bottle of finest malt in it for you.'

'I'm much obliged to you, sir,' Jakes grinned. 'You can count on me.'

Fisher nodded. 'Have the boy sent to me before chapel.' He went wearily back to his office. He was not relishing the task ahead.

His breakfast lay where he had left it, a congealing sea of fat and grease. His stomach churned in revulsion. After the morning's events, Jeremiah Fisher had lost his appetite.

Jack whistled as he carried the pile of logs in from the yard. It was a cool but sunny day. White clouds chased each other across a pale blue sky and rooks squabbled in the belfry of the grey-stone chapel.

He was slowly adapting to his new circumstances in the workhouse. It was a hard, grim life. The list of rules was long, and punishment for the slightest infringement harsh, but he received three meals a day, more than he'd had at home, and although he found the daily routine restrictive, it was not as bad as he'd imagined. He only had to keep his head down for two years and he'd be earning. Then he and his mother could leave.

'Hey, Jack,' one of the older boys called to him from across the yard. 'Fisher wants to see you before chapel.'

'What've you been up to?' whispered Jim, a thin, wiry lad of eleven who was helping Jack bring in the logs. Jack shrugged.

'Nothing, as far as I know,' he said. His heart sank. Jakes was the one who dealt with minor misdemeanours and meted out the relevant punishments. You had to have done something really bad to be called in to see Fisher. His mouth dry, Jack dropped his logs on the woodpile and, brushing bits of bark from his hands and shirt, slowly made his way indoors.

His heart thumped against his ribcage and he slipped his hand into his trouser pocket, drawing comfort from the feel of the paper against his fingers. Ellie-May's letter. Written in her scrawl, she had told him all about the Norris family living in his old house, *'They're nice enough,'* she'd written in her big, looping writing, *'and they've fitted right in but it's not the same as having you next door. I miss you, Jack. When are you coming home?'*

He had read her letter so many times the words were imprinted on his brain. He had wanted to write back, but he had no money for a stamp, let alone writing paper. He had already decided he would ask his teacher, Master Quin, if he would loan him the price of a stamp. He could tear a sheet of paper from his school book.

His throat as parched as a desert, his heart hammering in his chest, racking his brain in an effort to conjure up whatever infringement of the rules might have brought this summons from Fisher, Jack made his way down the deserted corridor like a man on his way to the condemned cell. Whatever his punishment, he only hoped it wouldn't prevent him from seeing his mother that afternoon. Her health had deteriorated so quickly. He was worried sick about her. She needed him, as she always had. He would gladly take a beating, as long as he would still be able to visit her that afternoon.

His footsteps slowed as he approached the custodian's office. The door was open, the crackle of the fire clearly audible.

'Is that you, Pickup?' a voice called before Jack had time to steel himself to knock.

'Yes, sir.' He took a deep breath and stepped into the office, coming to stand in front of the desk, head high, hands folded behind his back. To his surprise, Mr Fisher looked uncomfortable, rather than angry. A red flush had worked its way up his neck, spreading to his cheeks. He couldn't meet Jack's eye.

'Sit down, lad.' His voice was kind, sad, and Jack was instantly on his guard. He watched Mr Fisher with narrowed eyes as he leaned forward in his chair, spreading his fingers on the desk top. 'Pickup,' he coughed, clearing his throat. 'I'm afraid I have some bad news. It saddens me to inform you that your mother has passed away.'

Jack sucked in a ragged breath. His insides felt hollow and Mr Fisher's next words appeared to be coming from a long way off, the words disjointed, as if they were being spoken underwater.

'Do you understand what I'm saying, Pickup?' Mr Fisher asked, not unkindly. 'Your mother passed away during the night. She has already been buried in the chapel graveyard.'

'But, sir . . .' Jack wanted to scream that it wasn't true. His mother couldn't be dead. It was impossible. She had had a mild fever. How could she be dead?

'These things happen, lad,' Mr Fisher said softly, his gaze fixed somewhere above Jack's head. 'Fevers are unpredictable.

They can become worse in a matter of hours. There was no time to call you. I'm sorry.'

'May I see where she is buried, sir?'

'It's a communal grave, Pickup,' he said briskly. 'You'll only upset yourself.' He checked his pocket watch. 'It's almost time for chapel. Keeping busy is the best tonic for grief. You'll be on extra yard duties for the next week. You're dismissed.'

Numb, shoulders slumped in shocked disbelief, Jack slunk from the office. He couldn't cry, not yet. More than anything, he wished El was there. She would have slipped her hand into his and let him cry, her quiet presence the only comfort he craved.

Jack worked hard, falling exhausted into bed every night, the oblivion of sleep a balm to his grief and, as Christmas approached, the acute pain of loss receded, settling as a dull ache in his chest.

On Christmas Eve some local women decorated the refectory with garlands of holly and ivy, and brought sweet treats for the children. A grand-looking lady in a red-velvet dress, her snow-white hair pulled back in a neat chignon, played the piano and there was singing, and even dancing. Jack watched wistfully from the shadows, pining for El, and missing his mother, knowing how much she would have enjoyed the merrymaking.

CHAPTER FIVE

The start of the new year brought Jack another letter from El. It was filled with news of Church Street and the Bramhall family. Bert was away at sea, sending back postcards depicting exotic locations, and Bea and Jess were happy in their jobs. Young Arthur would be taken on at the shipyard come the summer, El wrote. She ended her letter as she had the previous one, '*I miss you, Jack. When are you coming home?*'

Jack loved school. Despite some initial hostility from the day pupils, in the months he had been attending St Cuthbert's, Jack's quick wit and natural intelligence had earned him the respect of his classmates and teachers alike, his English master, William Quin, in particular.

He finally plucked up the courage to approach his teacher about the loan of a stamp and a sheet of writing paper. William was only too happy to oblige.

'You write the letter, Jack, and I'll post it for you.'

'Thank you, sir.' Jack beamed.

'Jack.' William pursed his lips together. He wasn't a

handsome man, his features were doughy and out of proportion with each other, yet he had a pleasant nature that immediately put people at their ease.

About to head out to the schoolyard, Jack paused, turning to face his master, his gaze questioning.

'What are your plans for the future?' William asked him. He folded his arms across his chest and leaned against the desk. 'You'll be eleven this May. You'll be old enough to leave school when you're twelve . . . Have you thought what you might do for work?'

Jack shrugged. 'I expect Mr Fisher will find me an apprenticeship down the docks, sir.'

William pulled a face. 'You're a clever lad, Jack. I wonder, would you consider staying on at school for another two years after that, until you're fourteen?' He saw Jack was about to protest and he held up his hand. 'Hear me out. You're bright enough to qualify for a grant. You'll have to sit an exam, of course, but if you do well enough, the parish will provide the funds for you to further your education. The grant also includes your keep at the workhouse, so Mr Fisher will have no cause for objection.' William pushed himself off the desk and patted Jack on the shoulder. 'Think about it. You've got a quick brain. It would be a pity for you not to use it to your advantage.'

Jack spent much of the next few months thinking over William's words. By the time his eleventh birthday came around, unmarked by anyone but El, he was determined to apply for the grant. Mr Fisher proved surprisingly amenable to the idea when William called in to inform him that Jack had passed the exam with flying colours and would qualify for the grant when he turned twelve the following year.

'The parish council are keen for our boys to make the most of every opportunity,' Jeremiah told William over a cup of milky tea. 'It is the way of thinking these days that the better the education, the better the job prospects, which follows that the need for parish assistance in the future should be significantly reduced.'

'Quite.' William smiled, and noticeably relaxed. 'I have high hopes for Jack Pickup,' he said, swallowing a mouthful of tea and setting his cup in its saucer. 'High hopes indeed.'

It saddened Jack that his reunion with Ellie-May would be delayed but he was sensible enough to realize that, if he had decent qualifications, he would be better able to provide for her in the future. Swallowing her disappointment that Jack wouldn't be coming home any time soon, Ellie-May wrote to tell him she would be taking a job in a butcher's shop in Northam Road.

'*I'll have to get used to the smell and sight of blood,*' she wrote, '*but Mr Cartwright's offering a decent wage and I'll get every Wednesday afternoon off, as well as Sundays.*' With tears of longing pricking at her eyelids, she wished him well. '*I hope your studies go well. I'm tickled pink for you, Jack, I am, really.*

All my love, always,

El.'

CHAPTER SIX

1909

The bell on the wall clanged loudly. Ellie-May sighed, her breath clouding in the frigid air of the back room.

'Will you go?' Sixteen-year-old Frank Cartwright glanced up from the pig carcass he was deboning, the sharp edge of the meat cleaver glinting wickedly in the light from the oil lamp. He lifted his straw boater and ran a filthy hand through his blond hair. Despite the cold, his cheeks were red with exertion.

'I'll give you a kiss, if you go,' he quipped, using the back of his hand to wipe away the beads of perspiration that clung to the fine blond down of his upper lip.

'That's enough of your cheek, Frank Cartwright,' scolded Ellie-May. She grinned at him, her smile hiding the twinge of unease his words caused her. She was fourteen now and in the two years she had been working at Cartwright's Butchers, she and Frank had developed an easy friendship,

50

though lately she had begun to suspect Frank might be hoping for something more. He had started insisting on escorting her home each evening, despite her protestations that it was barely a five-minute walk from Northam Road to Church Street.

'I'll go and see what he wants,' she said now, wiping blood-stained hands on her apron. 'But if he needs to use his chamber pot I'm coming to fetch you.' She stepped through the doorway and climbed the narrow flight of stairs up to the flat above that Frank shared with his widowed father, Arnold. Her stomach muscles clenched at the prospect of dealing with her cantankerous employer at such an early hour. Barely twenty minutes had elapsed since Frank had left him to come downstairs. What on earth could the miserable bugger want now?

Pushing such uncharitable thoughts away, she plastered a smile on her face, and rapped on the door at the top of the stairs. Pushing it open, she stepped into the stuffy room, wrinkling her nose at the overpowering reek of stale body odour and alcohol fumes. 'Is everything all right, Mr Cartwright?'

'Where's Frank?' Arnold snapped, his mottled face clouding at the sight of Ellie-May standing in the doorway. He was a bloated toad of a man, with receding dirty-blond hair and loose jowls that shook with every laboured breath. His shiny cheeks were a web of broken veins and his bulbous nose glowed like a beacon. It was early September, yet a fire roared in the grate, causing Ellie-May to break out in a sweat.

'He's in the middle of a deboning a pig, Mr Cartwright,' Ellie-May explained, conscious of the perspiration trickling down her spine. She glanced longingly at the window, tightly shut against an overcast autumn sky.

'I haven't had my breakfast,' Arnold whined, his jowls wobbling as he struggled to sit upright. His huge stomach strained against the buttons of his fawn cardigan. He hadn't yet managed to put on his socks and Ellie-May looked in distaste at his gnarled feet, each scaly toe topped by a thick, yellow nail.

Suppressing a shiver of revulsion, she forced a note of brightness into her tone. 'Frank will have put the porridge on for you, Mr Cartwright, as he always does. It'll be keeping warm on the range.'

'How does he expect me to fetch it?' Arnold snarled. 'He knows my gout's playing up again, ungrateful little sod.'

Biting her tongue against the retort that sprang instantly to her lips, Ellie-May forced herself to remain calm. 'How about I fetch your porridge for you and make you a nice cup of tea?' Her gaze darted to the empty whisky bottle on the low table, the dirty glass. No wonder the miserable bugger suffered from gout. She felt no sympathy, her only concern being for Frank who, since his mother's death five years before, had borne the brunt of his father's foul moods.

Arnold's only response was to hawk up a glob of phlegm and spit it into a grubby handkerchief.

She escaped to the untidy kitchen, where she quickly washed her hands, wiping them dry on a none-too-clean tea towel, and set the kettle to boil. As expected, Frank had left Arnold's bowl of porridge warming on the small range. While she waited for the kettle, she gazed out over the row of small backyards, the alleyway that ran the length of the row, the sooty-brick terraced row beyond. Seagulls wheeled in the dishwater-grey sky, their mournful cries echoing over the rooftops. Frank's delivery bike was propped up against the privy wall.

She smiled. Even Arnold's unpleasantness couldn't put a damper on her happiness. Jack's monthly letters had been all Ellie-May had lived for over the past four years and now he had written to tell her he was taking up a position as a trainee bookkeeper for a department store in Above Bar Street. He was leaving the workhouse today, and he had promised to visit.

Her joyful thoughts were interrupted by the kettle coming to the boil and she busied herself making Arnold's tea, setting his cup and saucer on a tray beside the bowl of porridge and carrying it through into the other room.

'Here you are, Mr Cartwright.' She placed the tray on the low table, discreetly moving the whisky bottle to one side, and straightened up, her gaze taking in the mess and disorder. Frank did his best, God love him, but the flat clearly lacked a woman's touch.

Without so much as a word of thanks, Arnold picked up his spoon and began shovelling porridge into his mouth, lips smacking noisily.

'Right.' Ellie-May watched him for a moment, not

bothering to conceal her revulsion. 'If there's nothing else, sir, I'll get back to work.'

Arnold waved her away with a fat hand. 'I won't be down today,' he mumbled through a mouthful of porridge. 'You and Frank can manage without me.'

As we do most days, came the unspoken retort as Ellie-May bounded down the stairs.

Back in the cold back room, Frank was placing the cuts of meat on trays ready to take out into the shop.

'How is the old bugger?' he asked, as Ellie-May emerged through the doorway.

'His gout's giving him gyp,' she said, taking the two trays of neatly arranged chops Frank handed her and heading into the shop. 'He won't be down today,' she threw over her shoulder.

'Why am I not surprised?' Frank grinned as he followed her. 'I doubt the lazy bugger's done a full day's graft in his life. Mother kept this place going while she was alive, and it's been down to me ever since.'

In stark contrast to the flat upstairs, the shop was spotlessly clean. The previous evening after the shop closed at five, as she did every evening, bar Wednesday, Ellie-May had spent an hour scrubbing and sweeping until the place shone. The glass-topped counter gleamed and fresh sawdust covered the floor.

They worked in companionable silence, laying out the trays of mutton chops, fat pork sausages, mince, tripe and brisket ready for opening promptly at eight.

Conscious that Jack might appear at any moment, Ellie-May checked her appearance in the small mirror hanging behind the counter. A strand of auburn hair had fallen loose from her bun. She tucked it behind her ear. Her bright, carrot-red hair had turned a subtler auburn as she reached her teens. Her freckles had faded too, and though she did not realize it, she was maturing into a strikingly beautiful young woman. To Frank, she was one of the prettiest girls he knew.

He watched her now, his dark blue eyes lingering on her reflection as she fussed and titivated in front of the mirror. Her dull brown wool dress clung to her slim frame in all the right places and his heart skipped a beat as her gaze met his in the mirror. She grinned at him.

'Stop staring at me, Frank,' she said, keeping her tone deliberately light-hearted as she whirled round to face him. 'You'll make me blush.'

He laughed, embarrassed, the colour rising in his cheeks. His admiring gaze continued to follow her surreptitiously as she discarded her blood-stained apron for the clean one she wore in the shop, and went to unlock the door.

Ellie-May turned the CLOSED sign to OPEN, glancing down the street hopefully. Horses and carts lumbered up and down Northam Road. Already people were milling about on the pavements, children hurrying off to school, housewives with baskets over their arms, pedlars and beggars, the ladies particularly, keeping beneath the shelter of the shops' multi-coloured awnings as the mist turned to drizzle. A chill wind whistled down the street.

Rubbing her cold hands, Ellie-May had just ducked behind the counter when the doorbell jangled, heralding the arrival of the morning's first customer.

The steady stream of customers kept Ellie-May and Frank busy all morning and it was a relief when, at promptly midday, Frank stuck the CLOSED sign in the door and they could relax. He went upstairs to dine with his father, throwing down his daily invitation for Ellie-May to join them. As usual, she declined, preferring to eat her bread and dripping in the quiet shop. The mere sight of Arnold Cartwright snuffling and snorting his way through his mutton stew was enough to turn her stomach. She pitied Frank's wife one day having to take on Arnold. She had never known Caroline Cartwright, but from what little Frank had let slip, her life with Arnold had not been a happy one. It was common gossip amongst the shopkeepers of Northam Road that it was the despair and exhaustion to which Caroline had succumbed, rather than the influenza.

Ellie-May ate her dinner seated behind the counter, watching the passers-by. Each time a young man of Jack's height approached, her heart raced, only for her hopes to be dashed a moment later. She finished her meal, barely tasting her food, and visited the privy. She was just sliding back the bolts on the front door when Frank came thumping down the stairs, his expression livid.

'I'll swing for that man, so help me God!' he fumed, snatching his striped apron from the hook on the wall and tying it around his waist. His cheeks were tinged pink, his handsome features marred by his scowl of annoyance. 'He's only complaining the meat in his stew was tough and stringy. I told him to cook his own dinner in future if he's going to find fault all the time.' He rubbed his temples. 'He'll be the death of me, Ellie-May, I swear.'

'How is his foot?' asked Ellie-May. 'Any better?'

'Not if his temper is anything to go by,' Frank snorted. He sighed. 'I'll call in to Doctor Morton on my round later, see if he'll pop by.'

'I'll get everything packed up for you,' Ellie-May said, reaching for the order book. It was falling apart, the spine held together with tape. She flicked it open to the relevant page, and licked the tip of her pencil. Forcing herself to concentrate, she ticked off each item, wrapped it in paper and placed it in Frank's delivery basket.

'You all right?' Frank asked, lifting the delivery basket off the counter. 'You seem a bit distracted.'

'I'm fine, Frank,' Ellie-May replied, a faraway look in her eyes as she stared at the raindrops dripping from the awning.

'Right,' Frank said, unconvinced, 'I'll get these loaded and be on my way.' He glanced at the rain-splattered cobbles and pulled a face. 'I'd better wear my rubbers.' He peered over her shoulder at the orders. 'How far am I going?'

Ellie-May was just opening her mouth to reply when the bell over the door jangled.

She looked up, and the world stopped.

'Jack!' she squealed.

'Hello, El.' Jack grinned broadly as he stood in the door-way, rainwater dripping onto the floor.

Even though she had dreamed of this moment a million times over the years, Ellie-May hardly dared believe that Jack Pickup was standing in front of her, large as life.

'Don't look so surprised,' Jack chuckled. 'You knew I was coming.'

She slipped beneath the counter and flung herself into his waiting arms. 'I can't believe it's really you,' she breathed, gazing up at him. He had changed in the four years since he had left Church Street. He was a head taller than her for one thing. His wild, unruly mop of dark hair had been neatly trimmed and he was wearing a suit, clearly some-one's hand-me-down, but a suit nonetheless, under a long, dark coat.

Ellie-May's lip quivered. 'Oh, Jack, it's been so long!'

'You're telling me,' Jack grinned, oblivious to the rainwater puddling around his feet. 'Look at you, little Ellie-May all grown up.'

Ellie-May threw back her head and laughed, a blush colouring her pale cheeks. For a moment, they stared into each other's eyes, their silence saying so much more than any words. Frank glared at the tall, pleasant-faced boy dripping water all over the floor with a sinking heart. He coughed loudly, and Ellie May and Jack drew apart, the spell broken.

'I take it this is the famous Jack?' Frank said, sourly. He held out his hand. 'Frank Cartwright.'

'Of course.' Jack shook Frank's hand. 'El has mentioned

you in her letters. I feel as though I know you already,' he said pleasantly. 'Nice to meet you.'

Frank nodded, eyeing him warily. 'Likewise. Ellie-May has told me a lot about you, too.' Frank relaxed his shoulders slightly. 'You were close once?'

'We grew up together,' Jack explained, his eyes never leaving Ellie-May's face.

Frank watched them, his eyes narrowing as he took Jack's measure. If it came down to attractiveness, then he, Frank, with his cherubic, blond good looks would surely win hands down, and coupled with the fact that the butcher's shop would be his one day ... He mentally spread his hands in supplication. What did Jack have to offer a girl like Ellie-May? He was only a workhouse boy, after all.

'I can't believe you're really here?' Ellie-May exclaimed excitedly, once Frank had reluctantly gone off to do his delivery. 'And looking so smart.'

'I have to report to Chalke and Chase department store by six o'clock this evening. As I told you in my last letter, I start my training tomorrow. If I work hard, I could have a decent career with the company. Mr Chase and Mr Chalk have a good reputation for being fair to their staff. I'm looking forward to the challenge.'

'You always were a lot cleverer than me,' Ellie-May smiled. Her expression turned serious. 'You must be so relieved to be out of the workhouse?'

'I left the minute old Fisher had completed the

paperwork.' His stomach grumbled loudly and he grinned, the old familiar grin that Ellie-May had pictured in her mind so many times. 'As you can tell, I didn't even stop for dinner.'

'Here.' Ellie-May reached under the counter and lifted out a meat pie. She handed it to Jack. 'They're yesterday's,' she said when Jack started to protest. 'We're selling them off cheap. They'll only be thrown out otherwise.' She eyed him up and down as he took a bite of pie and chewed hungrily. 'You've filled out a bit. You were always such a scrawny kid. Mum was always trying to feed you up. She'll be tickled pink to see you again.'

They were still talking when Frank arrived back two hours later, wet and cold. Walking into the shop, rubbing his wet hair with a towel, his smile died on his lips to be replaced by a scowl at the sight of Jack still in the shop.

'I hope you haven't been distracting Ellie-May from her work,' he said pompously, glaring at him across the counter.

'It's been very quiet, Frank,' Ellie-May retorted. 'The weather's keeping people away.'

'I've got a few errands to run, anyway,' Jack said, with a nod in Frank's direction. 'What time do you finish, El?'

'Six.'

'Great. I'll report to my supervisor at Chalke and Chase and be back in time to see you home.'

'I walk Ellie-May home,' Frank said, a slight edge to his voice. Jack's brow furrowed and he turned his questioning gaze on Ellie-May. She flushed and shrugged.

'I keep telling him I'm perfectly capable of seeing myself home.'

'That's not . . .' Frank clamped his jaw shut, the blood suffusing his cold, damp cheeks.

'Jack can walk me home this evening, Frank,' Ellie-May said firmly, fixing the blond-haired boy with a stern gaze. 'Mum and Dad will want to see him, and so will Arthur.'

Frank scowled, but had no option but to acquiesce. After all, it wasn't as if he and Ellie-May were courting yet. He flicked the wet towel over his shoulder and disappeared out the back.

'I'll see you later, then, El,' Jack said, as the bell jangled and Mrs Harris, the vicar's wife, blew in on a gust of icy cold rain.

'Good afternoon, Mrs Harris,' Ellie-May greeted her, her gaze following Jack as he darted between two carts across the street. 'What will it be? A couple of sausages for the Reverend's tea?'

'Six pork chops, if you please, Ellie-May,' Mrs Harris replied, straightening her hat which the wind had blown askew. 'I've got the bishop coming for supper.'

'The bishop?' said Frank, emerging from the back. 'How very grand.'

'But very wearying,' replied Mrs Harris with a grimace. 'He's a rather tedious man whose supper conversation tends to revolve mostly around himself. Still, what can you do? He is my husband's boss, after all. Thank you, my dear.' She took the neatly wrapped chops from Ellie-May and tucked them in her basket. 'Good afternoon to you both.'

The doorbell jangled as she left, and two more customers entered. After that there was a steady flurry of customers and both Ellie-May and Frank were kept busy. It was with relief when, finally, six o'clock came and Ellie-May could finally hang up her apron and put on her hat and coat.

'I suppose I'll see you tomorrow then,' Frank said sullenly as he watched Ellie-May pull on her gloves.

'Yes. I'll see you in the morning, Frank. Have a good evening.'

Frank didn't answer. He watched her leave with a scowl on his face. He wasn't sure he was comfortable with the idea of Ellie-May walking home with the likes of an ex-workhouse lad like Jack Pickup. His scowl deepened. There was the look of the gypsy about him, too. Definitely not one to be trusted.

A loud banging above his head only served to darken his mood even further. While Jack got to spend a pleasant evening with Ellie-May, what did he have to look forward to? Skivvying for his old man, that's what, and putting him to bed once he'd drunk himself into oblivion. He just hoped the old bugger hadn't wet himself again; he just wasn't in the mood to deal with that carry-on tonight. With a snort, Frank turned out the light, and tramped up the stairs, his mood growing darker with every step.

It had stopped raining, though a thick blanket of cloud remained, obscuring the moon.

Jack was leaning against the lamppost opposite the shop, hands in his pockets. The gaslight hissed, its yellow glow forming a halo of light around his head. He pushed himself upright when Ellie-May emerged into the swirling mist.

'I hope you haven't been waiting long,' she said as Jack approached. 'It's rather chilly for September.'

Jack replied with a grin, stamping his feet. 'I've only just arrived. Anyway, I'm used to it. The workhouse was always freezing in winter. We had to break the ice on the water in order to wash, most days.'

Their breath clouded between them. Out to sea a foghorn blared. The fog swirled around them, muffling the sounds of the street. A horse-drawn tram trundled by, crammed with commuters.

Jack offered Ellie-May his arm. 'Shall we?'

Slipping her arm through his, Ellie-May felt instantly at ease. It was as if the past four years had never been as they laughed and chattered, oblivious to the cold, and the fact their teeth were chattering.

'Our Bea is walking out with the head porter of the Grand Hotel,' she told Jack. Their footsteps sounded loud in the foggy stillness. 'Ivor, he's called. He's Welsh. And Jess is smitten with a chap who works at Woolworths, though she suspects his affections lie elsewhere.'

'Poor Jess,' Jack chuckled, remembering Jess as a petulant fourteen-year-old, too fond of her own way.

'Well, yes,' agreed Ellie-May wryly. 'Poor Jess indeed. Bert's still at sea, currently somewhere in the Adriatic, according to his last letter, though they take so long to arrive, he could be somewhere else by now. Arthur's working down the shipyard with Dad, as I told you, and our Nora leaves school this summer. She's already been promised a position with W. H. Smith and Son. She'll be up the road from you.'

They turned into Church Street. The streetlights sputtered in the fog. Light shone from cracks in the curtains of the terraced houses.

'Does it feel strange being back?' Ellie-May asked as they paused outside number 10, gazing at the freshly painted front door.

Jack shrugged his shoulders. 'It hit me just now when I turned the corner,' he admitted. 'Despite all her faults, Ma and I were happy here.' A shadow crossed his face and Ellie-May groped for his hand in the lamplight. 'You didn't say much in your letters, but I got the impression it was very grim.'

'I kept my head down,' he said, after a short pause. 'Did as I was told and worked hard.' He forced a smile, not wanting to burden her with the nights he'd cried into his pillow for his mother, or endured a beating for some minor infringement of the draconian rules. That part of his life was behind him now. He had a good job, which came with a decent place to live and, the greatest blessing of all, he was back with his dearest El.

'Jack Pickup!' exclaimed Sid coming out of the kitchen as Ellie-May opened the front door and ushered Jack inside. 'Ah, lad, you're a sight for sore eyes and no mistake.' He shook Jack's hand warmly. 'And how you've grown. Hasn't he grown? Eileen, look who's here.' Sid bundled Jack into the warm, cosy kitchen where Eileen was ladling great dollops of cottage pie onto rose-patterned plates.

'He's a strapping lad,' Eileen agreed, her flushed, damp face beaming as she hugged him fiercely, her eyes glistening with tears. 'Verity would be proud of you.'

'Thanks, Mrs Bramhall,' Jack said. He thrust out his hand. 'Arthur, it's good to see you, mate, and little Nora, not so little anymore.' Eleven-year-old Nora giggled, while Arthur, a big lad of sixteen, rose from his seat.

'Jack, good to see you again.' The two boys shook hands with genuine warmth while Eileen, bustling around like a mother hen, urged them all to sit and eat.

'This calls for a celebration,' Sid said, nipping into the pantry and returning with a bottle of his homemade elder-flower cordial. He poured everyone a glass. 'Cheers, Jack,' Sid raised his glass. 'Welcome home, lad. Welcome home.'

CHAPTER SEVEN

1910

Spring had arrived in all its glory that March. The ancient churchyard was awash with daffodils, their golden heads nodding jauntily in the breeze. Fluffy white clouds scudded across a milky-blue sky and the sun was warm on Ellie-May's face as she emerged from the church to see Frank loitering across the street. He spotted her immediately and his expression brightened. Ellie-May watched him cross the street towards her with growing disquiet.

'Ellie-May.' He tipped his hat. He was wearing a brown suit and his hair was neatly slicked back. 'Morning, Mrs Bramhall, Mr Bramhall.'

'Good morning, Frank,' Eileen smiled, making her way down the steps behind Ellie-May. Sid and Nora followed, deep in conversation. Sid nodded. 'Morning, Frank.'

Ellie-May started down the street and Frank fell into step

beside her. 'I thought you might like to take a walk. It's such a lovely day.'

Eileen raised an eyebrow. Her Ellie-May had another admirer. Did Jack realize he had a rival for her daughter's affections, she wondered, smiling to herself.

Unable to think of a suitable excuse, Ellie-May reluctantly accepted. They walked in silence towards the park, drawn by the sound of children playing. They had reached the wrought-iron gates before Frank finally spoke.

'Thank you for agreeing to come,' he said, a hint of pink colouring his fair cheeks. 'I was afraid you might turn me down.' He gave a self-conscious laugh.

'It's just a walk,' Ellie-May murmured. Two little boys in sailor suits ran past them in the direction of the pond, each carrying a toy sailing boat. Frank cleared his throat.

'Ellie-May, you must realize how I feel about you?' He stopped walking and took hold of her hand, forcing her to stop and look at him. She saw the hope in his blue eyes and winced inwardly. 'I know you're not fifteen yet, but I'd like to ask your father's permission to court you.'

'Oh, Frank.' Ellie-May shook her head in dismay. She had suspected for some time that Frank's feelings for her were growing into something more than friendship, but had purposely ignored the signs, not wanting to spoil their relationship.

Frank sucked in a lungful of fresh spring air, dredging up every ounce of his courage. He had to make Ellie-May understand how much he loved her. Ever since Jack had appeared on the scene, he had felt her slipping away from him. He was losing her and the thought terrified him. With a sense of urgency, he cupped her face in his hands, looking into her eyes.

'Tell me you feel the way I do.' Seeing only pity reflected in Ellie-May's eyes, his smile faltered. 'You do like me, don't you?'

She looked away, unable to bear the pleading look in his eyes, and fixed her gaze on the two boys at the water's edge. They had been joined by a black Labrador. It frolicked in the water, barking madly and sending a shower of droplets into the air.

'I'm sorry, Frank.' She forced herself to meet his gaze, hating the hurt and disappointment, the crushed hope she could see in his eyes. 'You're a dear friend, and I'm very fond of you, but . . .'

'But you can't love me?' Frank finished her sentence, a bitter edge to his tone.

'No, Frank, I'm sorry.'

A shrill whistle pierced the air and the Labrador shot passed them like a bullet, sending a spray of muddy water over Ellie-May's navy wool skirt.

'Give me a chance,' Frank wheedled, pouting petulantly as Ellie-May brushed droplets from her skirt. 'I think about you all the time. I . . . I love you.' He took Ellie-May's hand in his, his expression earnest. 'Please, just give me a chance to show you how much you mean to me. You'll learn to love me. I know you will.'

Ellie-May smiled sadly. She hated hurting his feelings, but rather that than lead him on.

'I'm sorry,' she said again, gently withdrawing her hand. A cloud passed over the sun and she shivered as a gust of wind ruffled the grass.

'I should be getting back. Jack's coming around for supper and . . .'

'*Jack?*' Frank cried. 'Jack, Jack, Jack! It's always bloody Jack isn't it? He's all you talk about. Anyone would think you were sweet on the bloody gypo.'

'Frank!' Ellie-May's mouth fell open in shock. 'Jack is my friend.'

'Yes, I know.' Frank rolled his eyes. 'I've heard it all before – what a great friend he is, how he was always looking out for you when you were kids. Well, Ellie-May, I hear things when I'm delivering to the posh houses and I made it my business to find out a bit more about your precious Jack.' He spat the name in distaste, hurt and disappointment making him mean-spirited. 'Gypo Jack,' he sneered.

'I grew up with the rumours about Jack's dad being a Romany,' Ellie-May shrugged her shoulders. 'So what?'

'But what about his mother? I bet you didn't know she was Lord Farquharson's daughter?' He laughed, a strange, strangled sound, and raised one eyebrow. 'Huh?'

'Verity Pickup, the daughter of a lord?' Ellie-May frowned, remembering Jack's mother, thin and unkempt with sad, world-weary eyes. 'I know she spoke a bit posh, but ... Where'd you get that from?' She strode on, forcing Frank to increase his pace in order to keep up with her.

'A kitchen maid who used to work for the family.'

Ellie-May whirled round, hands on hips.

'So, you're telling me, Jack is related to gentry? The grandson of Lord so-and-so?'

'Well, yes,' Frank faltered. 'But it's nothing to be proud of, is it? She brought shame on the family and was disinherited.' He smiled coldly. 'So, you see, Ellie-May, your precious friend Jack is nothing but the son of a common trollop and a dirty gypsy. No wonder he ended up in the workhouse.'

Ellie-May regarded him coldly. 'You'd better not let Jack hear you calling his ma names, Frank Cartwright,' she said, her tone icy. 'I don't give two hoots who his father is or was, but you really are a nasty piece, aren't you? As callous and judgemental as your father.'

Frank shoved his hands deep into his trouser pockets, an angry flush creeping up above his collar and spreading to his cheeks. 'I'm nothing like my father,' he retorted vehemently. 'Nothing at all.'

Fuming, Ellie-May strode off along the path, the soles of her shoes crunching on the gravel. Frank hurried after her, his expression mutinous, keeping pace as they walked in the direction of Church Street, both silent and resentful.

They parted at the entrance to the alleyway that led around the back of the terraced houses.

'Give your parents my best,' Frank said curtly. 'I won't come in.'

Still seething with annoyance, Ellie-May didn't bother to reply.

Her family were all in the backyard, along with the Norris family and Stan Wilson from number 14. The grizzled old man was seated on a green-painted straight-back chair, Nellie, the latest addition to the Norris family, gurgling contentedly on his lap.

Her mood lifted instantly at the sight of Jack playing cards with Sid and Tony. Sid had dragged the small card table outside and set it up against the high stone wall, behind which loomed the grey-stone edifice that was the Methodist chapel, its plain-glass windows aflame with the reflection of the afternoon sunshine. Feeling Ellie-May's gaze, Jack caught her eye, relief written all over his face when he saw she was alone.

'You were longer than I expected,' Eileen said as Ellie-May perched herself on the edge of the raised flowerbed. A clump of yellow daffodils stood proudly to attention amidst a cluster of purple and white crocuses. 'Frank not come in with you?' Eileen was sitting on a kitchen chair beside Rose Norris, darning Sid's socks, her mending basket at her feet. The three older Norris children were playing marbles, supervised by Nora.

'No, he didn't,' Ellie-May replied shortly.

'Well, your dinner's on the stove,' Eileen went on, pausing to bite the cotton with her teeth. 'Eat it before it dries out.'

'I'll have it later,' Ellie-May replied. 'I'm not really hungry.' She could feel Jack's eyes on her, but when she looked his way he quickly lowered his gaze, his brow furrowing as he pretended to concentrate on his hand of cards.

'He seems a pleasant enough chap, that Frank,' said Rose, winding up her knitting and getting up to take baby Nellie from old Stan. 'If a bit full of his own importance.'

The heat rose in Ellie-May's cheeks. 'He's my boss's son, Aunty Rose, we're friends, nothing more.'

Eileen and Rose exchanged a knowing smile. It had been blindingly obvious to both women that since the moment Jack had waltzed back into their lives, no one else stood a chance of winning Ellie-May's affections. She was clearly smitten with Jack, and, unless Eileen was very much mistaken, he felt the same way about her.

'I think Frank's a little sweet on you?' Rose teased, settling herself back on the chair, Nellie cradled against her chest. 'He's a good catch. The girl who marries him will have a comfortable life.'

'Marriage?' Sid's ears pricked up, as Ellie-May caught Jack's eye. She pulled a face, making him grin.

'Who's talking about marriage? You're not yet fifteen, girl,' Sid scowled at her over his cards. 'Far too young to be thinking along those lines.'

The clock tower at the end of the street chimed two o'clock. Eileen stirred herself. Laying her needlework aside, she got up to collect the tea cups. 'Anyone for a refill?'

'It won't make things awkward for you at work, will it?' Jack asked Ellie-May some time later when she had relayed the entire conversation between her and Frank to him. He sat beside her, his long legs stretched out in front of him. The sun was low above the rooftops now and the yard was shrouded in shadow. The air had cooled considerably and Ellie-May was glad of her shawl. Sid and Eileen, and Rose and Tony Norris had gone indoors. Arthur had returned home from visiting his young lady and was standing with Stan beside the coal bunker, both enjoying a smoke as they swapped stories about life working down at the shipyard, while watching the children at play.

'I hadn't thought of that.' Ellie-May bit her bottom lip. 'It shouldn't do. At least I hope not.' She shook her head. 'I don't think Frank's the type to hold a grudge, do you?'

Jack shrugged. 'You know him better than I do. I've only met him a couple of times. I thought he seemed a decent enough chap, a bit arrogant, maybe, but after what you've told me, I don't know. Just don't let him bully you. If he makes a nuisance of himself, let me know. I'll sort him out.'

Truthfully, Jack had thought Frank a bit of a pompous idiot, but he supposed he was biased. He had to admit though, it had come as something of a shock to realize that Ellie-May was no longer his little El, his faithful little shadow, willing to do whatever he asked without question, but an extremely beautiful young woman – something Frank had clearly noticed. The thought that someone else might have designs on his El gave him a queer sensation in the pit of his stomach.

It had taken him no more than a minute to fall for her.

Expecting a girl, he had been shocked to the core to see the lovely woman she had become. Even her blood-splattered apron and flushed, shiny face hadn't detracted from her allure. And if it had taken Jack a minute to fall headlong in love with Ellie-May, it had taken her half that time. But they had still not admitted to each other what everyone else, including Frank, had begun to suspect. Jack and Ellie-May were in love.

'Do you think there's any truth in what he said about your mother?' Ellie-May asked now, not wanting to think about Frank or what tomorrow might bring.

Jack thought for a moment. 'I doubt it. I know Ma's family were well to do and they threw her out without a penny, but the daughter of a Lord?' Ellie-May nodded. 'Nah, it's a bit of a stretch by anyone's imagination, isn't it?'

The following Thursday, Frank came back from his deliveries in a particularly bad humour, having been given a good telling off by the housekeeper of a new customer for having the audacity to knock at the front door of the house instead of going around the back.

'She spoke to me as if I were a common servant,' he complained to Ellie-May.

With his ego severely bruised, he wasn't best pleased to see Jack come striding in, a broad grin on his face, his dark hair plastered to his skull, his coat dripping puddles of water on the sawdust.

'Jack.' Ellie-May couldn't hide her delight at his

unexpected appearance. 'Why aren't you at work?' She was conscious that she wasn't looking her best – her hair was coming out of its bun, and her face was flushed and sweaty – but as Jack stood there, rain lashing the glass behind him, he thought that she'd never looked so lovely.

'Yes,' barked Frank. 'What do you want, Pickup?' He scowled. He was still smarting over Ellie-May's rejection and the atmosphere in the butcher's shop had been decidedly frosty all week.

Jack afforded Frank a curt nod. The animosity between the two young men was palpable. Leaning against the counter, he focused his attention on Ellie-May. She gazed back at him expectantly, her green eyes wide.

'Mr Chase is organising an Easter dinner for his staff and I've been sent to discuss his meat order with you. I've got a list here from Mrs Peat, his cook.' He delved inside his coat and brought out a folded sheet of paper, which he handed to Ellie-May. 'These are the quantities we'll need.'

'Of course,' smiled Ellie-May. 'I'll get the order book.' She made to delve under the counter but Frank placed a restraining hand on her shoulder.

'I'll deal with this, Ellie-May,' he said, whipping his pencil from behind his ear. 'What will it be, Pickup? Lamb? That's the usual choice for Easter.'

Before either Jack or Ellie-May could respond, Arnold Cartwright came lumbering through the doorway, oiled hair glistening across his shiny pate, his face like thunder.

'What's this I hear about you getting Mrs Cutter's delivery

wrong yesterday?' he snarled at Frank, giving his startled son a clip around the ear. The blow took him by surprise, causing him to stumble against the counter, embarrassment turning his cheeks scarlet.

'Sorry?' Frank mumbled sullenly, his hand pressed against his throbbing ear.

'The cook had to revise her entire dinner party menu.'

'I made a mistake,' Frank muttered, trying not to quail under his father's anger.

'You're a useless sod,' Arnold bellowed as Ellie-May and Jack exchanged uncomfortable glances. Ellie-May knew Arnold was free with his fists where Frank was concerned, but he'd never hit him in front of her before. 'You'll get back on your bike and take Mrs Cutter a cut of our prime beef, and the cost will come out of your wages.' He turned back to the stairs. 'Woe betide you if we lose their business because of your stupidity.'

Frank's shoulders slumped. Burning with shame at being chastised in front of Ellie-May and her bloody workhouse boy, he snatched up the steak and stormed out of the shop, not wanting Ellie-May or Jack to see his tears of humiliation.

Ellie-May waited until Arnold's heavy footsteps had retreated up the stairs before apologizing. 'Sorry about that. Mr Cartwright can be a bit rough on poor Frank.'

Jack shrugged, embarrassed at having to witness his rival's humiliation at the hands of his brute of a father.

'Right,' Ellie-May said brightly, taking the ledger from under the counter. 'Let me sort out that order for you.'

They spent the next few minutes working out prices. Ellie-May bent her head over the ledger and wrote it down carefully in her neat handwriting. Jack's fingers brushed against hers, sending a tingle down her spine. She raised her head, cheeks flaming, to find herself staring straight into his eyes.

Nothing was said but something passed between them, something that neither of them could ignore and in that moment Ellie-May knew there would never be anyone for her but Jack, ever.

Two weeks later, Jack was round at Ellie-May's. It was another beautiful spring day. Skylarks and swallows swooped in a cornflower-blue sky. The surrounding streets echoed with the sound of children at play.

Jack took Ellie-May's hand in his. 'So, are we officially courting?' he asked her, his dark eyes boring earnestly into hers.

'You'd better ask my dad,' Ellie-May replied with a grin of her own. 'I'm not fifteen for another six weeks.' Her grin broadened at Jack's frown of concern. She was confident that asking Sid's permission would be a mere formality. Both her parents adored Jack. They'd be thrilled to bits.

'I'll speak to him on my way out,' Jack promised. They talked quietly for a while. The sun sank below the rooftops and it grew colder, the first evening stars emerging in the east. Arthur and Stan finished their game of draughts and went indoors.

'Ellie-May.' Eileen appeared in the doorway, just as Rose appeared at hers to call the children in for their tea. 'Nora's waiting to have her bath, love.'

'All right, Mum.' Reluctant to let the day end, Ellie-May got to her feet. 'I've got to go,' she said. 'It's my job to fetch and heat the water for bath night.'

'Then I'll say goodnight.'

Ellie-May walked with him as far as the back door.

'I'll have a word with your dad now,' Jack promised, giving Ellie-May's hand a squeeze, then, quick as a flash, he leaned forward and kissed her quickly on the lips. She barely had time to react or close her eyes before it was over. Breathless with the thrill of her first kiss, her fingers on her tingling lips, she stood motionless on the threshold until her mother's voice brought her back to earth.

Eileen stood in the kitchen in her floral apron, a smile playing on her lips. The kiss had not gone unnoticed, and she knew Jack was speaking to Sid now, the two of them closeted away in the parlour. Jack was a good lad. Ellie-May could do a lot worse for herself. She shook herself. The evening was slipping away. 'Are you fetching that water or what?' she called out to her daughter, her gruff tone tempered by her indulgent smile.

The memory of Jack's kiss lingering on her lips, Ellie-May snatched up the bucket, and headed for the tap.

CHAPTER EIGHT

1914

'You heard the news, Jack?' Chalke entered Jack's office, closing the door quietly behind him. It was a warm day in late June. The windows were open and the noise of the street wafted up on the breeze.

'No, sir.' Jack sat back in his chair. As senior bookkeeper he had an office to himself. It wasn't very big, little more than a broom cupboard really, but it was tastefully furnished with a broad walnut desk, a teak filing cabinet and two comfortable chintz chairs for visitors. It was into one of these that Chalke now settled himself. He crossed his long legs.

In his early sixties, he was a distinguished-looking man with a mane of snow-white hair, the deeply tanned complexion of a man fond of outdoor pursuits and startlingly blue eyes that missed nothing.

'Damn dreadful business,' Chalke said, reaching across the desk to pass Jack the latest edition of the *Southampton Echo*.

'The heir to the throne of Austria–Hungary, Archduke Franz Ferdinand, has been assassinated in Sarajevo. This could start a war.'

Jack scanned the article, his expression sombre. 'Sobering news, sir. Do you think we'll be drawn into it?'

'I'm not sure we can avoid it,' Edward replied with a sigh, rubbing the bridge of his long nose. 'Well,' he got to his feet, smoothing the creases from his trousers. He gave Jack a wry smile. 'I just wanted to let you know what's going on. I must get a move on. I believe Miss Masters in the haberdashery wants a word before I leave for my luncheon appointment.'

'Of course, sir,' replied Jack, half rising from his seat.

Once Chalke had gone, Jack leaned back in his chair. He steepled his fingers, a deep frown etched on his brow. A war would certainly disrupt his carefully laid plans. He would volunteer if it came to it, of course. His conscience wouldn't allow him to do otherwise. He sighed. El wouldn't like that and she'd be sure to let him know it, in no uncertain terms.

A smile played on his lips as he thought about his beloved El. He was planning to propose. He had seen a ring he liked in the jeweller's shop down the street, Heinz and Son. Nothing ostentatious, his El wasn't like that, but it would use up a good chunk of his savings, nonetheless.

His smile broadened at the thought of the little nest egg he had squirreled away in his savings account. It would come in handy when he and El set up home together. She was putting things away in her bottom drawer as well, so they'd be comfortable.

Jack was proud of his savings. Having grown up with little more than the clothes on his back, the fact that he had a savings account at all felt like a great achievement, and he had Edward Chalke to thank. The day he joined Chalke and Chase, Chalke had sent Jack along to the bank with his secretary, Miss Jackson, to open a savings account. Mr Chalke insisted that his apprentices spent only what money they needed to live on, and saved the rest.

'You'll thank me in the long run, young man,' Chalke had told him with a knowing smile when Jack had protested. And thank him, Jack had, on many occasions.

His needs were simple and, unlike El, he had no family to help support. He shared a small attic room with Jimmy, another of Chalke's apprentices, also a former workhouse boy.

Jack was brought out of his reverie by a knock on the door. It opened immediately, and Jimmy came in, his face pale.

'Have you heard the news?' he asked, sinking into the chair so recently vacated by Chalke. He was a wiry young man with an unruly mop of curly fair hair which no amount of hair oil could keep in check. 'They're saying downstairs that there might be a war. Will we have to fight, do you think?'

Jack leaned forward, resting his chin on his hands as he regarded his roommate solemnly, a knot of anxiety forming in the pit of his stomach. He wasn't scared, exactly, but he forced down the anxiety that rose like bile in his throat.

'Let's hope it won't come to that,' he answered Jimmy in what he hoped was a reassuring tone. Jimmy, God bless him, was a timid soul, always anxious, like a cat on hot bricks most of the time. Goodness knows how he'd cope on a battlefield. Not that Jack could say with any certainty how he would react either, he thought wryly. Who ever knew how they'd behave under such pressure?

'Alice has got a brother and two cousins in the army,' Jimmy said, his pale grey gaze moving to the window. A pigeon crouched on the sill, silhouetted against a Mediterranean-blue sky. 'She lost an uncle in the Boer War. You can imagine how she's feeling.'

Jack nodded. Alice worked in Ladies' Fashion. She was a sweet-natured girl, a little plump perhaps, with a mane of raven-black hair and bright blue eyes. She was sweet on Jimmy – and while her feelings were reciprocated, Jimmy, to Jack's continued frustration, was too shy to do anything about it. Perhaps, Jack thought now, the threat of war might be just the thing to spur his friend on.

In the butcher's, Ellie-May had also just heard about the goings on in Sarajevo. Making one of his increasingly rare appearances downstairs, Arnold leaned heavily on the counter, on which a crumpled edition of that morning's newspaper was spread. He read the article out aloud, for once his words not slurred by alcohol.

A lengthy pause followed. Ellie-May felt sick to her stomach. Would Bert and Arthur have to fight? And Jack? She went cold at the thought.

'It won't affect us, Father,' Frank said at length, with more confidence than he felt. 'Our army will sort them out quick as you like. All this speculation about volunteering, it's just scaremongering.'

'I hope you're right, son,' Arnold said gruffly but with little conviction. The thought of his son enlisting sent terror shooting down his spine. He hadn't been a good father to the boy, he would be the first to admit it, but Frank was all he had, and he'd do whatever he could to keep him safe.

Talk of the assassination was everywhere as the threat of war hung over the town like a black cloud.

'I can't see how events so far away could affect us so,' Ellie-May frowned.

'It's complicated,' Jack replied with a sigh. 'Politics always are.'

'You won't join up, will you?' Ellie-May asked. They were walking through Mayflower Park. Couples and families, and the occasional person on their own, milled between the giant oak trees. Children ran about, chasing each other, or sailed their boats on the satin-smooth waters of the lake. The sky was a cloudless blue and it was almost impossible to imagine that a political crisis was raging that would affect all of their lives.

'Mr Chalke believes war is inevitable,' Jack said after a moment's pause. He didn't want to alarm Ellie-May, but he wouldn't lie to her either. 'There will be a recruitment drive, though I doubt anyone will be forced to fight.' *Yet*, he added under his breath.

'Promise me you won't do anything stupid,' Ellie-May

said, turning to look into Jack's face, her eyes clouded with worry. 'Arthur's driving Mum mad with all his talk about enlisting, and Bert wrote in his last letter that he'll join up if it comes to it, even though he's bound to be still needed as a merchant sailor. Mum's frantic.' Ellie-May swallowed, her throat dry. 'I can't bear the thought of Bert and Arthur putting themselves in danger, but I'd die if you went, Jack.'

'You know I couldn't sit back and do nothing,' Jack said softly, taking her in his arms. She pressed herself against him, tears spilling over her pale lashes.

'But you could be killed,' she whispered into his collar.

'I'll be fine,' Jack said, releasing her and holding her at arm's length so he could look into her eyes. 'Anyway, the powers that be might find a way to resolve things without a war so don't give up hope.'

She nodded, desperate to cling to what little hope she could. They continued their walk. Jack tried hard to lighten the mood but for Ellie-May, the beautiful Sunday afternoon had been thoroughly spoiled.

Ellie-May scattered fresh sawdust on the flagstones and wiped her hand across her sweaty brow. Yesterday a welcome thunderstorm had brought a brief respite from the heatwave that had gripped the country but today the heat had returned, as oppressive as ever. Wiping her dusty hands on her apron, she looked out the window. The mood on the street was sombre, the expressions on the faces of the passers-by tense and apprehensive. Nerves were on a knife-edge after the events of the past months. Only a week before, on July 28th, shots had been fired by the Austro-Hungarians. Germany had invaded Belgium and Luxembourg and were moving towards France. It was only a matter of time before Britain became involved.

The shop had been quiet all day, a combination of the unpleasant heat and uncertainty keeping customers away. Ellie-May returned to the counter, wafting away a large bluebottle. Keeping flies off the meat was a full-time occupation in the summer.

Despite the open door, the shop was hot and stuffy. What little air drifted in from the street smelled of horse dung fermenting in the heat. She took a handkerchief from her skirt pocket to mop her shiny face. Sweat trickled down her spine and she walked over to stand in the open doorway. A tram rumbled by, its red-faced occupants fanning themselves. The air was hot and heavy. She wondered idly where Frank was. Their relationship had been forever altered since the day she'd rejected him four years before. They were courteous to each other now, but that was all.

The front step needed sweeping, again. With a weary sigh, Ellie-May took up the broom and went outside, grateful at least for the shade provided by the striped awning. She flicked the broom lethargically across the pavement, flicking dust into the hot, dry air. She straightened up to wipe the sweat out of her eyes. There seemed to be no escape from the heat. The sun bounced off the cobbles. A horse and cart rumbled by. The poor horse looked almost ready to collapse in the heat. Leaning her broom against the doorframe, she scanned the near deserted street, squinting against the dazzling sunlight.

A loud shout of alarm ripped through the still air. A young newspaper seller came tearing up the street, waving frantically, his face crimson in the heat.

'War! War!' he screamed. 'Britain is at war!' He paused and glanced at Ellie-May, his expression grave. 'Did you hear me, miss? We're at war with Germany!'

CHAPTER NINE

'We knew it would happen,' Sid remarked soberly over the supper table that evening. 'It was only a matter of when.'

'It's ridiculous,' Eileen fumed, banging down her knife to emphasize her point. 'Grown men acting like children, and it's the likes of us who'll pay the price.'

Ellie-May tried to swallow but her food caught in her throat, the meat and potato pie turning to sawdust in her mouth. Jack would certainly enlist, he'd hinted as much. The thought turned her stomach and sent icy fingers of fear running up and down her spine.

'It says in the paper that recruitment offices are springing up all over the country,' Arthur said, reaching across the table for a slice of bread. Of all of them he appeared the least perturbed by the news.

'I hope you're not thinking of doing anything silly?' Eileen said, her beady gaze fixed on her younger son.

'Two chaps from our news department have already enlisted,' Nora said, flicking a strand of auburn hair out of her clear green eyes. 'They went down to the council offices the minute they heard the news. Mr Barlow was awfully upset.'

'Hopefully they'll get enough volunteers without having to bring in conscription,' Sid said quietly. The thought of his country being at war sickened him. At forty-seven he was too old to join up, but terror for his sons gnawed at his belly.

'They're saying it'll likely be over by Christmas,' Eileen said. She shot Arthur a warning glare. 'So, don't you go rushing off like a bull in a china shop, my laddo. Wait and see what happens, eh? I doubt you can be spared from your job anyway.'

Arthur refrained from replying, chewing calmly on a hunk of bread, his gaze focused on his meal. Ellie-May's stomach contracted painfully. She knew her younger brother Arthur too well; knew he'd always craved adventure. From an early age, he could be found with his nose buried in his *Boy's Own* magazines, revelling in stories of derring-do. Now the chance had presented itself for him to be a real-life hero, it would take a lot of persuading to deter him from enlisting, and Ellie-May had no doubt the realities of war were far different from those portrayed in a child's storybook.

'Well, I hope our Bea and Jess put their foot down with their husbands and they don't go volunteering. They've got the little ones to think of, especially now Jess has another on the way.' Eileen said, half rising from her seat to replenish her cup of tea. 'A top-up, Sid?'

'Yes, thank you.' Sid raised his cup.

'Rose next door was saying that if they do have to bring in conscription, married men will be exempt,' Eileen went on as she sank back into her seat with a sigh, her thoughts turning to her eldest child, Bert, out on the high seas. She sent up a quick prayer for his continued safety. 'This city's only just getting over the *Titanic* tragedy,' she muttered softly. Around the table they fell silent. Old Northam had been particularly devastated by the sinking of the ship two years before. So many of their neighbours had lost husbands, fathers and sons in the disaster. Eileen hadn't had a moment of peace since, knowing Bert was out there at the mercy of the elements. Her stomach a knot of anxiety, she pushed her plate aside. 'I've quite lost my appetite.'

'Will Jack enlist, do you think?' Eileen asked Ellie-May as they washed the dishes some time later. Sid and Arthur had gone to sit outside, enjoying the pleasant coolness of the evening after the stifling heat of the day.

'He says so,' replied Ellie-May dully, handing the dried plate to Nora to put away in the cupboard.

'I'm glad I haven't got a boyfriend,' remarked Nora earnestly. 'I couldn't bear watching him go off to war.'

'I doubt anyone will find it easy, Nora,' said Eileen mildly. She wiped her soapy hands on a tea towel and patted Ellie-May's arm. 'Jack's a sensible lad, love, perhaps he'll change his mind.'

'You've done it then?'

Late evening sunlight streamed in through the parlour

window. The carriage clock on the mantelpiece ticked quietly. The bowl of lilies on the sideboard gave off a heady scent, a cloying smell that made Ellie-May think of death and destruction.

A terrible sense of foreboding filled her heart as she stared at Jack. At least he had the grace to look shamefaced.

'I can't believe you'd do this to me,' Ellie-May hissed. 'To us!'

'El, please. You've got to understand. I don't want to leave you any more than you want me to go but I can't, I *won't*, stand by while other blokes go off to fight.'

They were sitting in the front parlour. Eileen had taken one look at Jack's face when she'd opened the door that warm Tuesday evening and her heart had sunk to the floor.

'Good evening, Mrs Bramhall, may I see El for a few minutes?'

Her shoulders slumped in resignation. She'd replied with a long, shuddering sigh, 'Of course, lad. Come into the parlour. I'll get her for you.'

The moment her mother had come out into the yard, her face sombre, it was like all the colour had leached from Ellie-May's world. Her heart in her mouth, tears already threatening, it had been by sheer force of will that she had managed to walk into the parlour where Jack was waiting.

They were sitting side by side on the red velvet sofa, their upper bodies angled towards each other.

'I'm sorry, El,' Jack said. He took her hands in his. He genuinely regretted hurting her but his mind was made up.

'I've enlisted now so there's nothing I can do. I can't change my mind, even if I wanted to. Which I don't.'

'Why didn't you speak to me first? We should have discussed it.'

'We have discussed it, El. I've made no secret of my intention to volunteer should war be declared. Jimmy and I have joined up together. They're saying that they're going to make sure we all go with chaps we've grown up with. Jimmy and I'll stick together.' Jack grinned. 'We'll be all right, El. And they're saying it'll be over by Christmas, anyway, so I'll hardly be gone at all. I won't have finished my training by then, so I might not even get to leave England before it's all over.'

Ellie-May forced down the lump in her throat. 'When do you leave here?' she rasped, her mind in a turmoil of emotions. She was proud Jack had enlisted, proud he was brave enough, yet furious he would place himself in danger seemingly without a care for her own feelings.

'On Friday.'

'That's three days away!'

'We're being sent to a training camp in Sussex.' He squeezed Ellie-May's hands. 'Mr Chalke has released me from work from today. Will you ask Mr Cartwright for the time off so we can spend the time I've got left together?' Jack asked with a quiver in his voice. Despite his bravado and determination to do his bit, the thought of leaving his El would prove to be one of the hardest things he'd ever had to do.

*

The next three days flew by in a blur and before Ellie-May could catch her breath, she was standing on the platform surrounded by wives, mothers, girlfriends, all come to wave their brave men off to war. Some of the young men boarding the train barely looked in their teens. They crowded against the carriage windows, trying to be brave and pretending not see the tear-stained faced of their mothers.

Ellie-May clung to Jack, biting her lip until it hurt, but she was determined not to make a show of herself. She would do her sobbing later, once she was alone. The sound of weeping echoing up and down the platform almost broke her resolve.

'Hey, El.' Jack gently prised himself out of her grip. Taking her by the shoulders he looked into her green eyes. 'I'll be back by Christmas and in the new year we'll go and see the vicar, set a date, hmm?'

Ellie-May nodded, unable to speak for the lump in her throat.

'I love you, El. I always will.' He tapped the breast pocket of his shirt. 'I've got your picture and I'll look at it every day, I promise.'

The train whistled and the uniformed officers, with gruff voices and faces like granite, barked the order to board the train.

After one quick, final kiss which left Ellie-May gasping at the suddenness of it all, Jack was gone, swallowed up in the mad scramble for the train. She searched for him at the windows which were crammed with men, each hoping for a final glimpse of their loved ones. Anxiously she scanned each face, a variety of expressions, fear, bravado, cocky confidence, uncertainty.

The train began to move, slowly at first, then gathering speed.

'Jack!' Ellie-May shouted, shoving her way through the crowd as the train lurched out of the station, her eyes frantically searching the sea of pale faces. 'Jack!'

'El!' She turned her face towards the sound. It was the merest glimpse that was all, the flash of his face, but it was enough to give her a small measure of comfort before, her vision blurred by tears, she made her way out of the station and into a city reeling with the shock of being at war.

A week later Sid returned home from work to find his wife red-faced and screaming at his youngest son.

'You're a bloody idiot!'

Arthur stood with his head bowed. It was the reaction he'd expected from his mother but it didn't make it any easier to bear. He loved her, and hurting her was the last thing he'd wanted to do but ...

'I'm doing my bit for King and Country, Mum,' he said calmly. 'You should be proud.'

'*Proud*?' Eileen shrieked, her face puce. 'When you're lying dead on some foreign battlefield, do you think I'll be proud then?' She rounded on Sid who smiled at her sadly.

'Now, love, don't go on so.'

'Do you know what your son has gone and done?' she fumed, her face flushed.

'Aye, I heard,' replied Sid mildly, sitting down and untying his shoelaces. 'I'm proud of the lad. He's twenty years old, Eileen, a man. He has to do what he believes is right.'

Eileen stared at her husband incredulously. 'You're happy with the fact he's going off to be maimed or even killed, are you?'

'Mum!' She waved away Arthur's protest.

'Well?' Hands on hips, Eileen glared at her husband.

'I'm not happy about it, Eileen.' Sid sighed. 'Don't talk daft. But I am proud. There's a difference.' He pulled on his slippers, his balding pate gleaming in the light coming in through the kitchen window. 'Parents all over the country are having to say goodbye to their sons, Eileen. Why should we be any different? If our boy wants to do his duty, then I, for one, am not going to stand in his way.' He turned to Arthur. 'Good for you, lad.'

Arthur nodded. 'Thanks, Dad. I appreciate the support.'

Eileen's shoulders sagged and she sank onto a chair, defeated. Tears streamed down her face. She felt as though her heart were breaking.

'What will I do if anything happens to you, Arthur?' she wept.

Arthur put his arms around her. 'Mum, I'll be all right. Remember the newsreel we saw at the cinema the other night? The training camps look a right laugh. The gym instructor appeared to be a bit of a tyrant, but just think how fit I'll be with all that physical training,' he teased. 'You're always saying I need more exercise.'

'Oh, Arthur!' Eileen was in no mood for humour.

'Cheer up, love.' Sid patted Eileen's hand. 'When do you leave, lad?'

'The day after tomorrow,' Arthur replied, carefully avoiding his mother's gaze.

She let out a low moan. 'I wish you'd change your mind, Arthur.'

'I can't, Mum. Don't be upset, please,' he begged. 'I'll be all right, I promise.'

'You can't make such promises,' Eileen shouted, fear fuelling her anger.

'We're home,' Ellie-May's voice rang out and a moment later, she and Nora bustled into the kitchen. 'Mr Cartwright sent some sausages ...' Ellie-May stopped short, the paper-wrapped package in her outstretched hand, her green eyes taking in the scene, the cold hand of fear squeezing at her insides. 'What's happened?' Panic gripped her. 'Is it Jack?'

'Your brother's only gone and enlisted,' Eileen said bitterly. 'That's what's happened.' She dragged herself wearily to her feet. 'Tell Mr Cartwright, thank you for the sausages,' she said dully, as Ellie-May stared at her brother in dismay.

'Oh, Arthur.'

He held up his hands. 'Don't say anything, Ellie-May. Like I've been telling Mum, I need to do my bit.'

Ellie-May sighed and met her father's gaze. He slowly shook his head, warning her not to say anything more.

'More and more men are joining up every day,' Nora said. 'The recruitment offices are just across from where I work.

The queue's all down the street before they even open in the morning, and lads are still queueing up when I leave to come home.'

'I don't want to hear about it,' Eileen snapped, rattling the pan on the range. 'Will you take over, Ellie-May? I've lost my appetite and the grate in the front room needs blacking.'

'It doesn't need doing now, Eileen, love,' Sid chided her gently.

'Yes, it does,' came Eileen's sharp retort. She had to keep busy, and the smell of the cabbage boiling rapidly on the range was making her feel quite ill.

'Let her go, Dad,' Ellie-May said softly. She knew exactly how her mother felt. She felt the same. As long as she kept busy she could forget for a while that her Jack was training for war.

While Eileen disappeared into the other room with her blacking brush and a pile of old newspapers, Ellie-May finished the supper, her mind whirling. Now she had Arthur to worry about, as well as Jack. And God alone knew where Bert was.

'There wasn't any mail for me today, was there?' she asked, draining the cabbage, a cloud of steam billowing around her. All she'd heard from Jack so far was a hastily scribbled postcard to let her know he'd arrived safely at the camp in Sussex.

'No, love, sorry.' Sid straightened the cutlery Nora laid before him. 'I expect they keep them busy at that training camp. Not much time for letter writing,' then, catching sight of his daughter's crestfallen expression, he gave her a reassuring smile. 'Not to worry, love, perhaps one will come tomorrow.'

She kept Jack's postcard in her skirt pocket. It was creased and fading from her reading it so often. She missed him so much but she had to be brave. Millions of women and girls were in her position. She only hoped it was right what they were saying. That it really would be all over by Christmas and Jack, and Arthur, would be able to come home.

CHAPTER TEN

It soon became clear that the war would not be over by Christmas. Every day the newspapers published appeals for more young men to join up. Trains were arriving in Southampton every hour and the port was crammed with ships waiting to ferry troops across the Channel to France. It seemed as though half the city had turned out to wave them off.

The common had been taken over by the military and rows of white tents stood where once families had picnicked. Everyone who owned a horse was being asked to give it up to the cause. Poor Nora had been devastated when the two beautiful dray horses from the brewery up the street from W. H. Smith and Son had been commandeered by the army. Since she'd started working there she'd gotten into the habit of feeding the gentle giants apples and sugar lumps, loving the sensation of their big, hairy lips on her hand. Standing in the doorway, she hadn't been able to stem the flow of tears as the horses were led away, their owner, Eddie, staring after them, cap in hand, crying unashamedly.

In late August came the grim news that a total of 1,600 British soldiers had been killed, wounded or reported missing at the Battle of Mons.

Arthur was now at some training camp in the Midlands. His letters were infrequent and heavily censored, much to Eileen's immense annoyance.

'How's anyone supposed to make sense of what he's saying when every other word is blacked out?' she fumed to Sid, once her initial excitement at hearing from her son had waned. Bert, they had last heard, was somewhere in the Adriatic, but heading for home. Though he hadn't been specific, his letter had hinted at dangers lurking beneath the water and then Eileen had read a newspaper article about submarines and underwater bombs. She hadn't known a decent night's sleep since.

'It doesn't feel a bit like Christmas, does it?' Nora remarked to Ellie-May early on Christmas Eve afternoon. Snow covered the ground, turned to slush by the passing wagons and carts, pulled by the few remaining horses too old or too small to be of use to the military. The air was biting cold, the sky a dull grey.

'Not much,' Ellie-May agreed. They had joined the crowds in Above Bar Gate where clusters of children cooed over the pretty window displays. In front of the Bargate itself, the Salvation Army band played a rather mournful rendition of 'Come All Ye Faithful'.

'We're collecting for the war wounded,' a young woman

in uniform called to them, rattling her tin under Ellie-May's frozen nose. She rummaged in her purse for a few pennies and Nora did the same. No one in Southampton could remain naïve about the horrors of what was happening across the Channel. Boatloads of wounded soldiers were arriving daily, and every day the newspaper shared photos of men who had lost limbs or their sight, and those who were so shell-shocked they didn't know who or where they were. With each passing day, Ellie-May became more fearful for Jack and Arthur.

At present they were both still in England. Jack wrote every week, but his letters lacked the humour they once had. He was clearly growing bored with camp life and was itching to get over to France to do his bit. New recruits were arriving at the camps every few days and there were not enough uniforms or weapons to go around, the new arrivals being forced to train with pitchforks and broom handles.

'Oh,' Nora sighed as they paused outside Chalke and Chase. In its brightly lit windows a dazzling array of toys tumbled artfully from a life-size wooden sleigh. 'Let's go inside.' She grabbed Ellie-May's arm, her cheeks pink with cold. She was looking very grown up in her new maroon coat, hat and muff, but if she noticed the admiring glances she was attracting from passing gentlemen, she gave no sign. Ellie-May looked down at her own drab winter coat. It was looking a little threadbare. She'd seen one she liked in the shop window down the street from Cartwright's, a lovely plum-coloured wool. Perhaps she'd treat herself in the

January sales. She certainly couldn't afford anything from Jack's old store.

They spent a pleasant half hour wandering around the various departments, fighting their way through crowds of shoppers searching for bargains.

'We'd better head along to the market now,' Ellie-May said as they emerged into the cold street, 'or all the best trees will have gone.' Nora tucked her gloved hand in the crook of her sister's arm and they set off at a steady pace, their breath billowing in the frigid air.

Despite the ongoing war, the mood at the street market was festive, as if the people of Southampton were determined not to let the fighting spoil their Christmas. The aroma of freshly baked mince pies and cinnamon wafted from various stalls.

'What are those women doing?' Nora asked as they paused to buy mugs of mulled cider. Ellie-May followed her sister's gaze.

'They're handing out white feathers,' she said with a grimace. They watched a particularly pretty young girl stride up to a young man in a brown overcoat and thrust the feather under his nose.

'You ought to be ashamed of yourself,' the girl hissed angrily, her cheeks colouring with the depth of her disgust and contempt. 'Be a man and do your duty!'

The young man, flushing to the roots of his fair hair, turned tail and practically ran from the street, followed by the jeers of passers-by.

'They assume anyone who isn't in uniform is a coward,' Ellie-May enlightened Nora as they continued on their way, cold fingers curled around warm mugs. 'Frank got given one the other day. He came back in a foul mood, I can tell you.'

'Well,' declared Nora stoutly. 'They should be ashamed of themselves. Why should our Arthur and your Jack risk their lives when other men take life easy at home?'

I'd rather Jack was a coward and here with me than a dead hero, Ellie-May thought miserably. Every night she prayed the war would end before Jack was sent to the front, but every day it seemed increasingly unlikely. Recruitment posters were everywhere, urging young men to join up without delay.

'Frank's not thought of joining up, then?' Nora asked, as they browsed the rows of Christmas trees on offer.

Ellie-May shook her head. 'No. He says he's needed to run the shop.'

'He has a point, I suppose. What about this one?' Nora brushed a scattering of snow off the branches of a little pine tree. 'We should get it home between us.'

Ellie-May agreed. She paid for the tree and they set off for home. It had begun to snow again. The cold leached through the soles of her boots, the sharp pine needles snagging on her woollen gloves as they trudged onwards, heads bowed against the swirling snow.

'Frank will be in for a shock if they bring in conscription,' Nora said through chattering teeth, returning to their previous conversation.

'I just wish those in charge of this stupid war would come

to their senses and stop sending our boys overseas as cannon fodder,' Ellie-May retorted bitterly. She lived in a constant state of anxiety, worrying about Jack. And she knew her mother was beside herself over Bert and Arthur. There had been news of merchant ships being torpedoed, so Bert was in no less danger than those on active duty.

There would be no Christmas cheer at number 6 Church Street this Christmas, Ellie-May mused sombrely as she and Nora trudged past the house with its curtains tightly drawn. The youngest Doyle boy, Robbie, had been killed only last week. His older brother, Kenneth, had been one of the many Northam men to lose his life aboard the *Titanic*.

'Were we expecting company?' Nora asked. 'The parlour light's on.'

'I don't think so,' replied Ellie-May as the front door opened and a man in army uniform stepped out into the swirling snow.

'*Jack*!' she screamed. Letting her half of the tree drop into the snow, she flung herself into his arms, sobbing and laughing all at once.

'Get indoors, you daft pair,' Nora chided them, her eyes smiling with happiness for her sister. She knew how much she had missed Jack. After all, she was the one who listened to Ellie-May crying into her pillow every night.

'Yes, come on in. You're letting the heat out.' Sid stood in the doorway, beaming. 'Let me give you a hand with that tree, Nora, before you drag all the snow in with it.'

The parlour was warm and cosy. A fire blazed in the

hearth and the aroma of spicy gingerbread and mince pies wafted from the kitchen.

While Ellie-May and Nora divested themselves of coats, hats and scarves, Eileen bustled in with the tea tray.

'Isn't he a sight for sore eyes?' she laughed, handing round a plate of mince pies. 'And so handsome in his uniform.'

Jack grinned and helped himself to a pie. 'You flatter me, Mrs Bramhall.'

'I just wish our Arthur were here as well,' Eileen added wistfully. A silence descended on the room as their thoughts drifted to Arthur and Bert.

'Come on now,' Sid chided them. 'It's Christmas Eve and we're blessed to have Jack with us.'

'You're right, Sid.' Eileen rallied herself. 'Our Bea and Jess will be here for dinner tomorrow with their little ones. Kiddies always make Christmas that bit more special. Sid, love, you and Jack get that tree up. Ellie-May, the presents for the children are in the trunk at the foot of our bed. Would you fetch them? Nora, nip next door and see if you can tempt Stan round for a cup of tea and a mince pie.'

'I wish you could stay longer,' Ellie-May whispered into Jack's ear later that evening. The fire had died down, its glowing embers sending shadows leaping up the walls. Sid and Eileen had gone up to bed. The stockings hung above the fireplace, bulging with treats. Larger packages were piled around the tree.

'It's so unfair you've got to be back on Boxing Day,' she

pouted, sulkily. Now that Jack was home, she couldn't bear to let him go again.

'At least we've got tomorrow,' Jack said, burrowing his face in Ellie-May's neck, and making her giggle. 'And I'll get leave again before we're sent to the front.'

'When do you think that will be?'

'A few weeks at most,' Jack said with a shrug.

Ellie-May's stomach cramped with fear, but she was determined not to spoil the short time they had together by being miserable. With effort, she changed the subject to something more cheerful . . .

They were startled a few minutes later by a loud banging on the door.

'What on earth?' Jack got to his feet. Nora came in from the kitchen where she had been putting the finishing touches to the Christmas cake. She looked at Ellie-May with frightened eyes.

'Who can it be at this time?'

They heard footsteps overhead, and Sid's voice. 'Was that the door?'

The banging came again, more frantic this time. Nora went to the window and drew back the curtains.

'*Arthur!*' she screeched, flying to the door, shouting, 'Mum. Dad. It's Arthur. He's home.'

Arthur stumbled in, surrounded by a flurry of swirling snow and blast of cold air. He was blue with cold.

'Welcome home, mate!' Jack slapped him on the back, as Nora and Ellie-May took turns to hug him.

'You're freezing,' Ellie-May cried, hastening to put more coal on the fire. 'Nora, put the kettle on.'

'Arthur, oh it's so good to see you.' Eileen came hurrying down the stairs, bustling into the room in her dressing gown, her hair in disarray, her face wreathed in smiles as she enveloped her youngest son in her arms. 'You're frozen stiff, lad. Get yourself in front of the fire. Nora,' she barked. 'Where's that tea? Sit down, lad. I'll get you a blanket.'

'Don't fuss, Mum,' Arthur laughed, despite his chattering teeth, waving away his mother's concern. In spite of the fact he couldn't stop shivering, he was as pleased as punch to be home. And it was great to see Jack as well. Good to have someone who understood where Arthur had been, the life he now lived.

'I would have been here sooner,' he explained, between gulps of hot, sweet tea. 'But the train got stuck in the snow just outside Basingstoke and we were brought the rest of the way by cart. That was hard going, I can tell you. The horse was an ancient old nag – no wonder the army didn't want her – and we had to keep shovelling through snow drifts. My greatcoat kept out the worst of the cold and wet,' he said, nodding at the heavy coat which was now draped in front of the fire to dry out. He grinned. 'At least I made it home for Christmas.'

'Yes, you did, lad,' Sid agreed. 'And we're glad about that, aren't we, Eileen?'

'I'm tickled pink to see you, Arthur, I really am.'

'How did you find life in the camp?' asked Jack.

'Not quite what I was expecting,' Arthur admitted truthfully. 'A bit like PE lessons really, only more demanding. I only got given my uniform last week. I haven't even held a real rifle yet.'

'All that's set to change,' Jack told him soberly. 'I think they'll be shipping us out over the next few weeks.'

'So I've heard.' Arthur nodded in agreement.

'Can we not spoil Christmas by talking about this blasted war?' Eileen fumed, hands on her hips.

'Sorry, Mrs Bramhall,' Jack apologized.

'Sid, get that bottle of sherry we've been keeping for a special occasion. I reckon two of the lads getting home for Christmas is as good as cause for celebration as any.'

As Sid fetched the sherry, the clock chimed midnight.

'It's Christmas,' said Jack, pulling Ellie-May into his arms and kissing her gently on the lips and whispering softly, 'Merry Christmas, my love.'

Jack's leave flew by all too quickly. It seemed to Ellie-May that she had barely taken a breath before she was standing on the railway platform waving yet another tearful goodbye.

'Write as soon as you get to camp,' she called, blowing a final kiss towards the carriage window as the train began to pull away. She kept her gaze focused on Jack's face until it disappeared in a cloud of steam.

With the now familiar ache of loss sitting heavily in her chest, she turned into Church Street to see the telegram boy peddling away from her house. Gripped by a terror so strong, she broke into a run, oblivious to the slush that splashed up her stockings, and soaking the hem of her blue wool skirt.

'What's happened?' She burst into the house, her heart racing, to be greeted by Nora, her eyes red from weeping.

'It's our Bert,' she gasped. 'His ship was torpedoed three days ago. He's dead.'

She fell into Ellie-May's arms. Numb with shock, all Ellie-May could do was pat Nora's back, while her stunned mind tried to make sense of what had happened. Her darling big brother was dead? It was inconceivable. With one arm draped around Nora's quivering shoulders, Ellie-May manoeuvred them both through the narrow doorway into the warm kitchen.

Arthur was leaning against the sink, arms folded across his chest, his face ashen. Despite the five-year age gap between them, he and Bert had been close. Sid, deathly white, was trying to comfort Eileen. She buried in her face in her apron, and rocked to and fro, inconsolable in her grief.

'Ah, lass.' Sid met Ellie-May's anguished gaze. 'It's a bad do.'

'I can't believe he's gone,' she croaked, her numb brain still unable to process the news.

They were oblivious to the knock on the door until it opened to reveal the shawl-draped form of Rose Norris.

'I saw the telegram boy ... ?' She broke off, biting her bottom lip, her sympathetic gaze travelling around the room.

'It's our Bert,' Sid sighed heavily. 'His ship has been torpedoed. No survivors.'

Rose groaned. 'Sid, I'm so sorry. Ah, Eileen, love.' Casting off her shawl, she came to crouch at Eileen's side. 'Ellie-May, get the kettle on, love. Nora, run next door and tell my Davie to go fetch your sisters. Your mum needs you all here. You should all be together at a time like this.'

Wiping the tears from her eyes, Nora did as she was told. Ellie-May made the tea automatically. She barely noticed when she splashed a drop of boiling water on her hand, turning the pale skin an angry red.

Neighbours began to arrive to offer their condolences, knowing all too well that tomorrow it could be them getting the dreaded telegram. Ellie-May and Nora were kept busy dispensing endless cups of tea and handing round slices of leftover Christmas cake no one ate. Bea and Jess, seven months pregnant, arrived by hansom cab twenty minutes later. 'Damn the expense,' declared Bea defiantly. 'This is an emergency.' Their faces were blotchy from crying, their eyes red-rimmed and swollen. They had left the children at home in the care of their fathers.

'You should have brought Tommy,' Ellie-May said to Jess, as they huddled in the kitchen, needing a reprieve from the endless visitors. 'It might have cheered Mum up having him here.'

'Maybe in a day or two I'll pop round with him. I doubt anything would cheer her up today. God, what a thing to happen. And we had such a lovely day yesterday, too. I feel awful now, us having such a good time while our poor Bert was . . . at the bottom of the sea.' She burst into tears. Her own tears rolling down her cheeks, Ellie-May reached across her sister's swollen belly in a clumsy embrace.

'Oh, don't,' wailed Bea, coming into the kitchen to replenish the teapot. 'You'll start me off again.'

'Mum's going upstairs to lie down,' Nora said, joining her sisters in the kitchen. They huddled around the table, united in their grief. Ellie-May closed her eyes, despair like a heavy blanket settling across her hunched shoulders. She could hear the low rumble of voices in the room next door, the soft, weary tread of Eileen's footsteps as she hauled herself up the stairs, the creak of bedsprings overhead.

The front door closed and Sid came into the kitchen, shoulders hunched, his face grey. He appeared to have aged years in the last few hours. 'That's the last of them,' he said, rubbing a weary hand across his brow. 'They mean well, but . . .'

'I know,' Ellie-May replied with an understanding nod. 'Everyone's been very kind.'

'I'll be off home now, my loves,' Rose said, coming in with a tray of dirty teacups. She set them beside the sink and reached for her shawl. 'Will you be all right to finish the tidying up, only I must get back to Tony and the kiddies.'

'Of course, Mrs Norris,' Bea assured her. 'You've been a godsend.'

'Yes, you get off home, Rose, love,' Sid said. 'And thanks.'

'Well, if you need anything, you know where I am.' She smiled sadly. 'And let your mum sleep. It's the best thing for her. I'll pop around in the morning, see how she is.'

She shut the door behind her and silence descended on the small kitchen.

'I'm going down the pub,' Arthur said, suddenly feeling as if the walls were closing in on him. He slammed the door behind him, his grief erupting in a burst of anger.

Sid collapsed into the armchair by the fire, staring into the distance, his mind filled with the horrifying image of his son floundering in a burning sea, waving, screaming, burning, drowning. He squeezed his eyes shut, willing them away yet knowing that such images would haunt his dreams for years to come.

CHAPTER ELEVEN

The new year brought more bad news. On New Year's Day the Royal Navy battleship, HMS *Formidable* was sunk off Lyme Regis by a German U-boat with the loss of 547 lives. Then, just two weeks later, two German Zeppelins bombed Great Yarmouth and King's Lynn. Four people were killed and several buildings left in ruins. Civilians sporting black armbands and the front doors of the more affluent houses adorned with black wreaths were becoming commonplace.

Rose Norris's brother, Stephen, was part of the British Grand Fleet that defeated the German fleet in the North Sea at the end of January, sinking the German armoured cruiser, SMS *Blucher*, with a loss of 792 sailors, and disabling the German battleship SMS *Seydlitz*. Sitting in the Bramhall's kitchen, Rose read Stephen's heavily censored account of the battle.

'At least you know your brother's safe,' Eileen said, forcing aside her own overwhelming grief to reach across the table and give Rose's arm a squeeze.

'Yes, but for how long?' Rose replied with a sigh. She refolded the letter and placed it back in its envelope. 'So much for it all being over by Christmas. God knows how long this blasted war's going to last, or how many of our young men will end up paying with their lives.'

Eileen bit her lip, her cheeks pale in the weak winter-morning light.

'Arthur says it's likely he'll be sent to France within the next few weeks,' she said, wrapping cold fingers around her teacup. Despite the fire burning cheerfully in the grate, she couldn't get warm. Her heart was heavy with grief and a deep sense of foreboding. Would God be so cruel as to take Arthur from her too?

'I'm just so thankful my Davie is too young to enlist,' Rose said. 'I know it's selfish of me, but I can't help it.'

'I don't think you're selfish at all, Rose, love,' Eileen smiled sadly. 'I would have done anything to keep my boys safe. I'm thankful your lads will be safe, for a few years at least.'

'I hear boys of fourteen are lying about their age and joining up,' Rose nodded. 'That's my Davie's age. Their mothers must be frantic with worry.'

'I know. It's shocking the way the recruitment officers are turning a blind eye. Some have been sent home again, though.'

'Well,' said Rose with a humph. 'They should be thanking their lucky stars, the idiots. War's no bloody picnic.'

A small figure caught their eye, darting past the window. Someone hammered loudly on the back door.

'What the . . . ?' Eileen yanked the door open, and peered down at the snotty, tear-stained face of five-year-old Freddy Reed from number 15. Her heart sank. 'Freddy, love, what is it?' she asked, glancing at Rose, who was already out of her seat and reaching for her shawl.

'It's our Michael,' he sobbed, as Eileen bundled him into a motherly embrace. 'Mum's had a telegram. She says can you come straight away?'

'Of course, sweetie. You run on home. Me and Mrs Norris will be right behind you.'

The little boy sped off down the yard, his feet slithering on the frosty ground.

'Another family destroyed?' Eileen sighed, buttoning up her coat. 'When will it end?'

Ellie-May surveyed the tidy shop with an air of satisfaction. Fresh sawdust covered the floor, the tiles shone, the counter glass gleamed. She slipped into the back room, the frigid air taking her breath away.

'You ready to go then?' Frank asked, with barely a glance in her direction. He was scrubbing the table, the water in his bucket a deep crimson, pink bubbles dripping onto the stone floor. An icy draught rattled the windows in their frame and howled under the back door.

'Yes. I've finished up out front.' Ellie-May bundled up her apron and reached for the coat she had bought in the sales. Dark green, with a brown fur trim at the cuffs, it complemented her pale skin, and highlighted her eyes. Frank looked up, a scowl on his face, jealousy churning in the pit of his stomach. He had hoped that with Jack out of the way, he and Ellie-May might have stood a chance, but no such luck. It was 'Jack did this' and 'Jack said that'. He wanted to scream. She was obsessed with that bloody gypsy boy.

'Would you like me to look in on Mr Cartwright before I go?' She finished buttoning her coat and pulled on her gloves. 'I could make him a cup of tea if you're going to be a while.'

'You're all right, I'm almost done here. You get on.'

'I'll see you tomorrow, then.'

'Yes.'

She made her way back into the shop, and was about to turn out the light when someone banged on the door. She crossed the floor with a weary sigh. Why couldn't people read? The sign clearly said the shop was closed. She slid back the bolts and yanked open the door, her sarcastic response dying on her lips at the sight of Jack's grinning face.

'Jack! What are you doing home again so soon?' The words were barely out of her mouth when comprehension dawned. She clamped her hand across her mouth, her euphoria at seeing him extinguished like a flame doused in water. 'You're being posted?' she whispered through her fingers. Jack took her in his arms, the door swinging shut behind them.

'When?' Ellie-May whispered into his greatcoat. The material was cold and rough against her cheek.

'I've got three days,' he replied softly, his own voice choked with emotion. Now that the time had come to leave

England, he was filled with cold dread. 'I was hoping your Mum would let me kip in the kitchen for a couple of nights.'

Despite herself, Ellie-May smiled. 'Don't be silly. You can have Bert—' the name caught in her throat, '. . . and Arthur's room. I'll warm the bed for you. It hasn't been slept in for a while, it'll be damp.' Then, her lip trembling, she said tearfully, 'I wish you didn't have to go.'

'I know, El, but I do, so we'll make the most of the time we've got, hey?'

'I thought I heard voices.' Frank stood in the doorway, drying his hands on an old towel. 'So, are they finally shipping you out?'

Jack gave Frank a curt nod. 'We sail on Saturday.'

Ellie-May clutched Jack's arm as the two men eyed each other with open hostility. Frank sucked in a breath and blew out his cheeks. He took a step forward and stretched out his hand, a look of grudging respect on his face.

'I know we'll never be mates but, well, good luck, yeah?'

Jack shook Frank's hand. 'Thanks. I reckon I'll need all the luck I can get.'

'Take the next few days off, Ellie-May,' Frank said, smiling magnanimously. Ellie-May's eyes widened.

'Are you sure?'

'Yeah, I can manage.'

'Thanks, Frank.' Jack slapped Frank's shoulder. 'I appreciate that.'

Frank closed the door and watched through the misty glass as they stepped out into the cold February night. He could afford to be generous, what with Jack soon to be out of the picture. He rubbed his hands, grinning as he shot the bolts.

He'd soon persuade Ellie-May he was the better bet.

Huddled together, Jack and Ellie-May were oblivious to the bitter cold as they navigated their way home by the moonlight. The streets were treacherous and Ellie-May was glad she had Jack to cling onto as they slipped and slithered on the icy cobbles.

'Are you scared?' Ellie-May asked in a small voice as they rounded the corner into Church Street.

'Only an idiot wouldn't be scared,' replied Jack, his breath clouding in front of his face. Ellie-May tightened her grip on his arm. 'All I can promise you is that I'll not take any unnecessary risks.'

'I shall pray for you every night,' Ellie-May whispered, as they approached the front door of number 12. The blackout curtains were firmly drawn and not a chink of light spilled out into the street.

She fumbled at the doorknob with fingers numb with cold, and they fell into the porch.

'Is that you, Ellie-May?' Sid called from the warm kitchen.

'Yes, Dad,' she called back, divesting herself of her wraps, 'and I've got a surprise for you all.'

Sid appeared in the doorway with Nora. 'Ah, Jack.' Sid shook Jack's hands. 'Good to see you again, lad.'

Norah flung herself at Jack with a grin. 'Gosh, Jack, you

grow more handsome every time we see you. Our Ellie-May's a lucky girl.'

'Don't tease me, Nora,' Jack grinned back at her.

'Come on in where it's warm,' Sid urged, ushering them into the kitchen where a good fire burned in the grate. 'Nora's about to make some toast. Sit yourself down, lad. You too, Ellie-May, you look half perished.'

'Where's Mum?' Ellie-May asked, sitting down at the table. She slipped off her boots and massaged her frozen feet.

'Michael Reed's been reported MIA,' Sid told her soberly. 'Mum and Rose are sitting with Mrs Reed until her husband can get home.'

'Missing in action? Thanks, Nora.' She accepted the mug of steaming hot tea gratefully. 'There's a chance he's all right, then?'

Sid shrugged wearily. 'There's always hope, I suppose.'

They fell into a melancholy silence, the only sounds the rattling of the window in its frame as the wind shrieked through the yard, and the crackle and pop of the burning coals. Nora knelt in front of the fire, toasting thick slices of bread. Ellie-May fetched butter and jam from the pantry under the stairs, anxiety churning in her stomach. She wouldn't be able to bear it if anything happened to Jack. She'd rather die herself than live without him.

'Hey, come on.' Jack grabbed her hand, and looked into her eyes. 'I've only got three days. Don't let's waste them being miserable.'

'Jack's right, love.' Sid stretched his stockinged feet

towards the fire. 'Much as we feel sorry for the Reeds, we've got to focus on the living. God knows how much time any of us have got left. We owe it to those we've lost to make the best of it.'

The three days passed by all too quickly. On his last night in England, Jack sat in the Bramhalls' kitchen staring into the dying embers. The kitchen was in darkness but for the glow of the coals. His armchair was close to the fire. Ellie-May sat on his lap, her head resting against his chest. She was fast asleep. His nostrils were filled with the scent of her hair, and the lavender soap she used. With a heavy heart he watched the gentle rise and fall of her chest. Her dressing gown had fallen open and he could see the lace frill of her nightdress, the navy ribbons he had earlier pulled open to reveal the creamy mound of her breasts. Heat flooded his veins as he recalled the moment they had come together in front of the fire, their passion made more urgent by the knowledge that their time together was so short. When it was spent, they had clung to each other, the heat of the smouldering embers warm on their skin. In the firelight, his El resembled a mythical goddess, her alabaster skin taking on a golden hue in the light of the flickering flames.

Sleep eluded him, and he was glad. He didn't plan to miss one second of his last night with El by sleeping. His heart was like a rock in his chest. Not for one second did he regret his decision to join up; he would do his duty to God and country, but the prospect of leaving El behind for what might be months, years even, terrified him more than the thought of the trenches.

He blinked, his eyes gritty, and yawned. Outside a cat yowled, echoed by another further away. A dog barked once, then fell silent. The cat yowled again, a haunting sound that made the hairs on Jack's arms stand on end.

Ellie-May stirred. 'Jack?' she whispered sleepily.

'Shush,' he hushed her, gently stroking her hair. 'I'm here. Go back to sleep.'

He woke her in the cold hours of the early morning, and sent her up to bed. Quietly unlocking the back door, he stepped out into the icy darkness. Dawn was a pale smudge in the east, the cold, black sky studded with stars. He leaned against the cold concrete of the coal bunker. He could smell the sour stench of the privy. That very night, he would be on his way to France and God alone knew when he would be back. The thought filled him with a heaviness he hadn't experienced since the day Fisher told him his mother was dead.

He lost track of time, his mind wandering until the sound of the back door opening brought him back to himself.

'Morning, Jack? Can't sleep?' Sid walked towards him in the grey dawn light, and held out his pack of Woodbines. Jack shook his head. Sid stuck a cigarette between his lips, a match flared and died. He inhaled deeply, flinging the spent match over the wall into the church yard.

'It's a bit parky out here,' he said, shivering despite the heavy coat he'd pulled on over his pyjamas. 'You don't want to catch cold, lad.'

'I'm all right,' Jack replied, gritting his teeth in an effort to stop them chattering. 'I just wanted to . . .' He shrugged his shoulders helplessly, at a loss for words. How could he explain that he wanted to drink in everything about home – the star-lit sky, the brooding monolith that was the Methodist church, the crumbling wall, and yes, even the stink of the privy. Sid laid a calloused hand on Jack's shoulder.

'I understand, lad,' he said softly, his breath billowing on the frosty air. 'Since Eileen and I lost our Bert,' he went on in his gentle tone, 'well, lad, it's an ache that never goes away.' He stared into the distance for a moment, lost in thought. Jack coughed and Sid started. He smiled. 'What I'm trying to say is, for God's sake, look after yourself. For our Ellie-May's sake, if not your own. I won't even pretend to imagine the kind of hell you're heading to, and my Arthur won't be far behind, God help him. Do your best to keep yourself safe, hey?'

'I'll do my best, sir.' Jack's laugh sounded hollow even to his own ears. Sid slapped him on the back. 'You'll be in our prayers, you know that?'

'Thank you.'

They stood in companionable silence for a while, the smell of cigarette smoke sharp in the cold air.

'If anything . . .' Jack paused and cleared his throat. 'If anything should happen to me, sir, I've got some post office savings. I've made a will, the army insist on it, and well, everything goes to El of course.'

Sid nodded, his expression grave. 'Let's hope it won't come to that.'

'What on earth are you two doing out here?' Eileen stood in the doorway, tying the belt to her gown and surveying the two men with a look that said she thought they'd lost their minds. 'Get inside before you catch your death, you idiots.'

The quayside was a sea of uniforms. The sound of weeping could be heard all along the docks. The Salvation Army band had struck up a rousing tune, designed to encourage patriotism and drown out fear and doubt. Many of the soldiers – young men, most only in their late teens like Jack – were white-faced and stiff-lipped. Their impending departure was made worse by the fact that, only an hour before, a ship had docked, bringing home the seriously wounded. The men waiting on the quayside had tried not to see the stretchers, the blood-soaked bandages. The shell-shocked. The heartbreaking sight had a sobering effect on even the most patriotic of those assembled, and a hush fell over the quay as the distressing procession made its way to waiting ambulances.

Ellie-May's stomach turned as she contemplated the difficult road to recovery the poor men faced; men who'd sacrificed so much for their country. She offered up a silent prayer that they would not be abandoned by their loved ones, knowing without a doubt that, as long as Jack came back to her alive, she wouldn't care what bits he was missing.

Jack stiffened and Ellie-May's heart contracted with fear. The time had come to board.

The ship loomed above her. Seagulls wheeled overhead,

their haunting cry echoing the wails of those gathered along the quayside. The air smelled of the dark and forbidding sea and the sky was a cold grey. The noise was incredible; they had to shout to make themselves heard above the cacophony of the loading and unloading going on around them.

The gangplank was lowered and there was a surge as the first wave of soldiers shuffled forward to embark. A sob caught in Ellie-May's throat and she gripped Jack tighter.

'God bless you, lad,' said Eileen, giving him a hug. Jack held onto her for a moment, breathing in her warm, motherly scent. Eileen had always been more of a mother to him than his own. 'You look after yourself, and stay safe.' Eileen held him at arm's length. 'You hear me, Jack Pickup?' Her lip trembled as she spoke, her eyes glistening with tears. She was still grieving her beloved Bert. Losing Jack too would be a bitter blow.

'I'll keep my head down,' Jack promised her. Reluctantly, Eileen let him go, and he turned to Ellie-May. She clung to him, sobbing into his heavy coat, her heart breaking, anxiety sitting like a rock in the pit of her stomach.

'I'll write as often as I can.' He cupped her chin, raising her face so he was looking into her eyes. 'I love you, El.'

Ellie-May was crying so hard she could barely speak. She nodded, tears streaming down her cheeks. 'I love you too, Jack.'

Jack wiped her cheek with his thumb. 'And when all this nonsense is over, I'll come back and marry you.' Jack grinned. She managed a weak smile. 'There, that's better,' he said softly, as he held her tight, oblivious to the crowd jostling around them. If it weren't for the war, they'd likely have been married by now, but the prospect of leaving her a widow and perhaps with a child, too, had strengthened his resolve to wait until the war was over. There was still hope that it would be over sooner rather than later, and they'd have the rest of their lives to be together.

The order came for Jack to embark and he gently prised himself free from Ellie-May's grip. He looked into her devastated face and gave her a brave smile, glancing to Eileen for support. She nodded, her own eyes red with unshed tears.

'You go on, Jack, love, and Godspeed. Come on, Ellie-May, sweetheart. Jack's got to go now. Come on, be brave, there's a good girl.'

With immense effort, Ellie-May choked back her tears. After one final, lingering kiss, she let him go. She tried to keep him in view, but all too soon he was swallowed up by the crowd. Her eyes blurred with tears. With Eileen's arm tight around her quivering shoulders, the cold February wind tugging at her coat, she watched the soldiers embark. They swarmed up the gangplanks like ants, filling the decks high above their heads, bodies pressed against the railings, each one desperate for a final glimpse of a loved one, eyes desperately seeking a familiar face amidst the sea of waving hands.

The cold seeped through the soles of her shoes and chapped her damp cheeks, but like everyone else, Ellie-May and Eileen stood rooted to the spot, oblivious to the discomfort, not daring to leave until the ship was clear of the harbour. The band struck up another rousing song and some of the onlookers even joined in with the chorus. A few waved flags and banners, reminding Ellie-May of how they had gathered here almost three years before to wave the *Titanic* off on her maiden voyage.

Clutching Eileen's arm, Ellie-May strained her eyes, desperately trying to pick Jack out from the waving throng. The band ceased playing and a heavy silence fell over the onlookers, broken only by the occasional sob and the melancholy calling of the gulls.

They stood together huddled against the wind; wives, mothers, sweethearts, watching until the ship disappeared over the horizon.

CHAPTER TWELVE

Jack squinted into shards of broken sunlight. The latest barrage of bombs and bullets had ceased, leaving the expanse of frozen mud known as No Man's Land eerily silent to allow the stretcher bearers to bring back the dead and dying. Although it was early March, the godforsaken landscape bore no hint of spring. No birds sang. The only birds Jack had seen since his arrival were the carrion crows that fought with the rats to feast on the dead bodies. Every tree and shrub for miles around had been obliterated, leaving only desolation; mile upon mile of packed-hard mud, splintered with broken ice, dissected by great lengths of impenetrable barricades of wickedly sharp barbed wire.

'It's brass monkey weather today, that's for sure.' Larry Potts slapped at his shoulders in an effort to warm himself up. He was a lanky, quiet, unassuming young man of twenty, and Jack had warmed to him instantly. Friendships were formed quickly in the trenches. Jack's friend and co-worker, Jimmy, with whom he had enlisted, had been sent further up the line the day they'd arrived, and Jack hadn't heard anything of him since.

Jack dropped down from the ladder, his boots landing with a dull thud on the frozen mud. 'I prefer it cold than raining,' he replied to Larry's comment, his hands shaking as he lit a cigarette. Smoking, and receiving letters and parcels from home, were the few comforts of life in the trenches.

Jack had been at the front for just over a week and he was slowly becoming used to the ever-pervading cold and the stench of blood and death. His first sight of the trenches had sent terror coursing through his veins and it had taken all his strength and determination not to turn tail and run. No wonder men deserted, poor sods. He'd only been in the trench for five minutes when he spotted his first rat. It was the size of a domestic cat, yellow eyes glinting malevolently, its face a crusty rust-brown colour. Upon realizing why, Jack had emptied his stomach there and then, much to the mirth of his more battle-hardened comrades.

The noise was the worst: the enemy shelled them relentlessly; bombs crashed into No Man's Land; bullets whistled overhead. But Jack soon learn that it was when the bombs and bullets fell silent that the worst was to come. The haunting screams of the wounded and the dying could drive a man mad if he weren't careful. Sleep was impossible, and Jack had grown used to getting by on a few snatched minutes of shut-eye.

He exhaled and flexed his shoulders in an effort to relieve

the tension and stamped his frozen feet, knowing he needed to keep the blood flowing if he wanted to keep his toes.

'It'll be us next,' he murmured to Larry, inclining his head to indicate the high, solid-mud wall of the trench. He clenched his teeth, trying to control the nervous tremor in his cheek. Many times over the past week, Jack had watched his new-found friends go over the top, some never to return.

'Yeah,' Larry nodded, as terror bleached his face of all colour. Jack noticed that the hand that brought Larry's Woodbine to his lips was shaking, and made a conscious effort to control his own nerves.

'Are you scared?' Larry croaked, as they crouched against the mud wall. All along the trench, men were dozing or writing letters; some merely staring into space. All were waiting.

'Terrified,' Jack replied softly.

'I wish the food was better,' Larry said, making Jack smile.

'Yeah,' he agreed. He reached into the pocket of his greatcoat and retrieved the photograph he and Ellie-May had had taken when he'd first joined up. They had gone to a photographer in Above Bar Street; a stooped little Jewish man who was rushed off his feet photographing newly enlisted soldiers with their sweethearts, or mothers. Jack and Ellie-May had posed together, stiff and formal in their Sunday best in front of a gaudily painted background. He studied it now, a smile playing on his cold lips. He was sitting in a straight-back chair, El standing primly beside him, and looking ravishingly beautiful, one gloved hand resting on his shoulder, in front of a backdrop of a flowering oak tree.

Ellie-May's letter had been filled with news of her new niece, Grace Elizabeth, born the first week of March. It had been a long and difficult labour, she wrote, but Jess was recovering well. Eileen had gone to stay for a few days to look after Gordon and little Tommy.

'That your girl?' Larry leaned against Jack in order to get a good look. 'Cor, she's a bit of all right, isn't she?'

Jack grinned. 'She's a diamond. We're going to be married once all this is over.' He waved his hand to encompass the trench.

'You're lucky to have someone waiting for you,' Larry said, in a somewhat wistful manner. 'I've never had a girlfriend. Too shy.'

'You're young,' Jack assured him, giving his arm a playful punch. 'You've plenty of time to meet the right girl.'

Larry's ghostly cheeks coloured slightly, then his eyes widened, his gaze fixed at something further along the trench. Jack turned to follow his gaze, his own heart plummeting as anxiety and fear began to gnaw at his stomach as viciously as any trench rat.

'Right, lads, let's be having you.' Captain Reginald Axe was a tall, distinguished-looking man in his early thirties, with a pencil-thin moustache and slate-grey eyes. There was a scramble in the trench as men clambered to their feet. Letters were refolded and tucked safely into breast pockets, half-smoked cigarettes extinguished to be enjoyed later.

'This is your first time over the top, lads,' Reggie said, his words tinged with kindness. 'And I know no amount of training can prepare you for what you are about to experience.' He strode up and down the trench, hands clasped behind his back, holding the attention of every man present.

Jack swallowed. His throat felt as dry as sandpaper and his palms were clammy.

This was it.

It crossed his mind fleetingly to wonder whether he'd be alive by sunset, but he shook the thought away, forcing himself to concentrate on his captain's words.

'I'm going to reiterate what you'd have been told when you first arrived,' Reggie said. 'Once you go over the top, you keep moving.' His voice was as clear as a bell in the cold, crisp air. 'You don't stop for anything. Stop moving and you'll be killed. If your mate goes down, you step over him and keep moving forward.' There was a rumble of dissent at this, and Reggie swung his beady gaze along the assembled men. 'I mean it,' he said sternly. 'You leave your fallen comrades for the stretcher bearers and the medics. There's nothing you can do for them except get yourself killed alongside them. Is that clear? A second's hesitation can be the difference between you ending up dead or making it back here.' His eyes blazed as he demanded harshly, 'Got it?'

A murmur of 'Yes, sir,' rippled along the trench.

'Good.' Reggie glanced at his watch. 'You go in an hour.'

The next sixty minutes dragged. A few chaps attempted a game of cards, or told bad jokes. A couple prayed, begging the Holy Virgin for her protection. Jack and Larry huddled together and shared a final cigarette. Jack rubbed his hands together. He could barely feel his feet in his boots despite the two layers of socks he wore.

The last of the clouds dispersed, leaving an azure sky in their wake. The sun was almost at its zenith. Jack inhaled a lungful of smoke. Neither of them spoke. What was there to say?

The order was sudden and brutal. Jack leapt to his feet, flinging his cigarette butt to the ground. Before his brain could form a coherent thought, he had clambered up the ladder, and taken his first step into Hell.

Ellie-May crossed the street and hurried passed the angry mob that had gathered outside Heinz the Jewellers. A window had been smashed and someone had daubed rude slogans on the wall.

'We're not German, we are Czechoslovakian.' Reinhold Heinz leaned out of an upstairs window and tried to reason with the baying crowd. His bald pate gleamed in the spring sunshine, his long comb-over flopping down the side of his face as he pleaded with the screaming crowd intent on destroying his livelihood. His wife Hilda's tearstained face appeared beside him.

'Please, we have children,' she cried. The children's frightened wails could be clearly heard over the baying mob.

Sick with disgust, Ellie-May bowed her head, and scurried along the street. Reinhold and Hilda were second-generation immigrants, born and bred in England, but she knew they weren't the only family to be persecuted in such a misguided display of patriotism. The *Echo* was filled with stories of immigrant families who had been similarly targeted, their homes and businesses defaced and vandalized. The local authorities were going so far as to detain immigrants with German connections, interring them in camps along the south coast.

Ellie-May sucked in a breath and exhaled slowly, trying to banish the image of Hilda Heinz's terrified face from her mind.

It was a beautifully mild Saturday morning in early March. Clouds scudded across a sapphire-blue sky and the sun was warm on her face as she ducked down the alley and entered the yard of Cartwright's Butchers.

Frank was hunched over a pig's carcass. He looked up, his cheeks red and shiny with perspiration, blood up to his elbows. 'What's all the commotion?' he asked.

'There's a mob outside Heinz the Jewellers,' Ellie-May informed him, shrugging out of her coat. She hung it on the peg behind the door and tied on her apron. 'They've smashed the window.'

'You can hardly blame them,' Frank said, straightening up and wiping his hands on a bloody towel. 'Sentiments are running high.'

'It's cruel. Mr Heinz and his wife aren't even German.' She fetched the broom and went into the shop. She had the floor to sweep and scatter with fresh sawdust before they opened.

Frank followed her, twisting his hands together, a clear sign he was nervous. Ellie-May eyed him curiously.

'What's the matter?'

'There's a concert at the Mayflower tomorrow evening,' he said, clearing his throat, a blush colouring his cheeks. 'I wondered if you might go with me?'

'Frank, I'm engaged!'

'No, I don't mean like that,' Frank lied quickly. 'I meant as friends. It's for a good cause. It's a fundraiser for wounded soldiers. Mrs Jones practically bullied me into buying tickets when I dropped off her order yesterday afternoon. Her son lost both his legs at Mons last year.' He splayed his hands and shrugged sheepishly. 'I could hardly refuse, could I?'

'It's disloyal to Jack, Frank. I'm sorry, I can't.'

'I've got three tickets,' Frank persevered. 'You could invite Nora as chaperone.'

Ellie-May sighed. She chewed her bottom lip thoughtfully. 'All right then,' she gave in with a sigh. 'If it's the three of us, I suppose it will be all right.'

Frank's face brightened. 'Excellent. The concert starts at seven o'clock sharp so I'll call for you both at six. We'll get the tram.'

'All right,' Ellie-May said again. She was already regretting her decision. 'You'd better get back to work or we won't be ready to open on time.' She flicked a pile of sawdust with the broom. 'How's Mr Cartwright?'

'As cantankerous as ever,' Frank replied over his shoulder. 'His foot was up like a balloon this morning. The doctor's due at eleven. Show him up when he arrives, will you?'

*

133

As a rule, Saturday was their busiest day of the week and that day proved to be no exception. The hours flew by and it seemed Ellie-May had barely had a chance to draw breath before it was six o'clock and she was locking and bolting the door.

In the back room, she sluiced the floor and scrubbed the table before putting on her coat and hat. Calling a cheery goodbye to Frank and reaffirming their plans to meet at six the following evening, she stepped out into the growing twilight. Already, the first evening stars were visible in the velvet-blue sky. A pair of house martins, newly returned from warmer climes, swooped over her head, and dived into their nest tucked neatly under the eaves.

Her footsteps sounded loud in the stillness of the evening, as she made her way home. There were few people about, the growing darkness and the cold evening air driving people indoors.

'Where's Mum and Dad?' she asked Nora as she entered the kitchen.

'At church,' Nora replied. She added a shovelful of coal on the fire and shut the door. A pot of pea soup simmered on the range. 'The kettle has just boiled,' Nora said. 'Tea?'

'Yes, please.' Ellie-May rubbed her cold hands and sat down to unbutton her boots. 'Any news?'

'A letter came from Arthur this morning. It's behind the clock on the mantelpiece.'

Ellie-May set her boots to one side and went to fetch the letter. Arthur had left for France in the middle of February and Sid and Eileen had taken to going to church every evening to light candles for him and Jack.

'He sounds cheerful enough,' Ellie-May said, as she skimmed Arthur's untidy scrawl. The letter had been heavily censored and it made for difficult reading, with every other word or sentence erased in thick black ink.

'He's got to, hasn't he?' Nora replied drily. 'He's hardly going to tell us how bad things are.'

'I suppose not. I haven't heard from Jack in ages. I hope he's all right.' Ellie-May nipped her lip anxiously and Nora turned her attention from the bubbling pot of soup to give her sister an encouraging smile.

'Try not to worry. A lady I work with, Mrs Duke, hadn't heard from either of her boys for weeks, and then she got four letters all at once.'

'It's hard not to worry,' Ellie-May sighed, folding Arthur's letter carefully along the creases. 'I saw the telegram boy going down Peel Street this morning on my way to work.'

Nora shook her head. 'We live in anxious times,' she agreed, handing Ellie-May her mug of tea, and coming to sit opposite her.

'Oh, I almost forgot. Frank's got tickets for some benefit concert tomorrow evening at the Mayflower. Do you fancy it?'

'Why not?' Nora inclined her head. 'It'll be nice to dress up a bit and go out for a change.' She raised an eyebrow quizzically. 'I take it you're going as friends?'

'Of course,' replied Ellie-May crossly. 'I only accepted

because Frank said I could invite you.' She glared at Nora over the rim of her mug. 'Anyway,' she added with more confidence than she felt, 'I'm sure whatever feelings he used to have for me are long-dead.'

Nora raised her eyebrows quizzically. 'As long as you're sure,' she said, draining her mug.

The concert turned out to be very enjoyable, and moving. There was barely a dry eye in the house by the time the curtain came down, as the thoughts of those in the audience turned to loved ones far away. The lights came up and, struggling to control her own emotions, her cheeks stained with tears, Ellie-May followed Nora and Frank out into the cool night air.

As the throng of concertgoers poured down the steps, Ellie-May heard Frank swear under his breath and she suddenly became aware of the women with their feathers. They were a common sight on the streets of Southampton these days, their sole purpose to shame and embarrass any young man not in uniform. Frank ducked his head and hurried down the steps, his hat pulled low over his eyes. Ellie-May and Nora exchanged glances, rushing to keep up with him.

'Sir, excuse me, sir!' the young woman cried, scurrying after Frank. She was attractive and well-to-do, judging by the cut of her expensive-looking black coat. She wore a black hat and veil and her mouth was set in a grim line, her heels clicking rhythmically on the cold pavement. 'Sir,' she said again, catching up with him when her determination finally forced

Frank to admit defeat and stop. He whirled round to face her, his expression angry, his cheeks inflamed in embarrassment.

'Go away, woman!' he hissed through clenched teeth. Ellie-May and Nora huddled behind him, their own cheeks flaming with shame as passers-by paused to stop and stare.

'Sir,' the woman's voice was steady and clear. She raised her chin, and looked Frank straight in the eye. 'I would like to present you with this white feather as a symbol of your cowardice.' She thrust the long, snow-white feather under Frank's nose 'Men like you make me sick,' she snarled venomously, forcing him to take a step backwards. 'Here, take it.' She waved the feather in his face, a mocking smile playing on her lips. With an equally mocking leer, Frank snatched the feather from her dainty, gloved hand, and let it fall to the floor, where he ground it into the dirt with the heel of his shoe.

'That is what I think of your feather,' he snorted. 'You're pathetic, all of you.' He nodded to where other women were moving amongst the dispersing crowd. 'Now get out of my way.' He brushed passed her. 'Are you two coming?' He glowered at Ellie-May and Nora over his shoulder. Mortified, Ellie-May and Nora could only nod, as heads bowed in shame, they hurried after him.

Feeling the young woman's gaze boring into her back, Ellie-May felt compelled to turn back. 'My fiancé is at the front.'

'Then you should be ashamed of yourself,' the woman snapped. 'Gallivanting with a coward while your man risks his life.' Taken aback, Ellie-May had no time to protest, or explain. The woman spat at her feet in disgust and turned away in search of her next target.

'Take no notice,' Nora said, tucking her hand into the crook of her sister's elbow.

'No,' Ellie-May said. She was shaking. 'That woman is right. I shouldn't have come tonight. It was disloyal to Jack. I shan't go anywhere with Frank again. And,' she lowered her voice as they neared the tram, 'he is a coward. He uses the shop as an excuse as to why he can't enlist, but Mr Cartwright can easily afford to employ someone to help me until the end of the war, which, *please God*, won't be far off.'

As she and Nora settled themselves on the crowded tram she glanced across the aisle to where Frank sat slumped in his seat. He was clearly brooding, his chin almost resting on his chest, his hat pulled low over his eyes. He would be a in a foul mood tomorrow, of that she was in no doubt. She leaned back in her seat and closed her eyes, thinking of Jack.

CHAPTER THIRTEEN

The recent thaw and days of torrential rain had turned No Man's Land into a sea of glutinous mud. The trenches were inches deep in filthy water, and duck boards had been laid down in an attempt to make movement easier.

Jack rolled a cigarette. He had to make a conscious effort to stop his hands from shaking. The bloated body of a dead rat floated close by, but he barely noticed it. After the horrors of the past weeks, he could scarcely be bothered by a dead rat. He yawned. His eyes felt hot and gritty from lack of sleep and he was grateful for the lull in fighting – however brief – that allowed for the stretcher bearers and medics on both sides to retrieve the wounded and the dead.

He hunkered down on his haunches and inhaled contemplatively, the nicotine taking the edge off his shattered nerves. He had grown used to the monotony of life in the trenches. He'd even grown used to the stench of blood and death, and the relentless hail of bombs and bullets. What he still hadn't managed to get used to, however, were the screams of the wounded and the dying. Even when they had fallen silent, he could still hear them in his head. Sometimes he wondered if he had already gone mad.

He leaned against the damp mud wall of the trench. Soldiers' worst enemy was boredom; it played havoc with a man's imagination. There was little to do except write letters, play cards, smoke, and worry about the next time it was your turn to 'go over the top'.

Glancing sideways at the sound of approaching footsteps, he grinned to see Larry making his way along the treacherously slippery duck boards towards him. His friend's face was pale and he sported dark smudges beneath tired, bloodshot eyes. He hunkered down beside Jack and took the proffered cigarette with a nod of gratitude.

They sat in companionable silence for a while, sharing the cigarette and half listening to the snippets of conversation drifting up and down the trench, punctuated by the occasional splash, as someone missed their footing and ended up ankle-deep in the filthy, stagnant water.

'How are you holding up?' Jack asked. 'You're very pale. You're not sickening for something, are you?' He cast a sideways glance at his friend, hoping he wasn't coming down with dysentery or something worse.

Larry shook his head. He was trembling all over and there was a distinct smell of vomit emanating from his tunic. When he finally replied, his voice quivered. 'I saw Roly drown right in front of me.' His shoulders heaved as he fought to banish the horrific image from his mind. 'He

slipped over in the mud and went down. We tried to . . .'
He faltered, his lips trembling at the memory. 'We tried
to pull him out, but it all happened so fast. One minute
he was screaming and cursing, the next, he was . . . he
was . . . gone.'

Jack squeezed Larry's shoulder. 'That's tough, mate,' he said.

'He was drowned by his own equipment,' Larry said,
his voice shaking. He managed a hoarse laugh. 'I'm afraid I
rather embarrassed myself by throwing up.'

'I don't blame you, mate.' Jack took out his tobacco and
rolled another cigarette. 'Do you want to go and see the
medic? A few days away from this hellhole might do you
the world of good.'

'What's the point?' Larry drew hard on the cigarette Jack
handed him, exhaling a cloud of smoke. 'They'll just tell me
to pull myself together and get on with it.'

'Incoming!' The shout reverberated down the line. Jack
and Larry pressed themselves against the walls of the trench
as a barrage of shells crashed over their heads, their ears
ringing with the sound of explosions, and the screams of the
men and horses caught in the onslaught.

Hours later, bone-weary, Jack forced his fatigued legs up the
ladder. The rungs were slippery with mud and treacherous
underfoot. With immense effort, he heaved himself over the
top. The mud sucked at his boots like quicksand as he pushed
himself forward, his bayonet at the ready. Shells whistled and
exploded around him, lighting up the night sky.

Sweat coated his skin, his heart pounding his ribcage. His breath came in ragged bursts. He swallowed hard.

'Keep moving forward. Keep moving forward.' He repeated the mantra to himself as his companions fell around him. He had to steel himself to keep going, to step over friends, focusing his gaze on the distant goal. A sudden shriek caught his attention, and he turned his head a fraction. He could see a horse in his peripheral vision, a magnificent beast, which, in its former life, would have been drawing a fine carriage, or being ridden to the hunt by a wealthy gentleman. Now it made for a pitiful sight. Silhouetted against the fiery backdrop, it had become tangled in the barbed wire. It rolled its eyes in terror as it screamed and thrashed its hooves. The broken body of its rider lay in the mud, one foot caught in the stirrup.

'Keep going, Jack,' a voice shouted in his ear. 'There's nothing you can do. Keep going.'

Swallowing the bile that rose in his throat, Jack forced himself to move forward. The mud sucked at his feet, making each step feel as though his legs weighed a ton.

He risked a sideways glance at Larry. His friend's face was grim and determined, his skin gleaming and ghostly white in the light of the exploding shells. Jack stepped forward, forcing himself to concentrate on their objective, to keep moving forward and capture the ridge. His foot hit a stone and he stumbled, but quickly regained his footing. He pressed forward, always moving forward.

A scream reverberated in his ears, strangely distant. The

sky around him lit up bright orange and Jack felt himself lifted off his feet. His mouth stretched open into a silent scream as he returned to the ground. The wind was knocked from his body and he couldn't breathe. As he struggled to suck air into his tortured lungs, he was aware that something soft and heavy had landed on top of him. Forcing his eyes open, he found himself looking directly into Larry's vacant stare.

Jack screamed, frantically clawing at the choking mud until he sank into merciful oblivion.

Ellie-May leaned back on her heels and wiped her mouth with her hand. With mounting dismay, she stared at the contents of the chamber pot. Getting unsteadily to her feet, she opened the window, letting the smell of vomit drift away on the breeze. She placed her trembling hands on the sill and leaned out, breathing in the cool spring air. The brisk March wind chased fluffy white clouds across a pretty cornflower-blue sky. Tendrils of smoke curled from a myriad of chimney pots, pale sunlight dancing on slate roofs, sparkling with dew.

She pressed her knuckles to her forehead in an attempt to ease the headache gnawing at her temples. This was the fourth time she'd been sick in as many days and she didn't need to be a genius to understand the reason why.

When she'd first missed her monthlies she'd quashed her anxiety by convincing herself it was out of worry over Jack and Arthur. But when she'd missed for the second month in a row, she could delude herself no longer.

The bedroom door flew open and Ellie-May turned, startled. She had thought herself alone at home.

'Gosh, it stinks in here,' said Nora, wrinkling her nose in distaste and flouncing into the room, the petticoats under her dark blue skirt rustling. She peered disdainfully at the chamber pot. 'Ellie-May, you're ill.'

'What are you doing here?' Ellie-May snapped irritably. 'I thought you were at work.'

'I'm on the late shift,' Nora replied. She had quit her job at W. H. Smith & Sons to work at a munitions factory. The work was hard and dangerous, but the pay was good, and she enjoyed the comradery of the other women, deliberately not dwelling on the warnings of the unpleasant side effects like losing her hair, or having her skin turning yellow, not to mention the fact that the slightest mistake could see her blown to kingdom come.

The bed sagged as she sat down and she studied her sister quizzically, taking in the deathly pale skin, the shadows beneath her eyes. 'You look awful. Shall I run and fetch Mum?'

'No.' Ellie-May shook her head. She was leaning with her back against the windowsill, the cool air pleasant on the back of her neck.

'Will you be able to go to work?' Nora frowned. 'I can pop over and let Frank know you won't be in?'

Ellie-May closed her eyes and breathed in deep, her nostrils flaring. The thought of going into work filled her with dread. Lately, the smell of blood and raw meat turned her stomach something terrible. She'd had to run to the outside privy three times the day before.

'I'm not ill,' she whispered.

'What?' Nora frowned. 'But ...' Her words trailed away as comprehension dawned. Her eyes widened as she stared at her sister in shock, her hand flying to her mouth. 'You're expecting!' she gasped.

Ellie-May nodded miserably.

'Ellie-May! Mum and Dad will go mad.'

'I know.' Ellie-May sank down on the bed bedside her sister. Nora put a comforting arm around her shoulder.

'Is it Jack's?' she asked.

'Of course it's Jack's,' Ellie-May snapped. 'How can you even ask?'

'Ellie-May, what were you thinking ... ?' Nora cleared her throat, and looked directly into Ellie-May's eyes.

'We weren't thinking, not really,' Ellie-May replied in a small voice. 'Nora, he was going to war. He might be killed. We needed to be together.' She raised her eyes, looking at Nora beseechingly. 'Do you understand what I mean?' She twisted her hands in her lap. 'And we were careful.'

'Not careful enough, clearly,' scoffed Nora drily. She sighed. 'You must set a date as soon as possible. If you write to Jack he may be able to get compassionate leave to come home and marry you. A woman at work's daughter got herself in the family way, and her young man was granted four days' leave for the wedding. Of course, people will talk when the baby comes early, but at least you'll be a married woman by then. The busybodies will soon turn their attention to someone else.'

'Don't tell Mum,' Ellie-May begged Nora. 'Not yet, anyway. She'll die of shame. At least let me write to Jack first. I'll tell Mum and Dad once we've set a date. That'll go some way to calming them down.'

'I won't say anything,' Nora promised. 'But you'd better write to Jack today. You must be two months along at least. You'll want to be married before it becomes glaringly obvious.'

Three weeks later, Eileen had scrubbed the washing in the tub and put it through the mangle. She was chatting to Rose across the washing line, when her attention was diverted by a loud knocking on the front door. At once, the colour drained from her face as she met Rose's worried gaze.

'The telegram boy would come around the back, Eileen,' Rose assured her, though her own frightened expression belied her words. Eileen nodded. Wiping her damp hands on her apron, and leaving the laundry basket on the flagstones, she hurried through the house to the front door.

'Mrs Bramhall?' A tall, distinguished-looking man stood on her doorstep. He had white hair and piercing blue eyes. He had a kind face, the sort of face one would expect to be always smiling. But he wasn't smiling now. His expression was sombre. He held his hat in his hands, and gave a little bow. 'I'm Edward Chalke. Jack Pickup worked for me before he enlisted?'

Eileen nodded, her breath catching in her throat. 'Yes, sir. He's mentioned you.'

'May I come in?'

'Yes, I'm sorry. Please, do come in.' Flustered, Eileen stood aside to allow Chalke into the tiny porch. 'Please, come through to the parlour.' She indicated the door which stood ajar, her gaze alighting on the car parked outside her house. A Ford, its paintwork gleamed in the sunlight. It was surrounded by a gaggle of awestruck young children. A car parked outside Eileen Bramhall's house? Whatever next? That would cause tongues to wag, she thought drily as she shut the door firmly, a sense of foreboding causing her heart to sink to the soles of her slippers, and followed her visitor into the chilly parlour.

'I'm afraid I haven't lit the fire,' she apologized, wincing as she caught a glimpse of her reflection in the mirror over the mantelpiece. Her cheeks were flushed from the steam of the wash tub, and her hair had come lose from its pins.

'Mrs Bramhall,' he said softly. 'Please, sit down.' He glanced about him, taking in the dark-wood furniture, the heavy blackout curtains. 'Is your daughter, Ellie-May, here?'

'She's at work,' Eileen croaked, perching nervously on the edge of the sofa, icy fingers of fear running up and down her spine. Dread squeezed her heart like a vice.

Edward Chalke sat opposite her, his expression one of great sorrow. 'Mrs Bramhall.' He reached across and took Eileen's hands in his while looking her straight the eyes. Eileen held his gaze, her heart banging painfully against her ribcage. 'When Jack left for France, he put me down as his next of kin. It is standard practice for any of my employees who came from the workhouse. It makes things easier.' He cleared his throat. 'I'm sorry to tell you, but Jack has been killed.'

Eileen stared at him in silence. She had known the moment he'd introduced himself that something had happened to Jack. She shuddered as she was engulfed by a great wall of sadness. 'Oh, poor Jack,' she whispered. 'And poor Ellie-May.' She raised her eyes, her desperation plain to see. 'Oh, Mr Chalke. How will I tell my Ellie-May? Oh,' she buried her face in her hands. 'Oh, Ellie-May, my poor, darling girl.'

Ellie-May smiled with pleasure to find Sid waiting for her after work that evening.

'Hello, Dad. This is a nice surprise.' She ran to him, but stopped short, her smile dying on her lips as she registered his sombre expression.

'Dad?' Her voice sounded small and she started shaking like a leaf. '*Arthur?*'

Terror gripped her heart as Sid gently shook his head.

'Oh, no!' She wailed. 'Not *Jack*? No! Dad, please, it can't be Jack.' Without a word, Sid opened his arms and Ellie-May fell into them, sobbing as if her heart would break.

'How will I go on without him?' Ellie-May sobbed, blowing her nose. She and her dad were sitting on a low wall close to

Baker's Wharf, near where she and Jack had once scavenged along the water's edge. The sun was sinking over the roof-tops and the flaming sky was reflected in the swiftly flowing water, transforming it into a river of molten gold. A family of swans huddled on the shingled bank. A gust of wind swept up from the water, and Ellie-May shivered.

'You'll do as your mum and I have had to do every day since we lost our Bert,' Sid said in reply to her question. He took Ellie-May's gloved hand in his own. 'You go on.' He sighed, his gaze focused on a large seagull pecking disconsolately at a tangled clump of seaweed. 'I won't lie to you, lass, it won't be easy. There are days when I can barely get out of bed of a morning. But I do, for you and Mum, and Bea, Jess and Arthur, and the grand-kiddies. Somehow, I find the strength, and you will too.'

'I don't think I can, Dad,' Ellie-May sniffed, wiping her eyes. The cold wind stung her damp cheeks.

'It doesn't feel like it now, Ellie-May, but you'll manage it, even if only for the sake of those who love you.'

She stared out over the water. Boats bobbed on the waves, dark, silent shapes in the encroaching twilight. The water lapped rhythmically against the shore. Faint accordion music drifted from one of the nearby taverns, a burst of laughter. It seemed incongruous that life could be going on as normal when Jack was gone. Never again would she feel his arms around her, or see his cheeky grin. She would never kiss his lips . . .

'Surely, I should have felt something,' she whispered. 'I

should have known.' Jack was her soulmate. It was inconceivable that he could have left this life without her knowing. It was though a part of her had died too. She gently removed her hand from Sid's, and with shaking fingers, unfolded the telegram.

REGRET INFORM YOU PRIVATE JACK
PICKUP KILLED IN ACTION 28 MARCH
AT LENS STOP

There it was, in black and white; the words etched on her memory.

'I already miss him so much.'

'I know, lass.' Sid put his arm around her and pulled her against him. 'I know.' He held her as she cried, soaking his jacket with her tears.

CHAPTER FOURTEEN

Ellie-May sank onto an upturned crate, desperate for a respite from customers and the nauseating smell of meat and blood. Although her bouts of morning sickness had all but passed, she occasionally became light-headed while on her feet all day. And the smell of raw meat still had the tendency to turn her stomach.

She tilted her weary face to the sun. It was unseasonably warm for May and the skin beneath her corset was damp with perspiration. She placed a tentative hand on her stomach. She was almost four months now and beginning to show. From a contact she had gotten from work, Nora had given her the address of a woman in Northam who promised to make her a corset that would conceal her condition for a few more weeks. She glanced down at her stomach ruefully. It wouldn't be long before even the corset maker's expertise could prevent her shame from being revealed. Yet, despite the shame she would bring upon her family, she was desperately grateful for this child. Jack's child. He or she would be a part of him, and her joy that he was not completely lost to her overrode any feelings of shame or embarrassment she might otherwise have felt.

Her letters to Jack had been returned to her, the word DECEASED stamped starkly across the envelope. She had fed them into the fire, one by one, tears streaming down her cheeks.

Two magpies landed on the back wall. *Two for joy*, she whispered to herself, closing her eyes. She had almost driven herself mad weighing up all her options, even going so far as to consider moving to another part of the city where no one knew her and bringing up her baby alone. After all, there were so many war widows and women whose husbands were away at the front that mothers raising their children alone were becoming the norm. But Ellie-May was not a widow, and as such, would not be entitled to any compensation. If only she and Jack had married before he went away, she thought wistfully. Edward Chalke had brought over Jack's post office savings book and had gone with Ellie-May to have the money transferred to herself. It was a blessing with the baby coming, but not enough to live on long term.

It was six weeks since she had received the news of Jack's death and her grief felt as strong as ever. Fresh tears brimmed in her green eyes, squeezing out beneath her closed lashes and trickling down her cheeks.

'Are you all right?'

She quickly wiped her eyes as Frank stepped out into the yard. He was still wearing his blood-splattered apron and the coppery scent of it caused the bile to rise in Ellie-May's throat. She quickly swallowed it down, forcing a smile as Frank hunkered down beside her, his brows knitted together in genuine concern.

'Yes, thank you,' Ellie-May nodded. 'I'll be there in a minute. I just needed some air.'

'Are you sure you're all right?' Frank pressed. 'You've been looking pale and washed out for days. Is it just grief, or are you sickening for something? I'll speak to Father; get you a few days off. I'll make sure you don't lose your wages.'

'Thanks, Frank.' Ellie-May placed her hand over his and gave his fingers a squeeze. 'That's kind of you, but I'm fine.'

'You don't look fine.' Frank scrutinized her quizzically. 'Look, Ellie-May, I know we've had our differences but I'm your friend. You can talk to me.'

Moved by the kindness in his tone, Ellie-May welled up. Suddenly, the need to confide in someone other than Nora was overwhelming. 'Oh, Frank,' she whispered, desperately. 'I'm in trouble.'

'Trouble?' Frank frowned, perplexed. 'What sort of trouble?'

She gulped back tears. 'I'm going to have a baby,' she said softly, not wanting to be overheard by any passers-by. She looked Frank defiantly in the eye, daring him to respond.

He swallowed hard, his cheeks flushing a dark shade of crimson from his neck to the tips of his ears.

'You're having a baby?'

'Yes, Jack's baby.' She watched him as a myriad emotions flashed across his face. 'Please don't sack me. I can't afford to lose my job, especially now. I shouldn't start to show, not properly, for another couple of months yet. At least let me stay on until then.'

'What sort of man do you think I am?' Frank scowled. 'Of course I'm not going to sack you.' He got to his feet, his brow furrowed, his mind racing. He had not been elated, exactly, upon learning of Jack's death, even he wasn't that callous, but he couldn't deny that with Jack permanently out of the way he had allowed the rekindling of his hopes that he and Ellie-May might . . .

His heart sank. A baby put things in a different perspective. He frowned at her. 'Just don't let my father find out. I'm not sure he'd be as charitable as I am.'

Ellie-May dropped her head in her hands, wondering what on earth she was going to do.

In the cool of the shop, Frank wrapped up a quarter pound of bacon and handed it to Mrs Thomas.

'Thank you, Frank, love.' Vera Thomas and her husband, Ted, lived in the next street. Her children, Joseph and Eleanor, had been at school with Frank. 'Did I tell you I got a letter from my Joey this week?' Vera asked as she tucked the parcel of mince into her basket. 'He got the chocolates and the socks I sent him.' She looked Frank straight in the eye. 'You're not intending to join up, then?'

Frank gritted his teeth. 'I've got to run this place, Mrs Thomas,' he replied with forced jollity. He was finding it tedious, constantly having to defend his decision not to enlist to smug-faced mothers and sweethearts. He bet there wasn't one among them who wouldn't have kept their menfolk safe at home had they been able to dissuade them from joining up.

'My Ted tells me they'll be bringing in conscription soon.' Vera smiled as she adjusted her hat on her cloud of steel-grey hair. Her blue eyes twinkled with mischief. 'You'll have no excuse then, Frank, love. I'll see you tomorrow for some of those lovely sausages. Remember me to your father, won't you? Good day.'

She sailed out into the sunshine, leaving Frank scowling after her.

He banged the metal meat tray on the counter, his lip curling in dismay. Articles calling for conscription abounded in the newspapers and, deep down, he knew Vera Thomas was right. It was only a matter of time before he would be called up. The very thought of being conscripted into the army gave him clammy palms and palpitations of the chest.

He wiped his hands on his apron, his brows knotted together in concentration. He folded his arms across his chest and leaned against the wall, idly watching a gaggle of children chase a hoop past the window, their shrieks of uninhibited delight drifting through the open doorway.

God, what he wouldn't give to be a kid again.

His reverie was broken by Ellie-May's return. She had washed her face, and she smiled at him as she took her place behind the counter, opening the order book to plan the afternoon deliveries.

Frank watched her as she bent over the counter, the end of

the pencil resting gently on her lower lip, her eyes downcast, one slender finger working its way down the page, her face screwed up in concentration.

He opened his mouth to speak then closed it with a snap, an idea forming in his head. When, for it was a case of 'when' now, and not 'if', conscription was brought in, it would be the single men who were called up first. The war might even be over by the time the powers that be extended conscription to include married men.

'I'm just popping out the back for a minute,' he said, brushing past Ellie-May in haste.

'All right, but don't be long. You've got quite a few deliveries this afternoon, and you know Mrs Hunt leaves for her bridge game at two.'

'I'll be a minute at the most.' Frank waved away Ellie-May's concerns. So what if the old bat was out when he arrived? He actually preferred it that way. It offered him the chance to flirt with her housemaid.

He smoked a quick cigarette in the backyard, enjoying the warmth of the early afternoon sun on his skin. The sky was an unblemished blue. A train whistled in the distance. He inhaled deeply, his thoughts drifting to Mrs Hunt's housemaid. Daisy Smith was curvaceous and blonde with an eye for the lads. Before Jack's death, Frank had seriously been considering asking her to walk out with him, but now Ellie-May was free, Daisy's attractiveness paled into insignificance. She was nothing compared to Ellie-May.

He'd decided to bide his time with Ellie-May, allow her a

few months to grieve before making his intentions known, but now her condition had well and truly messed things up, it gave him pause for thought.

He rested his heel against the wall. He picked at the moss sprouting in the crevices of the crumbling brickwork with his fingernail, the other hand holding the half-smoked cigarette to his lips. Was he really prepared to raise another man's bastard child? On the other hand, he loved Ellie-May. He'd tried to get over her, God knows, he'd tried. There had been several others, but none of the young ladies he'd courted had been a patch on Ellie-May.

She might not feel the same about him, but he was confident she would soon come to love him as he loved her. In the meantime, she was desperate enough to grab any lifeline that was handed to her. And he, Frank Cartwright, could be that lifeline. Of course, his motives weren't completely altruistic. As a married man, he might avoid the conscription board for a while longer.

The resolution firmly planted in his mind, he crushed his cigarette butt underfoot and pushed himself off the wall. Whistling cheerfully, he returned to the shop.

'I've packed the first four deliveries,' Ellie-May said when she saw him. She indicated the neatly wrapped bundles lining the countertop. 'I'll have the second lot ready for you by the time you get back.'

'Ellie-May,' Frank said, his voice rising an octave with a sudden attack of nerves. He could feel the heat rising in his cheeks. Ellie-May looked at him suspiciously.

'Are you all right?' She made to turn away from him, but he grabbed at her hand.

'Ellie-May,' he blurted out, as her gaze dropped to their entwined fingers. 'I've worked out a solution to your predicament.' Now it was Ellie-May's turn to flush beetroot-red. She cast a startled glance at the empty doorway, and then at the door to the staircase up to the flat above, thankful to note that it was firmly shut.

'What are you talking about?' she hissed, snatching her hand away angrily. Her heart raced. Why had she ever thought it a good idea to confide in Frank? She turned away from him, her cheeks burning and pressed her palms against the cool glass counter, willing her emotions under control.

'Ellie-May, listen to me,' Frank tried again. 'Look, you're in trouble, and I can help.'

She rounded on him, her eyes wide, her mouth a grim line. 'Oh, no, Frank,' she said, her voice low and firm. 'I'm not going to one of those women. I'm not letting those ...' she cast around for a suitable word, but couldn't think of one, 'those women, anywhere near me.'

Taken aback, Frank stared at her in stunned silence as comprehension dawned. 'No, I mean, it is an option, of course, but ...' The look on Ellie-May's face cut him short. He had the grace to look shamefaced. He cleared his throat. 'I'm offering to marry you, Ellie-May. I'm prepared to raise your child.'

Ellie-May blinked and swallowed hard. 'You want to marry me?' She wasn't sure she'd heard him right.

'Yes.' Feeling rather pleased with himself, he drew himself to his full height, even going so far as to puff his chest out a little. His ego deflated slightly at the sight of Ellie-May's confusion. He'd expected her to practically bite his hand off with gratitude.

Instead, she frowned, puzzled. 'Why?'

'You know how I feel about you,' Frank said, coming to stand beside her. 'How I've always felt about you.' She looked at him uncertainly as he took her hand in his. His fingers were warm and clammy against her skin and she had to force herself not to recoil.

'But the baby . . . ?' Her frown deepened.

'Like I said, I'm prepared to accept it as my own.'

'People will know it's not yours,' said Ellie-May. 'They're not stupid, they'll work it out.'

'Only your neighbours. People around here won't be any the wiser. And even if they do, they'll only think well of me for taking on another man's b–'

'*Don't!*' Ellie-May snapped, jerking her hand free.

'I was going to say *baby*,' Frank chided her mildly. 'Another man's *baby*.'

Ellie-May looked away, her mind reeling. In so many ways, Frank's proposal was the answer to her prayers. As a respectable married woman, she would be able to hold her head up high. Her child would have a name, a father, a stable home life. Though she had never thought for one moment that her parents might turf her out once they learned about the baby, the fact that they would be shamed in the eyes of their neighbours would hurt Ellie-May more than anything anyone could do to her.

'It'll be a quiet wedding,' Frank was saying, taking her silence as acquiescence. He released her hand and began to pace the shop floor. 'Your parents and sisters, my father, if he can be bothered. A brief service at St Peter's followed by luncheon at the Belvedere Arms.' He stopped his pacing to smile at his soon-to-be bride. The fact that she looked a little shocked did nothing to dampen his enthusiasm.

'You've taken me a bit by surprise,' Ellie-May managed to say. Her emotions were in turmoil. Could she really spend the rest of her life with him?

'I need a bit of time to consider . . .'

'What is there to consider?' Frank wheedled petulantly. 'I'm offering you a way out, Ellie-May,' he said coldly. 'I can't believe you'd be so ungracious as to throw it back in my face.' His lip curled sarcastically. 'For someone in your position, time is not really on your side, is it, my dear?'

He stood in front of Ellie-May. She could smell the tobacco on his breath. He was handsome, there was no doubting it, yet there was something there, lurking behind his eyes, something cold and unpleasant . . .

'The way I look at it,' he said, running his thumb gently across her flushed cheek as she grit her teeth, willing herself not to flinch at his touch. 'You don't have much of a choice, do you?' He grinned. 'You should be grateful to me. Not many men would be willing to take on another bloke's leftovers, not to mention his kid.'

It gave him a slight feeling of satisfaction to see how Ellie-May flinched at his words, and his grin broadened. Feeling no compulsion to mention his own dalliances with members of the opposite sex, he gave Ellie-May's cheek a gentle pinch. 'I'll give you until the end of the afternoon to decide. If you can't give me an answer by the time we close the shop, consider my offer withdrawn. I won't be taken for a mug and kept dangling. So, think on it.'

Left alone in the shop, Ellie-May leant against the counter. She was in a quandary. Her options were somewhat limited, she had to admit. She would not give up her child, Jack's child, nor could she manage as an unmarried mother. She had witnessed first-hand Verity's callous treatment at the hands of so-called friends and neighbours. It was only due to her friendship with Eileen, who was well-respected and liked by her neighbours, that Jack's mother had been tolerated at all. Young as she was, Ellie-May hadn't been immune to the snide comments or the way other women looked down their nose at Verity, and her ears still rang with the sound of Jack being called names. Until he'd grown big enough to shut them up with his fists, of course.

She pressed her knuckles on the glass counter. The trays of meat glistened below, nestled amongst tufts of green parsley.

She had no doubt that her parents would support her, once they'd recovered from the shock. She'd had it all worked out in her head. Eileen would mind the baby while she, Ellie-May, went out to work, but, and this was the downside, she would always be the subject of gossip and derision, and by association, so would her parents – and she couldn't bear them to be part of her shame. And her child, Jack's child, would be forever branded a bastard.

She shook her head. She didn't want that for her son or daughter. She couldn't raise Jack's child as a bastard. She owed it to him to do her best by their unborn child, and if that meant marriage to Frank, then so be it.

Ellie-May took a deep breath, trying to still her beating heart. She was under no illusions that marriage to Frank would be a bed of roses. Quite the contrary: upon marrying Frank she would be taking on the full-time care of his father, as well as helping to run the shop, whilst caring for a baby. She sighed in resignation. She had never been afraid of hard work, and she was prepared to do whatever it took to give her baby a good life.

'Well?' demanded Frank the moment he walked into the shop at twenty-five minutes past five, his face flushed with the exertion of peddling his bike halfway around the city in the heat. His sandy hair was damp and there was a whiff of dust and sweat about his person. 'Have you made up your mind?'

Ellie-May drew herself to her full height and breathed deeply. Perspiration trickled down her spine and she was aware of a dampness beneath her armpits. Folding her hands piously in front of her, she held her breath for a long moment, the only sound the rush of blood in her ears, before exhaling slowly. Forcing herself to look Frank full in the face, her heart racing, she braced herself to say the words that would change her life for ever.

'I would like to accept your offer, Frank. I will be your wife.'

Frank expelled a gasp of relief. All afternoon he had been in a state of heightened anxiety that Ellie-May might turn him down after all. Placing his hands on her shoulders, he kissed her gently on the lips.

'You've made me the happiest man alive,' he grinned. Ellie-May smiled, but her heart wasn't in it. *I'm so sorry, Jack,* her heart whispered. *Please forgive me.*

She realized that Frank was talking, his voice high-pitched with excitement. 'Let's go upstairs and tell Father,' he said, taking hold of her hand and raising it to his lips. 'We'll tell your parents together, this evening. Tomorrow I'll speak with the vicar. We can be married as soon as the banns have been read. Oh, Ellie-May, you've made me so happy. You'll want for nothing, I promise you.' He kissed her again and led her upstairs.

Arnold was slouched in his chair, his swollen, purple foot resting on a low stool. He looked up in surprise. Fighting down a wave of nausea, Ellie-May was suddenly aware of a gentle fluttering in her stomach, like the sensation of beating butterfly wings. She placed her hands on her stomach, a huge lump forming in her throat as she felt her baby, Jack's baby, moving for the first time.

CHAPTER FIFTEEN

They were a small group gathered in the Church of St Peter that balmy day in late June. Ellie-May wore a pale blue calico dress sprigged with navy-blue flowers that Bea had spent several evenings altering to encompass her sister's thicker waistline. She was almost five months gone now and starting to show, despite her clever corset.

She stood beside Frank, blinking back tears. Her posy of freesias shook wildly. Frank looked debonair in his dark suit, his hair slicked into a neat side-parting, and reeking strongly of eau de cologne.

Eileen and Sid, still shell-shocked by both the news they were to be grandparents again and Ellie-May's sudden marriage, sat stoically in the front pew, dressed in their Sunday best. Arthur, on leave from the army, smart and looking somehow older in his uniform, sat soberly between them and Nora, who flashed Ellie-May an encouraging smile. Bea and Jess, with their husbands and children filled the second pew. Frank's father, Arnold, his right foot heavily bandaged, sat alone across the aisle.

The service was mercifully brief, and Ellie-May was relieved when they emerged a short time later into brilliant sunshine and a shower of confetti. Sid shook Frank's hand, and Eileen hugged him stiffly. Ellie-May stood rigid, her lips parted in a rictus of a smile, as she accepted the lukewarm congratulations of her family.

Arnold treated them all to luncheon at the Belvedere Arms. The food smelled delicious, but Ellie-May could barely bring herself to eat anything. She sat at Frank's side, toying with her food, cheeks burning throughout Frank's clumsy speech, after which Arnold, already part-way drunk, proposed a toast to the 'happy couple'.

She caught Eileen's gaze and looked quickly away, reaching for her glass of cordial, her face flaming. She could still picture the stunned disbelief on her parents' faces the evening she and Frank had turned up on the doorstep to announce their engagement.

'It's very sudden,' Eileen said softly, as she ushered Ellie-May into the kitchen. 'Are you sure? It's just, well, Jack's not been gone that long. Don't you think you're rushing things a bit?'

'I'm having a baby,' Ellie-May had blurted out.

'Oh, Ellie-May,' was all Eileen said, the disappointment in her green eyes tempered with pity. On hearing the news Sid had shaken his head sorrowfully.

'Ah, now, lad,' he'd said, directing his words at Frank. 'You've put the cart before the horse there, haven't you?' He glowered at Frank disapprovingly. Frank bristled, his grip on Ellie-May's hand tightening.

'I think you'll find, sir,' he said, icily, 'that it wasn't *me* putting the proverbial cart before the horse. People will talk, of course, when the baby comes early, but I am prepared to claim Ellie-May's child as my own and the gossips be damned.'

'Thank you, Frank.' Sid clapped the young man on the shoulder. 'There's not many men would be so gallant.'

'Mr Bramhall,' Frank had assured him, clearing his throat. 'I love your daughter, and I promise you, I shall look after her to the best of my ability.'

'That's all I can ask, lad,' Sid said gruffly. 'That's all I can ask.'

Frank had stayed for supper, during which plans were made. Nora pretended surprise at the news, offering her hearty congratulations at the news of the impending marriage.

Later, after Frank had gone, Eileen cornered Ellie-May outside by the privy.

'Are you certain you want to go through with this?' she asked quietly.

'I haven't got much choice, have I, Mum?' she replied, her voice dull.

'No.' Eileen sighed heavily. 'I suppose not.'

Then she held Ellie-May while her daughter cried, the sound of children's carefree laughter reverberating around the rows of terraced houses. 'Frank's a good man,' she said, running her work-roughened hands down her daughter's thick, auburn hair. 'He works hard; you'll have a comfortable life.' Eileen hugged her tight. 'You're going to have to make the best of it, love. Do your best to be a good wife to Frank, and you'll be all right.'

Ellie-May had nodded, her stomach twisting with anxiety. She was already regretting her decision, but what else could she do? What other choice did she have? As the saying went, she'd made her bed and now she had to lie in it.

Now, sitting beside Frank, his hand resting proprietorially on her thigh, Ellie-May fixed a smile on her face, and forced herself to join in the stilted conversation. Jess, cradling baby Gracie in her arms, while keeping one eye on three-year-old Tommy who was playing on the stained, pockmarked carpet with his cousins, three-year-old Shelly and thirteen-month-old Poppy-Jo, smiled across the table at Ellie-May, her wide, generous face devoid of censor. 'I've put a bag full of bits and pieces aside for you,' she said. 'You can send Frank around to pick them up once you're settled. Bea's got a crib you can borrow, too. Poppy-Jo will soon be in the bed with Shell.'

'Yes,' Bea confirmed, breaking off her conversation with Nora on hearing her name. 'You're welcome to it.'

'You won't need a crib, yet,' Eileen interjected. 'A bottom drawer will do for the first few months.'

'You're all very kind,' Frank said, giving his new wife's thigh a squeeze. 'But I plan to take Ellie-May to Tyrell and Green in a few weeks' time. We'll buy whatever we need for the baby.'

There was a moment of uncomfortable silence around the

table. In the neighbourhood Ellie-May had grown up in, people didn't go shopping for baby's things. They borrowed from family and friends, with cribs, clothing, prams, being second-, third-, fourth-, even fifth-hand.

'Oh, right,' Jess pouted, sounding decidedly put out. Ellie-May blushed.

'There's no need to spend money,' she said, turning to Frank. 'If Bea and Jess are happy to lend us things they no longer need . . .' Her words trailed away as Frank waved away her objection.

'No,' he said firmly, the determined set of his chin making it perfectly clear to all concerned that the subject was closed. 'No one will say that Frank Cartwright can't provide for his family,' he intoned a touch pompously, Ellie-May thought, as the rest of her family exchanged glances. 'Your son, or daughter, will have only the best.'

'Oh, well,' said Trevor, draining his pint. 'If our stuff's not good enough . . .' He glanced down the table. 'Gordon, another pint?'

Gordon nodded and got to his feet. Bending to kiss the top of Jess's head in an effort to placate her, he followed his brother-in-law to the bar. Eileen cast Ellie-May a look. She shrugged. Frank was her husband now. She had to abide by his say-so.

Sid and Arthur joined Trevor and Gordon at the bar to get another round in while Frank, seemingly impervious to the slight he had caused, launched into a lengthy dialogue with Arnold regarding the prices of meat on the black market until, having worked his way methodically through several jugs of red wine, Arnold let out a long groan, and promptly fell asleep in his trifle.

'He's dead to the world and snoring like a steam train,' Ellie-May said drily, emerging from her new father-in-law's bedroom and closing the door softly behind her. She set down the bowl of water and towel she'd used to bathe his swollen foot, and wrinkled her nose. She'd thrown the sash windows wide open hoping the fresh, summer air would dispel the sour, stale smell that lingered about the room.

'We won't hear a peep out of him until morning,' Frank said with a leer. He folded his newspaper and reached out his hand, pulling Ellie-May onto his lap. She landed clumsily, bruising her chin on the top of Frank's head.

'Careful, Ellie-May.' Frank cupped her head in his hand, and brought her lips to his. His breath smelled of wine. She let him kiss her; after all, he was her husband now.

'Oh, El,' he whispered, and Ellie-May froze. Drawing back her head, she looked at him with narrowed eyes.

'Please don't call me that, Frank.'

'Why not? I've always considered Ellie-May's such a mouthful.'

'Call me Ellie, then,' she conceded. 'Just not El.'

Frank's gaze narrowed, a dark flush creeping up his neck. 'Oh, yes, I forgot,' he said, coldly. 'That's what *he* called you, isn't it?' He groaned, as if in pain. 'Are you thinking about him now? On our wedding night?'

'No,' Ellie-May lied quickly as Frank closed his eyes, breathing deeply. 'I would just prefer it if you didn't call me, El, that's all.'

Frank exhaled, nostrils flaring. 'Fine.' He held up his hands. 'I'll call you *Ellie*. But you've got to forget about Jack. You're married to me now.'

'Of course I am,' Ellie-May said, winding her arms around Frank's neck. 'I'm sorry.'

Frank grunted. He kissed her again, his breathing growing more ragged as the kiss progressed.

'Let's go to bed,' he growled. Ellie-May's insides turned to water. With legs like jelly, she allowed him to lead her into the bedroom.

It was a man's room, drab and bare. Ellie-May's nightdress lay folded on the pillow where Eileen had placed it earlier when she'd brought round Ellie-May's things. 'Just to make you feel at home,' she had said.

Ellie-May's clothes hung in the wardrobe beside Frank's, her hairbrush and comb had been placed on the dusty dressing table. Her dressing gown hung on the hook behind the door.

The blackout curtains were open; the heavy material barely stirred by the warm breeze wafting through the open window. It was gone half past eight, yet the room was a bright as day. Dust motes swirled in the shards of sunlight slicing across the brown candlewick bedspread. A framed photograph of Frank's mother hung on the otherwise bare walls.

Despite the balminess of the evening, Ellie-May found

her teeth were chattering as she slowly unbuttoned her dress. Turning her back on Frank, she let it fall to the floor. Her shaking fingers began to undo the stays of her corset. Behind her she heard the squeak of bedsprings. Ellie-May swallowed the lump in her throat, fear gnawing at her belly. The corset finally came away in her hand, and she slipped her nightdress over her head and got quickly into bed. She lay on her back, the covers pulled up to her chin, staring up at the ceiling, her teeth clenched in an effort to stop them chattering.

Frank rolled over and placed a hand on her breast. She froze, every muscle clenched. She turned her head, her wide eyes radiating fear.

'Frank,' she whispered, panic clawing at her throat. 'The baby . . .'

Frank drew back. Staring at her, he wrestled with his conscience. With great effort, he took his hand away and rolled onto his back, letting out a long, shuddering sigh.

'I'll leave you alone until the baby is born, Ellie,' he said, his voice hoarse with unspent desire. 'But then I will insist on my rights as your husband, and you'd better not deny me. Goodnight.' He rolled onto his side, and was soon snoring loudly.

Ellie-May lay awake for hours, watching the shadows creep across the room. When the sun had completely disappeared below the roof tops, she slipped silently out of bed and padded to the window, gazing up at the night sky. Since the Zeppelin raids had started over London in May, there was the very real worry that Southampton, being an important port, might be next. But the sky over the city was clear. She could see the searchlights in the distance, cutting great swathes of light across the empty night sky. In one swift movement, she closed the curtains, plunging the room into blackness, and made her way back to bed. Careful not to disturb her sleeping husband, she slipped in beside him, falling asleep just before dawn.

CHAPTER SIXTEEN

Ellie-May soon settled into a routine and, if not exactly happy, she found, if she tried really hard, she might grow to be content. Frank was polite and courteous, but had affected a certain air of distance in his manner, which she put down to the baby growing inside her.

She rose early each morning to make breakfast for Frank and her father-in-law, before going downstairs to prepare the shop for the day's business. She was blossoming, filled with energy, accepting congratulations from surprised customers with a cheery smile. She was determined to make the best of her new life.

She was still prone to the occasional bout of intense grief, so powerful that she would grip the counter with both hands to prevent herself crumbling with the intensity of it. But, for the most part, she managed to keep her grief at bay; a dull, nagging ache in her heart.

Frank proved as good as his word and one Wednesday afternoon they took the tram to Tyrrell and Green in Above

Bar Street and purchased a new crib. It was a fancy affair, bedecked in ribbons and lace, the likes of which no one in Church Street had never owned before, Bea said enviously, running a finger over the smooth, white woodwork the following Sunday afternoon when she called round with the children.

'I would have been happy with an orange crate,' Ellie-May said, placing a plate of buttered scones in front of her sister. 'But you know Frank, he's got pretensions above his station.'

'As long as he can afford it,' Bea replied, somewhat ungraciously, slathering strawberry jam on her scone and taking a bite. 'Our bottom drawer's done all right for our Shell and Poppy.' She glanced over to where the two little girls were sprawled on the floor, playing with their wooden blocks.

'How are Mum and Dad?' Busy as she was all week, what with looking after Frank and his dad, working in the shop and keeping the flat clean and tidy, when Ellie-May did have time to spare, Frank seemed reluctant for her to spend too much time at Church Street.

'If you visited more often you'd see how they are for yourself,' Bea scolded.

'Bea,' Ellie-May rebuked her. 'You know I'm rushed off my feet here.'

'There's always Sundays,' Bea retorted, licking cream from her fingers. 'Why don't you and Frank come back to Mum's for your tea? Mum would love to see you.'

'I can't,' Ellie-May said, her eyes clouding a little. 'Frank likes us to spend time together on Sundays.'

'You see him every minute of every day! Can't he share you, just for a couple of hours on a Sunday afternoon?' Bea cocked a sceptical eyebrow.

'Shush!' hissed Ellie-May, casting a furtive glance towards the door that separated the kitchen from the parlour where Frank and Arnold were playing cards. 'He says that's different. We're both so busy all week; Sunday is the only day we can relax together. We're going for a walk around Andrew's Park later. Frank fancies having our tea at their new tea shop.'

Bea shook her head. 'I'm surprised at you, Ellie-May. You never used to be such a pushover.'

Ellie-May lowered her gaze, the freshly baked scone turning to sawdust in her mouth, shame washing over her like a wave. Bea was right: she had neglected her family in the weeks since her marriage to Frank, but the truth was, arguing with Frank just wasn't worth the aggravation. It had become clear to her during the first weeks of her marriage that, for some unfathomable reason, Frank felt jealous of her family. Whenever she suggested spending time with them, he would find some excuse. On the odd occasion Ellie-May had defied him and gone anyway, he had sulked for days.

'Honestly, Bea,' she said slowly. 'It's just not worth the argument. I promise I'll speak to him about the bank holiday picnic,' she added, in an attempt to redeem herself in her sister's eyes.

'Make sure you do,' Bea said, eyeing her sternly. 'The whole street will be going. It'll be a bit of light relief in the midst of all the bloody carnage. Mum got a letter from Arthur the other day, did she say?'

'How is he?' Ellie-May asked, relieved to move away from her increasingly difficult relationship with Frank.

'As well as can be expected, I suppose,' said Bea slowly, reaching for her teacup. 'He puts a brave face on things, but reading between the lines, you get the idea it's pretty grim over there.'

'Another of our customers lost a son last week,' Ellie-May said with a sad shake of her head. 'When will it ever end?'

'God knows. I had hoped that when the Germans sank the *Lusitania* it might have spurred the Americans to help us,' said Bea, pushing a strand of hair from her face. She scraped back her chair back. 'Well, I'd better get going. I told our Trevor I wouldn't be long.'

'It's been lovely to see you.' The two sisters hugged warmly, their earlier argument forgotten. 'Tell Mum and Dad I'll try to pop in soon.'

'See that you do,' Bea said, standing in front of the mirror to put on her hat. 'They miss you. Come on, girls. Say bye-bye to Aunty.' Shelley and Poppy scrambled to their feet, their little faces upturned for Ellie-May's kiss.

She walked them to the back gate and watched as they made their way down the narrow alleyway behind the row of shops. She climbed the stairs to find Frank in the kitchen waiting for her.

'Thank the good Lord,' he said as Ellie-May began to clear the table. 'I thought she'd never leave.' He came and stood behind her at the sink, his hands circling her expanding waistline and kissed the back of her neck. In spite of herself, Ellie-May felt herself stiffen. Frank noticed it too. 'If we're going for that walk we should go now,' he said curtly, his hands falling to his sides. 'Leave the dishes. You can do them when we get back.'

CHAPTER SEVENTEEN

Eileen removed the apple pie from the oven and placed it on the trivet to cool. Sid peered over his newspaper, sniffing the air appreciatively. 'That smells good, love. I shall look forward to that later.'

The small kitchen was warm with the smell of baking. With food shortages beginning to take effect now that the bombing of merchant ships was becoming all too common, the windfall apples from the neighbourhood allotments were a welcome treat.

'Will you have a cup of tea?' Eileen asked, dusting off her floury hands and setting the kettle on the hob. A red-breasted robin hopped along the windowsill, making her smile. The Lord knew she didn't have much to smile about these days. Hundreds of civilians were being killed in air raids over the east coast and London. The casualty lists in the newspapers grew longer day by day and, as if that wasn't bad enough, the *Echo* had reported that Edith Cavell had been executed for treason. Eileen shook her head in disbelief.

She had been a nurse, for Heaven's sake! It would appear no one was safe from the enemy's insatiable quest for murder and mayhem.

Her life revolved around Arthur's letters, each one bringing only a modicum of relief, for by the time a letter reached her, she fretted, *he may be dead now.* She lived in constant dread of the telegram boy. Often, she would see him coming, hardly daring to breathe until he'd passed the house, and then being overwhelmed by feelings of guilt and anguish, as yet another neighbour was sentenced to a lifetime of grief.

There had been a brief squall during the night, and the flagstones glistened in the October sunshine. Spiders' webs sparkled on the washing line. In the raised flowerbed, the potato plants were bent and bowed, some lying flat upon the sodden soil.

The kettle came to the boil and she made the tea. Settling herself at the table, she pulled out the matinee jacket she was knitting for Ellie-May's baby. She had barely seen Ellie-May since the August bank holiday when she and Frank had joined them for the annual picnic. It had been clear to Eileen that Ellie-May and Frank had argued. Ellie-May had been all forced cheerfulness and haunted eyes, while Frank had been moody and distant. It had been a relief to everyone when they left early, citing Ellie-May's swollen ankles as an excuse.

'What's the big sigh for?' Sid lowered the paper, peering at her through his spectacles.

'I'm sorry,' said Eileen. 'I hadn't realized I'd sighed.' Her knitting needles clicked rapidly. 'I was thinking about our

Ellie-May.' Eileen rested her knitting in her lap. 'Do you think she and Frank are happy?'

'I reckon they rub along well enough,' Sid replied after a moment's consideration. 'Why do you ask?'

'Frank seems very controlling. Bea thinks he deliberately keeps Ellie-May from seeing us as much as she'd like. I mean, the only time I get to see her these days is if I go around there, and even then I get the impression I'm intruding.'

'They're newlyweds,' Sid reminded her with a grin. 'It's only natural he wants to keep his wife to himself for a bit. Wait until the baby comes along. We'll never get rid of them then.'

'I hope you're right,' sighed Eileen, holding up the tiny white jacket that would match the pair of booties and bonnet she'd packed away in tissue paper with the other items she'd knitted.

They settled into silence, the only sounds the crackle of the fire and the rhythmic clicking of Eileen's needles, with the occasional rustle of Sid's newspaper, as the weak autumn sun shone in through the window.

When the knock came, they looked at each other with frightened eyes. Eileen's heart began to pound painfully against her ribcage. Reluctantly, she forced herself to her feet. Sid laid a staying hand on her arm. He shook his head solemnly. 'I'll go.'

He set his paper aside, the hammering on the door coming again. On wooden legs, he walked from the kitchen, Eileen close behind him, her heart in her throat. The relief when they opened the door to see the cheery postwoman instead of the telegram boy they had expected, was overwhelming.

'Good morning,' she said cheerily, handing them the letter. 'Gorgeous day, isn't it?' With that, she moved on up the street, whistling cheerfully. Like so many occupations, the postal service had begun employing women to take the place of the young men who had enlisted, many of whom would never come home again.

'It's addressed to our Ellie-May,' Sid said, with a frown. 'Postmarked Dorset.'

'Give it here.' While Sid shut the door, Eileen took the letter, inspecting it with trepidation. After the briefest moment's hesitation, she whipped a hairgrip from her hair and slit it open. Ignoring Sid's exclamation of shock, she pulled out the single sheet of writing paper and unfolded it.

'Oh, no!' she wailed, the colour draining from her face, as she scanned the contents. 'Oh, no! Oh, please God, why now?' Her knees buckled and Sid had to hold her up in order to prevent her falling to the ground.

'What is it?' he whispered, terror tearing at his throat. 'Is it our Arthur? Is he hurt?' He didn't dare give voice to the dread building up in his gut.

'It's Jack,' Eileen gasped, shock almost robbing her of speech. She fixed her stricken gaze on her husband. 'It's a letter from Jack. He's alive.'

CHAPTER EIGHTEEN

It was cosy in the parlour above the butcher's shop. A cheerful fire crackled in the grate and the lamp cast a cheery glow over the room. Ellie-May was seated in an armchair, her swollen ankles resting on a small stool. She set down her knitting and massaged her aching back. She was only a few weeks off her due date, and although the thought of giving birth terrified her, she was finding this last stage of pregnancy very taxing. With one hand resting on her stomach, she glanced over to where Frank was pouring over the day's news reports in the *Echo*.

They had settled into a form of contented domesticity. After supper, Frank and Arnold would play cards while Ellie-May knitted, or tended to her seemingly never-ending pile of mending and darning, until Arnold finally nodded off. Frank would manhandle him to bed, and they would spend an hour in companionable silence, before heading to bed around half past nine.

She listened to her father-in-law's snores reverberating

through the wall. Earlier that evening, when the wind had stilled, they had been able to hear the sound of heavy guns, far out to sea, carried on the breeze.

'We're heading for our second Christmas at war,' Frank remarked, folding the paper and setting it aside. He glanced across at his heavily pregnant wife, a small frown creasing his brow.

'Yes,' Ellie-May didn't look up from the baby bonnet she was knitting. 'Those poor boys.'

'We'll send a parcel through the Red Cross,' Frank said. He was more than happy to salve his conscience with a few chocolate bars and a pair of warm socks. He was feeling decidedly queer this evening. The newspaper editor had again raised the subject of conscription, and it was looking very likely that all single men between the ages of eighteen and forty-one would be called up as early as January next year. Thank God he was a married man. But it was rumoured that married men could be called up as well, and the thought terrified him. It wasn't that he held any objections of conscience, like the Quaker family in the next street, he just wasn't prepared to risk his life, and as for the conditions endured by the poor blokes on the front, well . . . He shuddered at the thought.

'Are you cold?' Ellie-May asked, glancing up from her knitting, her face lit up by the flickering lamplight. Firelight danced up the walls, tiny sparks flying as a lump of coal fell from the grate.

'No.' Frank got up to retrieve the lump of coal before it scorched the carpet. 'I was just thinking about the boys in

France.' He sat back down. He'd put on a bit of weight since his marriage to Ellie-May and was getting quite a rounded belly. Too much good home cooking. 'Where's your brother Arthur these days?' he asked conversationally.

'Near Ypres,' Ellie-May replied, winding up her ball of knitting wool and placing it on the table beside her. She rubbed her stomach, wincing as the baby kicked her hard in the ribs.

'Mrs Croft has asked all us ladies to knit socks for the boys fighting on the front, which I'm happy to do, of course. At least I feel I'm doing my bit for the war effort.'

'Is that a dig at me?' Frank leaned forwards, scowling.

'Of course not,' she said warily. 'I'm merely saying I'm happy to play my part.'

Frank snorted and settled back in his chair. 'You know I can't enlist. You'd never manage this place on your own once the baby comes, and Father's a dead loss. He'd bankrupt us within weeks if he was in charge.'

'If they start calling up married men, you'll have to go,' Ellie-May pointed out. Frank pouted.

'You make it sound as though you want to get rid of me,' he said petulantly.

'Oh, Frank,' Ellie-May sighed in exasperation. 'Of course I don't. I'm just saying what the papers are reporting: conscription is highly likely, and if the war goes on much longer it won't be just the single men who are eligible.'

'We'll just have to hope to God it won't come to that then, won't we? I'm going to bed. Are you coming?'

Ellie-May nodded with a sigh. Frank would sulk for days now, which would mean the silent treatment. Wearily, she got to her feet, and followed her truculent husband through to their bedroom.

In the back bedroom of number 12 Church Street, Eileen was unable to sleep. She lay on her back, in the pitch darkness, listening to Sid snoring gently beside her.

She was in turmoil over what to do about Jack's letter. He was alive, and in some sort of convalescent home in Dorset. She couldn't tell Ellie-May, it would destroy her. How would she live, knowing Jack was alive, yet she was tied to Frank? She railed silently at God's unfairness, tears cascading down her cheeks and seeping into her pillow.

Why, God? she cried.

She sighed deeply, a long shuddering breath as a plan began to formulate in her mind. Finally, in the early hours of the morning, enveloped in a sense of calm peacefulness, she slipped out of bed, wrapped herself in her old dressing gown, and crept downstairs.

Fetching the writing pad from the dresser, she sat down at the kitchen table. Shivering in the chill air, squinting in the flickering candle light, her heart heavy with regret, she put pen to paper, and wrote a letter to Jack.

Jack stared out of the bay window at the beautiful Dorset countryside. The trees that hid the lane from view were a riot of russet reds, golds and browns. The lawns of Wyke

Hall sparkled with dew in the autumn sunshine. A gentle breeze ruffled the surface of the ornamental lake, upon which glided a pair of orange-beaked moorhens. A group of village children were collecting conkers beneath the massive horse chestnut tree, kicking mounds of sodden leaves into the air. They came often, and Jack enjoyed watching them.

It was warm in the library. Dust motes swirled in the rays of autumn sunshine streaming in through the tall bay windows. A fire roared in the ornate fireplace. It was Jack's favourite room. He enjoyed the smell of the ancient leather-bound books that lined the shelves, but most of all, he enjoyed the quiet. Prone to violent headaches, which could be brought on by any loud noise, he was grateful for the solitude.

The road to recovery had been long and slow. From the first frightening weeks when his life had hung in the balance to the daunting, terrifying months where he hadn't known even his name.

The staff at the hospital had kept referring to him as Larry, and while the name sounded familiar to him, from somewhere deep in the recesses of his mind he had been convinced it wasn't his name.

His head wound had been severe, and the doctors had warned him that he would be prone to headaches for the rest of his life, but it was the loss of his memory that had been the most frightening.

When he had finally recovered his memory just two weeks ago, he had been appalled to find that he had been reported as 'killed in action'. His first thought was that he must go to Ellie-May immediately. He couldn't imagine how devastated she must have been to learn of his death. To his dismay, his injuries were such that he was forced to content himself with writing to her instead but he quelled his impatience, picturing how tickled pink she'd be to hear he was still alive.

He had written to Larry's parents as well. They had lost a fine, brave son and Jack had wept many tears for his lost friend.

A flurry of falling leaves danced and spun in the sunlight. The children's uninhibited joy was clear in the way they scooped up piles of the fallen leaves, throwing them in the air, dancing like wood nymphs. Jack smiled at them fondly. Ah, to be a child again, he mused, scratching his aching leg. Physically, apart from the trauma to his head, and his memory loss, he had escaped relatively intact.

Once his convalescence was complete, he would be sent back to France. He was hoping Ellie-May would agree to marry him before then. He strained his eyes, his hungry gaze focused on the wrought-iron gates at the end of the long, gravelled driveway. His letter to Ellie-May had been sent five days ago and he was eagerly awaiting her reply. He half hoped she hadn't bothered to write and instead was on her way to Gillingham. Some kindly farmer or market trader would be more than happy to give a pretty girl like El a lift from the station in their cart.

There was a flash of movement between the grand gateposts, and Jack's heart quickened as the postwoman wheeled her laden bicycle purposefully up the drive. She was a buxom woman of around thirty; a spinster from the neighbouring village who had taken on the role when her brother enlisted.

Caching sight of Jack by the window, she waved. He lifted his hand in acknowledgment, hope rising when she gave him the thumbs up, before bounding up the steps with her bundle of letters.

'There's one for you, Jack.' Molly, a pretty young VAD from Lancashire, said, entering the library a few minutes later. She held out the letter and Jack held his breath. He had written to Mr Chalke as well, to let him know he was alive. It would be a crushing disappointment if the letter was from him. He took the letter from Molly with a shaking hand, and frowned. The writing was unfamiliar. He turned the envelope over. The return address was right: Church Street.

'I'll leave you alone to enjoy your correspondence,' Molly said, straightening the blanket that covered Jack's legs. 'I'll be back in a bit to bring you a cup of tea.'

Jack nodded, barely noticing her departure. He slit open the envelope and pulled out the single sheet of pale blue writing paper. He read the short missive with growing disbelief, as all the light drained from his world.

Dear Jack,

We are made up to hear you are alive and well, after all.

There's no easy way to say this, Jack. Ellie-May and Frank were married in June, and are expecting their first child.

I know this will come as a huge shock to you, but I beg you not to try to get in touch with Ellie-May. She is happy, and wishes you all the best for the future.

> *Affectionately yours,*
> *Eileen*

CHAPTER NINETEEN

1918

The worst war in the history of mankind was over. Sitting tall on her father's broad shoulders, Penelope Cartwright looked out over the cheering, waving crowd that had gathered outside the city hall. The Salvation Army band played a rousing hymn and strings of hastily erected bunting flapped noisily in the breeze.

Yesterday Penny had celebrated her third birthday, but today was an even more important day than that. Today was the day the war had stopped.

She clapped her little hands, swept along by the air of celebration. Her face crumpled when she noticed her Nanny Eileen was crying. She was dressed in her best black coat and hat, and held a handkerchief to her face, her shoulders shaking. Penny sucked her thumb, her expression sombre.

Eileen bowed her head, unable to stop the tears coursing down her face as she remembered her beloved Bert, her sense of loss undiminished by the passing years. She felt a gentle pat on the top of her black fur hat and looked up, smiling through her tears at her granddaughter's grave expression. Penny was a source of great joy to Eileen, a soothing balm to her heartache and a reminder that there was hope for a happier future.

No family, it seemed, had escaped the war unscathed. As well as their loss of Bert, Arthur had returned home an invalid after being severely wounded in 1916 at Verdun. Blind in one eye and partially deaf, he was also trying to come to terms with the loss of his right arm.

Bea's husband, Trevor, was in a sanatorium somewhere outside London, suffering from severe shellshock, and was likely to remain there for the foreseeable future. By some miracle, Jess's husband Gordon had made it through the war safely and would be returning home in the next few weeks, after almost eighteen months away.

Frank had managed to escape the war altogether. When conscription was extended to include married men at the end of May 1916, he had taken himself off to old Dr Morton, the Cartwright family doctor, and whether by fair means or foul, he had managed to convince the old man that he was suffering from a weak heart.

Feigning disappointment, Frank had gone immediately to the conscription office with his medical certificate, where he had procured an unconditional certificate of exemption. He had left the recruitment office with a smile on his face and a spring in his step, but all the relief he felt at dodging the draft dissipated as soon as he arrived home and saw the contemptuous expression on his wife's face. No enemy bullets or bombs could have wounded him as much as the look of disappointment in the eyes of his beloved Ellie-May.

When Penny mentioned her daddy's weak heart to Nanny Eileen, her grandmother had made a derisive snorting noise in the back of her throat and rolled her eyes.

Penny loved her Nanna Eileen and Grandpa Sid. Mummy had to work a lot in the shop with Daddy, so Penny spent much of her time at her grandparents' house or down on the allotment with Grandpa Sid.

The allotment had belonged to Sid's neighbour, Tony, but Sid had taken it on when Tony was conscripted, and Penny loved it there. She enjoyed the feeling of soil between her fingers and the thrill of watching things grow. She enjoyed unearthing the first potatoes of the season, or hunting for slugs and snails under the rhubarb leaves.

After a productive afternoon spent at the allotment, Penny would clamber into the wheelbarrow, her dress tucked into her knickers, soil clinging to the hem of her petticoat, and Sid would wheel her home, surrounded by whatever produce the modest patch of land had yielded that day.

'We'd better not let your mum see you looking like that,' Eileen would say when Penny would arrive at Church Street covered in dirt, bramble twigs caught in her thick, dark curls, her wide, dark eyes shining with merriment. So Sid would drag the old tin bath into the kitchen and Eileen would scrub Penny from head to foot before Ellie-May arrived to collect her.

*

Standing beside Frank, Ellie-May smiled up at her daughter. Her darling Penelope, born on a stormy November night after a quick and easy labour that had both her sisters exclaiming with envy. It had been love at first sight. At just a few minutes old, Penny's resemblance to Jack had been blatantly obvious, and for a while Ellie-May had been afraid Frank would take against her, but although he had visibly blanched at the first sight of his new daughter, he had quickly recovered his equanimity and, while he remained emotionally distant, materially Penny wanted for nothing.

As a provider, Ellie-May couldn't fault him, but as a husband and father, he was difficult: prone to bouts of insecurity and jealousy, he even seemed to begrudge the time she devoted to caring for her child. But Ellie-May tried to make the best of things. She was expecting another baby in a few weeks and was hopeful that giving Frank a son or daughter of his own would go some way to laying Jack's ghost to rest.

She cast her gaze around the sea of people. Most were wearing black, and the celebrations were tinged with sadness. Happiness that the long war was over was deeply marred by so much loss and suffering. Already Ellie-May had grown used to the sight of wounded soldiers loitering on street corners, many missing limbs and being forced to beg for a living after being rejected by their families. She thought of her sister Bea, struggling to make ends meet on Trevor's meagre pension, not knowing whether her husband would ever be well enough to return home and live a normal life.

'Shall we get off, then?' asked Sid, moving towards her as the crowd began to disperse. Like many of the men around them, he was sporting a black armband. He reached up to lift Penny down from Frank's shoulders. 'Are you coming back to ours?' he asked Ellie-May as Penny snuggled against his neck, content in her grandpa's arms. 'We could have a bit of a celebration tea?'

As had become her habit, Ellie-May looked to Frank for confirmation. He shrugged. 'I should get back to the shop,' he said. 'But if you want to, I can spare an hour, I suppose.'

'Don't put yourself out,' muttered Ellie-May under her breath, turning to smile brightly at Sid. 'We'll come for a little while, Dad.'

'Lovely.' Sid squeezed his granddaughter's legs, pleased at the prospect of spending some time with Ellie-May. He hardly ever saw her these days, Frank was that possessive. He turned around, his eyes scanning the scattering throng, calling to Nora, Jess and Bea, who were standing a few feet away with the children. Bea wore black, her swollen, tear-blotched face concealed by a black lace veil.

Sid swung Penny into the air and she squealed in delight. She loved it at her grandparents' house. It was much more fun there than at home, and today she would have her cousins to play with and, if Uncle Arthur was in a good mood, which wasn't very often because she knew he wasn't very well, he might even help them build a fort out of Nanny Eileen's spare blankets . . .

*

Close to the Dorset–Wiltshire border, news that the war was over was slow in filtering through to the tiny villages. It was well into the afternoon of November 11th when Jack's housekeeper, Ida, came puffing down the garden path, her plump cheeks crimson with the exertion.

'Mr Pickup,' she panted, a hand to heaving bosom as she paused to catch her breath. 'Mr Pickup.'

Jack, one foot on the lower rung of the five-bar gate, turned from stroking the whiskered face of his nanny goat, Bertha. He raised a single eyebrow questioningly. Meg, his young Border Collie, sat beside him, ears pricked.

'It's over, Mr Pickup,' Ida gasped, coming to a halt as soon as she was close enough for Jack to hear her. His hearing wasn't what it had once been. 'They were talking about it in the village,' she said, excitedly. 'The Armistice was signed at eleven o'clock this morning. Oh, Mr Pickup, isn't that the best news?'

Tears sparkled in Ida's eyes and Jack reached for her hand, giving it a squeeze. Ida had lost both her sons in the first few months of the war.

'That is certainly cause for celebration, Ida,' Jack replied. 'We deserve a cup of tea at the very least.' He lifted his leg down and, leaning heavily on his cane, followed her buxom figure up the path, Meg close at heel.

The war had ended for Jack in 1917 at Passchendaele when two German bullets smashed into his femur. For several hours, he had lain in agony on the battlefield, bullets and bombs whizzing above his head, before the medics reached him. By then he was delirious with pain and infection had set in. It had taken six months for his leg to heal, and as a result, his left leg was noticeably shorter than his right. Even with the special built-up shoe he wore, he would always walk with a prominent limp.

Hobbling as fast as he could, he followed Ida into the small cottage, a chicken casserole bubbling in the oven, filling the kitchen with its meaty aroma. Salome, a sleek tabby cat that had wandered in one wet August night and made herself quite at home, lay curled up in the shabby armchair closest to the range. Meg flopped down on the hearthrug with a soft sigh, her long nose resting comfortably on her paws, her dark gaze focused on her beloved master.

Jack sank heavily into the other armchair, grateful to take the weight off his bad leg. It was now, as the days were growing cold and damp, that his leg plagued him the most.

'Perhaps this calls for something more than tea,' he suggested, massaging his leg while Ida filled the kettle. 'Maybe a nip of whisky?'

'That would be a treat, Mr Pickup.' While Ida disappeared into the small sitting room to fetch the bottle, Jack closed his eyes, letting the news sink in. He could scarcely believe it. The war was over, at last.

After receiving the heartbreaking news from Eileen that Ellie-May and Frank were married, all Jack had wanted to do was catch the next train to Southampton and see her, but Molly, the sweet VAD nurse had managed to persuade him otherwise. What did he expect to achieve? she'd asked. He had to accept the truth: Ellie-May had chosen another.

As soon as the doctor declared him fit, Jack had returned to the front. With a heroism that had bordered on foolhardy, he had risked his life time and again, earning himself the Victoria Cross for bravery after rescuing three members of his troop whilst under enemy fire. After Passchendaele, Jack had spent months undergoing treatment, first in hospital, and then in a rehabilitation centre near London. One of his few visitors had been Edward Chalke, his old employer.

'I don't want to be a bookkeeper anymore, Mr Chalke,' Jack had told him straight-up when Edward had assured him in no uncertain terms that his job would be waiting for him when he was able to return to work.

'What would you like to do, Jack?' Chalke had seated himself beside Jack's bed, arms folded across his chest. The ward resounded with the groans and moans of the injured. Some men had lost their faces and were totally unrecognizable to their loved ones. The majority were missing limbs. To Jack's mind, losing a couple of inches off your leg was not too much to cry about.

'I had a lot of time to think while I've been laid up here, sir, and I really don't want to go back to Southampton.' He didn't want to risk bumping into Ellie-May with Frank. 'I quite liked Dorset when I was at Wyke Hall. I'm thinking of trying for a job somewhere around there, though what I can do with a gammy leg I'm not too sure,' he smiled ruefully.

'You should ask for your savings back,' Edward Chalke said, thoughtfully. 'I'm surprised Ellie-May never sought to return your money to you, Jack. She never struck me as the sort of girl who would keep something that wasn't rightfully hers.'

'That struck me as strange, too,' Jack agreed. 'El is as honest as they come. But I shan't be asking for it back.' Much as it irked him to think of Frank spending his hard-earned money, he could never begrudge Ellie-May his money. After all, she had received it in good faith.

Edward Chalke patted Jack's shoulder. 'I doubt there would be much left by now anyway,' he said. 'Give me a couple of weeks. I'll put out some feelers, see if I know anyone looking to recruit.'

'Thank you, sir.' Jack sank back against his pillows, nodding gratefully. 'I'd appreciate it.'

Two weeks later Chalke had visited again. Jack was sitting in the day room by the open French windows overlooking a daisy-strewn lawn. The budding trees were garlanded with pink blossom against a pale blue sky. Chalke laid a thin cardboard folder on Jack's lap.

'What's this, sir?'

'Open it.'

Puzzled, Jack flipped it open, his frown deepening as his quick gaze scanned the document.

'I don't understand, Mr Chalke,' he stammered. 'This is a rental agreement, and it appears to be in my name.'

Edward leaned against the wall, arms folded, his lined face wreathed in smiles.

'Wayside,' Edward said, enjoying Jack's confusion. 'It's a smallholding I've bought, not far from a little hamlet called

Boyne Mead in Dorset. As the crow flies, it's about eight miles from Wyke Hall where you convalesced. I'll own the land, but you'll be my tenant, manager, whatever you want to call yourself. It's not very large, just a few acres. The very sweet housekeeper, Ida Martin, comes with the cottage. She's a widow who lost both her sons at Mons.'

Jack had stared at Chalke, stunned. His old employer grinned, sunlight catching his silvery-white hair. 'My wife and I were never blessed with children, Jack. You workhouse lads are the closest thing to family I've got. It tore my heart out when Jimmy got himself killed.' Jack nodded in acknowledgment. He had been gutted to learn the fate of his old workmate. Edward Chalke cleared his throat.

'Well, what do you say? Will you manage Wayside for me?'

Jack hadn't needed to think about it. He grabbed Chalke's hand. 'Yes, sir. Thank you for your faith in me. I shan't let you down. I promise.'

That had been six months ago. Simon, the fourteen-year-old son of the local vicar, worked alongside Jack, helping with the heavier chores he couldn't yet manage, though he was growing stronger with every passing day, thanks to the fresh Dorset air and Ida's cooking.

His reverie was interrupted by Ida bustling into the cosy kitchen brandishing the bottle of whisky and two glasses.

'I don't usually imbibe, Mr Pickup,' she said, coyly. 'But as this is a celebration, a little nip won't hurt.'

'Indeed it won't, Ida.' Jack took the glass and downed the

amber liquid in one gulp, relishing the heat flooding his body as the alcohol hit his veins. He sighed and held his glass out for a refill. 'One more and then I must see about digging up those turnips. I take it you've sent young Simon home?'

'I have, Mr Pickup. He was sluicing out the cowshed when I got back. His three older brothers are still God knows where and, well, he needs to be with his family today. He'll be here bright and early tomorrow.'

'Of course. He must be with his parents today of all days,' Jack agreed amiably, downing his second whisky. 'Please God, let all three of his brothers make it home safely.'

'Oh, listen, Mr Pickup, can you hear it? The church bells! They're ringing.' Ida sighed, her shoulders sagging as if she had finally been relieved of a huge weight.

In number 12 Church Street, Penny was also listening to the bells ringing out across the city. Nanny Eileen's house was bursting at the seams. Rose from next door had come over with her four younger children; Davie, now a strapping lad of seventeen, had yet to return from the shipbuilder's yard. Bea and Jessie were there with the cousins, and even old Stan from next door had popped in for a celebratory cup of tea. He was sitting beside Arthur who, to Penny's great disappointment, was having one of his low days and was not inclined to build a fort nor, in fact, spend any time with his nieces and nephews at all.

'Your Uncle Arthur is thinking of his old friends who were killed in the war,' Ellie-May had whispered to her when Penny complained about Arthur's lacklustre response to her request to play. 'You need to play quietly with your cousins today, sweetheart. I know it's a day for celebration, but we mustn't forget that a lot of people are mourning those who were killed, like your poor Uncle Bert lost at sea, or hurt like Uncle Trevor, stuck in that hospital.'

'Arthur should stop feeling sorry for himself,' Penny heard Frank mutter as he squeezed past them, earning himself a sharp look from Ellie-May. Penny cringed. She did hope they weren't going to spoil the day with one of their arguments.

'Perhaps if you'd been man enough to fight, instead of hiding behind your so-called "weak heart",' Ellie-May hissed, following him into the empty kitchen, 'you'd be more understanding.'

Frank flushed an angry red and turned away.

In the noisy, crowded parlour, Penny hunkered down on the hearthrug where Neville Norris was playing with his toy horses, blinking back hot tears. She hated it when Mummy argued with Daddy. It gave her a horrible sick feeling deep in the pit of her stomach.

It was awkward playing on the floor amongst the grown-ups' legs. Twice, Nora and Eileen, who were moving between the two rooms, dishing out cups of tea and plates of fairy cakes, almost tripped over them. Finally, Eileen lost patience and chased all the children outside to play.

As night approached, the street took on a carnival atmosphere. As the grown-ups began to spill from their houses, someone dragged out a piano and there was a rousing sing-song, songs that had given them hope and strength through the long, weary years of war, the cobbles glowing with pools of light shining out of windows that had been dark for so long.

People were dancing and Penny was happy to see her mummy and daddy arm in arm, swaying merrily along to the music. She smiled sleepily as the moon rose up behind the rooftops, stars sparkling in the crisp, cool night air. People's breath billowed in clouds as they laughed and sang.

There was sadness, of course. There was barely a house in the street that had been spared, but now there was the tangible hope that life would get better.

CHAPTER TWENTY

Four days later, Penny was sitting on the hearthrug playing with her doll. She placed it in the little cigar-box bed Sid had made for her, tucking her under the tiny bedclothes sewn by her Aunty Nora. Late autumn sunshine filled the room.

Her mother was sitting close to the fire, knitting as usual, her brow furrowed in concentration. Mummy had been feeling tired all day, and Daddy had warned Penny not to make too much noise. She must play quietly. Mummy needed her rest.

Penny glanced over to where Daddy sat in what had once been Grandpa Arnold's favourite chair, reading the newspaper.

Arnold had been taken earlier in the year by a particularly virulent strain of influenza. Penny had been packed off to stay with Eileen and Sid, safely out of harm's way. To the family's immense relief, neither Ellie-May nor Frank had come down with the illness, and once the flat had been properly fumigated, Penny had been allowed to return home.

She had found it strange at first, without Grandpa Arnold's solid presence in the corner of the room. He had always been there, a big lump of a man, emanating a queer smell, his huge, swollen foot propped up on a stool, his bulbous nose glowing. But despite his yellow teeth, bad breath and rheumy, bloodshot eyes, he had been inordinately fond of his little granddaughter, and she hadn't minded sitting on his lap as he bounced her up and down, the resulting coughing fit the usual signal to Penny that the play session was over.

A pigeon landed on the windowsill with a flutter of wings, distracting Penny from her play. She glanced up just as her mother let out a sharp cry, pain causing her to bend double, her knitting falling to the floor.

'Ellie!' Frank was on his feet at once. He took hold of Ellie-May's arm, steadying her as she got heavily to her feet, her face as white as a sheet.

'The baby's coming,' she said through clenched teeth, groaning loudly as her womb contracted painfully.

'I'll get one of the lads from next door to go for your mum,' Frank said, panic in his voice. He helped Ellie-May to bed, Penny following in wide-eyed fear.

'It's all right, Penny.' Frank swung her into his arms. 'Mummy's having her baby, that's all. It'll all be over soon.' He carried her down the stairs to the shop and out into the backyard, his own heart beating a nervous tattoo in his chest.

He was at once nervous and excited, nervous for the suffering his Ellie was about to endure, but excited about the fact that at last he would have a son or daughter of his own.

Penny was a daily reminder that Ellie had loved another before him. She was the image of her father through and through. She didn't have anything of Ellie in her, and at times, much as he attempted to hide it, he found the fact he was looking into Jack's face daily, damn hard to swallow.

The air was cold, a biting wind sweeping down the alleyway as he leaned against the fence that separated his property from the grocer's next door, shouting to catch the attention of the lanky delivery boy, Del.

'Del!' Frank panted, relief flowing over him in waves when Del finally appeared in the doorway, blinking against the low autumn sunlight. 'The baby's coming,' Frank explained quickly, shifting Penny from one arm to the other. 'Will you take our Penny around to Church Street and fetch Eileen?'

Del nodded and grinned at Penny over the fence.

'Of course, Mr Cartwright. Come on, Pen–Pen. Let's go get your grandma.'

They found Eileen in the backyard talking to Rose. She took one look at her granddaughter and the young lad and nodded.

'I'll get my hat and coat. See you later, Rose.'

'Tell your Ellie-May I say good luck,' Rose smiled. She patted Eileen's arm. 'She's a strong, healthy girl. She'll be fine. Look how quick she was with Penny.'

Eileen nodded, her face grim. She had a bad feeling about this baby. Forcing such thoughts from her mind, she smiled down at Penny.

Sending Del off home, she settled Penny in the kitchen

with Sid and Arthur, before grabbing her coat and hat and hastening to Ellie-May's bedside. One look at her daughter's pain-ravaged face warned her that this was a far cry from the easy time she'd had with Penny. Despite his protestations, she shooed Frank out of the room.

'Go and fetch the midwife,' she told him, shutting the door firmly in his face. She perched beside Ellie-May's side, pressing a soothing hand to her fevered brow.

'There, now,' she crooned, forcing a smile as she fought to keep all feelings of foreboding away. 'Don't make such a fuss,' she said cheerfully. 'Remember how quick and easy it was with Penny.'

'This is much worse, Mum,' Ellie-May panted, grimacing in agony. She felt as though her entire insides were being ripped apart, crying out in pain with each contraction. It was a relief to them both when the midwife, a capable woman with a beaming smile and friendly manner, arrived to take over.

It was a long, difficult labour and darkness was falling by the time Ellie-May's little boy made his way into the world.

'You have a son,' the midwife told Frank, a smile plastered on her weary face as she let him into the room. Haggard and pale from worry, tie askew, eyes bloodshot, Frank couldn't conceal his joy. The room was stale with the smell of sweat and blood. The midwife yawned, gathering up her bags, and slipped silently from the room, declining Eileen's offer of a cup of tea.

Frank barely noticed the exchange. He was staring at the tiny bundle Ellie-May cradled in her arms, mesmerized by the tiny form. He smiled at his wife. Ellie-May was deathly pale, dark shadows beneath her eyes. Her lank, greasy hair fanned the pillow. She barely had the strength to smile back as she handed Frank his son.

'He's beautiful, Ellie,' he breathed, cradling his newborn son, his eyes bright with love and pride. 'You clever girl,' he whispered. 'He's an absolute diamond, Ellie, a diamond.'

'I think we've all earned a cup of tea,' said Eileen, dragging her weary body off the chair. 'I'll put the kettle on.'

Frank Arnold Cartwright lived for just eight hours. They buried him on a bleak mid-November day. Clutching Penny's gloved hand in hers, Ellie-May watched dry-eyed, the cold wind scouring her cheeks, as they lowered her infant son's coffin into the unforgiving ground. Frank stood at her side, his expression like granite. At the vicar's nod, he stepped forward and took the proffered spade. As the first clod of earth hit the tiny coffin, he burst into noisy, agonising tears. Sid gently prised Frank's fingers from the handle of the spade and he flung himself against Ellie-May. She wrapped her arms around him, feeling the solidness of him, the force of his grief causing his shoulders to shudder. In the cold, windswept graveyard, they clung to each other, united in their inconsolable sorrow.

CHAPTER TWENTY-ONE

Penny clung tightly to her mother's hand. Eileen and Sid walked slowly in front of them. Both were dressed in their finest clothes. Nora, proudly sporting her 'VOTES FOR WOMEN' sash, her hand tucked into the crook of Arthur's arm, brought up the rear. Frank, to everyone's relief, had chosen to stay at home.

'Someone's got to mind the shop,' he'd snorted coldly when Ellie-May had asked him why he wasn't coming.

'Too ashamed to show his face, more like,' Nora had muttered to Eileen when Ellie-May had made his excuses. Eileen had nodded sagely.

'There'll be all those crippled soldiers and widows. No wonder he feels ashamed.'

Nora tugged the collar of her black coat tighter around her slender throat. Now an attractive young woman of twenty-two, she took pride in her appearance. Her dark auburn hair was cut into a sleek bob, emphasising her elfin face and large, green eyes. Since leaving the armaments factory at the end of the war, she had taken a job working for the suffragette movement. She worked at their office close to the Guildhall, helping to produce and distribute literature furthering the cause of women's rights. She loved her job and wore her sash with pride, despite the disparaging looks it earned her from the local constabulary.

Now she strode proudly with her family towards the newly erected cenotaph in Watts Park. The structure was breathtaking in its simplicity, yet awe-inspiring in its beauty.

Ellie-May picked Penny up, craning her neck to take in the whole structure. Right at the top was the prone figure, a fallen soldier, below a carved wreath and a lion. A stone pine cone mounted on urns stood on either side.

Although they had come early, a large crowd had already gathered in front of the cenotaph. The mood was sombre. Many of the men wore black armbands. Many women, Eileen included, wore veils. It was a poignant day, a day to remember the thousands of men and women who had made the ultimate sacrifice.

After only a few minutes, Ellie-May set Penny back down. Her little girl was almost five now, and heavy. She rubbed the small of her back. The two years since the end of the war hadn't been easy. The loss of their baby had hit Ellie-May and Frank hard, and they'd just been getting back on an even keel when the influenza pandemic had swept across the country, slaying people in their thousands. The Spanish Flu had taken Jess's husband, Gordon, three months after his return from France. As fit as a fiddle at breakfast, by teatime he was gone.

Davie Norris had succumbed, as had Stan Wilson. Families who had rejoiced when loved ones were returned to them after the war, now mourned their cruel deaths from influenza. Men, women and children, rich or poor – the Spanish flu had killed indiscriminately.

As well as the devastating effects of the flu epidemic, there were the heart-breaking images of wounded soldiers begging on the streets. It broke Ellie-May's heart to see once-proud men being treated so abysmally by the very country for which they had sacrificed so much. She didn't wonder that political unrest was rife.

Penny stood on tiptoe, trying to see through the throng. Seeing her, Sid hoisted her onto his shoulders so she could have a better view.

A hush fell over the assembled onlookers as a distinguished-looking man climbed the stone steps and cleared his throat. He was Major General John Seely. After a lengthy speech and a two-minute silence, the band played the last post, and the crowd were invited to inspect the cenotaph.

Ellie-May pushed her way through the crowds to the foot of the imposing structure on which 1,793 names were engraved.

The names of Southampton's brave men and women who had died during the war.

'Here's Bert,' Nora breathed, her gloved fingers gently brushing the name carved into the cold stone. 'Bramhall. A. G.,' she read out softly, choking back a sob as her family crowded around her, tears sparkling in their eyes. Eileen sniffed and wiped her eyes with a handkerchief. Sid blew his nose. Arthur, who had been subdued throughout the ceremony, turned away. He had been very close to his brother, and still felt his loss keenly.

The damn war, he scowled, anger churning in his gut like a bubbling cauldron. It had destroyed his family.

Bea had taken the children and moved up to St Albans in order to be closer to Trevor. He had shown little sign of improvement and doctors were losing hope that he would ever recover sufficiently to lead a normal life. Jess, now a widow with two children to support, had moved to Doncaster to be closer to Gordon's elderly parents. Gordon had been an only child, and since his death his parents had gone downhill rapidly. Jess felt it her duty to take care of them in their old age.

'It's what Gordon would have wanted,' she had told Eileen firmly when her mother questioned the wisdom of taking herself and the children off into the unknown. 'And anyway, it's time the children got to know their paternal grandparents before it's too late.'

Arthur shoved his hands in his trouser pockets and walked away, kicking through the fallen autumn leaves, his good eye screwed up against the dappled sunlight. Sid caught up with him and put his arm around his son's shoulders.

'So many of my mates, Dad,' Arthur said, his voice quivering. 'And our Bert . . .'

'I know, lad,' Sid said gently. 'I know.'

Jostled by the crowd, Ellie-May frowned. She had

scrutinized the surnames beginning with P, but there was no Pickup listed.

'Jack's name isn't here,' she said, more to herself than anyone else. How was it possible Jack's name been left off the memorial? She glanced around her, puzzled and that's when she noticed a few other people murmuring in consternation.

'It's probably a clerical error,' one man was saying in an attempt to console his clearly distraught wife. 'I intend to take it up with the council first thing Monday morning.'

'Excuse me.' Ellie-May approached them nervously. 'Has someone in your family been left off the roll of honour?' she asked, clutching Penny tightly by the hand.

The man nodded, and cleared his throat. 'Our son. I gather there are several other names not included.'

'But why?' Ellie-May asked, bewildered. The man's wife dabbed at her eyes, and attempted to stifle her sobs.

'That's what I intend to find out,' the man said firmly, taking his wife's arm.

'And so they're going to approach the war memorial committee about having the missing names added,' Ellie-May told Frank later that evening. Penny was in bed and Nellie Melba was playing on the gramophone. Ellie-May sat with her mending on her lap. A fire crackled in the grate and the curtains were drawn against the night. 'If that doesn't work they will go to the newspaper and start a campaign.' She looked across at Frank and frowned at finding he was staring into the fire, stony-faced.

'What's the matter?' she asked with a sigh, genuinely puzzled by his reaction. 'Doesn't it bother you that some of our brave soldiers aren't being honoured as they should be?'

'What's bothering me,' said Frank heavily, 'is the fact you're so concerned over Jack's name being missing. Your brother was honoured, surely that's all that should concern you?'

'But Jack ...' The words died on her lips as Frank jumped to his feet and rounded on her with a ferocity that made her jump.

'Jack, Jack, Jack,' Frank snarled, flecks of spit flying from his lips. 'I'm sick to bloody death of hearing that name. What did he do, huh, except get you in the family way and bugger off to France? Do you ever stop to consider where you and Penny would be without me?' He advanced towards her, apoplectic with rage. Genuinely frightened, Ellie-May shrank back in her chair. Frank inhaled, nostrils flaring, all his deeply buried shame erupting like a burst dam.

'I've never been able to live up to your memory of him, have I? If I hadn't married you, you and your bastard would have ended up in a tenement somewhere eking out a living, shunned by anyone with half an ounce of respect. But instead of being grateful, I constantly feel like you're comparing me to him and I'm sick of it, do you hear me? I'M SICK OF IT!'

'Frank.' Ellie-May forced herself to be calm, but her hands were shaking. She'd never seen Frank this angry before. He was moody and prone to long bouts of sulking if he didn't get his own way, but this was something new, and it scared her. 'You're being unreasonable. Of course I'm concerned that Jack's name has been left off the roll of honour. He deserves to be recognized, but that has nothing to do with our marriage.'

'It has *everything* to do with our marriage,' screamed Frank. 'You're married to me, not him. If he'd cared so much about you, he'd have married you before he went away, instead of just taking advantage of you. You are my wife and I don't want to hear the name Jack bloody Pickup mentioned in this house again. Understand?'

'But Frank . . .' Ellie-May rose.

'Shut up!' Frank screamed at her. 'Shut up, do you hear me? Just shut up!'

The slap took her by surprise. She fell back heavily into the chair clutching her throbbing cheek, eyes wide with shock.

Frank was instantly contrite. 'Oh my God, Ellie, I'm so sorry. I didn't mean it. I'm sorry.' He fell to his knees in front of her, his horrified expression begging her forgiveness. A frightened cry brought them both up short. Penny stood in the doorway to her bedroom in her pyjamas, her hair tousled with sleep.

'Penny, darling.' Pushing Frank aside, Ellie-May got to her feet, plastering a smile on her face as she crouched down to cuddle the terrified little girl.

'Darling, don't cry,' Frank said, shamefaced. 'Mummy had a little accident. She tripped and banged her face. She's going to be fine.' He cringed at the sight of his daughter's anxious, tear-stained face. Ellie-May shot him a filthy look and he averted his gaze, unable to bear the contempt in her eyes as she scooped Penny up and carried her back to bed, leaving him alone to wallow in his shame.

The following morning Frank was filled with contrition. Ellie-May entered the kitchen, her heart full of trepidation, to find Frank stirring the porridge, a pot of tea on the table and the smell of freshly made toast filling her nostrils.

'I'm so sorry, Ellie.' She forced herself not to flinch as Frank planted a kiss on her swollen cheek. An ugly bruise was forming around her left eye. She wouldn't be showing her face in church that morning, that was for sure.

'Hey, Pen-Pen,' Frank said jovially. 'Why don't you and me go to the park this morning and look for conkers, let Mummy have a bit of time to herself?'

Penny nodded happily, ladling a spoonful of porridge into her mouth.

'What do you say, Ellie?' Frank looked at her anxiously, his eyes begging her forgiveness.

For Penny's sake, Ellie-May forced herself to sound cordial. 'That sounds lovely.' She smiled at Penny, and patted her hand. 'You be a good girl for Daddy, and this afternoon you can go to the allotment with Grandpa Sid. You can stay for your tea.'

'Are you coming?' Penny asked, taking a sip of milk and licking the cream from her upper lip.

'No, sweetheart,' her mother replied with a shake of her

head, knowing she could never explain away her bruises. 'I feel like staying in today. You'll have a lovely time with Grandpa and Nanny. Daddy will fetch you before bedtime.'

Ellie-May washed up the breakfast things while Frank and Penny got ready for their walk in the park. For Penny, a morning off Sunday school was a joy in itself. Miss Prince, her Sunday school teacher, was a bit of a disciplinarian and, much as Penny enjoyed listening to the stories of Daniel and David, and Peter and Paul, looking for conkers beneath the giant horse chestnut trees, and perhaps chasing a squirrel or two was, to her young mind, a much preferable way to spend a Sunday morning.

'We'll be off then,' Frank said, standing in front of Ellie-May, twisting his cap in his hands. He looked at her beseechingly. 'Please say you forgive me,' he begged.

Ellie-May gave a curt nod. What else could she do?

Frank glanced around, making sure Penny was preoccupied with buttoning up her boots. He reached out and placed a hand on Ellie-May's arm, his anguish evident on his face.

'I just want you to love me the way you loved Jack,' he whispered.

'Come on, Daddy.' Penny tugged at Frank's sleeve, saving Ellie-May from having to answer. Frank gazed down at his stepdaughter's little face, bright with excitement and reluctantly released his grip on Ellie-May. 'We'll see you later, then,' he said heavily.

Ellie-May nodded, and followed them to the top of the

stairs, stooping down to kiss Penny goodbye and wind her scarf more snuggly around her neck.

'Have fun,' she said, as they disappeared down the narrow staircase. Penny's voice drifting back up the stairs.

'This is much more fun than going to church, Daddy, isn't it?'

Though it wasn't his custom, Jack was attending church that morning. He sat in a narrow pew in St James Church in Boyne Mead, next to Ida. The tiny Saxon church was packed to the rafters for the unveiling of the memorial plaque in honour of the twelve local boys killed in the war.

Peter Briggs, the woodcarver who had lovingly carved the decorative plaque, had lost his own son, Mathew, in the final few days of the war. It was a poignant service and the vicar's sermon was punctuated by bouts of muted sobbing. Ida, the names of her own dear boys plainly visible amongst the carved vine leaves, was openly crying, tears spilling unchecked down her soft cheeks. Jack, too, had a recurring need to blow his nose.

Wiping her eyes, Ida cast a sideways glance at her employer. In the three years Jack had been at Wayside, she had come to love him like a son. And she wasn't the only one to have grown fond of him; there was barely a farmer's daughter around whose heart hadn't been set aflutter by Jack's charm and rather exotic appearance.

Ida sighed. Folding her handkerchief, she took a shuddering breath in an effort to pull herself together. Daily, she thanked God for giving her Jack. He'd never replace her boys, God rest them, but he went a long way to filling the empty space they'd left in her heart.

Now that the war was long over, and things were returning to normal, she had decided it was high time her surrogate son found himself a wife. He was only twenty-five or thereabouts and she couldn't for the life of her understand why he hadn't taken up with one of the willing young local lasses.

What with the war and then the terrible flu pandemic, eligible young men were few and far between. Her Jack could have his pick of young women. Despite his limp and the slight deafness he suffered in his right ear, he'd be a catch for any girl. And in Ida's opinion, the streak of white in Jack's fringe, caused by shock so the doctors had said, only served to make him more attractive.

The vicar announced the final hymn and she rose along with the rest of the congregation. Thank the good Lord that all the vicar's sons had returned from the war in one piece. The eldest, Adam, was due to marry his childhood sweetheart in the spring.

Opening her mouth to sing, Ida sent up a quick prayer that her Jack, too, would soon find a young lady and settle down. Wayside was in dire need of a family and Ida found the idea of becoming a surrogate granny thoroughly appealing.

Beside her, leaning heavily on his cane, Jack caught the eye of the young organist. She smiled at him shyly, and as Jack found himself grinning back, he felt something stir deep within his soul. He had spent the past five years pining for Ellie-May; perhaps it was time to let her go and start living again.

Catching the brief exchange, Ida supressed a triumphant smile. Perhaps her prayers were to be answered after all.

CHAPTER TWENTY-TWO

1925

'Grandpa, what's a bastard?'

Startled, Sid glanced across the allotment to where nine-year-old Penny was filling her wicker basket with broad beans, the warm June sunshine picking out the chestnut highlights of her dark, wavy hair. Scratching his head, Sid got stiffly to his feet. He was fifty-eight now and not as supple as he had once been. Straightening up, he massaged his aching back and frowned.

'It's a nasty word,' he said gruffly, leaning on his fork. 'Where'd you hear it?' he queried, although he could hazard a guess.

'Daddy and Mummy were arguing again,' Penny replied in such a matter-of-fact tone it broke Sid's heart. That such domestic strife should be part and parcel of his beloved granddaughter's daily life grieved him deeply.

She spun around to face him. Her face and arms were as

brown as the proverbial berry and she was the spit of Jack Pickup. Sid sighed inwardly. It was no wonder she got under Frank's skin.

'Daddy said that if it wasn't for him, Mummy and her bastard would be out on the street.'

'Like I said, it's a nasty word.' Sid shrugged his shoulders. He was at a loss as to what to tell the child. 'I'm sure Daddy didn't mean anything by it. Now then, how are you getting on with picking those beans? Your nan will need a good basketful for tonight's supper. Your Uncle Arthur eats like a horse, as well you know.'

As Penny returned happily to the task at hand, Sid watched her with a sympathetic smile. The poor lass, she had it hard at home. Despite the loving father act Frank put on for the world, he had never taken to his stepdaughter.

Perhaps if he and Ellie-May had had a child of their own but, well . . . no use crying over spilt milk.

Four little graves in the churchyard, four little boys, none of whom had lived longer than a few hours. There would be no more babies for his Ellie-May, the doctor had made that clear. It had been a bitter pill to swallow, and Frank particularly had taken the news hard.

Ellie-May didn't confide much in Sid and Eileen, but they were astute enough to realize that the Cartwright household was not a happy one. His daughter and granddaughter spent much of their lives walking on eggshells around Frank, never knowing what might set him off. His jealousy of Jack bordered on the pathological and Penny, bless her heart, served as a daily reminder of him. God alone knew how Frank would react if he ever discovered Jack was alive.

Even now, almost ten years on, the letter, tucked in the back of Eileen's Bible, haunted him. He had spent many a sleepless night over the years questioning the decision he and Eileen had taken all those years ago. And what of Jack? How had he reacted to Eileen's letter?

Sid grunted, forcing such thoughts from his mind. *What's done is done*, he sighed, putting his foot to the fork and turning over a handful of rosy-red beetroots. Shaking them free of earth, he placed them in the basket.

They walked home hand in hand, Penny skipping alongside him in a manner that warmed Sid's heart. She loved spending time with her grandpa on his allotment. She enjoyed the feel of the dry soil between her fingers; loved growing things, crowing in pride when her own carefully nurtured produce surpassed even her grandpa's in both size and taste. Nanny Eileen had suggested she enter her carrots in the vegetable competition at the church summer bazaar. Grandpa Sid's carrots had won first prize the last three years running, and this year Penny was determined to beat him.

The dark rooftops were stark against the dazzlingly blue sky. Starlings and swifts soared overhead, and the haunting cries of the ever-present seagulls were calling. Sunlight glinted on windows. Children were playing in the sun-kissed streets, and women stood on doorsteps gossiping with neighbours, everyone enjoying the warm summer air.

Nanny Eileen was in the kitchen, her sleeves rolled up

above her elbows, slathering butter on thick slices of bread. A warm honeysuckle-scented breeze wafted in through the open door. The Norris's large ginger tomcat crouched on the high, mossy back wall, eyeing up the two crows squabbling on the sloping roof of the Methodist chapel.

'What lovely beetroot,' Eileen exclaimed. 'And such fat broad beans.' She took the baskets of vegetables from her husband and granddaughter and dumped them on the draining board beside the sink. 'What a feast we'll have later.'

Penny flung her arms around her grandmother's ample waist, burying her face in her apron and inhaling the warm, familiar scent of flour and rose water.

'Did you have a good time?' Eileen asked Penny, as the young girl helped set the table. Penny nodded.

'She's a grand little worker, aren't you, Pen?' Sid grinned and ruffled Penny's unruly mop of hair. Settling himself in the armchair beside the empty fireplace, he opened the paper.

'I enjoy it,' Penny replied seriously. 'I might get a job as a gardener when I'm older,' she pondered thoughtfully. On a recent trip to the library she had paged through a book that pictured the gardens of some of England's grand houses and had been awestruck at how creative the gardeners had been with their planting of various species of exotic flowers and shrubs.

'I think Daddy has other ideas for you,' Eileen said, pursing her lip as Penny pulled out a chair and sat down.

'I think the child should be allowed to decide for herself,' Sid interjected from behind his copy of the *Echo*.

'I don't want to work in the butcher's,' Penny pouted, resting her chin on her hands and peering at her grandmother under her fringe.

'Well, you've plenty of time to think about your future,' Eileen said in a placatory tone. 'You're not even ten yet.'

'I will be in five months.'

The sound of voices emanated from the backyard and Penny glanced up in time to see Arthur passing the window, his empty shirtsleeve pinned across his chest. There was a young woman with him. She was tall and slender, her dark hair cut into a fashionable bob, and she was wearing one of the close-fitting cloche hats that had become popular of late with fashionable young ladies. Arthur was laughing, his black eye-patch giving him a rakish air.

'Hello,' he said, poking his head around the doorframe and gently drawing the young lady forward. 'This is Victoria Howard. Victoria – my mum and dad and my niece Penny.' Sid got hastily to his feet, shoving his newspaper aside, to offer Victoria his hand which she shook firmly.

'I'm pleased to meet you all,' Victoria smiled. She had a pretty face, and was wearing a fashionably short frock of bright green. A string of glass beads, also green, hung from her slender, swan-like neck. The way they caught the light every time she moved fascinated Penny.

'You're very welcome,' Eileen said, a lightness in her heart. She worried terribly about her only surviving son. He was prone to bouts of depression, and she was often afraid he might do something drastic. Perhaps Victoria would be the tonic he needed. 'Penny, lay another place for Miss Howard.'

'Oh, it's Victoria, please,' Victoria said as Penny hurried to do as she was told. 'There's no need to stand on ceremony, surely? Now,' she glanced around the small kitchen, 'what can I do to help?'

'So where did you two meet?' Sid asked a short time later as they all took their places around the table laden with freshly baked bread, baby lettuce and plump, juicy tomatoes, all courtesy of the allotment. Sid hadn't seen Arthur so animated for a long time and it gladdened his heart.

'We met in April at a benefits concert in aid of wounded soldiers,' Victoria answered. 'I'm on the committee.'

'I didn't know you'd been to a benefits concert?' Eileen raised an eyebrow as Victoria reached across the table, perfectly at ease, and began to cut Arthur's food into manageable chunks.

'Yes, well,' said Arthur. 'Thank you.' He smiled at Victoria, spearing a slice of tomato with his fork. 'I'm thirty-one years old, Mum, I don't have to tell you everything I do.'

'Well, no, I don't expect you to,' Eileen conceded, flushing slightly with guilt. Because of Arthur's disabilities, she was perhaps inclined to mother him more than she should.

'We've seen each other a few times since then, haven't we, Arthur?' Victoria smiled.

'Yes,' Arthur replied shortly, apparently disinclined to discuss his blossoming romance with his family.

'I'm friendly with Nora,' Victoria continued. 'We work in the same office. It was she who persuaded Arthur to come along to the concert.'

'But our Nora works for some women's rights place,' Sid piped up, wiping tomato juice from his chin with his handkerchief. 'Are you one of those suffragettes as well, then?'

Victoria smiled across the table at him beguilingly. 'I believe in equal rights for women, Mr Bramhall, yes. After all, so many women proved themselves to be quite capable of doing a man's job during the war. It's unfair to expect them to simply go back to being housewives and mothers, surely, and having absolutely no say in the running of the country.'

'Good on you, love,' Eileen said before Sid could open his mouth. 'I'm dead proud of our Nora.'

'She'll end up an old spinster,' Sid said dejectedly. Penny looked up from her plate.

'What's a spinster, Grandpa?'

'A woman who is not married,' Victoria explained, a smile playing on her lips. 'I'm sure there are some married women who would envy them their freedom.'

'You wouldn't want to stay a spinster, would you?' Arthur asked, his blush deepening as he realized he had spoken his thoughts out aloud. Victoria laughed.

'Is that a proposal, Arthur Bramhall?' She grinned at him across the table.

'No.' Arthur dropped his gaze. 'I mean, well, not yet, but . . .' He looked up, feeling as though he might be having a heart attack, such was his difficulty to draw breath. Victoria reached across the table and patted his hand.

'I'm teasing you, Arthur,' she said softly, the expression of love on her face causing Eileen and Sid to exchange a hopeful glance. If Victoria would be willing to take on Arthur, well, it would make Eileen's heart glad.

'I got a letter from our Bea this morning,' Eileen said, changing the subject as she retrieved a creased sheet of blue writing paper from her apron pocket. She pursed her lips, her gaze travelling around the table. 'It seems she's met someone.'

'Met someone?' Arthur raised an eyebrow. 'As in a bloke?'

'Yes. He's a widower with two grown-up children. I gather he's quite a bit older than our Bea.' She scanned the letter. 'He works as an orderly at the sanatorium.'

'But what about Trevor?' Arthur sat back, appalled that his sister could take up with another man while her husband was so ill. Penny listened with fascination. She couldn't remember her Uncle Trevor. She had only been a baby when he'd gone off to war. There was a picture of him and Aunty Bea on their wedding day on the mantelpiece in the parlour. He looked a nice man, with kind, smiling eyes, but that was all he had ever been to Penny, a nice-looking man in a photograph.

'Trevor's never going to recover, son,' Sid said gently. 'I know you got on well with him. We all did, he was a good lad. But that person is gone, and if this chap, Duncan – is that his name, Eileen?'

His wife nodded. 'Duncan Sheppard.'

'Good for her, I say,' Sid went on. 'Life is short, as you well know. A person has to grab happiness where they can.'

'Will she divorce Trevor?' Arthur wanted to know.

'I don't know,' Eileen admitted, with a frown. 'It's still early days. At least where she's living now no one knows about Trevor, so she would avoid a scandal. On another note, our Shelley has got herself the promise of a scullery maid position at some posh house in Knightsbridge for next year when she turns fourteen, and the housekeeper promised Bea she'd put a word in for Poppy-Jo as well, soon as she's old enough.' Eileen folded the letter and shoved it back in her pocket. 'At least the two girls will be well settled.'

'That will be a weight off her mind, then.' Sid pushed his plate aside and leaned back in his chair with a sigh of satisfaction. 'Take some of that beetroot home with you, when you go, Penny,' he said, smiling at his granddaughter. 'You work really hard on that allotment. It's only right that you have your share of the rewards.'

Penny smiled, pleased with the praise. She hurried home from school each weekday, and would be waiting by the shipyard gates when the whistle blew, hopping impatiently from one foot to the other until she saw Sid emerge. On Saturdays, she was at her grandparents' back door by eight, in time for a cup of Eileen's strong, sweet tea and a slice of toast before walking with Sid to the allotments, as they had that morning, to spend a pleasant few hours at one with nature. On occasion they were joined by Tony Norris. He had hurt his back in the war and had declined Sid's offer of the return of the allotment, preferring to spend the odd Saturday morning sitting on a bench enjoying the sun while watching Penny and Sid work.

Lately Frank had started insisting Penny spend more time helping in the shop. As yet, he hadn't exactly forbidden her to go to the allotments after school, but Penny was anxiously aware that it was only a matter of time before her freedom was curtailed. After all, she was nearly ten years old, too old to need babysitting by her grandparents.

'Arthur and I are planning to take the tram over to Hamble this afternoon,' Victoria said, breaking through Penny's thoughts. 'Would anyone care to join us? It's such a perfect afternoon.'

'You're all right, pet,' Eileen said, waving the invitation away with a flap of her hand. 'You two go and enjoy yourself. I've got plenty to keep me busy here.'

'That's kind of you, lass,' Sid agreed, 'but I'm going to tackle the flowerbed in the yard this afternoon. With all the rain we had last week the weeds are having a field day. You'll give me a hand, won't you Pen-Pen?'

'Of course, Grandpa.' Grinning in delight, Penny slid off her chair and began to help Eileen clear the table.

CHAPTER TWENTY-THREE

Ellie-May wiped her hands on her apron and groaned. It was oppressively warm in the shop, and she was uncomfortably aware of the sweat trickling down her spine. A motor car rattled up the street, horn honking loudly, drawing Frank from the back room. He'd been on about buying a car for weeks. He had taken a fancy to the relatively new, reasonably priced Austin 7. So far she had resisted his entreaties. As far as she was concerned, motor vehicles were noisy and dangerous. Just recently the newspapers had reported a horrific accident in Yorkshire where a coach full of families on a day trip from York to Bolton had crashed through a bridge, killing seven people. The story had turned her stomach.

'I really wish you'd reconsider, Ellie,' Frank wheedled now, turning from the window, a deep frown puckering his brow. He had recently turned thirty-two and looked even more handsome than ever. Ellie-May hadn't failed to notice the admiring glances he attracted from their female customers. *If only they knew what he was really like*, she thought with a toss of her head.

Frank shoved his hands deep in his trouser pockets and cocked his head in what he hoped was an endearing manner. 'It's not as if we can't afford it.'

'They're dangerous,' Ellie-May replied. She pressed her hands on the counter top, and bit her lip. 'I don't want Penny riding in a car.'

'The only people who have crashes are the reckless idiots who either don't know what they're doing or are show-ing off,' Frank said disparagingly. 'Like that fool, Johnson, around the corner. He was driving too fast, and hit a tree. He admitted as much to me himself. It was entirely his own fault and . . .' He broke off as a tall, smartly dressed gentleman stopped outside the open door. He glanced upwards, brow creased, nodded and removing his hat and leather driving gloves, stepped into the shop.

'Good afternoon, Mr Cartwright, Mrs Cartwright.' He inclined his head slightly in greeting.

'Good afternoon, Mr Turner,' smiled Ellie-May. 'Frank, this is Mr Turner, our Penny's teacher. What can I get you, sir?'

'A couple of your fine pork chops, if you please.' Barry Turner smiled at Frank. 'I saw you admiring my car,' he said jovially.

'You've got a fine-looking machine there, sir,' Frank replied, not quite succeeding in hiding the wistful envy in his voice.

'She's a good little runaround,' Barry agreed, enjoying Frank's envy. 'You thinking of buying one yourself?'

'Thinking about it,' Frank grinned. 'Got to convince the wife first, though.'

'You'd love it, Mrs Cartwright,' Barry said, turning his attention to Ellie-May who had wrapped his chops and was awaiting payment. She laughed easily. She liked Penny's teacher; he made her laugh with his easy manner and charming good looks. He was not handsome in the usual sense of the word, but he had an open, pleasant face, and bright blue eyes that appeared to be always smiling. He was wearing a cream shirt, with the sleeves rolled up to show off tanned forearms, and brown trousers. His whole manner was relaxed and casual, a complete contrast to Frank whose uptight, buttoned up manner was reflected in his style of dress. Ellie-May couldn't remember ever seeing her husband with his sleeves rolled up, not even when they had a rare day out at Weston Foreshore.

'Maybe I'll convince you to go for a spin one day,' Barry was saying with a cheeky grin as he handed over the money for his purchase. Ellie-May laughed.

'I don't think so,' she said good-naturedly. She was astute enough to realize that Barry's almost flirtatious manner was a cover for his natural shyness. He was happily married to Gladys, and they were both regular attendees at St Peter's. Ellie-May was fond of them and she spent a pleasant couple of minutes chatting with Barry about nothing in particular.

'Give Mrs Turner my regards,' she said when he turned to leave. 'I hope she recovers from her cold very soon.'

'Thank you,' Barry nodded. 'Let me know when you're ready to buy a car, Mr Cartwright. I'd love to offer my advice.' Frank smiled thinly, and raised his hand in acknowledgement.

'You're very quiet,' Ellie-May remarked a short time later as they prepared to close the shop for the evening. She was wiping the meat trays. Frank had been in and out of the shop all afternoon, his expression sullen, his blue-grey eyes slate-like in their intensity. His response to her attempts at conversation had been curt at best. Ellie-May frowned at him. 'Is something the matter?'

'You tell me,' Frank snarled as he locked the door, slamming the bolts across with unnecessary force. Ellie-May felt the familiar sick feeling in her stomach.

'What do you mean?' she asked, unable to disguise the nervous quiver in her voice. Genuinely puzzled, she followed him up the stairs to the flat above. They had barely gone through the door when Frank rounded on her.

'You disgust me!'

'What?' Taken aback, Ellie-May could only stare at her husband, open-mouthed in shock. 'What do you mean?' she asked in a small voice.

'Your behaviour earlier; the way you were carrying on with that Turner chap!'

'*What?*' Incredulous, Ellie-May could only stare at him. 'For goodness sake, Frank, he's Penny's school teacher. We always have a laugh when he comes in here; he's that sort of person. His wife is the same.'

'It's demeaning,' Frank spluttered. 'And *humiliating*.' He stood in the centre of the room, silhouetted against the dusty sunlight streaming in through the windows. He was visibly shaking. 'You do it on purpose, don't you, to humiliate me?'

'Do *what*? Frank, I don't know what you mean.' Ellie-May rubbed her throbbing temples.

'You're determined to rub it in my face, aren't you?' he snarled, spit flying from his lips. 'You're determined to humiliate me because I'm not the one you wanted.'

Ellie-May opened her mouth to reply, but the words wouldn't come, she was so flabbergasted by Frank's accusations.

'I've always been second-best. You treat me like dirt because I'm not bloody Jack!'

'Frank . . .' Ellie-May whispered, her hand flying to her mouth. 'That's not true. I've been the best wife to you that I can be.'

'Oh, yes?' Frank snapped. 'You really believe that, do you? Then how do you explain this?' He turned on his heel and marched into the bedroom, Ellie-May hurrying after him, her heart thumping.

'What are you doing?' she demanded in genuine distress as Frank yanked the drawer out, throwing her underwear to the floor.

'Ah, here we are. I knew you had it squirrelled away somewhere.'

'You've been through my *things*?' Ellie-May was aghast.

'You're my wife,' Frank said angrily. 'I have every right to search your drawers.' He waved the photograph in front of Ellie-May's face. Her heart contracted at the sight of Jack's face. It was the studio photograph she and Jack had had taken before he went away to France. A sob caught in her throat. Contrary to what Frank clearly assumed, she hadn't looked at the photo in years and it was a shock to see it now.

'You were his whore,' Frank said, his face puce with anger. 'Well, guess what, Ellie-May, he's dead! Gone. He left you in the lurch, carrying his brat. He used you and buggered off.'

'No . . .' Ellie-May blinked back tears. 'It wasn't like that.'

'If he'd really cared about you he'd have married you before he went away. Draw your own conclusion. I reckon if he'd lived he'd have moved on to the next easy lay without giving you a second's thought.'

'That's not true,' Ellie-May gasped. Too late, she saw his open palm coming towards her. She let out a cry as the blow knocked her backwards. Frank stood over her, a sinister leer on his face. Very slowly, his features twisted in a triumphant sneer, he methodically ripped the picture into pieces, Ellie-May watching in quiet dismay as they fluttered to the floor.

'I'm going to the pub,' he said, glaring down at her coldly. 'You might want to clean yourself up. Jack's bastard daughter will be home soon.'

CHAPTER TWENTY-FOUR

Penny bounded up the stairs to the flat and burst through the door.

'Hello, Mummy, Grandpa sent you some beetroot . . .' She stopped in the doorway to the kitchen, immediately aware that something was wrong. 'Mummy?' Her voice quivered. Ellie-May looked up from where she had been sitting with her head in her hands, a noticeable bruise across her left eye. She stretched her lips into a semblance of a smile.

'Hello, sweetheart. Did you have a good time at Nanny and Grandpa's?'

Penny nodded. She noticed that her mummy's voice sounded thick, as if she'd been crying. 'Uncle Arthur's got a girlfriend. She's called Victoria and she works with Aunty Nora.'

'That's nice for Uncle Arthur,' Ellie-May said, getting wearily to her feet. She had hit her hip on the doorframe when she went down, and now her movements were stiff and painful.

'What have you done to your eye?' Penny asked, a sick feeling in the pit of her stomach.

'I walked into the door,' her mother said, her voice sounding brittle. 'Have you had your tea?'

'Yes.' Penny frowned as her mother winced with pain. 'You sit down, Mummy. I'll make you a cup of tea.' She set the basket of beetroot on the table and busied herself making the tea.

'You're a good girl, Pen-Pen,' Ellie-May said tiredly, rubbing her throbbing cheek.

'Where's Daddy?' Penny asked, warming the teapot.

'He's gone out,' Ellie-May replied, trying not to let the relief show.

'What's this?' Penny's sharp eyes spotted the torn shards of a photograph laying on the top of the bin, nestled between potato peelings and damp tea leaves. She picked up a few pieces, curious. 'It's you.' She looked at her mother in surprise. 'Who's that man in uniform?' Penny squinted at the man's face. 'It's not Uncle Bert, is it.'

Her mother dragged her hands down her face. 'No,' she said dully. 'It's not Uncle Bert.'

'Who is it, then?' Still holding the torn section of photograph, Penny climbed onto one of the four spare chairs. 'Why did you tear it up and throw it away?'

Ellie-May sat back with a sigh. 'It's someone I knew a long time ago,' she said softly. 'An old friend. He was killed in the Great War.'

Penny stared at the smiling young man soberly. He wasn't

handsome, but he had a nice face and ... She screwed up her face, puzzled. There was something familiar about him.

'You look very pretty, Mummy.' Penny held the two jagged edges of the photograph together. Whoever the man was, it was clear by the way her mother was looking up at him that she had been very fond of him.

'Yes, well.' Ellie-May pushed back her chair and snatched the tattered bits of photograph from her daughter's fingers. 'It was a long time ago.' Without allowing herself even the briefest glance at Jack's face, she tossed them into the bin with the rest. 'Go and get your spelling book. You can have twenty minutes to read over your words and then I'll test you.'

'But, Mummy, I know my spelling words. You know I do.'

Ellie-May gave an impatient shake of her head. 'Just do as I say, Penny, for once,' she snapped, close to tears.

Chastened, Penny slid off her seat and did as she was told.

'Have you noticed how much the bloke in that picture looks like you?' remarked Nellie Norris, shielding her eyes from the glare of the late afternoon sun as she studied the photograph in Penny's hands. Sensing that the photograph had once meant something to her mother, Penny had carefully fished all the pieces from amongst the rubbish and painstakingly taped them together, and although the photograph was crisscrossed with tiny cracks, Nellie was certain the man with Ellie-May must be related to Penny. They looked so alike.

The two girls were sitting on top of the coal bunker

outside Nellie's house, having just returned from buying Grandma Norris her weekly ration of stout. Grandma Norris had recently moved into number 10 with her son and daughter-in-law. Penny was terrified of the old crone. She'd sit propped up against the pillows, a black shawl draped around her bony shoulders, staring out of the window and glaring at the children playing in the street. For the boldest children, it had become a game, daring each other to see who was brave enough to peer in the window, before running shrieking down the street when the old woman banged on the glass with her stick, shouting curses after them. For an elderly woman, Penny had heard her grandpa remark on more than one occasion that old Mrs Norris Senior's language could be as choice as the coarsest docker.

At fifteen, Nellie was the youngest of the Norris brood, and so it fell to her to walk down to the Belvedere Arms to buy the stout. For this errand, Grandma Norris would begrudgingly give her a few pennies.

It was gone six o'clock and the old woman was contentedly sipping her mug of stout in her bed, allowing her long-suffering family a few moments respite from her constant demands.

'So, is he a relation?' Nellie asked, scrutinising the photograph. 'He looks a lot like you.'

'Mummy said he was an old friend ...' Penny replied, frowning at the picture. 'He died in the war.'

'I think he was more than just a friend.' Nellie wrinkled

her nose thoughtfully. She was a pretty girl with dark brown eyes and wavy dark hair, worn in a neat bob. 'They look like they're in love . . . Why don't you ask Eileen?' she suggested.

'Ask me what?' Eileen said, emerging from the privy.

'We were wondering who this chap is with Penny's mum.'

Eileen took the photo from Nellie and the colour drained from her face. 'Where did you get this?' she whispered, her hand going to her throat.

'It was in the bin at home,' Penny replied in a small voice. 'I kept it because Mummy looks so lovely . . .'

'Who's the chap?' Nellie persisted. 'Is he an old flame of your Ellie-May's? Only, he looks a lot like Penny so we wondered if he was a relative.'

'He's no one.' Feeling the blood rushing in her veins, Eileen briefly considered keeping the photograph but that would only raise Penny's curiosity even further. Seeing Jack's face again after all these years was a shock and guilt and shame washed over her like a wave. Forcing herself to calm down, she handed the photograph back to Penny. 'Does Mummy know you've got this?' she asked sternly. Penny shook her head. 'Well, don't go bothering her with it. He was someone she knew a long time ago, before she married your daddy.'

'Mummy said he was killed in the war.'

'Yes,' Eileen lied. 'I'm afraid he was.'

As Eileen went back inside, Nellie's older sister, Hattie, stepped out into the yard. She leaned against the wall of the house and lit a cigarette.

'What are you two up to then?' she asked Nellie, inhaling a lungful of smoke. 'What have you got there?'

Nellie showed her.

'Ah, it's your mum, Penny, with poor old Jack.'

'Mummy's friend,' Penny said. Hattie raised her eyebrows.

'Well, he was more than her friend, he was her fella. She was heartbroken when he was killed. It came as a huge shock and surprise to everyone when she upped and married your dad a few months later.'

'How soon?' asked Nellie, her quick mind working fast. Hattie's brows rose even further. 'Soon enough to cause some folk around here to raise an eyebrow or two.'

'I knew it,' Nellie hopped off the coal bunker. 'It's all coming back to me now. I heard Mum and Mrs Bramhall talking once, when I was little. You were just a baby, Penny, but Mum made some remark about your colouring and I remember your nan went a bit red and said something about Frank not being your proper dad. That's why this Jack fellow looks so familiar. You look just like him.'

'Shut up, Nellie,' Hattie snapped, crushing her cigarette butt underfoot. 'Mind your own business.'

'Jack's Penny's real dad, isn't he?' She ducked, just missing being clouted by her older sister. 'I'm right, aren't I?' Nellie pouted while Penny stared at the two Norris girls in shocked silence.

'What do you mean?' she asked in a small, shocked voice. 'Frank's my daddy.'

'You take no notice of Nellie,' Hattie said kindly. 'She's

a born troublemaker.' She shot her younger sister a ven-
omous glare.

'Doesn't mean it's not true, though,' Nellie said petulantly.

'Is that what people are saying?' Penny asked Hattie, her
little face pinched with worry. 'That my dad isn't my dad?'

'Some people have nothing better to do than gossip about
other people's lives,' Hattie replied.

Penny's lip quivered. She was remembering all the
fights, the nasty words flung about by her father. 'I want
to go home.'

'Now look,' Hattie fumed at Nellie. 'You've upset her.'

Nellie shrugged. 'She deserves to know the truth.'

'You have no idea what the truth is, Nellie Norris. You're
as bad as the gossipmongers.' Turning to Penny, Hattie laid a
gentle hand on her shoulder. 'Listen, love, maybe you should
talk to your mum instead of listening to rumours.'

Penny nodded.

Mumbling an excuse to her surprised grandparents, she
ran home as if the devil himself were after her. Heart pounding, cheeks burning, she only stopped when she reached the
alley behind the shop. Gasping for air, she slumped against
the wall, her lungs on fire, her cheeks burning from the exertion, her heart racing. She stared up at the upstairs windows,
afraid suddenly to go inside, knowing instinctively that her
life was about to be turned upside down.

Ellie-May sank wearily onto the sofa. The shop had been
busy all day and she had been rushed off her feet. She

rubbed her aching temples and closed her eyes, listening to the pigeons squabbling on the windowsill. A warm breeze drifted in through the open window, bringing much-needed relief from the oppressive heat.

She could hear Frank banging about downstairs. Knowing he would be up in a minute, she let out a long-suffering sigh, relishing the brief respite. Her bruised eye might be almost healed, but her bruised heart would take a lot longer to mend.

As usual, Frank had been full of remorse. He had been as attentive and affectionate as a husband could be over the past week. If he made her one more cup of tea, Ellie-May fumed now, listening to his heavy tread on the staircase, she might just throw it in his face.

'Penny!' Ellie-May exclaimed as Frank came into the room, ushering Penny before him. 'Sweetheart, what's the matter?' Alarmed, Ellie-May got immediately to her feet and crouched in front of her daughter, feeling her forehead with the palm of her hand. 'Are you ill? You're awfully hot and clammy.' She glanced up at Frank. 'What happened?'

Frank shrugged.

'I found her in the yard. Someone's upset her but she won't say who.' He scowled at his daughter.

'Pen Pen, what is it, darling? Tell Mummy. Has someone hurt you?' The question came out more sharply than she intended and Penny reeled back, her eyes widening. She shook her head.

Ellie-May hugged her close. 'Are you feeling sick?' Again, Penny shook her head, a fat tear rolling down her flushed cheek. Ellie-May looked up at Frank with a frown. 'I'm going make her some beef tea and put her to bed.' She shot her husband a scathing look as she led Penny towards her bedroom. 'Are you going out?'

'The lads are expecting me,' Frank said, almost sullenly. 'I can't let them down.'

Since it had become certain that Ellie-May and Frank would have no children of their own, he had begun to drink heavily, spending most evenings down at the Belvedere Arms. It would be close to midnight before he returned. Not that she minded, the less Frank was at home the better, as far as she was concerned.

'No,' Ellie-May replied, shooting him a withering look. 'Of course, you can't.' Without another word, she helped Penny undress and get into bed. The bed creaked as Ellie-May sat down beside her. 'Can't you tell me what's upset you, sweetheart? You won't be in any trouble, I promise. Did Nanny Eileen tell you off? Or did that Nellie Norris say something nasty to you? She can be a bit sharp, that one.'

'I just want to be left alone,' Penny said, pulling the bed-clothes over her head. She was desperate to ask her mother about Jack, but her courage had deserted her.

Ellie-May sighed, completely at a loss. Penny was usually such a happy-go-lucky child. This sullen, silent, scarlet-faced child frightened her. Reluctantly, she got to her feet.

'Try to sleep, sweetheart,' she said softly, gently stroking Penny's shoulder through the sheets. 'I'll check on you in a little while and see if you want anything.' She bent over and kissed the top of Penny's head. Pulling the bedroom door to, she returned to the sitting-room where Frank was pouring himself a large brandy.

'One for the road,' he leered, lifting the glass of amber liquid in a mock salute. Ellie-May ignored him.

Penny lay staring up at the ceiling. It was still light outside, the longest day being only a week away, and despite the thickly lined curtains, her bedroom was bright. She had heard her father leave a few minutes before. He had already been slurring his words when he'd said goodbye to her mother. Her mother's reply had been too low for Penny to catch, but no doubt it had been something disparaging. She sighed and rolled over, seeking a cool spot on her pillow. She knew her mother and father weren't happy. Not like Nanny Eileen and Grandpa Sid, or Rose and Tony Norris. She seldom heard her mum and dad laugh or joke with each other like her grandparents did, and Mummy didn't sit on Daddy's knee like Rose sat on Mr Norris's, always jumping off with an embarrassed giggle when Penny and Nellie caught them unawares.

She might only be nine and three quarters, but she was astute enough to know that her parents' marriage wasn't made in heaven, and instinctively, she knew her father was at the root of all their problems. Penny heard her mother cough softly. She could hear the clickety-clack of her knitting needles over the gentle tick on the carriage clock, and, plucking up her courage, she threw aside the sheets and swung her legs onto the floor.

It was too warm to bother with a gown or slippers, so wearing just her nightdress, she padded barefoot into the living room. She stood in the doorway watching her mother in the dusty sunlight. Her head was bent over her knitting. Penny was shocked at how sad she looked. Then she glanced up and her expression changed. Smiling, Ellie-May laid down her knitting aside and held out her arms.

'Pen-Pen,' she said with obvious relief. 'You look so much better.'

Penny went to her mother's side, letting her arms enfold her. She rested her head against her shoulder.

'Would you like something to eat?' Ellie-May scrutinized her daughter closely. Penny shook her head. Her heart was pounding, and nerves had robbed her of her appetite.

'Mummy, is Frank my real daddy?'

'*Pardon?*' Ellie-May stared at Penny in surprise. 'Why would you ask such a thing?'

Penny drew back, looking her mother directly in the eye. 'Hattie said I must ask you about Jack.'

'Did she now?' Ellie-May murmured with annoyance. *The little madam!* She made a mental note to have words with that Harriet Norris. Ellie-May would give her what for, meddling in her private business.

'Is Jack my dad?' The confusion on Penny's face broke Ellie-May's heart. She cleared her throat, playing for time, and sighed, her shoulders sagging in resignation.

'I was waiting until you were older.'

Penny's stomach did a funny little flip.

'Pen-Pen, Frank loves you, and as far as everyone is concerned, he is your father.' She swallowed. Taking Penny's hands in hers, she looked into her eyes. Her heart lurched. How like her father she was. For a moment words deserted her. 'But, yes, Jack Pickup is your biological father.' She looked at Penny earnestly. 'Do you understand what that means?' Penny nodded.

'My real daddy, Jack,' she savoured the name on her tongue, 'died ... so you married Frank.'

'Well, yes,' Ellie-May replied, colouring slightly. Of course, Penny would understand, Ellie-May acknowledged. Born into a generation where so many children had lost their fathers in the war, there were many stepfamilies in their neighbourhood.

'Jack and I were very much in love,' Ellie-May explained softly, her lips buried in Penny's cloud of dark, bed tousled hair. 'We wanted to get married, and we would have, if Jack hadn't been killed.'

Penny remained silent, digesting what her mother was telling her. 'But ...' She frowned. Drawing back her head, she scowled at her mother. 'But you weren't married,' she queried accusingly. 'How did you have a baby?'

'Oh, Pen-Pen, this is why I didn't want to explain things until you were older. You'll understand when you're grownup, but let's just say, the war changed things; people did things they probably wouldn't under normal circumstances. I was so happy when I found out I was expecting you. I wanted you more than anything in the world and that is all you need to know; that you were wanted, very much. And Jack would have loved you, so, so much.'

'You would have married Jack, but he died, so you married Frank instead?'

Ellie-May winced. 'Well, put like that it sounds a little callous, but yes, I suppose that is exactly what happened.' She kissed Penny on the forehead. 'It's hard for a woman to have a baby on her own. People can be cruel, to the woman and her child. I wanted you to have a good home. Sweetheart, I know Frank can be difficult, but he does love you.'

'I found this in the bin.' Penny scrambled off her lap and scampered to her bedroom, reappearing a minute later clutching the photograph.

'Oh, Penny,' Ellie-May murmured sadly when she realized what it was.

'I rescued it,' Penny explained. 'And taped it back together. May I keep it?' She gazed at her mother anxiously. Ellie-May stared at the photograph for a moment, a faraway look in her eye. Then she smiled.

'Of course you can,' she nodded. 'Just don't let Frank know, okay?'

Penny nodded. 'I look like Jack, don't I?'

'You do, darling, very much so.' Ellie-May ruffled Penny's hair. 'We went to a photographer's studio. It was a day or two before Jack left to go to the training camp.' The faraway look in her eyes returned as she gazed into the empty fireplace. 'I hope he had it with him when he died,' she murmured softly.

'Will you find a frame for it?' Penny asked, stroking her

dead father's image with her finger. 'I'll keep it in my drawer where Daddy won't see it and get upset.'

'All right, sweetheart,' Ellie-May agreed. 'We'll go to the emporium on Saturday afternoon and buy one.' She smiled at her daughter, her green eyes bright with unshed tears. 'Jack would have been very proud of you.'

PART TWO

CHAPTER TWENTY-FIVE

1939

Jack was stretched out in front of a roaring fire in the snug of the Quill and Ink pub. For a bitter February night, the place was heaving. His dog Star, one of the late and much-lamented Meg's grand-pups, lay across his feet. He sipped his pint of bitter and leaned back in his chair, letting the conversation from the bar wash over him like the ebb and flow of the tide, Britain's souring relationship with Germany and the possibility of another war, being the overriding topic.

The village of Boyne Mead had only just started to recover from the last conflict – would they really be called upon to sacrifice another generation of young men? Jack let out a long sigh, his thoughts turning to the women of the village, middle-aged spinsters now, whose hopes of marriage and motherhood had been so cruelly snatched away by the Great War. He allowed himself a wry smile. He'd turned a few heads when he'd first arrived in the village over twenty years before but, while he'd been happy to flirt a little, his heart hadn't been in it, much to Ida's dismay, who had made no secret of the fact she thought it was high time he found himself a wife and started a family.

Ah, Ida. Just thinking about his housekeeper brought a smile to his lips. God bless her, where would he be without her? She bossed him about shamelessly and played merry hell with him if, God forbid, he did anything to vex her. She was like a mother to him, and he loved her to bits. Mindful of the fact that she had recently celebrated her sixty-third birthday, he had begun dropping subtle hints about her retiring, but she wouldn't hear of it.

'Jack, my friend!' Jack recognized the loud, guttural tone instantly.

'Deon,' he grinned, getting awkwardly to his feet and extending his hand to the enormous, ruddy-faced man towering before him. 'Good to see you again. When did you get back?'

Star raised her head and growled a welcome, her feathery tail beating the worn hearth rug.

Deon du Randt was built like a barn, with broad shoulders and the thick bull-like neck of a rugby player. The hand that grasped Jack's was the size of a shovel. He held a pint of cider in the other, his fingers curled around the glass like fat sausages.

'We docked three days ago,' he replied, lowering himself into a chair adjacent to the fireplace. 'We arrived in the village this morning.'

Jack cocked an eyebrow. 'We?' He sat down and took a sip of his pint.

'*Ja,*' Deon replied, his nostrils flaring. 'My sister, Jennette. She came with me.'

'I shall look forward to meeting her,' Jack said, licking froth from his upper lip and wondering idly how closely Jennette resembled her brother in looks.

'Don't worry,' Deon grinned, as if reading his friend's mind. 'Fortunately for my sister, we look nothing alike. Jennette takes after our mother.'

'A relief for the young lady, I'm sure,' Jack teased. 'It's really good to see you, Deon.'

'And you, Jack.'

Deon had occupied the bed next to Jack's in the military hospital. His recovery from a shrapnel wound in his back had been much swifter than Jack's and when he'd been discharged, the two of them had kept in touch. At the end of the war, Deon had decided not to return to his native South Africa but had followed his friend to Dorset, where he made a living for himself as a wheelwright.

Deon sighed. 'It'll be a sad day indeed if this Hitler fellow plunges us all into another war.' The chair creaked ominously as he adjusted his position. He ran a huge hand through his straw-like hair, causing it to stick up like that of a scarecrow.

'Let's hope Chamberlain's policy of appeasement has the desired effect,' Jack remarked, unconvinced. A power-hungry man such as the German Chancellor would be unlikely to take notice of the British Prime Minister, and how much more of Europe was Chamberlain prepared to sacrifice before the British people finally said enough was enough?

He rubbed the bridge of his nose. Simon, his dear friend, and much-depended upon farmhand, was a strapping man in his early thirties now. If there were a war, Jack deemed it likely Simon would join up. The thought gave him an unusual pain in his chest. He had grown fond of Simon and it would be a wrench to lose him.

After all, he hadn't forgotten how distressed his employer, Edward Chalke, and the Bramhalls had been when he'd made the decision to enlist back in 1914. And El had been distraught. He pushed thoughts of Ellie-May aside, unwilling to allow painful memories to mar his pleasure at seeing his friend. Deon drained his pint. He held up his empty glass, signalling to Jack he was going to the bar for a refill. Jack declined with a shake of his head.

'I'd better be on my way.' He got to his feet, leaning on his stick. Star jumped up, tail wagging eagerly. 'Why don't you and your sister join us for supper tomorrow? Ida would love to see you.'

'Thank you.' Deon extended his hand. 'Until tomorrow, my friend.'

Jack shook his hand, hailed the barman a cheery 'good evening,' and, turning his collar up against the cold, damp air, set off at an ungainly pace along the lane. Star bounded ahead, pausing every few minutes for a lengthy sniffing session. A badger snuffled close by, startling the dog. She barked loudly and Jack shushed her. He quickened his pace.

The damp was making his leg ache and he was eager to get into the warmth.

Jennette du Randt stood in front of the full-length mirror, her attractive features distorted by a deep frown of consternation. Now thirty-three, seven years younger than her brother, her mother was worried she was in danger of becoming an old maid. She was the opposite to Deon in both looks and temperament. She was petite, with wide blue eyes and a cloud of blonde hair the colour of sun-ripened corn. The hot South African sun had tanned her skin the colour of honey, a stark contrast to the pale, winter skin of Boyne Mead's residents. In her bright, colourful clothes she felt like an exotic butterfly amongst a colony of drab brown moths.

Her distinctness from the rest of the community was why she was lingering in front of the mirror this evening. Was her blue dress too much? It was new, bought from one of Cape Town's most fashionable department stores before boarding the ship, and she had not yet had occasion to wear it. Falling to mid-calf, the slimline dress in vibrant peacock-blue, hugged her slender figure. Coupled with a matching blue hat, trimmed with navy-blue ribbon that perfectly matched her silk gloves, she cut a fine figure. But she couldn't help wondering if it was too much for a supper in a farm cottage.

'Come on, Jen,' Deon chided her impatiently, filling the narrow doorway with his broad frame. Jennette smiled. She couldn't get over how small everything seemed to be in England compared with the spaciousness of her native country. Why, the labourers on her parents' vineyard lived in larger cottages than the one she now shared with her brother.

'I'll just be a minute,' she said, twisting a blonde curl around her finger and leaning forward to peer critically at her reflection. Deon always spoke highly of Jack, and she was looking forward to meeting him. She was keen to make a good impression.

Deon's impatient sigh was like a gust of wind. 'I haven't the patience for all this primping,' he said irritably. 'I'll bring the trap round and wait for you out front.'

With a toss of her shaggy mane, the little Welsh pony set off at a jaunty pace, the clip-clop of her hoofs muffled by the swirling fog that rendered the winding lanes silent and eerie. Skeletal branches crisscrossed overhead. Jennette tugged the collar of her coat tighter around her throat against the damp. To her relief, it wasn't long before a light appeared in the distance, a glowing beacon drawing them on.

Nothing Deon had told her about Jack had prepared Jennette for her reaction to the tall, sturdy-looking man lurching towards them. He carried a lamp, and was accompanied by a collie dog, barking a welcome, tail wagging frantically. She felt a fission of excitement down her spine. Despite the obvious limp, and the fact his features might be described as rugged rather than handsome, she felt an instant attraction to Jack. She was grateful for the darkness as she found herself blushing.

'Miss du Randt,' Jack said, offering Jennette his hand as

she stepped down from the trap. 'Welcome to England, and to Wayside.'

'Thank you, Mr Pickup.' She smiled demurely. 'My brother has told me a lot about you.'

'I bet he has. Please, call me Jack.'

'And I'm Jennette.'

Jack flashed Deon a grin as he ushered his guest towards the house. 'Come on in.' He hadn't quite known what he had been expecting but he certainly hadn't been prepared for the dainty, pretty woman now standing in the steam-filled kitchen and being welcomed enthusiastically by Ida.

'Sit yourselves down,' she said, busying herself with the various pans bubbling on the hearth. 'Supper will be ready in a minute.'

'Thank you, Jack,' Jennette smiled graciously as Jack pulled a chair out for her before taking the one opposite her. Throughout the meal she watched him surreptitiously from beneath her lashes, noting his weathered complexion, the dark, curly hair, salted with grey, and his scar which, in Jennette's opinion, only served to enhance his looks rather that detract from them. The streak of white above his forehead she found intriguing. Sensing her scrutiny, Jack met her gaze, and she flushed, embarrassed to be caught staring like a besotted schoolgirl. Yet that was how she felt, like a giddy schoolgirl. She hadn't been as attracted to any of her previous suitors the way she felt drawn to this man opposite her. A man she'd known for less than an hour, yet she was already smitten.

*

Later that night, once Deon and Jennette had left, Jack sat in the dark parlour staring into the dying embers, Star snoring softly at his feet. Ida's cooking and one too many glasses of port had left him feeling drowsy and nostalgic for the past. Over the years he'd learned to suppress his feelings of anger and hurt caused by Ellie-May's betrayal, yet in his quieter moments the memory of her flooded his mind, leaving him with an emptiness in his soul that no amount of female company had ever managed to fill. Ellie-May had been his life, his soulmate, he had never before even imagined he might want to spend his life with someone other than her, until now.

The memory of Jennette's flushed face swam into view. Although the total opposite to her loud, brash brother, Jack had found Jennette pleasant and entertaining company, and something stirred deep inside him.

CHAPTER TWENTY-SIX

August had been wet but the first days of September had turned unusually warm. It was a quarter past eleven on Sunday 3 September, two months before Penny's twenty-fourth birthday. In their upstairs flat, Frank, Ellie-May and Penny huddled sombrely around the radio. Penny was thinking of her cousin, Tommy, and Donny Norris, both of whom planned to join up the moment war was declared. Ellie-May pursed her lips in dismay, wondering at the madness of men who would subject the people of Britain to another war.

Ever since Germany had invaded Poland two days before, they had been expecting the inevitable. The threat of war had been hanging over them for months, yet it made the announcement, when it came, no less difficult to bear. Prime Minister Neville Chamberlain's clipped tones resounded across the airwaves:

'This morning the British Ambassador in Berlin handed the German government a final note stating that, unless we heard by 11 o'clock that they were prepared to with-draw their troops at once from Poland, a state of war would exist between us.

'I have to tell you that no such undertaking has been received, and that consequently this country is at war with Germany.'

'Well, that's that then,' said Frank, rubbing his hands across his face. 'Put the kettle on, Ellie.'

'I can't believe we've got to do it all over again,' Ellie-May said dully. 'Did no one learn anything the last time?' She pushed her chair back with a weary sigh.

'Stay there, Mum,' Penny said, shooting Frank a dirty look. Couldn't he see how tired her mother looked? The skin beneath her eyes was bruised with dark shadows. Sleepless nights worrying over what war would mean for Penny and for the menfolk in her family had taken its toll. 'I'll make the tea.' She kissed the top of Ellie-May's head and went into the kitchen, grateful for something to do. While she waited for the kettle to boil, she pressed her hands on the windowsill and gazed out over the rooftops of Northam.

She had already planned to volunteer for the Women's Land Army, whether Frank liked it or not. She could pin-point the exact moment her relationship with Frank had soured and she'd started calling him by his name instead of 'Daddy'. It was a few months before her fourteenth birthday when he'd scuppered her long-cherished dreams of becoming a trained horticulturist by refusing to allow her to stay on at school. Her headmaster had even paid Frank and Ellie-May a visit in an attempt to persuade Frank to change his mind. He'd told them over a cup of tea and a slice of Battenberg that Penny was one of the brightest students he had ever taught; that it would be a terrible waste of her natural ability if she were to leave school without any qualifications.

Elie-May had been bursting with pride at the man's glowing praise and, while Frank had grown ever-more tight-lipped in response, she had never for one moment imagined that he would refuse to pay the fees.

'I am not paying for Penny to go to high school,' he'd said, rounding on Ellie-May the moment the headmaster was out the door. 'There's the tram fare there and back every day, not to mention the cost of the uniform.'

'We can afford it,' Ellie May had argued tearfully, seeing her dreams for Penny's future slipping through her fingers. 'We've got savings.'

'That's for our old age,' Frank countered firmly. 'I will not waste it on an education Penny doesn't need. She'll only go and get married and that'll be money down the drain. If you'd given me a son,' he'd said, a cold edge to his voice, 'he would have taken over the running of this shop, but as it is, it will go to Penny and her husband.'

'Penny hates the shop, Frank,' Ellie-May protested. 'You know that.'

'She'll do her duty and carry on the family business,' Frank said firmly. Ellie-May had opened her mouth to say more but

Frank held up his hand, signalling the conversation was over. 'The matter is settled,' he said. 'I'll hear no more about it.'

'My real dad would have let me stay on at school,' Penny had wept when Ellie-May had sorrowfully relayed the disappointing news that Penny would be leaving school at the end of the summer term to work full time in her parents' butcher's shop. Frank had overheard Penny's comment and there had been an almighty row between him and Ellie-May. For a while Penny had seethed with resentment towards Frank but her natural exuberance for life had soon come to the fore and she set her dreams aside and resigned herself to life as a butcher's assistant, at least for the foreseeable future.

That had been ten years ago. She still helped Sid on his allotment when time allowed, gradually taking on more of the heavy work as he grew older. He was seventy-two now, yet his vegetables still won prizes in the Romsey Show held each year on the Broadland's estate.

The allotment was still Penny's go-to place in a crisis, and that was where she needed to be now. She swallowed the last of her tea and scraped back her chair.

'I'm going to see Grandpa,' she said, unable to stand the simmering silence, the argument she knew would erupt the moment she was out of earshot. Frank said nothing, his lips a disapproving line. Sid was a bad influence on Penny, as far as he was concerned. Her duty was to him and the shop, not digging around in the mud, pandering to an old codger who should know better than to interfere in his granddaughter's life.

'Tell Grandpa and Nanny Eileen I'll be over later. I expect they'll be in a bit of state after Chamberlain's announcement.'

'We're all in a "bit of a state",' Frank retorted sourly.

'I will, Mum,' Penny replied. Pulling a thin cardigan over her navy and white polka-dot frock, she hurried down the stairs without a backward glance.

'You won't get away with your dodgy heart this time,' Ellie-May said with obvious contempt. She could never forgive Frank for his cowardice when so many brave young men like Jack had made the ultimate sacrifice. 'You won't fool Doctor Ellis like you did old Doctor Morton. You'll have to fight.'

'Don't talk rot, woman,' Frank snarled. 'It says in the paper, the age range for enlisting is between eighteen and forty-one. I'm too old.'

'You're only forty-six. There's talk they'll raise the age to fifty-one.'

Frank gave a derisive snort but Ellie-May could tell she had rattled him. She sighed wearily, knowing he was probably right. It seemed that Frank was one of those people for whom the odds always swung the right way. For him, the war would probably turn out to be little more than an inconvenience.

Leaving Frank slumped in front of the wireless, Ellie-May went to check on the chicken roasting in the oven. She set about preparing the vegetables Penny had brought back from the allotment. Bless her, her daughter loved nothing more than getting her hands dirty, and she was such a help to Sid, who was getting on a bit now. His old joints weren't what they used to be.

She paused in her chopping and slicing, knowing the morning's announcement would bring back bitter memories for her parents. Her sister, Jess's son, Tommy, had vowed to enlist the minute war was declared. Thankfully, Arthur's son, Barney, only eleven, was too young, but who knew how long the war would last? Please God, it wouldn't last as long as the last one. She was just grateful Penny didn't have a young man to fret over. She couldn't bear the thought of Penny's heart being broken the way hers had when she'd lost Jack.

War! She slammed the saucepan down angrily. The politicians might make the decisions but, as always, it was the normal folk who suffered.

Penny arrived at her grandparents' house to find a tearful Eileen being comforted by Rose.

'It's terrible news, isn't it, Penny?' Rose said, looking perilously close to tears herself. 'My Hattie's already talking about having her kiddies evacuated.'

'I don't blame her,' Penny said. 'Being a major port, Southampton's bound to be a target. And your boys?'

'Oh, they'll enlist, of course,' Rose snorted with a toss of her head.

Leaving Eileen in the capable hands of her best friend, Sid and Penny set off for the allotment. It was a bright, early autumn day. The trees in the park were just beginning to turn. Some boys, too young to be overly concerned with talk of war, were playing cricket on the grass, the gentle tap of ball on willow, drifting on the breeze.

'Our Tommy will join up,' Sid said, his calm tone belying his anguish at the thought of his grandson facing the horrors of war. 'He'll be down the recruiting office first thing tomorrow morning, you mark my words. There's nothing cowardly about our Tommy.'

'They seem to think it's a *Boy's Own Adventure* story,' Penny said. 'Didn't we learn anything the last time around?'

'When do we humans ever learn?' Sid replied sadly, scratching his head. 'Bea's getting an Anderson shelter. Rose and Tony are thinking of getting one too. Apparently, they can accommodate up to six people so they've said we'd be welcome to use it as well.'

'Frank's on about getting one but Mum's adamant she won't go in it. You know how claustrophobic she gets.' Penny pushed open the gate to the allotments, and led the way between rows of runner beans, pumpkins and cabbages. The air hummed with the sound of insects. 'Grandpa, I haven't said anything to Mum or Frank yet, but I'm going to volunteer for the Women's Land Army.' She had seen the posters at every bus stop and train station. The Women's Land Army had been formed in June as the threat of war became increasingly likely, coupled with the government's need to increase food production on British farms.

Sid nodded slowly. 'I'm proud of you, lass. You'll thrive

on a farm and your experience with butchery will stand you in good stead. Make sure you mention it when you apply.'

'I will.' Penny kissed his whiskery cheek, inhaling the familiar scent of Old Spice and the Polo mints he kept in the pocket of his tweed jacket.

'It'll be hard work.'

'I'm not afraid of hard work, Grandpa,' Penny grinned, reaching for the hoe. 'That doesn't trouble me at all.'

Deon found Jack down by the pigpen. He was leaning on the fence watching his two black and white sows waddle off into the woods where they would spend the next few weeks growing fat on acorns and roots.

'Well, my friend, I'm afraid this is goodbye for the foreseeable future.'

Jack turned to his friend, his eyes heavy with regret. 'Are you sure?'

Deon rested his thick arms along the top of the three-bar gate, staring contemplatively towards the trees.

'It's only a matter of time before South Africa declares war on Germany. It is only right I enlist and do my duty.'

Jack slapped him on his broad back. 'We are no longer the impetuous, naïve young men we were a quarter of a century ago, my friend.'

'No indeed. We're older and, one would hope, a little wiser.' Deon rubbed a huge calloused hand over his ruddy face. His expression turned serious. 'You'll look after Jen for me?'

'That goes without saying.'

'She's very fond of you.'

'And I her.' It was true, Jack reflected. His attraction to his friend's sister had grown as the months progressed, and he was certain she felt the same way. He could see it in her eyes; and the way her face lit up when he spoke to her. He rubbed his chin, the stubble rasping against his palm. He thrust out his hand.

'Stay safe, Deon.'

'I'll do my best,' Deon grinned, grasping Jack's outstretched hand.

'I had considered sending Jen home but, if they target passenger ships, well, I think she'll be safer here for the time being. If anything should happen to me ...'

'I'll see she gets home safely,' Jack promised. Deon nodded.

Jack watched him walk back up the gently sloping paddock, his broad form silhouetted against a cobalt September sky. Star panted softly at his feet. The surrounding trees and hedgerows resounded with birdsong and the rolling Dorset hills, dotted with grazing sheep, were bathed in hazy sunshine. In such a peaceful, tranquil setting it was inconceivable to fathom that the country had been plunged, once again, into war.

CHAPTER TWENTY-SEVEN

A bitter wind swept through the churchyard that grey and bleak November afternoon, a week after Penny's twenty-fourth birthday. She clutched the collar of her black coat around her throat as she fought to hold back the tears. Beside her, supported by Frank looking dapper in a dark pinstriped suit, his thinning Brylcreemed greying hair plastered across his scalp, her mother was weeping quietly into a handkerchief. An assortment of relatives huddled around the open grave, pale faces etched with pain as they watched the coffin being gently lowered into the cold earth. Grandpa Sid stood opposite Penny, supported by his twin daughters, Bea and Jess, both looking sombre in thick black coats and veils. Sid's face was drawn, his sparse white hair blowing in the wind, clutching his hat in his shaking, liver-spotted hands, his rheumy blue eyes glistening with unshed tears.

He'd always thought he'd be the first to go, had prayed for it even. He couldn't contemplate life without his Eileen. How would he go on? It had been a stroke that took her.

One minute they'd been listening to a programme on the wireless, the next, he'd turned to make a comment about the presenter and she had just been sitting there, staring straight ahead, unable to move or speak. She had died two days later without regaining consciousness.

It had been a blessing in a way. He comforted himself that she hadn't suffered.

The vicar brought his brief sermon to a close, and, swallowing the huge lump in her throat, Penny turned to follow her parents and the rest of her extended family along the frosty gravel path towards the George Hotel.

Eileen had been well liked and respected by friends and neighbours alike and the hotel's reception room was heaving. Penny shed her heavy coat, and wound her way through the black-clad mourners to where her eleven-year-old cousin, Barney – Arthur and Victoria's eldest child – was sprawled in the window seat, reading a *Beano* comic. He was the spit of Arthur. His younger sisters, Catherine and Elizabeth, nine and seven respectively, both resembled their mother.

He flashed Penny a grin and scooted along to make room for her to sit down. She gazed out of the mullioned window at the stark, leafless trees, silhouetted against a sombre winter sky, the haunting cry of seagulls echoing over the rooftops, and let out a long sigh of relief. The worst of the day was over.

'I thought you could do with a cuppa.' Victoria appeared at her side, bearing two cups of tea, one of which she handed to Penny. 'How are you feeling?' she asked, genuine concern in her eyes.

'Better now,' Penny replied, taking a sip of the tea. It was hot and sweet, just what she needed. 'Move along, Barney,' she ordered her young cousin. 'Let your mother have some space.' Without tearing his gaze from his comic, Barney shuffled further along the window seat until he was pressed up against the rose-patterned wall.

'A fitting day for a funeral,' Victoria remarked, following Penny's gaze out the window to the windswept lawn.

'Hmm,' Penny agreed. 'It matches my mood perfectly.'

'How's your Mum?' Victoria eyed Penny over the gold rim of her teacup. 'Arthur's been pretty upset. He and Eileen were particularly close, being the only surviving son.'

Penny nodded. 'mum's bearing up all right. You know what she's like, stiff upper lip. No, thank you.' She shook her head, waving away the plate of cucumber sandwiches brandished by the young waitress. Victoria helped herself to a couple, frowning at Barney, who'd grabbed a handful.

'It's very good of you and Uncle Arthur to go to this expense,' Penny said, sipping her tea. 'I know Mum was hoping Frank would contribute, but . . .' She shrugged.

Victoria waved away Penny's thanks. 'It's the least we could do,' she said, taking a dainty bite of her sandwich. 'I thought the world of Eileen. And let's face it,' she smiled, the skin around her blue eyes crinkling, 'you'd never have got all these people in your grandparents' front parlour.'

'It's heartening to see how many people have turned out,' Penny agreed.

Victoria nodded. Brushing crumbs from her dark skirt,

she got to her feet. 'I must go and see if Arthur's all right,' she said. 'He was going outside for some fresh air. You know how he finds crowds difficult.'

Penny watched her aunt disappear into the crowd. In her early forties now, she was still an attractive woman, although no longer as slim as she had once been, but she had retained her sense of fashion and was always immaculately dressed and coiffed. She had passed on the name of her hairdresser to Penny, who now sported a fashionably short hairstyle, her natural curls making her the envy of many of her friends who complained incessantly about the sleepless nights they were forced to endure with their hair tied up in rags in order to achieve the same effect.

Finished with his comic, Barney sloped off in search of more food.

'Are you all right, love?' Ellie-May emerged from the throng and sat down beside her daughter. 'It's a good turn-out, isn't it? I bet Nanny Eileen's having a right old chuckle looking down on us.' Despite her mother's bright smile, the tears sparkling in her eyes didn't go unnoticed. Penny placed her hand on her mother's arm.

'We all miss her, Mum,' she said softly. 'She was one in a million.'

'That she was,' Ellie-May agreed with a sigh, catching sight of her husband moving amongst the mourners, playing the role of host perfectly. After twenty-four years of marriage, Frank's jealousies and insecurities had only grown worse. He had aged well, despite putting on a few pounds.

At forty-six he could still elicit an admiring glance from women of a certain age.

He was talking to Jess and Bea now. Now in their late forties, the twins could not look less alike. Jess had grown more matronly with the passing years, bowed down first by the loss of her husband and then the sole responsibility for the care of her in-laws. After they'd both passed away, it seemed as though Jess might, at last, have a life of her own, but then her eldest daughter, Gracie, had fallen pregnant. The boy in question, the son of Gracie's employer, had denied all responsibility and Jess had ended up caring for the child, Lizzie, now a lively eight-year-old, herself. Three years previously, Gracie had married a successful architect from Manchester, Alister Glass. To Jess's dismay, the marriage proposal had not included little Lizzie.

Gracie and her husband had not made the journey down to Southampton, but Lizzie was there with Jess. She stood shyly beside her grandma, while Frank discussed what the newspapers were calling 'the phoney war' with Duncan, Bea's common-law husband.

Bea clearly spent more time and effort on her appearance than her twin. Wearing a black dress that fell just below her knees and lizard-skin shoes, she looked to Penny as though she had just stepped out of a magazine. Her pale red hair was cut very short, and she had, to her late mother's dismay, taken up smoking. She held a long cigarette holder in one gloved hand, a string of black glass beads glittering at her throat.

Trevor still lingered on in the sanatorium, but it had been months since Bea had visited him. As she told Eileen in a letter her mother had received a few days before her death, 'One feels like one is visiting a stranger.' Trevor had no recollection of Bea, or his children, and spent his days staring vacantly into space. Bea had confided to Ellie-May on a brief visit the previous year that it would be better for all concerned if Trevor were to die peacefully in his sleep.

'What is the point of God keeping him alive?' she'd lamented tearfully more than once. The whole family felt for poor Bea. She had refused to divorce Trevor, even though she and Duncan were, for all intents and purposes, married. It was accepted amongst their neighbours that they were man and wife. When Trevor, God bless him, did finally pass away, they intended to slip quietly down to the registry office and make their union official, but until that day came, both Bea and Duncan were content to continue as they were.

'Did Grandpa tell you he'd received a letter from our Nora?' Ellie-May said now.

'Oh, no, he didn't.' Penny adjusted her position on the padded window seat. A gust of wind rattled the windowpane, a sudden squall spattering the glass with drops of rain. 'He's still a bit shell-shocked by Nanny Eileen's death, I think.'

Ellie-May grimaced. 'Poor Dad. He'll be completely lost without Mum.'

They were both quiet for a moment, each lost in their own memories, before Penny asked: 'So, what did Aunty Nora have to say? Is she happy?'

'She seems to be,' replied Ellie-May. 'Obviously the letter was posted before she received the telegram about Nanny Eileen.' She pulled a handkerchief out of the sleeve of her black wool dress and wiped her nose. 'It sounds like she's having a wonderful time; elephant safaris and tiger hunts. Very exciting and exotic.'

Earlier in the year, Nora, approaching her forty-first birthday and having never been inclined to marry, had boarded the P&O passenger ship SS *Narkunda* and set sail for India to act as governess to the two young daughters of an English diplomat stationed in Bombay.

'It'll be hard for her now, though,' Penny said, 'having no one to share her grief. At least we've all got each other.'

'That's true.' Ellie-May lifted her cup to her lips, eyeing her daughter over the gold rim and thinking what a lovely young woman she had become. Her father, God rest his soul, would have been so proud of her.

'I told Grandpa you'd go around and help him sort through Nanny Eileen's clothes and things next week,' Ellie-May said, setting her cup on its saucer. 'Jess and Bea have trains to catch first thing tomorrow and I'm not sure I can face it just yet. Would you mind?'

'Of course not.' Penny laid her hand on her mother's arm, and smiled. 'I'll leave it a couple of days, perhaps until Wednesday or so. I'll see how Grandpa is then. I won't do anything if he's not ready.'

'Thanks, Pen-Pen. I'd appreciate it.'

*

Sid already had the kettle on when Penny arrived at her grandparents' house the following Wednesday morning.

'I'm sorry I've no cake or anything to offer you,' he said apologetically, as she followed him through to the kitchen. 'I'm on my own now, you know.'

Penny gave him a hug and kissed his whiskery cheek. 'I do know, Grandpa, and I think you're managing wonderfully well,' she reassured him. She smoothed down her skirt and took the proffered cup of tea gratefully, wrapping her frozen fingers around its welcome warmth.

It was perishing outside. A cold wind howled up the narrow, cobbled street and sleet lashed the windowpane. Beyond the garden wall, the Methodist church rose up, menacing and dark against an even blacker sky, the skeletal branches of the giant oak in the churchyard bowing and creaking ominously in the gale.

Penny shivered. Despite the fire crackling in the grate, she couldn't shake the chill out of her bones. It was grief, she surmised. She missed Nanny Eileen so much it was like a physical ache. The house felt different without her grandmother's warm, welcoming presence; colder, somehow, and bereft, as if the house itself was mourning the loss.

She shook herself. It would do no good sitting here feeling morose. She had a job to do. 'Shall we make a start?'

'Aye, lass, sooner we start the sooner we're done,' Sid said, getting stiffly to his feet. Penny looked at him fondly. He appeared to have aged ten years in the ten days since Eileen's death.

It was cold upstairs, and dim. The counterpane on the big double bed was rumpled and her grandfather had neglected to open the curtains. Penny drew them back, staring down at the rain-slick street for a moment, biting her lip in an effort not to cry. She had to be strong for Sid. Pasting on a smile, she turned to face the old man, who, having opened the wardrobe was staring, teary-eyed at his wife's dresses, hanging neatly from the rail.

'Why don't you start sorting through Nanny's dresses while I make a start on the chest of drawers?' Penny suggested. Sid nodded woodenly, his heart clearly not up to the task at hand.

After making sure her grandfather was all right, Penny got started on the drawers. They worked in companionable silence for a while, making piles of what was to be thrown out, and what was to be put aside for the church bazaar.

Following a quick dinner and a much-needed cup of tea, Penny moved on to Eileen's bedside cabinet. She knelt down in front of it and pulled it open. It was filled to the brim with old birthday and Christmas cards, tickets stubs, which dated back to when Eileen and Sid were courting. There was the telegram from Nora informing her parents that she had arrived safely in Bombay. Tucked at the bottom of the drawer was an old leather-bound Bible. Penny lifted it out gently. It wasn't her grandmother's usual Bible that was on the top of the cabinet. Intrigued, Penny opened it up. On the flyleaf, written in perfect copperplate, was an inscription.

11 March 1887

To my dearest sister Eileen on the occasion of your marriage.
  With all my love and best wishes,
  Your loving sister,
  Jessie x

Penny gently stroked the decades-old ink, knowing the message was all the more poignant because Jessie, after whom Penny's Aunty Jess was named, had passed away unexpectedly just days after the wedding.

She went to replace the Bible in the drawer when something caught her eye; a piece of paper tucked in the back. Curious, she drew it out and carefully unfolded what revealed itself to be a letter addressed to Penny's mother.

Why is this in my grandmother's possession and not my mother's? she wondered. Her gaze darted to the bottom of the page and she drew in a sharp intake of breath, her fingers flying to her mouth.

Jack.

Inhaling slowly, she forced herself to calm down and read the letter from the beginning.

Wyke Hall, Dorset
October 1915

My dearest El,
  You must be tickled pink to hear that I am indeed very much alive. There is still some confusion over how it happened, even

I'm not clear on the facts. My head injury caused me to lose my memory for a while and I was bashed about quite a bit and had to spend a long time in hospital but, as you can see, I am now on the mend and in fine spirits, even if a little bored.

My darling, I long to see you. Please write straight away and let me know when I can expect you. You have no idea how much I long to see your face. My darling, it is all I dream about . . .

Penny read the letter in growing disbelief.

Jack Pickup, her father, had not died on the battlefield after all.

That would explain his name missing from the cenotaph, a fact she knew had bothered her mother for years, though she seldom dared mention it for fear of Frank's reaction. Penny's fingers shook, her incredulity growing as she reread the letter again, wanting to pinch herself to make sure she wasn't dreaming.

The letter went on to detail the train journey Ellie-May would have had to have made from Southampton to Gillingham in Dorset, ending with a further entreaty to her to write back immediately.

Please don't make me wait too long to see you, I grow more impatient with every passing hour. See you soon, my darling,
Until then, I remain,

Your ever-loving Jack

Penny sat back on her heels, shock rendering her momentarily speechless. Why? Why would her grandmother keep such a letter from her mother? And keep it a secret she obviously had, because Ellie-May clearly had no idea Jack was alive.

'What's the matter, Penny?' She started at the sound of her grandfather's voice, having completely forgotten his presence. 'You've gone very pale. If it's too much for you, we can give it a rest for a while. I . . .' His words trailed away as Penny held out the letter. 'Oh.' Sid sighed deeply. 'Penny, love . . .'

'Why?' Penny croaked. 'Why would she do this?'

'Now, Penny, love, you've got to understand.' Sid came towards her, arms outstretched. Penny pushed him away. Jumping to her feet, she rounded on the old man.

'You knew about this?' She waved the letter in front of his face. 'Are you part of the deceit as well?'

'I can explain, love,' Sid said, his heart breaking for his granddaughter.

'You've lied to me and Mum for my whole life.' Penny screamed. 'Why? Why would you do it?' She burst into tears, her life shattering around her. Everything she had ever believed was a lie. How could she ever trust anyone again?

'Pen-Pen, calm down and let me explain. Please?' Sid held out his arms. After a moment's hesitation, Penny fell against him, hot angry tears soaking into his fawn cardigan.

CHAPTER TWENTY-EIGHT

'You must understand, Penny, love. Your nan only did what she thought best at the time.'

They were in the kitchen, a bottle of sweet sherry on the table between them. Eileen had been partial to a drop of the stuff on High days and Holy days and, lacking anything stronger to take the edge off his granddaughter's shock, Sid had fetched the bottle from the pantry and poured them each a generous tot.

'By the time we got Jack's letter,' Sid went on, 'your mum and Frank were already married. It would have killed our Ellie-May to realize she'd just made the biggest mistake of her life.'

'She had a right to know,' replied Penny dully, swirling her sherry in its thick-bottomed tumbler.

'And what good would it have done, love?' Sid asked her gently. 'What could she do? Divorce Frank and suffer the inevitable scandal? Or stay with him and endure the misery of knowing Jack was alive, but lost to her anyway?' Sid sucked air in through his teeth.

'At least it would have been Mum's decision! I wasn't even born, when this letter is dated. If you and Nanny Eileen had told Mum the truth, whatever she decided to do, at least I'd have known my father. I'd have had a relationship with him.' She looked at Sid with eyes filled with sorrow. 'You robbed me of that.'

'And I'm heartily sorry for that, love. If I had the chance over again, I'd do things differently but hindsight's a wonderful thing. What's done is done, and can't be undone but if you had any idea how much your nan agonized over her decision, lass . . .' Sid shook his head sorrowfully. 'It broke her heart to write that letter to Jack. We were that fond of him.'

He raised his glass to his lips and took a sip, relishing the gentle heat at the back of his throat. 'I don't doubt our Ellie-May would've been a heck of a lot better off with Jack than she is with Frank.' He shrugged his thin shoulders, such a picture of abject misery that, despite her anger, Penny's heart went out to him.

'I've got to tell Mum,' she said. She had drained her glass and the sherry had left a warm glow in her otherwise pale cheeks. 'I can't keep this from her. It's not right.'

'She'll never forgive me.' Sid hung his head sadly as Penny buried her head in her hands.

'So many wasted years,' she whispered. 'For all of us. I've missed out on knowing my real dad.'

Sid reached across and took her hand in his. His skin was rough and calloused from decades of manual labour.

'No wonder Mum never got anywhere with the war

memorial committee . . .' Penny said with a sigh. Her eyes narrowed. 'She has a right to know, Grandpa.'

Sid gazed at her sadly. 'It's up to you, love, but sometimes, it's best to let sleeping dogs lie. You'll just open up a lot of old wounds.'

'I have to tell her, Grandpa. I couldn't live with myself and I need to find out what happened to Jack.' Penny held her grandfather's gaze. 'I've always felt like a cuckoo in the nest. Frank's always provided for me and I'm grateful, don't get me wrong, but he resents me, Grandpa. You know he does. I'm not stupid. I'm a constant reminder to him that Mum loved Jack first, and probably still does.'

She pushed aside her empty glass and leaned forward, her elbows on the table. 'I need to find my dad.'

Ellie-May leaned out of the upstairs window and shook the duster. It was a bright winter afternoon. If it weren't for the barrage balloons hanging over the city, one could pretend there wasn't a war on at all. Gulls soared in the pale blue sky, their mournful cries echoing over the frosty rooftops. The air was damp and smelled of coal fires. Ellie-May was about to close the window when she spotted Penny making her way up the street, shoulders slumped as if they bore the weight of the world.

Poor love, she mused, closing the window and hurrying through to the kitchen to put the kettle on. Clearing out Eileen's things must have taken a bigger toll on the poor girl than expected. After all, they had been very close.

She was pouring boiling water into the pot when she heard Penny's footsteps on the stairs.

'Sit down, love. The tea's just brewing . . .' Her words trailed away at the sight of Penny's stricken expression. Alarm clutched at her chest. 'What's happened? Is it Grandpa?'

Penny shook her head, glancing around the tidy flat. 'Where's Frank?'

'Where else would he be on a Wednesday afternoon?' Ellie-May snorted. 'At his club.'

'Good.' Penny slumped into a chair. Ellie-May sat down next to her.

'For goodness sake, will you tell me what's wrong.' Anxiety was tying her stomach in knots.

'Jack's alive,' Penny blurted out, her carefully rehearsed words deserting her.

'What?' Ellie-May gave a brittle laugh. 'I must have misheard you. I thought you said Jack was alive.'

The colour drained from her face and she pushed back her chair with such force it tipped over, crashing to the floor. 'No, I won't allow you to do this to me, Penny. I'm in no mood for cruel tricks.' She leaned against the sink, her breath coming in short, sharp bursts.

'Mum . . .' With trembling hands Penny took Jack's letter from her pocket.

Ellie-May practically snatched it from her. The only sound in the kitchen was her mother's ragged breathing as she read the letter. Her hand fluttered to her throat and she closed her eyes, tears squeezing beneath her lashes and sliding unchecked down her white cheeks.

'No, no, no!' she wailed, clutching the sink for support. Fearing her mother was about to faint, Penny wrapped her arms around her and helped her to a chair where she sat with her head in her hands, silent tears streaming down her face.

'I'm sorry, Mum,' she said softly, crouching at her mother's side. 'I didn't mean to upset you but I thought you'd want to know.'

'Where did you find it?' Ellie-May asked hoarsely, looking at Penny through a haze of tears. Her cheeks were blotchy and her nose was running. Penny breathed in deeply. This, she knew, would be the most painful part of the conversation.

'In Nanny Eileen's bedside drawer. It was tucked in the back of a Bible.'

'You mean Mum knew Jack was alive, and she didn't tell me?' Ellie-May stared at Penny with incredulity. 'She lied to me for twenty-four years?'

Her voice rose, anger suffusing her cheeks. She swallowed. 'Did my dad know?'

Penny's reluctance to reply was all the answer Ellie-May needed. She got to her feet, unable to contain the anger bubbling inside her like a cauldron. 'Why?' she shouted, trembling as she waved Jack's letter in the air. 'Why would they do that to me? Why? I'll never forgive them, never!' she screamed, her pain-ravaged gaze raking the worktops for something, anything, to throw. Her eyes alighted on a large glass bowl she used when making trifle. With one fluid movement, she swiped the worktop, sending the dish crashing to the floor. The sound of glass shattering sent Ellie-May to her knees. She sank onto the floor, sobbing as though her heart would break.

Penny crouched down and reached for her hand. It was ice cold.

'Why did they do it?' Ellie-May mumbled through her tears. 'They knew how much I loved him. They knew . . .'

Penny emptied out the cold, stewed tea and made a fresh pot, setting it before her mother, who was staring listlessly into the distance.

'There must have been a mix-up with identity,' Penny said. She poured Ellie-May a cup of tea, stirring in a generous portion of sugar for the shock. 'I'm angry with Grandpa and Nanny, too,' she said. She sighed. 'I know they meant well, and did what they thought was best.'

'Best for whom?' Ellie-May snapped. 'They kept me from the only man I will ever love, and you grew up never knowing your real father.' Ellie-May's voice trembled with suppressed emotion and she mopped at her red-rimmed eyes with a crumpled handkerchief. 'I can never forgive them for that.'

'Grandpa's really upset,' Penny said.

'And so he should be. He and my mother ruined my life.'

The letter lay on the table before her, now stained with tears, the ink running in places where Ellie-May had pressed it to her face, hoping some trace of Jack might remain but, of course, there was nothing there, just the faint smell of the scented paper her mother used to line her drawers.

'Jack would have been waiting for my reply? Why didn't he come here, once he was discharged, or write again. Why would he just give up on me? What?' she asked, warily, noting Penny's grieved expression.

'Nanny Eileen wrote to him. She told him you were married and asked him not to contact you again.'

'Oh, God!' Ellie-May buried her face in her hands, her stomach cramping painfully. Imagining Jack's devastation on learning that she had married Frank, she groaned in despair. She raised her head, her stricken gaze meeting Penny's. 'He must hate me,' she whispered.

'Oh, Mum, I'm so sorry.' For a long time, Penny held her mother close, her own cheeks wet with tears as both women cried bitter tears for the life they might have had.

'I've got an appointment with the recruitment office tomorrow,' Penny said some time later once they had both calmed down.

'What?' Ellie-May looked up at her in bewilderment.

'I haven't said anything before as I didn't want to worry you. I'm volunteering for the Women's Land Army. I'm seeing them tomorrow.'

'Oh, don't go, Penny. We need you here.'

'Now you sound like Frank,' Penny said with a tentative smile.

In spite of her misery, Ellie-May managed a small smile

in reply. 'I know. I'm sorry.' She sighed in resignation. 'I'm being selfish. You're a grown woman. Of course, you must do what you want.'

'I'm going to ask if I can be sent somewhere near Gillingham in Dorset.' She paused, waiting for her mother to comprehend the significance of her words.

'You're going to try to find him?'

'Yes, Mum.' Penny nodded. 'I'm going to find out what happened to Jack. I'm going to find my dad.'

The woman at the recruiting office for the Women's Land Army wasn't very sympathetic to Penny's request. 'You're not booking a holiday, Miss Cartwright,' she said brusquely. 'You'll go where you're needed.' Then, seeing Penny's crestfallen expression, added a little more kindly, 'But I'll see what I can do.'

Thanking her, Penny came away with renewed hope.

She rubbed her hands together as she made her way to the bus stop to catch the bus back to Northam Road. It was bitterly cold. Patches of washed-out blue sky were visible amongst the dark clouds and a murky sun cast its eerie light over the city. A few shops had started putting up their Christmas decorations, despite it only being the last week of November. The man in front of her lit a cigarette, flicking the spent match into the gutter. A seagull squawked loudly from atop a lamppost.

She squinted into the late-winter sun that had now appeared fully from behind a cloud. Her determination to find Jack was a yearning that couldn't be denied. Her breath clouded in front of her face as she stepped aside to make room for a nursemaid wheeling a large perambulator, her mind reeling with her newfound knowledge.

The woman in the recruiting office had said she should receive her call-up papers within a fortnight. In the meantime, she decided as the bus lurched through the drab, winter streets, she would write to Wyke Hall and see what information they could provide.

CHAPTER TWENTY-NINE

'You'll be away soon then,' Sid said matter-of-factly, his gnarled hands shaking as he poured tea from his flask into two chipped mugs. He handed one to his Penny and she curled her gloved hands around it gratefully.

They were sitting on an upturned crate in Sid's shed. The air smelled of mildew, damp and soil. Cobwebs clung to the corners of the sloping roof and the wind rattled the tiny windowpane. The floor was dusty underfoot.

It was two weeks before Christmas, and Penny's call-up papers had arrived that morning. To her delight, the recruiting office had granted her request and were sending her to a training farm about ten miles from Wyke Hall where Jack had convalesced.

'I have to report to Eastleigh train station on the third of January.' She sipped her tea, wincing as she scorched her upper lip.

She kept her voice calm yet she could hardly contain her

excitement. She would visit Wyke Hall the first chance she got, and start her quest to find her father in earnest.

'Ah, well, lass, you're a sensible girl. And you've been brought up right,' Sid said, drawing her attention back to the draughty shed. 'You'll do all right.' He smiled, his lips trembling slightly. 'You've no need to stand on ceremony, just be yourself and you'll be fine.'

'Thanks, Grandpa. I'm glad you're pleased for me. Mum's not happy about me going, but at least she understands. Frank's not speaking to me at the moment.'

'He doesn't know about Jack?' Sid slurped his tea noisily.

'That he's alive? No. I haven't said anything and I know Mum wouldn't dare.' Penny smiled fondly at the old man. She would miss him. 'Mum will come around, Grandpa,' she said. 'She's hurt and angry. She just needs some time to come to terms with everything. It's all been a terrible shock for her.'

'I hope you're right, lass,' Sid said gruffly. 'I don't like being at odds with her.'

It had taken Penny almost a week to forgive Sid for his part in the deception, but he had been so filled with remorse and had, she suspected rightly, only gone along with the subterfuge to please Eileen. And even she had done what she did with the best of intentions. She hadn't done it to be cruel. Penny understood that, not that it made the conse-quences any easier to bear. Penny had still grown up without her father.

'I'll miss you,' Sid added.

'Perhaps the war won't last too long this time around, and I'll soon be home,' Penny said hopefully. After all, what the newspapers were referring to as the 'phoney war' had failed to bring the bombings and air raids people had been dreading. Many children, evacuated to the country in August and September, were slowly returning home, Hattie's children among them.

'I think farm work will be right up your alley. You've never been happy in that butcher's shop, have you? It won't be easy mind. It'll be long hours and backbreaking graft.'

'You know I'm stronger than I look,' Penny grinned. A gust of wind shook the shed. From outside came the dull thud of a spade striking the frozen earth. She paused, stilling her racing heart. 'Jack's convalescent home is not far from where I'm going,' she said, keeping her tone deliberately light as she picked a speck of lint off her trousers.

Sid looked at her sharply. 'Ah, now, lass, are you sure you want to be opening that can of worms?'

'Grandpa, you know how I feel. I need to do this. For Mum, but mostly for myself.'

'What will you do if you find him?' Sid asked, chewing his lip thoughtfully. 'Have you thought it through? What if he doesn't want to know?'

'I have considered that possibility,' Penny replied solemnly. She had, constantly, and the idea terrified her. But it was a chance she was willing to take.

'What if he wants to see our Ellie-May?'

'That's up to Mum,' Penny said. She sighed. 'He only

convalesced in Dorset, Grandpa. He could be anywhere in the country.'

Sid regarded her gravely. 'Have you considered the possibility that he might no longer be alive?'

Penny nodded. 'I've prepared myself as much as I can.' She shrugged. 'I might find out nothing at all. It might turn out to be a wild goose chase.'

'I just don't want to see you hurt, Pen-Pen. You could be setting yourself up for an almighty fall.'

'I'm a big girl, Grandpa,' Penny grinned. She slurped down a mouthful of tea. 'I can take care of myself.'

'I hope so, lass.' Sid scratched his bristled chin. 'I sincerely hope so.'

Ellie-May wiped the kitchen table and threw the cloth in the sink. A rack full of Frank's damp shirts and underwear hung from the ceiling, lending the room a musty smell. Leaning her palms on the windowsill, she gazed down into the concrete yard. Frost sparkled on the roof of the privy and glinted on the top of the wall. Two gangly boys came running down the alleyway, their gasmasks bumping against their chests, woolly hats pulled low, ears and nose red with cold.

She sighed, her warm breath fogging the glass and obscuring her view. Jack hadn't died on the battlefield. No wonder his name hadn't been on the cenotaph. It hadn't been a clerical error after all. If only she hadn't given in to Frank's insistence she give up her correspondence with the war office. She might have found out about Jack much sooner. In the fortnight since Penny's revelation, Ellie-May had hardly eaten or slept. She snapped at Frank and was short with the customers. She hadn't been around to see Sid, terrified of what she might say should she give way to the anger that churned inside her like molten lava. The knowledge that Jack was, in all probability, alive and, believing she hadn't cared enough to wait for him, filled her with a misery that all but swamped her. Some mornings it was sheer willpower alone that got her out of bed.

She was dreading January when Penny would be leaving for the West Country. It was only a few hours away by train, but it might as well be the end of the earth. Still, she could console herself with the comforting fact that Penny was likely to be a great deal safer stuck down in rural Dorset than she would be in a city like Southampton.

She picked up the broom and busied herself sweeping the floor. Come January, it would be just her and Frank. The thought turned her stomach to water. Frank, as had become his habit on a Wednesday afternoon, was at his club in Kent Road. Not that she minded. She preferred it when he was out. He was giving both her and Penny the silent treatment at the moment, making no secret of the fact he didn't agree with Penny's decision to join up. Guilt, Rose had surmised when Ellie-May had bumped into her at the bus stop across the street.

'He feels guilty that he never had the courage to join up himself. She's showing him up, that's what it's all about, you mark my words,' Rose had told Ellie-May with a sniff of derision. Both Rose's sons and her sons-in-law had joined up as soon as war was declared.

While Ellie-May tried hard not to be disloyal towards her husband, she had to agree. Frank was forty-six years old. Four years below the cut-off age for enlisting. Yet Frank had returned from a routine visit to the doctor, a smug smile on his face, brandishing his exemption papers. Ellie-May had merely tucked them away in the dresser drawer along with the other important documents. Whatever the nature of Frank's heart complaint, it never seemed to trouble him during peacetime.

'I don't know what's gone on between you and Sid, Ellie-May,' Rose had added, just before boarding her bus, 'but he misses you something dreadful. Whatever it is, can't you put it behind you? He isn't getting any younger, you know.'

'I'll thank you to mind your own business, Rose Norris,' Ellie-May had snapped crossly, before turning away and marching off down the street, leaving her old neighbour staring after her in bewilderment.

She felt overwhelmed with shame every time she recalled the incident. Rose was very fond of Sid and had only been trying to help. Ellie-May understood that, but she was not ready to even talk to her father, let alone try to forgive him.

She flicked the broom across the linoleum floor. Much as she was dreading Penny's impending departure, she was proud of her. And her relief that Penny was finally getting shot of the butchers was heartfelt. Her daughter didn't belong here, she never had. If the rumours surrounding Jack's parentage were true, gypsy blood flowed through her daughter's veins. It was no wonder she felt at one with the land.

She leaned the broom against the wall and sat down, wondering at Penny's determination to trace Jack's whereabouts. She knew Penny had written to Wyke Hall but had yet to receive a reply. She pictured Jack as she had last seen him, looking dapper in his uniform as he waved from the train carriage window. Would Penny find him, she wondered, and how would she, Ellie-May, react if she did?

Christmas came and Ellie-May, Frank and Penny spent Christmas Day with Sid and the Norris family, squashed into Sid's front parlour. Carols played on the gramophone, but the festivities felt forced. If Frank noticed Ellie-May's frostiness towards her father, he didn't mention it.

In hushed silence, they gathered around the wireless to listen to the King's speech broadcast from Sandringham:

'I feel that we may all find a message of encouragement in the lines, which, in my closing words, I would like to say to you: I said to the man who stood at the Gate of the Year, "Give me a light that I might tread safely into the unknown." And he replied, "Go out into the darkness, and put your hand into the Hand of God. That shall be better than light, and safer than a known way." May that Almighty Hand guide and uphold us all.'

There wasn't a dry eye in the house. Even Frank had to blow his nose.

Nursing her grievances towards Sid, Ellie-May had drunk too much sherry. She'd argued with Frank on the drive home, both of them slightly worse the wear for drink. *There'll be tears before bedtime*, Penny had sighed inwardly, slumped in the back seat, listening to the crunch of the car tyres on the snow.

After depositing them both at home, Frank roared off down the street, leaving Ellie-May and Penny shivering on the pavement while Ellie-May fumbled with her keys, snow swirling around their heads.

'You need to talk to Grandpa, Mum,' Penny said as she made them both a cup of tea. 'You can't go on giving him the silent treatment.'

Ellie-May ignored her. 'Jack's mother was rumoured to be the daughter of Lord Farquharson,' she said instead, her unfocused gaze coming to rest briefly on Penny's face. 'She was seduced by a gypsy, so Frank heard.' She slurped her tea loudly. 'Caused a huge scandal, by all accounts.'

'Is it true, Mum?' Penny stared at her mother in wide-eyed astonishment. 'I'm the granddaughter of Lord Farquharson, the recluse?'

Ellie-May shrugged. 'Who knows? She had some fancy ways about her, Verity, and she always spoke very well. She stuck out like a sore thumb round Church Street, God rest her soul.' She laughed drunkenly. 'Of course, you'd never be able to prove it one way or the other, and I doubt it's true anyway. It's only gossip.' She got to her feet, grabbing the chair arm as she lurched unsteadily. 'It's been a long day, Pen-Pen, I think I'll get myself to bed.' She dropped a clumsy kiss on Penny's head and disappeared into the bedroom.

Lord Farquharson's granddaughter, Penny mused with a wry grin. Well, that would be something to bring up with Jack, if she ever got to meet him. It would be interesting to see what he might have to say on the subject of his parentage.

CHAPTER THIRTY

1940

The train station was bustling with young women from all walks of life, standing with their tearful mothers and stoic, disapproving fathers unable to understand why their well-brought-up daughters would wish to dash off to some godforsaken place in deepest Dorset to muck out cow barns and drive tractors. Several severe-looking women in uniforms, marking names off clipboards, shouted orders, raising their voices in order to be heard above the racket.

Ellie-May waited with Penny, a cold finger of fear running down her spine. Her mind travelled back to the day she had waved Jack off from this very station, for what she didn't know then would be the last time.

'I didn't expect there to be so many of us,' Penny said, loudly, forcing her mother to push her memories aside and smile bravely. She was determined not to make a show of herself, for Penny's sake.

Penny couldn't quell the growing sense of excitement that rose up from deep within her. She seldom ventured far from the city and was relishing the adventure. A cold wind howled the length of the platform and she tugged the collar of her thick winter coat higher around her neck, her breath clouding in the frigid air. She had already reported to Miss Potter and been ticked off her list. Now, the train whistle cut across the noise, signalling that it was time to board.

'Take care of yourself, darling,' Ellie-May said, finding she was suddenly fighting back the tears. 'Write as often as you can.'

'I will, Mum.' Penny hugged her back. 'Don't worry about me. I'll be fine.'

Giving her mother one last squeeze, Penny slung her gas mask over her shoulder, and boarded the train, making her way to the nearest available carriage. The three women already seated turned from the window to smile a welcome. Dumping her gas mask on a scuffed seat, she joined them in leaning out of the window, and spotted her mother immediately. Penny waved frantically as the train began to pull out of the station, its long, low farewell whistle reverberating down the cold platform.

'Hello, I'm Edie Wright. Pleased to meet you.' The tallest of the three girls, a big-boned redhead, thrust out her hand as they settled themselves on the seats, the train racing past drab sidings and mountains of grey ballast.

'Penny Cartwright.' Penny shook Edie's hand, and grinned around the carriage. The other two girls were

Anne Jones, a petite brunette with an open, pleasant face and Daphne Beaumont-Guy, a curvaceous blonde who told them, with complete modesty, that she had recently returned from finishing school in Switzerland and was engaged to the son of a Scottish earl.

'I'm afraid I'm rather in disgrace at home,' Daphne said in her clipped, upper-class voice. She lit a cigarette, holding it elegantly between long, tapered fingers, smoke drifting slowly upwards. 'I'm supposed to be planning the society wedding of the year with Mother, but instead I intend to "Lend a Hand on the Land" and do my bit. Father's refusing to speak to me at the moment.' She smiled wickedly. 'Not sure Tony is totally enamoured with my decision, come to think of it, but as he enlisted in October, he couldn't really make a fuss, could he?'

'I'm single and fancy-free,' offered Anne with a mock pout. She told them she was twenty-six, and had joined up to escape her job as paid companion. 'She was a miserable old so and so and I'm sure even a herd of cows shall prove to be much better company than that old witch.'

'My parents both support my decision to join up,' Edie volunteered with a smile. At twenty-one, she was the youngest of the four. 'My boyfriend, John, joined up just before Christmas. I used to work as a seamstress and I could have stayed on and made uniforms for our boys, but I fancied a change of scenery and decided to join up. Mum and Dad are happy I'm getting out of the city. Dad reckons they'll be hit quite hard once Hitler gets going.'

They were sober for a moment as the train raced through the frosty Hampshire countryside, thinking of the families they'd left behind.

'So, what about you, Penny?' Daphne drawled, exhaling a cloud of blue-tined smoke. 'What's your story?'

'I'm single and I've worked in my parents' butcher's shop since I was fourteen.'

'Cartwright's?' Anne said. 'In Northam Road? That's where my mum gets her meat. Nettie Jones?'

'Oh, yes,' said Penny. 'She's one of our regulars. Now you mention it, I can see the resemblance.'

'I wonder what sort of place they're sending us to,' Edie said, turning to gaze out of the window. Skeletal, wintery trees flashed passed, sheep huddled on windswept hills. The sky was grey and foreboding. They rumbled passed quaint stone villages, and grand country estates, vast expanses of open countryside. By the time they changed trains in the beautiful cathedral city of Salisbury, the sun had come out, bathing the tall cathedral spire in its pale buttery light, and the four women had become firm friends.

The train pulled into Gillingham's small station just after midday. In the time it had taken to travel the thirty-two miles from Salisbury, the sun had once again been swallowed up by thick clouds, and a light drizzle had begun to fall.

Penny gathered up her belongings, peering out the grime-coated window at the rain pooling on the platform, her mind whirring with excitement. Just knowing that her real father had more than likely once stood on this very platform caused her heart to soar.

The air was cold and damp and they stood shivering while a plump middle-aged woman in a grey coat and blue hat marched up and down, barking orders and ticking off names, before directing them to where two red buses waited to take them on the final leg of their journey.

It was a short drive along twisting lanes through the mist-shrouded Dorset countryside to Roanoke Farm where the girls would be billeted for the next few weeks. Penny stared out of the rain-splattered window at the long rows of huts surrounded by muddy grass and spindly, leafless shrubs. The farmhouse was some distance away, together with a selection of tumbledown barns and cattle sheds. To Penny's delight, the four of them were assigned to the same hut.

'This is a bit primitive, isn't it?' Daphne grumbled to Penny under her breath, as they squelched across the waterlogged ground to their temporary home. They opened the door and found themselves in a room barely larger than a garden shed. There were two sets of bunk beds, a chest of drawers, a small table and two rickety-looking wooden chairs. The floor was bare board and their footsteps echoed loudly as they crossed the small space to claim their bed.

'The mattress doesn't look very comfy,' Daphne said with disdain, dumping her hat on the rough, grey blanket of one of the top bunks.

'My cousin's a Land Girl,' Anne said. She was about to take off her coat but thought better of it. It was cold in the hut. 'She said that after the first couple of days we'll be so exhausted we'll sleep anywhere. Things like a lumpy mattress won't make any odds.' She shivered violently. 'Shall I light the stove? It's freezing in here.'

While she coaxed a good blaze out of the pot-bellied stove, there was a curt knock on the door and two strapping young women, dressed alike in loose-fitting brown trousers and olive-green jumpers, entered the room, their arms full of clothes, boots dangling from their laces.

'Hello, I'm Liz and this is Peggy. We've brought your uniforms. Two of everything.' They laid the pile of clothes on the table, the boots falling heavily to the floor. 'Your measurements have been matched to those on your application form, but if anything doesn't fit, you can swap them in the farm office this evening between four and six.

'Your uniforms are your responsibility,' Liz went on, as the four girls crowded around the table, holding up various items of clothing and examining them with a critical eye. 'There's a laundry on site; you may even end up working in there at some point.'

Liz went on to explain the working rules of the camp, the location of the ablutions and canteen. 'Breakfast is at half past four.'

Daphne blanched. 'Half past *four*?' she repeated, incredulous. 'We'll have to get up at four,' she said, shooting Penny a look of horror. She had never risen before eight-thirty in her life.

'You start work at five-thirty,' Liz said without a trace of sympathy. Born and bred on a dairy farm she had little truck with soft Townies. 'You'll soon get used to it. Get changed and join us outside in ten minutes for your tour of the farm. You'll be meeting the farmer, too, so make sure you're well turned out.'

'Not quite what I was expecting,' Daphne grumbled as they changed into their new clothes.

'You knew it would be hard work when you signed up,' Penny reminded her, buckling her belt and tugging the collar of her checked shirt out of her jumper.

'Well, yes,' Daphne bit her lip. 'But four o'clock? It's ridiculous.'

All early risers, the other three grinned at each other. With Daphne still muttering under her breath, they joined their fellow Land Army members in the muddy yard.

Roanoke was an example of farming on a large scale, Liz explained as she led them passed vast fields of pigs, cows and bored-looking sheep. Most of them would end up on smaller, family-owned farms but in the meantime, they would be taught the rudimentary basics of animal husbandry and general farm work. They were introduced to the farmer and his wife, a taciturn couple in their mid-forties, who appeared less than enamoured with the motley crew of new recruits, treating them with disinterest.

Anne's prediction had been spot-on, Penny mused ruefully a few days later as she collapsed into bed fully clothed, where she slept like the dead until awoken by the alarm.

The work was relentless. They were up long before dawn, working by lantern-light in freezing conditions. The work was backbreaking and mind-numbingly exhausting. Some evenings Penny was reduced to tears, her blistered hands red and swollen. The worst job by far, all the women agreed, was having to catch the huge rats that infested the cattle sheds. Penny would rather muck out, standing ankle-deep in filth, than do that. The communal bathroom facilities had come as something of a shock to many of the young women, but modesty was soon cast to the wind.

Penny had been at Roanoke for just over four weeks when she, along with Daphne, Anne and Edie were called to the farm office. Despite the harsh conditions, all four girls were flourishing. The outdoor air and good food had given them a healthy glow in their cheeks and put meat on their bones. Even though the work was hard, they each felt a sense of satisfaction, the comfort that they were doing their bit for the war effort.

The rather austere-looking woman they had met briefly at the station upon their arrival was seated behind the cluttered desk. She rose when the girls entered, and extended her plump hand to each of them in turn.

'I'm Doreen Hirst,' she introduced herself. 'Most of my girls call me Aunty Dor. You may do the same. Now,' she sat back down, shuffling papers, while Penny and the others exchanged glances. 'Ah, yes, here we are.' She scanned a sheet of paper, and smiled up at the waiting women. 'It is our tradition here at Roanoke to keep groups of friends together if we possibly can. It helps ease the homesickness and loneliness so I'm pleased to tell you that all four of you are being sent to the same billet.' She rustled more papers, regarding the four girls with her beady gaze. 'You'll be staying with Jim and Rosalind Mullins on Willowbrook Farm. It's not too far from here. Their farm hands enlisted six weeks ago and they've been struggling to cope ever since. Farmer Mullins will collect you at ten o'clock tomorrow morning. Make sure you're ready.'

'I hope they're nice,' Anne said, pulling her night dress over her head once they were back in their room. 'You hear such horror stories.'

'We can always come back here if we don't like it,' Edie pointed out. Her dark eyes flashed with mischief. 'And a little bird told me that Willowbrook Farm is close to the village of Butt's Mead.' The others looked at her expectantly. 'There is a military airbase not far from there.' She grinned triumphantly, running a hand through her tousled curls. 'An airbase means airmen,' she said with a triumphant flourish. 'Lots of dashing pilots.'

Leaving the others to their banter, Penny took the map she had been given by Doreen and spread it out on the bed. It took only a moment for her to locate Butt's Mead from where there was sure to be a bus to Gillingham. Penny hugged her excitement to her like a warm blanket as she cherished the hope that very soon she would be one step closer to discovering Jack's whereabouts.

CHAPTER THIRTY-ONE

In response to Penny's enquiries, the farmer, Jim Mullins, had informed her that the bus from Butt's Mead to Gillingham left from outside the Old Ship pub at 10 o'clock.

'Get off in the High Street and it's only about a twenty-minute walk from there to Wyke Hall.'

On her first Sunday off, Penny stood nervously outside the closed-up pub, her breath clouding in the cold air. She had been waiting for the bus for over twenty minutes and was starting to debate returning to the farm when, to her enormous relief, it rounded the corner. Penny paid her fare and, with a cheerful 'Good morning,' to the only other passengers – two middle-aged women, well wrapped up against the cold – took a seat midway down the aisle.

She leaned her forehead against the cold windowpane as the bus lumbered and swayed along icy lanes. She could barely contain her excitement. All her hope rested on her visit to Wyke Hall. With the outbreak of war, it had been requisitioned, once again, by the military. She had still received no reply to her letter so her hopes were resting on there being someone there who either remembered Jack or could look up any old records.

They pulled into Gillingham High Street twenty minutes later. Two boys were leaning over the bridge, throwing stones into the sluggish-flowing river.

The two middle-aged women disembarked, heading for the church across the street, and Penny made to follow them, but hesitated, and turned back to the driver.

'Could you tell me the way to Wyke Hall?'

'I'm going that way,' the bus driver replied pleasantly. 'If you don't mind waiting five minutes to see if I get any more fares, I'll drop you right outside the gates.'

'That's very kind of you. Thanks.' Penny sat back down and within five minutes they were on their way.

'You got someone convalescing there?' the driver asked as they turned down a long residential street.

'Oh, no.' Penny shook her head. 'I'm hoping to find out some information on someone who was there during the last war.'

'Ah, right,' the driver pursed his lips thoughtfully. 'It's an interesting place, Wyke Hall. Some parts date back to Tudor times. Henry VIII had it built for one of his favourite courtiers. Part of it was destroyed by fire in the seventeen-hundreds, and it was taken over by the Loxley family who own it to this day.

'Lord Loxley's only son was killed on the Somme in 1916 so what will happen to it once the old man goes, I don't know.' He shook his head. 'It'll be a shame to see it sold. It's a big part of our history. Anyway, enough of me prattling on. Here we are.' The brakes hissed loudly as the bus rolled to a halt. 'Wyke Hall.'

Penny drew in a long breath, mesmerized by the sight of the high lichen-covered wall and wrought-iron gates. How many times had Jack walked through those very gates?

'They won't be locked,' the driver assured her, as she hesitated. 'People come and go all the time.' He tipped his hat and grinned. 'Good luck. I hope you find who you're looking for.'

Penny thanked him for his help and leapt to the ground, the frozen mud crunching beneath her feet and approached the gates, her heart thumping in trepidation. Now that she was actually here, she was a bag of nerves.

The gate swung open on well-oiled hinges and a long, tree-lined drive stretched ahead of her, leading up to a large stately home, built from soft, buttery yellow stone, its many windows glinting in the cold winter sun. To her left was an ornamental lake, a solitary duck waddling across its frozen surface.

Excitement building, she made her way up the drive and climbed the wide, sweeping steps of golden Cotswold stone that led up to a pair of brass-studded doors, her heart ricocheting off her ribcage. She rang the bell. From within came the faint tinkle of piano keys.

The door was opened by a young nurse. Wisps of dark hair escaping from beneath her starched cap, her delicate elfin features creased into a smile as she looked up at Penny questioningly.

'May I help?' She had the sort of high-pitched voice Penny imagined might get on one's nerves after a while. 'Have you come to visit one of our patients?' she asked, taking in Penny's heavy coat and brown trousers, the heavy boots.

Penny took a deep breath to steady her nerves. 'I'm looking for information about a patient who stayed here during the last war. Is there anyone who might be able to help me? Are there any records I could look at?' She spoke quickly, hands flapping, as the young nurse chewed her lip thoughtfully.

'All records would have been removed when the house reverted back to the family,' she said. 'But Matron was here then. She may be able to help you. I'll see if she's free. You may wait in the library.'

Grateful to be out of the cold, Penny thanked her and followed her through an ornate entrance hall, her footsteps echoing on the black and white checked floor. A grand staircase swept upwards to a galleried landing. The nurse indicated a door off to the left.

'If you'd like to wait in there, I'll see if Matron is available.'

The library was overly warm and stuffy. A semi-circle of easy chairs faced an enormous marble fireplace, flames crackling in the hearth. The walls were lined with leather-bound books. Penny began browsing through the titles when she was startled by a voice.

'Good morning. I saw you coming up the drive. I take it you're not here to visit me?'

He had his back to her, seated in a scarlet wingback chair, in the perfect position to look out over the lake and grounds. His voice had a mocking edge to it and Penny, momentarily flustered, found herself blushing.

'Oh, no,' she stammered, her cheeks colouring from the oppressive heat of the room as well as embarrassment. 'I'm sorry. I didn't realize anyone was in here. I'm waiting for Matron.'

The man got to his feet, silhouetted against the pale, wintery light, and turned, causing Penny to take a step back in shock. His entire face was swathed in bandages. Only his mouth and eyes, which were an unusual slate-grey blue, were visible. He appeared to be smiling at her, but she couldn't be sure.

'I'm only teasing you.' He gazed at Penny with an intensity that caused her spine to tingle. 'Will you sit down?' He motioned to one of the many chairs set about the room. 'Matron may be some time. She's usually caught up in one crisis or another.' This time Penny could see the smile reflected in his eyes. 'You may as well be comfortable while you wait.'

Muttering her thanks, Penny shrugged off her coat and perched self-consciously on the edge of a chair, hands folded demurely in her lap. The man took the chair opposite.

'Caleb,' he said, thrusting out his hand. Despite his bandaged face, the rest of him appeared to be intact and Penny wondered idly what had happened to him. He was wearing brown corduroy trousers and a navy pullover. Tufts of brown hair sprouted between the folds of the bandages.

'Penny.' She gave his hand a brief shake. It was slightly surreal, she thought, to be having a conversation with a man whose face she could not see.

'A pleasure to meet you, Penny.' Caleb's words came out slightly slurred, which Penny assumed was down to the tightness of the thick dressing around his jaw.

'Likewise,' Penny replied, lowering her gaze as she felt herself redden beneath his scrutiny. A strange tingling sensation travelled up and down her spine, her heart hammering as they conversed, haltingly at first, but slowly growing easier with each other. It wasn't long before Penny felt as though she had known Caleb for years and it was with almost a sense of disappointment when the sound of approaching footsteps heralded Matron Molly Jones' appearance.

'You wanted to see me?' she barked at Penny without preamble, fixing her with her penetrating gaze. She was not an unattractive woman, but her expression was harried, her neatly plucked eyebrows tightly drawn over her slightly upturned nose. Penny guessed her to be in her early to mid-forties. Her blonde hair was scraped back into a tight bun, her uniform spotless and wrinkle free. She had high cheekbones and determined chin, which jutted out as she regarded Penny with her impatient, blue-eyed gaze. 'Matron Jones,' she said pleasantly enough. Miss . . . ?'

'Cartwright,' Penny stammered. Aware of Caleb's amused scrutiny, she cleared her throat and forced herself to calm down. In a firmer voice she said, 'Penelope Cartwright, Matron. I'm sorry to take up your time, but I'm looking for information on a former patient who stayed here in 1915. I understand you were working here then?'

'I was only a VAD back then,' Molly said with a hint of nostalgia. 'I can spare you a few minutes. Who is it you're interested in?'

'Jack Pickup.' Penny said his name in a rush of expelled breath. When Molly didn't answer, she gabbled on. 'I know you must have nursed hundreds of young men during that time, but if you can remember anything at all I would be so grateful. It is very important . . .' She broke off at the sight of Molly's smile.

'Ah, Jack,' Molly said, misty-eyed at whatever memory she was recalling.

'You remember him?' Penny breathed, giddy with excitement.

'Oh, I remember Jack all right,' Molly said with a genuine smile, her earlier irritability clearly forgotten. 'Lovely man.' She stared at Penny. 'Come to think of it, you look a lot like him. Are you a relative?'

'His daughter.'

'Oh!' Molly looked momentarily taken aback but, recovering quickly, said briskly, 'In that case, we should go to my office.' She glanced across at Caleb. 'Doctor said those bandages should be coming off at the end of the week. That's something to look forward to, isn't it?'

'If you say so, Matron,' Caleb replied, sounding as though it was the last thing in the world he was looking forward to.

About to follow Matron from the room, Penny paused in

the doorway. She felt strangely reluctant to take her leave of the intriguing young man. 'It was nice talking to you, Caleb,' she said. 'Good luck.'

Caleb raised his hand in reply and gave a curt nod. Their eyes met briefly before Penny turned away, hurrying to catch up with Molly.

'Poor chap,' Molly said quietly as she led Penny down a wide stone corridor smelling of boiled cabbage and disinfectant.

'What happened to him?' Penny asked, curious.

'Car accident. Caleb and his friend were returning to their base in Wiltshire after a night out when their car went off the road. His poor friend was killed outright. Caleb went through the windscreen. Cut his face to ribbons.' She shook her head sadly. 'It'll be such a shock for him when the bandages come off. Anyway,' she said briskly, 'we're in here.'

Molly's office had once been the housekeeper's sitting room. The walls were papered with pink cabbage roses, the furniture polished walnut. A watercolour depicting the White Cliffs of Dover hung on the wall behind a tidy desk. A gramophone player sat on top of a wooden filing cabinet.

'Take a seat,' Molly invited, settling herself at her desk and indicating the two green leather chairs opposite. She picked up a pen, twirling it between her fingers as she regarded Penny with interest. 'Jack has never mentioned a daughter.'

'He never knew about me.'

'I see,' Molly said, her tone devoid of malice or censure. 'Well, during his time here, I got to know Jack very well.

There was a girl. She broke his heart.' She looked at Penny questioningly.

'My mother,' Penny blurted out. 'It was a mistake, a misunderstanding . . .'

'It happens,' Molly said sympathetically. 'Especially in wartime.' She cleared her throat and put down her pen, lacing her fingers on the desk in front of her. 'We've kept in touch over the years, Jack and I, Christmas, birthdays, that sort of thing.'

Penny could barely contain her excitement. 'You're in touch with Jack?' she breathed. 'You know where he is?'

'I most certainly do.' Molly's eyes were kind, her smile bright. 'My dear Miss Cartwright, your father lives not ten miles from here.'

CHAPTER THIRTY-TWO

Several times over the next week, Penny studied Molly's scribbled directions until they were imprinted on her memory. The village of Boyne Mead was barely eight miles from Willowbrook. It hardly seemed credible that after all this time Jack was practically down the road. She closed her eyes, oblivious to the cold wind and wondered what, and when, she would tell her mother.

The days were dragging. It was bitterly cold and the skies were dull and grey with rain falling almost constantly. The girls were planning on going dancing on Saturday night at the Butt's Mead village hall and had talked of nothing else, but all Penny could concentrate on was going to see Jack. Her emotions seesawed up and down: elation one minute, gut-wrenching anxiety the next. What if he didn't like her? As far as Molly knew, Jack lived alone, with only his old housekeeper, but would he welcome Penny in his life or would she be a painful reminder of his past? These thoughts kept her awake at night and preoccupied during the day.

By Saturday morning, Daphne had had enough.

'Look, Penny,' she said, cornering her in the barn where she was sweeping up the old straw. Daphne snatched the broom from her hands. 'You've been less than useless all week, fretting about Jack. Why don't you go now? Take Jim's old bike, he won't mind.' She glanced at her watch. 'If you leave now, you can be there and back by teatime. I'll cover for you.'

'Are you sure?' Penny asked hesitantly.

'Positive,' Daphne replied with a smile. 'Go on.' She inclined her head. 'Off you go.'

'Thanks, Daphne.' Penny threw her arms around her friend. 'I'll make it up to you.'

'I'll hold you to that,' Daphne grinned after her. Thankfully Jim's wife, Rosalind, was nowhere to be seen as Penny hurried to her room. Taking only a few minutes to drag a brush through her hair and add a dab of lipstick, she raced down the stairs to retrieve Jim's bicycle from the lean-to and set off like the clappers down the muddy lane. She kept glancing up at the dark clouds rolling in across the fields, praying the rain would hold off. The last thing she wanted when meeting her father for the first time was to turn up looking like a drowned rat.

To her relief, while the sky came over all dark and menacing, the rain mercifully held off and forty-five minutes later she peddled over a small humpback bridge and into the sleepy hamlet of Boyne Mead. Clutching Molly's directions in one hand, she cycled passed a row of tumbledown cottages, smoke curling from chimney pots. She spotted the church, its spire silhouetted against the cheerless sky, a pair of rooks squabbling noisily in the belfry.

Dismounting, she wheeled her bike slowly down the street, passing quaint stone cottages with leaded windows and low-slung lintels. At the end of the street was the pub Molly had mentioned, The Quill and Ink. Pausing to catch her breath, she wondered if Jack ever drank there. The street was deserted yet she was conscious of the twitching of curtains. Even in wartime with evacuees, servicemen and Land Girls being billeted in every village, a stranger was bound to draw attention in such a tiny place as Boyne Mead.

She found the small stone memorial at the crossroads Molly had told her about, and took the road heading south. She cycled down a narrow lane, shrouded in shadow, and over another bridge and, through the skeletal branches ahead, she could see a sloping roof and chimney pots. Her heartbeat, already racing from exertion, beat even faster. The hedgerows gave way to an open gateway. One foot resting on the ground to keep her balance, Penny surveyed the cottage. Even in its drab, winter surroundings it looked almost magical; like something out of a child's fairy tale. A goat bleated and from a little distance away came the melancholy moo of a cow. A barking dog came hurtling around the corner of the cottage, a blur of black and white fur. It skidded to a halt in front of her, dropping to its haunches, eyeing Penny suspiciously.

*

Following clumsily in his dog's wake, Jack blinked in surprise at the sight of the nervous-looking young woman clutching the handlebars of a rather ancient-looking bicycle.

'Star, quiet!' The dog fell silent but her unwavering gaze remained fixed on Penny's face.

'Don't worry about my dog,' Jack said. 'She's a bit overprotective of me.' Leaning heavily on his stick, he bent down to pat Star's head. 'You're an old softie, really, aren't you, girl?' Star made a low whine and licked his hand.

Penny would have recognized Jack anywhere. He was older than in his photograph, of course. A small silver scar ran along one cheek, and his dark hair was streaked grey, and there was an unusual streak of white on his forelock. His eyes were kind, though his expression was puzzled as he watched her.

'Is everything all right, miss?' The sound of his voice shocked her to her senses. 'May I offer you a glass of water?' he asked, his brow creased in concern.

'Thank you,' Penny croaked hoarsely. 'I'm fine. You're . . . are you, Jack Pickup?'

Jack brow shot up in surprise. 'Yes, I am.' He studied the woman carefully. Come to think of it, there was something unsettlingly familiar about her.

Penny swallowed hard and licked her parched lips, her mouth dry, her carefully prepared speech entirely forgotten. She felt as though her heart might explode.

'Look,' Jack said. 'It's freezing out here. Would you like to come inside?'

Penny nodded dumbly, and followed him around the side of the cottage. Star, now accepting of Penny's presence, ran ahead. She was waiting outside the back door when Jack and Penny rounded the corner. Jack pushed the door open and Star ran inside.

'Please come in,' Jack said, holding the door open.

Propping her bicycle against the grey-stone wall, Penny ducked past him into the warm, cosy kitchen where a plump, grey-haired woman was hunched in front of the fire peeling potatoes.

'I didn't realize we were expecting company,' she said by way of apology, getting stiffly to her feet.

'An unexpected guest,' Jack smiled. 'Miss . . . ?' He looked at Penny questioningly.

'Cartwright. Penny Cartwright,' Penny said with an over-bright smile. She thrust out her hand.

'Ida,' the woman said, regarding Penny curiously as she wiped her hands on her apron before shaking Penny's hand. There was something about her . . .

'Ida is my housekeeper and a dear friend,' Jack was saying, but Ida barely heard him. 'I'll make us some tea,' she said, her mind whirring, as she began to busy herself with cups and saucers. 'Why don't you go through to the parlour and I'll bring it through.'

Her stomach churning with nerves, Penny ducked under the low beamed doorframe and into a warm parlour. A fire cackled in the grate. The blackened brickwork was festooned with red and blue rosettes.

'My dogs,' Jack said proudly, noticing Penny's interest as she crossed the room to perch on the edge of the two-seater settee. 'Most of them were won by Star's mother and grandmother. They're long gone now, of course, but they were quite something in their heyday.'

He sat down in a faded chintz armchair close to the fire. A book and a pair of reading glasses were balanced on the chair arm. Star flopped at his feet with a weary sigh, her nose resting on his foot.

'So, Miss Cartwright, what brings you here?' The furrow over his nose deepened. 'You seem to know who I am, which puts me at a slight disadvantage.'

Before Penny could speak, Ida came shuffling in with the tea tray, which she set down on the low coffee table in the centre of the room, sweeping aside pile of folded newspapers.

'Thank you, Ida,' Jack said pleasantly. Ida shot him a quick glance.

Has he noticed? Ida wondered. *Probably not.*

They were never as astute as women, men. But it was blindingly obvious to her. This Penny was the spit of Mr Pickup. It was on the tip of her tongue to say something, but she buttoned her lip and poured the tea, then left them to it, taking the newspapers with her.

The clock on the mantelpiece chimed the hour. Penny twisted her fingers in her lap, rubbing at a muddy stain on her trousers.

'You're a Land Girl, I see,' Jack said in an attempt to put Penny at her ease.

'Yes, at Willowbrook Farm?'

Jack nodded. 'The Mullins' place. I know of it.' He regarded Penny curiously. 'So, are you going to keep me in suspense or are you going to tell me who you are and why you're here. Not that I mind,' he added hastily. 'I don't receive many visitors so making a new acquaintance is always a pleasure.' He smiled warmly.

'I'm not sure how to say this ...' Penny said stumbling over the words.

Jack smiled at her, his dark eyes kind.

'I find it's better to just come out with it,' he said, leaning back in his chair and folding his hands across the back of his head.

'All right, well, here goes.' Penny took a deep breath. 'I'm ... I'm your daughter,' she blurted. She hardly dared breathe as Jack leaned forward in shock, his hands falling to his knees. In quick succession his expression moved from shocked surprise to disbelief, to astonishment, before settling on dismay. He regarded Penny sadly.

'My dear girl,' he said quietly. 'I'm sorry, but I'm afraid you've been misinformed. I don't have a daughter.'

'You knew my mother, Ellie-May.' She saw Jack grow pale.

'Of course,' he said, a sudden edge to his voice. '*Cartwright*. I thought your name rang a bell. You're Frank's daughter.' He got clumsily to his feet, groping for his stick as Star, alerted by her master's agitation, looked up at him, whining softly. 'Look, miss, I don't know what your game is, but ...'

'Frank's my stepfather,' Penny interrupted hastily, jumping to her feet.

Jack's dark eyes clouded in confusion. 'But if El was . . .' he rasped hoarsely, his expression one of desolation. 'If she was expecting, she would have told me.' He sank onto his chair, clutching the arms for support, his knuckles turning white as he fought to regain control of his emotions. Star whined again and he reached for her, trembling fingers tugging roughly at her silken fur.

'She did write,' Penny whispered. 'But she was too late. Mr Chalke came around and told them all you were dead. Mum's letters were returned.'

'But I wrote to her.' Jack got stiffly to his feet, his agitation clear. Aided by his stick, he crossed the room to the window, staring at the drab winter landscape, a kaleidoscope of memories filling his head. 'I explained that there had been some monumental cock-up, pardon my French, some confusion over identity. Eileen wrote back to tell me El had married Frank.'

His voice took on a bitter edge. He still had his back to Penny. She could see his shoulders shaking with the effort of maintaining control.

'Because Mum was expecting and she thought you were dead,' Penny told him. 'It was 1915. You know what life was like for unmarried women then. Frank offered her respectability.'

Penny laid her hand on Jack's arm, feeling him flinch. 'She never saw your letter, Jack. She never knew you were alive. My grandparents never told her.' Penny swallowed.

Jack turned to face her, his face a mask of agony. 'Does she know now? Does she know you're here?' he demanded, incredulous.

Penny nodded. 'She's hurt and angry, as was I when I first discovered the truth. I blamed Nanny Eileen myself but I can understand why she kept the truth from Mum, even if I don't believe it was the right thing to do. She knew Mum would have been devastated.'

'At least it would have been her decision, whether she stayed with him or not.' said Jack bitterly. 'So how did you find out?'

'After my nan died, I came across your letter hidden in an old Bible.'

'Eileen's dead? I'm sorry to hear that.'

Penny accepted his condolences with a nod.

'Your mother and Frank, are they happy?'

'Frank is . . . difficult.' Jack groaned and Penny realized that he was crying, silent tears sliding down his weathered cheeks. She went to him and wrapped her arms around him.

'Please don't be angry with Nanny Eileen. She only did what she thought best. She didn't have an unkind bone in her body. From what Grandpa Sid told me, she adored you.'

'Does El know you're here?'

'I wrote to tell her I had an address. She may not have got it yet, though.'

Jack sighed, his shoulders slumping tiredly. The first drops of rain splattered against the windowpane. 'All these years, I thought she didn't care, and never knowing I have a daughter ...'

Penny nodded, her eyes bright. 'It was a shock for me too. I know Mum loved you very much. I think she still does, in her heart. She kept your photograph.'

For the longest time father and daughter stared into each other's eyes. Jack held out his arms.

'Come give your old man a hug?'

Laughing through her tears, Penny fell into Jack's embrace. Pressed against his broad chest, she closed her eyes, savouring the sensation of being wrapped in her father's arms at last.

CHAPTER THIRTY-THREE

Jack sat in his chair brooding, the bleak weather matching his mood perfectly. Rain lashed the windowpanes and a cold wind howled through the trees. He yawned. He'd barely slept and his temples throbbed with the beginnings of a headache.

He rubbed his hand over his face and groaned in despair, the weight of so many wasted years settling heavily on his shoulders. If only he'd written to El sooner, he berated himself, but he'd been so ill, he hadn't even known his own name, never mind anything else. He reached for his teacup and took a sip, grimacing. It had grown cold while he had been lost in the past.

He had reconciled himself to his loss years ago, but meeting Penny, the discovery that he had a daughter, had ripped the wound wide open, the pain as intense as it had been the day he first read Eileen's letter. Lying awake all night, he had seriously considered tearing over to Southampton, but with the cold light of dawn, common sense had prevailed.

Nothing had changed and nor was anything likely to. El was Frank's wife. She was as lost to him now as she had ever been.

He massaged his aching temples. His head might understand that, but it seemed his heart still yearned for her. At least he had Penny, he consoled himself, smiling as the shrill ring of a bicycle bell snapped him back to the present. Penny came flying into the yard on her bicycle. She was drenched to the skin, her front wheel skidding alarmingly on the gravel as she let go of the handlebar to wave frantically before disappearing around the side of the cottage.

'I hope you don't mind me coming back so soon,' she apologized a short time later. She was wearing one of Jack's jumpers, hands cradled around a mug of steaming tea, watching Ida hung her sodden clothes over the maiden. 'I don't want to be a nuisance.'

'Not at all,' Jack said with feeling. 'We've got years to catch up on. I want to know everything about you.'

They moved to the parlour. Penny curled up on the settee, her bare feet tucked underneath her.

'I loved your mother very much,' Jack said.

'I know. She told me.'

He fixed his gaze on the logs crackling and popping in the grate. He would never love anyone the way he loved El, he mused dolefully. A love like theirs came along once in a lifetime. But things were moving along nicely with Jennette; she was great company, and they had a lot in common. If only he could get thoughts of El out of his head, he and Jennette might have a future ...

He adjusted his position, suddenly aware that Penny was scrutinising him.

'What are you thinking?' she asked.

'I was thinking about your mother,' Jack answered truthfully.

'I wrote to her again last night, and told her I had met you,' Penny said slowly.

'How do you think she'll react?' Jack asked. Common sense aside, he could imagine himself turning up at the butcher shop and sweeping El off her feet.

'I'm not sure,' Penny admitted. 'But Mum's very loyal,' she added as if reading Jack's mind. 'She would never betray her marriage vows.'

'Of course she is,' Jack agreed, swallowing down his disappointment. He'd half hoped El would be on the next train west. Instead he invited Penny to tell him about her childhood. 'Was it a happy one?'

'Relatively so,' Penny said. 'I wanted for nothing. Of course, for years I never knew Frank wasn't my real dad yet I always felt he resented me.' She shrugged. 'Understandable, I suppose, especially as he never had a child of his own. None of my little brothers survived.'

For the next hour Penny kept Jack entertained with tales of her childhood. He hung onto every detail. They were interrupted by a woman calling a cheery hello. Penny looked out the window. It had ceased raining and a thin, watery sun had broken through the clouds.

'That will be Jennette.' Rousing himself, Jack limped to the door.

'I'll bring you through a cup of tea in a minute, Jennette, love,' Ida said as a pretty, blonde-haired woman entered the room, looking slightly disconcerted as she eyed Penny with a look bordering on suspicion. Jack kissed Jennette's cheek warmly.

'Jennette, I'd like to introduce my daughter, Penny Cartwright. Penny, this is Jennette du Randt. She's a dear friend.'

'Your *daughter*?' Jennette's eyebrows rose to her hairline. 'You've never mentioned a daughter?'

'He only discovered I existed yesterday,' Penny replied apologetically, getting to her feet. 'I'm pleased to meet you.'

'It must have come as quite a shock,' Jennette said, sitting down, her gaze moving between father and daughter, 'discovering you have a grown-up daughter?'

'It was rather,' Jack grinned, winking at Penny, 'but a pleasant one.'

Ida chose that moment to bring in a fresh pot of tea. She smiled at Jennette. 'So, what do you think of our Penny?' she said, with a proprietorial air that made Penny smile. 'Peas in the proverbial pod, aren't they? I spotted it the moment I laid eyes on her.'

'There is definitely a family likeness,' Jennette agreed, turning to Penny. 'Do you live locally?'

'I'm billeted at Willowbrook Farm, near Butt's Mead.'

'I've heard of the village. And, are your family nearby?' she asked guardedly, the tiniest knot of anxiety forming in the pit of her stomach.

'My mother and stepfather live in Southampton,' Penny said. Jennette expelled a relieved breath and the tension left her face as she visibly relaxed.

Much as it was a shock to discover Jack had a grown-up daughter, Jennette considered as she quietly sipped her tea, as long as the mother wasn't in the picture, she was unlikely to threaten their future. She was no fool, she knew Jack would never love her as much as she loved him, but she was sure it was only a matter of time before he proposed. Once they were married, she'd been hoping to convince him to move back to her native country with Deon and fulfil her parents' dream of running the family vineyard. Hopefully Penny's unexpected presence in Jack's life wouldn't scupper her plans.

She stretched out her legs, crossing her dainty ankles, letting Penny and Jack's conversation wash over her. They were talking about relatives of Penny's mother; people Jennette neither knew nor had any interest in. As they often did in moments of inactivity, her thoughts turned anxiously to Deon. She was so deep in thought it took her a moment to realize Penny had asked her a question.

'Sorry,' she apologised. 'Miles away.'

'I was just wondering about your accent. Jack says you're from South Africa,' Penny repeated, genuinely interested.

'Yes, I came over with my brother, Deon. He's stationed in France at the moment so I'm rather stranded until the end of the war.'

'That's hard,' Penny said sympathetically. 'To be so far from your family.'

'It is, but Dorset has its compensations,' Jennette smiled, glancing coyly at Jack.

He appeared not to notice. Instead he asked hopefully, 'Are you able to stay for supper, Penny? It's only leftovers, but you'd be more than welcome.'

Penny shook her head with regret. 'I'd love to, but I'll have to be going soon.'

Jack wheeled Penny's bike down the drive. The clouds had dispersed and the winter sun had turned the sky salmon-pink.

'I already feel like I've known you all your life,' Jack said, earnestly, leaning on the gatepost.

'I know what you mean,' Penny agreed. 'I feel exactly the same.'

'Stay safe and don't be a stranger. You're always welcome here.'

'Thank you.' She threw her arms around Jack's neck and hugged him. Warmth flooded her veins as she felt his arms fold around her, holding her tight, hugging her back.

CHAPTER THIRTY-FOUR

Rain lashed the windscreen as Frank drove towards the train station through streets crammed with army vehicles. So far April had been wet and dull, the dark skies and low cloud perfectly suited to Ellie-May's mood. In the weeks and months since she found out Jack was alive, she had felt bruised to her very soul. Her anger towards Sid had dissipated over Easter when he had been taken ill with a bronchial infection. Ellie-May had nursed him through the night, listening as his ragged breathing grew fainter until, somewhere close to midnight on the Saturday, she had wept with the fear she was about to lose him, but he'd rallied on Easter Sunday. Later that afternoon, frail and wheezing, Sid had begged her forgiveness and she had given it to him. But though the anger had gone, the pain of betrayal remained.

She had said nothing to Frank about Jack, of course. Knowing he was alive would be like setting a torch to his very short fuse. He'd always been jealous. God alone knew how he'd react if he found out Jack was no longer a ghost, but a man, flesh and blood.

She pressed her fingers to her forehead. A dull ache was forming behind her eyes.

'Are you all right?' Frank asked, not taking his eyes off the road.

Ellie-May nodded, her gaze fixed on the station building up ahead. *Oh, Jack.* She raked her fingers down her pale cheeks, her heart heavy with regret. If only she had received Jack's letter before she'd married Frank ... Grief tightened around her chest like a vice. She had received Penny's letters, had memorized Jack's address and she had been tempted to write herself, telling herself she only wanted to explain, where was the harm in that? After all, not only had she loved him all her life, he was her dearest friend ...

'Here we are,' Frank said, breaking into her reverie as he brought the car to a halt alongside the kerb. 'Give Penny my love,' he added, as Ellie-May made to get out of the car. 'I'll see you this evening.' He leaned across the passenger seat and kissed her cheek. She tried hard not to flinch.

Dodging the raindrops, Ellie-May hurried up the steps. The station thronged with servicemen and women. Pigeons roosted in the rafters of the cavernous building and a cool draught blew across the platforms. Clutching her ticket, Ellie-May made her way to the relevant platform, her heart racing, as much from the deceit as with excitement at her daring. She boarded her train with just minutes to spare, and settled back in her seat to enjoy the journey.

As the countryside rolled by, wet and shrouded in mist, her confidence began to wane. Contrary to what Ellie-May had told Frank, Penny had no idea her mother was on her way to Dorset. Ellie-May planned to surprise her, once she'd seen Jack. Now she was besieged by doubt. What if Jack didn't want to see her? What if in spite of Penny's explanation, he still couldn't forgive her for marrying Frank and breaking his heart? She grew more despondent with every mile. By the time she changed trains in Salisbury she was so filled with misgivings, she was tempted to turn around and go back home. But common sense prevailed and as the sun emerged from behind the clouds just beyond Tisbury, bathing the countryside in golden light, some of her old optimism began to return.

The train pulled into Gillingham with a shrill whistle. Pulling on her gloves, Ellie-May stepped on to the platform. It was twenty minutes past ten and she was one of only a handful of passengers to alight at Gillingham. For a moment she stood shivering on the draughty platform, gripped by uncertainty. She took a deep breath and, giving herself a mental shake, made her way towards the exit, the soles of her damp shoes squeaking on the concrete and boarded the bus to Boyne Mead.

She rested her forehead against the window, her breath misting the cold glass as the bus lurched along narrow country lanes festooned with cow parsley and wild garlic. Her stomach was a mass of nerves. She chewed her bottom lip anxiously, butterflies in her stomach, their frenetic ballet growing more frenzied with every passing mile.

She had pictured this moment so many times over the past few weeks, seeing Jack's face as he had looked the last time she had seen him. In her dreams she could smell him, taste his kisses on her lips, she could feel his embrace, his presence so real that when she woke in the cold light of dawn, her disappointment was crushing, robbing her of breath.

She was jarred from her thoughts by the bus trundling into the sleepy village of Boyne Mead. Ellie-May recognised the pub, the Quill and Ink, outside which the bus rolled to a shuddering halt. The only person to get off in the village, Ellie-May got to her feet and lurched down the aisle.

'Could you tell me how to find Wayside, please?' she asked, pausing beside the driver.

'Follow the road round past the war memorial,' he said, pointing with his finger, 'and over the bridge. You can't miss it.'

Ellie-May thanked him and stepped down from the bus. There was a post office across the street. There was a large poster in the window encouraging people to SAVE FOR VICTORY. The bus driver gave her a cheery wave and trundled on down the street. Ellie-May took a deep breath, and started walking.

Jennette wiped her flour-covered hands on her apron and stepped outside. Dew sparkled on the grass and the air smelled of damp earth and woodsmoke. Star bounded down the bottom of the garden to bury her nose in the wood-pile. Until recently there had been a hedgehog hibernating amongst the logs and Star appeared determined to ferret it out. Washing stirred on the line and the hens clucked contentedly in their run. Jennette breathed in a lungful of fresh, country air. It was fresh, sparkling spring mornings like this that reminded her so much of home and she felt a pang of homesickness. Her gaze swept the tranquil scene, the rows of newly sprouting vegetables, the budding fruit trees, as she tried to picture Jack amongst rows of grape vines of her parent's vineyards nestling against the backdrop of majestic mountains. She had convinced herself that Jack would love the Cape, thrive even. And, she was certain, had Penny not appeared so unexpectedly in his life, Jack would have proposed by now. There was a connection between them, she had felt it the moment she laid eyes on him. If only she could exorcise the ghost of Penny's mother.

Thinking of Ellie-May had soured her mood. She went back inside to check on her scones. Jack had taken Ida to see her sister in Blandford. It was market day and he would be away most of the day, so Jennette had offered to spend the day, as she often did now, doing some of the chores in an effort to lighten Ida's load.

She was about to make herself a cup of tea when Star started to bark. Abandoning her futile hedgehog hunt, she raced around to the front of the cottage. Puzzled, Jennette slipped on her wellingtons and followed, raising her hand to shield her eyes from the sun's glare. A woman hovered uncertainly in the gateway, Star circling her legs in a frenzy of excited welcome. She was wearing a drab navy coat and hat, and looked to be some years older than Jennette. For a moment the two women regarded each other in silence. Jennette's stomach clenched. The woman's vague resemblance to Penny was such that she knew who she was even before Ellie-May opened her mouth. She blinked in disbelief. It was as if her thinking of Ellie-May had conjured up the woman in the flesh.

Ellie-May hesitated, wondering for a moment if she was at the wrong address, but the name was clearly marked on the gate post. She wondered if the lady might be Jack's housekeeper, but she thought Penny had said the housekeeper was older . . .

'Good morning.' She took a few steps towards the petite blonde woman. She looked fresh and carefree in her colourful frock. Ellie-May felt quite drab by comparison. She cleared her throat. 'I'm Ellie-May Cartwright. An old friend of Jack's.' Her gaze darted to the side of the quaint cottage. 'Is he home?'

'Ah, yes,' Jennette said, crossing her arms across her chest in a gesture of defiance. 'Penny's mother.'

'Yes, I am.' Ellie-May smiled. 'I don't believe Penny has mentioned you, Miss . . . ?'

'Du Randt,' Jennette said, cringing at the sound of her nasal twang. Her accent was always more pronounced when she was nervous. 'Jennette du Randt. I'm Jack's fiancée.'

The words of greeting froze on Ellie-May's lips, as she seemed to physically deflate before Jennette's eyes.

'You and Jack are engaged to be married?' she managed,

her voice hoarse with shock and disappointment. Forcing down her guilt at the lie, Jennette nodded.

'I'm afraid you've had a wasted journey, *Mrs Cartwright*, Jack is away from home today. I would invite you in, but I'm afraid he won't be home until late this evening and I do have quite a lot to be getting on with.' She smiled apologetically, hoping Ellie-May wouldn't have the presence of mind to confirm Jack's engagement with Penny.

'Of course,' Ellie-May whispered. She took a deep breath, forcing her emotions under control. 'Congratulations, Miss du Randt. I hope you and Jack will be very happy together. I'm sorry to have troubled you.'

Watching Ellie-May retrace her steps down the lane, the picture of dejection, Jennette almost felt sorry for her, but whatever she had once meant to Jack, Ellie-May belonged in his past. Jack's future lay with her, Jennette. All she had to do was bide her time until he came to the same realisation.

Tears rolling unchecked down her cheeks, Ellie-May followed the road back to the village, silently berating herself for being such a fool. What had she expected? That Jack would have put his life on hold? That he'd spent the last twenty-five-years pining for her? Angry at her own stupidity, she wiped away the tears, stumbling on the uneven ground. As she neared the village, she rummaged in her handbag for a handkerchief and blew her nose.

In the cloakroom of the Quill and Ink, she washed her

face and reapplied her lipstick, scrutinising her reflection in the mirror. Her dark auburn hair was streaked with silver, her face blotchy and her eyes red and puffy. She had over an hour to kill before the next bus to Gillingham. She sat in the deserted snug, nursing a pint of warm lemonade, and wondered how many times Jack had sat in this pub. The only pub in the village, he was bound to have frequented it on many occasions over the years.

Stop it, she told herself sternly. It was time she pulled herself together. She had wallowed in misery and despair for long enough. She would try to be happy for him, however painful, and get on with her own life. She wondered if Jennette would mention Ellie-May's ill-thought-out visit to Jack and Penny. Would they laugh at a middle-aged woman's foolishness? She herself resolved never to mention this visit to anyone. She had to put Jack out of her mind, once and for all.

Frank picked her up at the station. They drove through the pitch-black streets, the covered headlights of the car scarcely illuminating the road ahead. To Ellie-May's relief, Frank barely asked her about her trip, preferring instead to drive in silence, needing all his concentration to navigate the dark streets.

Seated beside Frank, listening to his muttered curses, as he hit first one kerb and then another, she wondered idly whether she would have left him, had Jack asked her. And the answer was, most probably, yes.

*

Jack returned from Blandford in a jovial mood. He had treated Ida and her sister to luncheon at the Crown Hotel. Seated in the attractive garden, enjoying the mild spring sunshine, the three had found themselves reminiscing about life before the Great War, back when life seemed simple. It was easy to look back with rose-tinted glasses, Jack acknowledged, for life with his mother had been very much a hand to mouth existence. It was El who had made his life bearable, El who had brought joy and warmth into his life, and by extension, the Bramhall family. There was many a night he would have gone to bed hungry if it hadn't been for Eileen's generosity and kindness to himself and his mother.

'Why don't you get in touch with Penny's mother?' Ida suggested, tucking into her cheese ploughman's with relish. 'You've never really gotten over the girl, have you?'

'It's not as though the idea hasn't occurred to me, Ida,' Jack pointed out, pausing to take a sip of his pint. 'But as she is still married to Frank, there seems to be little point.

'I have to confess, once Penny had explained why El married Frank, I was tempted to go rushing down there. I even got as far as calling in at the station to make enquiries but . . .' He shrugged.

'Well,' said Edie, Ida's sister. 'I don't see why you can't just meet up as friends. From what you've told me, the two of you go way back. You were friends before you were anything else. Her old man can't object to her meeting up with an old family friend, surely?'

'You don't know Frank,' Jack said with a wry grin. 'Jealousy's his middle name.'

'That's his problem, then, not yours.' Edie snorted.

'Perhaps you're right,' Jack said thoughtfully. 'I'll chat to Penny about it on her next visit.' He eyed Ida's empty glass. 'Right,' he said, getting to his feet. 'Who's for one more before we head over to the Punch and Judy show?'

Jennette had supper waiting when Jack and Ida arrived home just as dusk was falling.

'How was your day?' Jack asked, dropping a kiss on Jennette's forehead.

'Oh, uneventful,' Jennette said, busying herself at the stove, lest her flushed cheeks betray her. 'Tell me about your day. Ida, how is your sister . . . ?

As Jack got off the bus in Northam Street two days later, he was overwhelmed by a sense of déjà vu. How many times had he walked the length of this road on his way to meet Ellie-May from work? It was Wednesday, half closing day and, although just gone noon, many of the shops had already shut. Ignoring the throbbing ache in his leg, he made his way slowly up the street, suddenly overcome by a sense of trepidation that surprised him.

Ellie-May checked her appearance in the parlour mirror. Frank came up behind her and their eyes met. Ellie-May smiled, determined in her resolve to forget Jack and be a better wife to Frank.

'I thought we could stop for fish and chips after the pictures,' he said, combing his hair. 'It's been a while since we treated ourselves.'

'Yes, if you like.' Ellie-May turned to face him. She straightened his tie, her eyes darting towards the carriage clock. 'We'd better go if we're to make the first showing.'

They made their way downstairs and through the silent shop, breathing in the scent of freshly scattered sawdust.

'I heard a good joke in the club last night,' Frank said, unlocking the door, and stepping aside to let Ellie-May out, relayed the joke to her as he relocked the door. It was a weak joke but they both laughed. Ellie-May slipped her hand through the crook of Frank's elbow and they started down the street. Neither of them noticed the figure standing on the opposite kerb staring after them, his expression one of pure dejection.

The letter was waiting for Jack when he got off the bus later that afternoon. Morose and in no mood for Ida's questions, he was heading to the Quill and Ink when Joy Parker, the postmistress, came bustling out, calling his name. She was a short, buxom woman with a steely glare and short, greying hair.

'This arrived for you this morning, Mr Pickup, but your bus had already left.'

Jack took the envelope and thanked her, his breathing quickening as he read the postmark. Southampton. The letter could only be from El.

He hurried into the pub, barely acknowledging the greetings of the few patrons seated at the bar, and ordered a pint. He carried it into the snug, settling into almost the exact spot Ellie-May had sat just a few days before. In his haste, he tore the envelope. He threw it into the fire and unfolded the single sheet of blue writing paper.

My dearest Jack,

How do I put into words all the things my heart wants to say? I know Penny has explained my circumstances to you, and I'm sure you understand why I had no choice but to marry Frank. Jack, if only things had been different, if fate had not been so cruel, you know I would never have looked at another man.

I am so pleased Penny can now have the relationship with her father she has always dreamed of. I'm sure you'll agree we can be so proud of our daughter. She is a wonderful young woman.

Jack, you will always be my dearest friend, but after this there must be no further contact between us. I have my life here with Frank, and you have yours. I just want to say that I wish you all the happiness in the world. You deserve it.

Yours affectionately
El x

Jack felt the disappointment deep in his stomach. But after seeing El and Frank together earlier that day, he had been foolish to hope.

Jack rubbed his hand across his face, fighting the primeval urge to hit someone, preferably Frank Cartwright. Instead, he stared disconsolately into his beer. *Oh, El,* he groaned inwardly, feeling the familiar dull ache in his chest. And yet, common sense told him El was right. How could either of them ever settle for friendship alone? He had to forget about her and move on with his life. But, *dear God,* that would be easier said than done.

CHAPTER THIRTY-FIVE

Ellie-May checked that the blackout curtains were securely drawn before lighting the lamp. It had been a beautiful September day; clear skies and sunshine. Propped up against her pillows, she took her writing pad from the bedside table. She had started a letter to Penny earlier that day and was eager to finish it and get it in the post. She missed her daughter with an intensity that had startled her, and she was hoping Frank would agree to make the trip to Dorset to visit. It was unlikely Penny would be able to come home before Christmas. Ellie-May gathered from her daughter's letters that all they seemed to do on Willowbrook Farm was work and sleep.

She scratched a few lines then chewed the end of her pen, her skin prickling with apprehension. As always, when she wrote to Penny, thoughts of Jack filled her mind. She forced them away, resolved in her determination to forget about him.

The back door banged shut, and her stomach contracted

anxiously at the sound of Frank's heavy footsteps ascending the stairs. She laid down her pen, her eyes flickering nervously to the door.

'You're early,' Ellie-May said, licking her lips nervously as Frank appeared in the bedroom doorway. 'Is everything all right?'

'The pub was dead.' Frank leaned over and kissed her cheek. 'I had a game of dominoes with the landlord and called it a night.' His noticed the writing pad. 'You writing to Penny?'

'Yes.' Ellie-May swallowed. 'I thought we might go and see her some time.'

'We'll see,' Frank replied non-committedly. Ellie-May got out of bed. Throwing on her gown, she followed him into the parlour where he strode over to the sideboard and poured himself a brandy.

'I thought she'd have got fed up by now and come home where she belongs,' he said, settling heavily in Arnold's old chair. The clock on the mantelpiece ticked loudly. Voices drifted up from the street below. People making the most of the Indian summer.

'She's enjoying herself, Frank,' Ellie-May said. 'In spite of the long hours.'

Their conversation was cut off by the sudden shriek of the air raid siren. Down in the street, people started shouting. 'Is it the real thing this time, do you think, Frank?' Ellie-May gasped, frightened.

'Probably another false alarm,' he reassured her. Folding

up his newspaper, he got calmly to his feet, tugging down his cardigan. 'We'd better get to the shelter, though, to be safe.'

Reassured by her husband's calm demeanour, Ellie-May shook her head. Recovering some of her equilibrium, she said, 'You go if you want. I'll stay here. As you said, it's probably a false alarm. I'll be safe enough under the table.'

'Don't be ridiculous, woman!' Frank's brow creased in agitation. 'You'll be far safer in the Anderson shelter. They'll survive just about anything.'

'I'm not going in the shelter.' Ellie-May crossed her arms over her chest. 'I hate it in there. It's cramped and stuffy, and you know I'm claustrophobic. I'll be fine here. And anyway,' she said mutinously, 'if I'm going to die, I'd sooner die in my own home than in some grotty tin can.'

'You can be so damn stubborn, Ellie-May Cartwright!' Frank fumed. 'Fine. Suit yourself. I'm going to the shelter.' Snatching up his newspaper and hat, Frank crashed angrily out of the door.

Ellie-May heard his feet pounding down the stairs as she got up and lifted the blackout curtain ever so slightly to peer out the window. People were running down the street, heading for the nearest public shelter. It was not yet completely dark. If it were a real air raid, she couldn't believe the gall of the enemy to attack before dark. The anti-aircraft guns would soon send them packing, of that she had no doubt. She returned to her bed and tried to continue with her letter, but was unable to concentrate.

The sirens stopped abruptly. Ellie-May could hear the

clackety-clack of the anti–aircraft guns along the coast and her unease escalated. Perhaps this wasn't a false alarm after all, but the real thing. She laid her pen down and listened. Far in the distance, barely audible above the guns, came the distinct drone of aircraft.

She felt sick with fear, frozen to the spot. Then came a dull boom that rocked the room. She clutched the bedclothes in terror, her breath coming in short, sharp gasps. There was another loud bang, closer this time. The third blast shook the entire building. The light fittings trembled overhead and she heard the cups and saucers rattle on the dresser. Clutching at her throat in terror, and not even bothering to slip on her bedroom slippers, Ellie-May dashed from the flat, taking the stairs two at a time in her haste to reach the safety of the Anderson shelter.

She flung open the door to the yard and tripped over the threshold, falling into Frank's arms. Grateful for his support, for she was unsure whether her legs were capable of holding her up, she clung to his arm, as he dragged her across the yard and bundled her unceremoniously into the shelter, slamming the door shut.

'Thank God you came to your senses,' Frank growled, scowling at her in the lamp light.

Ellie-May choked on a sob of terror.

'I was just coming up to get you, even if it meant dragging you down here by your hair, you daft, stubborn woman.' He wrapped his arms around her shaking body, and she nestled against him, grateful for the comfort.

Huddled in the lamplight, they sat in terrified silence,

listening to the drone of aircraft overhead, punctuated by the sound of bombs exploding over their beloved city. During a lull in the bombing, Ellie-May noted that Frank had made the shelter look quite homely. There were two narrow bunks, a small table and a stove for heating a kettle. All in all, the confinement was bearable, as long as Ellie-May remembered to regulate her breathing.

A plane flew directly over their heads and Ellie-May held her breath. She gripped Frank's hand, her nails digging into his flesh, but he kept quiet, almost welcoming the pain, eyes wide as they listened to the whine of the falling bomb. There was an almighty bang and the world shook for what seemed an interminably long time. Ellie-May screamed, clinging to Frank, her face pressed against his shoulder. Cups fell to the floor and shattered.

'That was bloody close,' Frank croaked when, at last, the shaking ceased. Screams drifted from the streets and wisps of dust and smoke had made their way inside the shelter, making Ellie-May cough. Sirens sounded. Voices shouted, urgent and frightened. Terrified, Ellie-May huddled against Frank, his arms tight around her. She couldn't stop shaking. She had never felt so frightened in her life.

She lost track of time. For the time being it seemed, there would be no more planes, no more bombs. She made to open the door of the shelter, but Frank stopped her.

'It might not be safe,' he cautioned her. 'Better to wait until the all-clear sounds.' He peered at his watch. 'It's two in the morning. We should try and get some sleep.'

Reluctantly, Ellie-May climbed onto the narrow cot. 'No, don't,' she said when Frank made to blow out the lamp. 'Leave it on.' He nodded, understanding her fear of being shut in the dark. He swung his legs up on to his bed and lay back on the pillow, arms folded behind his head, and drifted into an uneasy sleep.

Ellie-May lay staring up at the shadows flickering on the corrugated tin roof, her ears straining for the slightest sound. She could hear muffled shouts further up the street and offered up anxious prayers for whoever's home had been hit. Please God the occupants had been safely in a shelter.

The all-clear sounded just before dawn. They emerged to find Northam Street forever altered. The air was filled with dust and rubble and bits of masonry littered the road. All that was left of Hanson's Drapers and Goldstein's Tailors was a smouldering ruin.

'Oh no,' Ellie-May wailed as her tired mind struggled to process what her eyes were seeing. 'Oh, poor Samuel and Alice. We must help them.'

Pausing only long enough to find her shoes and grab some blankets, she found Samuel Goldstein standing across the street from the charred shell of his shop. A blanket draped around his slumped shoulders, his white hair tinged with soot, he stared up at the blackened rafters in bewilderment.

'My birds,' he muttered as Ellie-May drew near. 'My birds.' She followed his gaze, her eyes widening in amazement at the sight of ten budgerigars perched along one of the exposed beams, their bright plumage a stark contrast to the smoke-blackened wood.

'Oh, Mummy,' came a small, frightened voice beside her and Ellie-May looked around to see Arnie, Alice Hanson's nine-year-old son, tugging at his mother's skirt. 'Oh, Mummy,' he said again, his hazel eyes wide in his pale face as he beheld his ruined home. 'What will Daddy say?'

Alice hunkered down, her face close to his. 'Daddy won't care about the shop, darling. He'll just be glad we're safe,' she told him, her eyes glistening with tears as she pressed him against her. 'I don't know what I'm going to do,' she whispered to Ellie-May, as a lady from the WAF took Arnie off to the van to get him a cup of tea and a slice of bread.

'Do you have any family who'll take you in?' Ellie-May asked, concern for her neighbour furrowing her brow. Alice shook her head.

'My parents are both dead.' She shrugged her shoulders, a look of resignation on her face. 'I'll have to go to Dave's mum's I suppose.' She gave Ellie-May a wry smile. 'We don't really get on.' Ellie-May gave her arm a squeeze. Across the street Frank was trying to coax Samuel over to the van, but he was refusing to go anywhere without his beloved budgies.

'The blast lifted the aviary roof,' one of the auxiliary firemen was saying, squinting up at the chirruping birds. His face was black with soot, his eyes bloodshot and swollen. He coughed, spitting soot and dust into a handkerchief. 'Sorry about that,' he apologized. He looked at the smouldering buildings where his colleagues were sifting through the rubble. 'Not much to salvage by the look of things,' he said apologetically to Alice. She nodded, too overcome with emotion to speak. Ellie-May took her arm.

'Come on. Let's get you a hot drink.' She led Alice over to the van where Arnie was sitting on the kerb, devouring his third slice of bread and dripping.

'Thank goodness you and Arnie weren't inside,' she said as they sipped mugs of hot, sweet tea, leaning against the van. Several windows in the street had been blown out by the blast but, thankfully, apart from a few scrapes and bruises, no one had been seriously injured. The new proprietor of the Belvedere Arms, a robust-looking man in his late fifties, stood in his doorway, arms folded across his chest, watching the somewhat unsuccessful attempts being made by Samuel Goldstein to coax his birds down from the roof.

'Where will he put them if he does get them to come down?' one of the firemen pondered out loud as he removed his helmet to run a hand through his thick, curly grey hair.

'I've got a mate who's got an aviary,' a special constable piped up, stifling a yawn. 'I'll ask if he's willing to take on some unexpected guests.' He frowned, gazing up at the budgies. 'At the very least, he can lend me a spare bird cage.'

While he went off to make enquiries about temporary accommodation for the homeless budgerigars, Ellie-May handed her blankets to one of the ARP wardens.

'Thanks, love,' said the warden with a tired smile. 'Three houses were hit two streets away. They'll be grateful for these at the shelter.' She turned to Alice. 'Have you and the boy somewhere to go, love?'

Alice shook her head. 'I'll send a telegram to Dave's mum in Cardiff.' She scratched her head, her eyes cloudy with confusion.

'There is a rescue centre in Millbank Street,' the warden said. 'You can stay there until you hear from your family.'

'It's all right,' Ellie-May intervened firmly, putting an arm around Alice's trembling shoulders. 'She can stay with me. I live over the butcher's shop. That's my husband over there with Mr Goldstein.'

The ARP warden looked to where Ellie-May was pointing, and nodded. 'Thank you. I'll leave Mrs Hanson in your capable hands then and see what I can do for the old boy. Bless him, he's more worried about his budgies than he is about himself.'

'He loves those budgies,' Alice said, momentarily forgetting her own sorry plight. 'He lost his wife some years ago and they never had children. They're all the family he's got.' The warden nodded. Her pretty face was marred by worry and exhaustion.

'We'll do our best to keep his birds safe,' she said. 'Right, I'll get these blankets down to the rescue centre.' She looked up at the clear blue sky. 'Hard to believe, isn't it? That such terror and destruction can come out of the blue like that.' She swore under her breath. 'Sorry, but it makes me so angry.' Ellie-May heard the catch in her voice.

'Are you all right?' she asked, laying her hand gently on the woman's arm. 'You look done in.'

'It's been a long night. They hit the gasworks ...' She smiled tearfully. 'Sorry, my boy's over in France fighting. It's the constant fear ...'

'My Dave's in the Atlantic,' Alice said softly, glancing around to make sure Arnie wasn't within earshot. She smiled briefly at the sight of him playing snap with an auxiliary fireman. 'It's a dread we have to live with.'

Ellie-May remained silent, thinking of her nephew, Tommy, who was somewhere in North Africa, and Rose Norris's boys, both in France. They were living in frightening times. But you didn't have to be abroad to be in danger. These days, danger came looking for you at home.

'Come on,' she said to Alice. 'Let's get you indoors. You and Arnie are welcome to Penny's room for as long as you need it.'

'You're so kind,' Alice replied, tears forging tracks down her soot-stained cheeks. 'Thank you.'

'No thanks needed,' said Ellie-May briskly. Calling a reluctant Arnie away from his game of snap, Ellie-May led Alice and her son down the street to the shop, where they found Frank in his hat and apron, unfurling the awning in readiness for the day's business.

Alice and Arnie soon became an integral part of the family. Ellie-May had worried at first that Frank might prove difficult, but he enjoyed their company, particularly Arnie's. In the evenings, Frank would set out his old tin soldiers and the two of them, man and boy, would spend a pleasant hour battling for possession of the living-room rug while Ellie-May and Alice watched with amusement.

Samuel Goldstein's budgerigars, Ellie-May learned a day or two later, had finally flown down from the rafters and had been found temporary homes, where they stayed until Samuel went to live with his sister in Norfolk, taking his beloved birds with him.

'I've been thinking,' Alice said to Ellie-May one evening three weeks later as they washed the dishes.

'Oh, yes?' Up to her elbows in soapy water, Ellie-May regarded the younger woman quizzically. Alice was only five years older than Penny, so for Ellie-May, her presence went some way to filling the void left by Penny's absence, and Arnie, bless him, was a breath of fresh air.

'I'm taking a job at the munitions factory,' Alice said. 'I feel I need to do something useful.' She put the plate she had been drying in the cupboard. 'It was impossible while I had the shop to run. I felt I had to keep it going so David would have something to come back to, but now . . .' Her shoulders slumped. 'Well, there's nothing to stop me, is there?'

'If you're sure?' Ellie-May dried her hands on a tea towel. 'I'm happy to watch Arnie for you.'

'Well, that's the thing.' Alice brushed a strand of hair from her face, a nervous gesture Ellie-May had come to recognise. 'I'm going to see about having Arnie evacuated.'

'Oh,' Ellie-May said, disappointment clouding her face.

'I know how fond of him you and Frank are,' Alice said

hastily, 'but I can't, in all good consciousness, keep him here. It isn't safe. We're down in the shelter every night. And now they're dropping bombs during the day! What if they come while he's at school, or if I'm at work and can't get home in time? I can't risk something happening to him, Ellie-May, I just can't.' Alice's voice broke and Ellie-May went to her, holding out her arms.

'Of course, you must do what you feel best. You're right. It isn't safe for him here. He'll be much better off in the country, all that fresh air and good food. Safer, too.'

'Thank you,' Alice whispered. 'I was hoping you'd understand.'

'Of course, I understand, love. I'd do the same if he were mine. I thank God every night that my Penny is well away from here.'

'Frank will miss him,' Alice said as they drew apart. She smiled shakily, blinking back tears. 'He dotes on him. Like a dad to my boy, he is, and Arnie loves him to bits.'

'Frank will understand, love. This isn't the time to be self-ish. He'll be safer in the country and Frank will know that.'

Just like he had, begrudgingly, accepted that Penny was better off down in rural Dorset. At least they could rest easy in the knowledge that Penny was safe. That was one less thing to worry about, thank God.

CHAPTER THIRTY-SIX

'Is it straight?' Daphne queried, peering over her shoulder and craning her neck in order to see her reflection.

'How can I draw a straight seam if you keep moving?' Penny muttered crossly, her face level with the back of Daphne's left knee, upon which she was attempting to draw a seam.

'It's dreadfully uneven,' Daphne snapped with a flounce of her golden curls. 'Wipe it off and start again.'

'Oh,' wailed Anne from across the room. 'I've overdone it with the gravy browning. Look how blotchy my legs are. No one will believe I'm wearing real stockings.'

'I don't know why you lot bother,' Edie said, puckering her lips and applying crimson lipstick. 'We're not fooling anyone for a minute. Men aren't idiots.'

'The magazine I was reading yesterday said it's important not to let standards slip,' Daphne huffed, twisting her leg sideways in order to inspect Penny's second attempt. 'Humph,' she snorted, somewhat ungratefully, thought Penny. 'That will have to do, I suppose.'

Penny got to her feet, smoothing down the skirt of her new blue dress. It was mid-December and they were getting ready for the Christmas dance in the Butt's Mead village hall. They had been working on their new frocks every spare minute they had.

Standing in front of the mirror, Penny admired the result of her handiwork, a pattern she had copied from the news-paper. It had taken her many evenings and brought her to floods of tears more than once, but the finished item was worth all the frustration and hard work. Made from a pair of pale blue curtains she had found in an old trunk, the short-sleeve dress fell just below her knees with a gathered bodice and a waistband that tied at the front in a dainty bow. She had added a frill to the collar and cuffs to achieve the look she had been hoping for.

Edie, her auburn hair shining like burnished copper, looked stunning in an emerald green ensemble, Anne wore a pale pink off-the-shoulder affair and Daphne, having shunned the offer of a new frock from her ever-indulgent father, had deigned to join in the fun and make her own dress too. The result was a rather fabulous creation in red silk that fell to mid-way down her shapely calves.

'You should consider becoming a dress designer when the war's over,' Penny told her now, their sharp words from moments earlier quite forgotten in the anticipation of the evening ahead. 'Your dress is amazing. I can't believe you made it without following a pattern. Incredible.'

They had attended several of the dances held at the village

hall which were regularly attended by the pilots from the nearby airbase. The fact that both Daphne and Edie were spoken for hadn't deterred them from enjoying the attentions of the dashing airmen.

'*I'm dreaming of a white Christmas . . .*' Daphne sang, crouching down to rummage under the bed for her shoes.

They called a cheery goodbye to Jim, who was settled in front of the fire with a whisky, and set off into the clear, moonlit night, linking arms as they made their way down the lane. Their breath billowed in front of their faces and the ground was slippery with frost. They could hear the distant sound of music, drifting through the frosty trees.

Caleb stared at his reflection in the washroom mirror. His was the sort of face that made people turn away in embarrassment and sent children running down the street, screaming for their mothers.

Since he had been sent to join his new squadron at Butt's Mead, apart from flying missions and the occasional unavoidable errand into the nearby towns of Blandford or Sturminster Newton, he barely left the base, preferring to stay in the barracks and read while the rest of his squadron enjoyed all the surrounding villages had to offer.

But tonight, with Christmas barely two weeks away, his mates had insisted he accompany them to the dance.

'We won't take no for an answer, mate,' his flight commander, George Ellis, had told him firmly. 'You're coming with us and that's an order.'

Reluctantly, Caleb had complied, and he'd regretted it the minute he walked into the brightly lit village hall. The steady hum of conversation had all but dried up when he followed the rest of his squadron across the room, and he had wanted the ground to open up and swallow him. Although they quickly tried to hide it, he saw the looks of horrified pity on the faces of the young ladies, and even some of the men, standing around edge of the hall. He had been about to turn tail and run, but had been stayed by a firm grip on his arm.

'Ignore them, Caleb,' Mark Collins whispered harshly. A tall, well-built man, Mark too, had not been blessed in the looks department. 'We're here to enjoy ourselves.' He cleared his throat and said more audibly. 'What can I get you from the bar, mate?'

Caleb asked for a beer, which he carried over to a dark corner and lit a cigarette. He smoked it quickly, wondering how long manners dictated he need stay before he could make his excuses to his mates and head back to the barracks. When the band struck up the first dance and none of the young ladies' hopeful glances swept his way, he had crushed his cigarette butt in his fingers, dropped it into his empty glass and headed for the toilets.

He splashed his damaged face with water and leaned against the washbasin, listening to the music filtering through the thin walls. Taking a deep breath, he opened the door and stepped out into the hall. People were dancing, girls with bright dresses like peacocks being spun about by men in uniform, watched from the sidelines by a handful of local boys, their noses clearly out of joint.

Caleb bought himself another beer, trying not to notice the look of pity that passed fleetingly across the barmaid's pretty face, and turned to watch the dancing. The door opened, letting in a blast of icy air – and then he saw her.

'I told you we'd be late,' Penny said, hanging her coat in the porch. 'You and your blessed seams!' Daphne threw a smile over her shoulder and pushed open the door. Penny followed her friends into the warm hall, buzzing with the hum of comfortable conversation. The ceiling was festooned with paperchains and the air smelled of cinnamon. A band was playing a lively number and couples were dancing. Daphne and Edie were immediately whisked onto the dancefloor, so Penny and Anne wandered over to the bar where they each bought half a pint of lemonade. Penny leaned against the wall watching the dancing, her frozen toes beginning to thaw.

'Did you find who you were looking for?' said a voice at her side.

'I beg your pardon, oh ...' Startled, Penny turned to the man beside her. He had suffered a horrible disfigurement and, just in time, she managed to conceal her pity with a bright smile. She frowned in confusion. There was something about the voice, something familiar ... 'Oh.' Her eyes widened in recognition. 'It's you. Last February at Wyke Hall. It was you.'

'Caleb Johnson.' He gave her a self-depreciating smile. 'I

didn't think you'd know me. I'm a bit of a mess without the bandages.'

Penny smiled. 'You must be glad to be out of that place. So,' she said, noting his uniform. 'You're a pilot?'

'Yes. Stationed just up the hill.'

'We can see the airfield from the farm,' Penny said. 'And in reply to your question, yes, I did. Long story, but I was searching for my father. He lives not far from here, as it turns out. In Boyne Mead.'

Caleb smiled. 'I'm glad. I often wondered. It's Penny, isn't it?'

Penny smiled, the fact he had remembered her name giving her an unexpected jolt of pleasure. She had thought of him often over the months, yet never had she imagined their paths would cross again.

'I'm impressed,' Caleb said.

'Why?'

'I haven't scared you off yet.'

Despite his air of nonchalance, Penny could read the fear in Caleb's eyes – fear of rejection, of humiliation – and her heart went out to him.

Caleb held his breath. Penny would never know the amount of courage he'd had to dredge up just to approach her. Since that day at Wyke Hall there hadn't been a day when he hadn't thought about her, and you could have blown him down with a feather when she walked through the door. He had almost bolted there and then, knowing a girl like her would never give someone like him a second glance, but something had stopped him; the memory of how at ease she had been with him last winter. Of course, his face had been heavily bandaged then. Even he, despite the warnings of the doctor, hadn't imagined the extent of the damage.

There was a smattering of applause as the song ended and launched into a jaunty ragtime number.

'I feel like dancing,' Penny said. 'Shall we?' Startled, Caleb looked at her.

He blinked. 'You want to dance? With me?'

'You do dance, don't you?'

Flustered, Caleb glanced around at the dancers taking to the floor. He felt the heat flood his scarred face and knew from experience that the rough ridges across his cheeks would be turning an angry scarlet. He shook his head, embarrassed, and began to turn away. Penny laid her hand on his arm.

'Please?'

Whether it was the look of genuine warmth he saw reflected in her eyes, or the sensation of her fingers on his arm, Caleb found himself leading Penny onto the dance floor. He took her in his arms and, awkward and self-conscious at first, he led her in the steps, his heart racing. He had always been a good dancer, and soon his natural rhythm overcame his reluctance. Penny matched his steps easily.

As they whirled across the dancefloor, dress spinning, arms and legs twisting in time to the music, Caleb almost forgot about his face. For the first time in months, he was actually enjoying himself. By the time the number came to an end, they were flushed and panting. The band announced that they were taking a break, so with his hand resting gently on the small of her back, Caleb led Penny over to the bar.

Clutching a second glass of warm lemonade, Penny leaned her back against the wall, and surveyed the hall. She spotted Daphne across the room, deep in conversation with a good-looking pilot. Anne and Edie were nowhere to be seen.

Caleb, holding a pint of mulled cider, suggested they step outside for a breath of air. 'I find I get a bit claustrophobic in crowds these days.'

'Of course. I could do with some fresh air myself.' Penny fanned her face with her free hand. 'It is warm in here.'

They fetched their coats from the entryway and stepped out into the crisp, cold night. The moon was high and full, surrounded by a halo of hazy white light. Frost glistened on the ground and nearby hedgerows. The star-studded sky formed a velvet canopy overhead.

'It's a bright night,' Caleb remarked drily. 'Perfect for Hitler's bombers.'

'Are some of your squadron out tonight?' Penny asked, tugging her coat tightly around her.

'Yes,' Caleb answered shortly. He stared into his glass. 'We lost a plane yesterday. Shot down over the Channel.'

'Oh, I'm so sorry.' Penny placed her hand on Caleb's arm. 'You must be devastated.'

'The only way you can cope is to put it behind you and keep going,' he said grimly. As he was wont to do, he stroked his scars absently, stopping short when he noticed Penny

366

watching him. He let his hand drop and glanced away, embarrassed.

'They're nothing to be ashamed of,' Penny said softly.

Caleb let out a harsh, mirthless laugh. 'It's not as though I earned them by any heroic deed though, is it? No, a flipping car crash.' Despite herself, Penny smiled. He was sounding like a sulky child.

'Matron told me your friend was killed in the accident. That must have been tough?'

'It was. When I first saw my face, I wished I'd been killed too.'

'You mustn't think that,' Penny chided him gently.

Caleb gave another harsh laugh. 'You're the only person who hasn't wanted to run away screaming at the sight of me,' he remarked bitterly.

They sat in silence for a while. Other couples had joined them out in the cold night. The tang of cigarette smoke hung on the frosty air. Inside the hall the band, refreshed after their break, began to play.

'You're cold,' Caleb said as Penny shivered. 'Shall we go back in?'

'In a minute,' she said. Her face was pale in the moonlight and Caleb thought he had never met such an attractive woman. He had thought her pretty when he'd first seen her at Wyke Hall, but tonight she looked even lovelier than he remembered.

'So,' he said, lighting a cigarette and inhaling deeply. 'Your father. What's the story there?'

Penny told him how her father Jack had been reported KIA during the Great War and how she had grown up believing him to be dead.

'We've been making up for lost time,' she said, rubbing her hands together to get the circulation going. 'I spend most of my days off with him, though over the summer, we were so busy I seldom got to bed before midnight, and we were up at dawn, I'm ashamed to say I spent most of my free time catching up on sleep.'

Caleb closed his large hand over both of hers. She stiffened briefly, aware of the rough callouses on her skin caused by the months of hard manual labour, but Caleb didn't appear to notice and she relaxed.

'It must have come as quite a shock to your mother.'

'Yes, it was,' Penny replied. 'She didn't speak to my Grandpa for weeks afterwards. It's funny though. Since last spring she hasn't mentioned Jack in her letters at all.'

'Perhaps she realized the past is best left where it belongs, in the past,' Caleb suggested.

Penny shrugged. 'Perhaps. I'll be seeing her at Christmas, anyway. It'll be the first time I've been home since I arrived and I'm really looking forward to it.'

An owl hooted nearby, and there was a flap of wings as it swooped overhead, a fleeting shadow on the moonlit ground. 'What about you?' she asked Caleb. 'Where are you from?'

'I'm afraid my life up until now has been pretty dull,' Caleb said, inhaling deeply on his cigarette. 'I was born and bred in Portsmouth, the second youngest of five: three girls and two boys. My mother died when I was five and Dad found it difficult to cope, so we were all farmed out to various relatives. I was sent to live with an old aunt. She was kind enough, if a bit stuffy and old-fashioned. She died when I was sixteen and I've been on my own ever since. My siblings and I are not close. In my pre-war life I was a shipyard welder.'

'Portsmouth has suffered a lot with the bombings,' Penny remarked.

'My father was bombed out of his house and is living with my oldest sister.'

'Is your brother fighting?'

'He's on HMS *Royal Sovereign* doing convoy escort work the last I heard. My eldest sister, Kitty, is the one who seems to make the most effort in keeping in touch with us all. We all get our news of each other from her.'

'Being an only child, I find it quite strange that you're not close to your family. I'd have loved brothers or sisters. My baby brothers all died in infancy.'

Caleb shrugged. 'Perhaps if we'd spent our formative years together it would have made a difference and we'd have bonded, but I didn't see any of them for almost ten years.'

'That's sad,' Penny said, shivering.

'Come on. Let's go in before you freeze to death.' He hoisted Penny to her feet. 'I enjoyed our chat.' He looked into Penny's eyes, and held his breath. In the semi-darkness his scars weren't so noticeable and he had been able to pretend, just for a short while, that they were a normal couple getting to know one another.

Slowly he bent his head to hers and kissed her gently on the lips. Penny closed her eyes, savouring the sensation of his lips on hers. It was over almost before it had begun, but it left Penny breathless and reeling. She laughed and ran up the steps, Caleb's hand firmly clasped in hers.

In the harsh brightness of the village hall, Caleb was all too quickly reminded of his disfigurement. A young woman brushed passed them, visibly recoiling as she caught sight of Caleb's face.

Anger and shame burned in his gut like a red-hot poker. He was a fool. Penny was being nice. She was that sort of girl, compassionate and kind, she wouldn't want to hurt his feelings. He cursed himself inwardly for being such an idiot. Penny was a lovely-looking girl indeed, she was the loveliest creature he'd ever laid eyes on, but there was no way she would want to be saddled with a freak like him, and nor would he expect her to. He shouldn't have kissed her.

When one of the local boys, a clean-shaven chap in his late teens, shyly approached Penny and invited her to dance, Caleb urged her to go ahead, claiming a headache. Soon afterwards he sought out his friends and made his farewells.

'Why did you scuttle off so early?' Mark asked him when he arrived back at the barracks shortly before their midnight curfew. 'You missed a great night.'

Caleb was lying on his bunk, a battered paperback novel lying face down on his chest, his hands behind his head, staring up at the ceiling and trying to ignore the general banter and laughter surrounding him as the returning men reminisced about their evening.

'I was tired,' he said, using the first excuse that popped into his head.

'That's a shame. That Penny was looking for you. She seemed a bit put out that you'd left without saying goodbye.'

Caleb felt a twinge of guilt. He should have said goodbye properly instead of running out on her like a coward.

'She seemed pretty keen.' Mark stripped off his shirt and trousers and swung his legs onto his bunk. 'She's a real looker.' He winked at his friend. 'I think you're in with a chance there, mate.'

Caleb closed his book and put it on his nightstand. 'She just felt sorry for me,' he muttered under his breath. 'I shan't be seeing her again.' He switched off his lamp and rolled onto his side, leaving Mark to shake his head in despair at his friend's stubbornness.

CHAPTER THIRTY-SEVEN

Late on the afternoon of 23 December, Ellie-May stood on the platform of Eastleigh Station, hunched against the cold, her shabby coat and headscarf offering little protection from the biting wind whistling down the track. She had come early, so as to be sure not to miss the train, only to discover it was running nearly an hour late. It was almost dark by the time it finally rumbled into the station.

'Oh, Pen-Pen!' she cried, seeing Penny step down from the second-class carriage, swept along by a tide of returning servicemen and women. She pushed her way through the crowd towards her.

'Mum!' Penny fell into Ellie-May's open arms.

'Oh, Pen-Pen, I've missed you so much,' Ellie-May said, letting the tears fall unashamedly down her face.

'I've missed you too, Mum. How have you been?'

'It's tough but we're managing.' Ellie-May smiled, holding Penny at arm's length. 'You look well. The country air obviously agrees with you.'

'Is that your tactful way of saying I've put on weight?' Penny laughed, tucking her arm through her mother's as they headed for the exit.

'You've filled out,' Ellie-May affirmed. 'You were always such a skinny little kid, like your ...' She bit off the end of the sentence, shooting Penny a sideways glance, but Penny was glancing back over her shoulder and appeared not to have noticed.

'You look tired, Mum,' Penny said as they stepped into the bleak December afternoon. 'You're working too hard.'

'It's not the work, so much,' Ellie-May replied as they joined the queue for the bus. 'It's these blessed air raids. I haven't had a decent night's sleep in weeks. I was half tempted to tell you not to come. It's so dangerous here now.'

'You know I'd have come anyway,' Penny replied with a grin. Her smiled faded. 'I saw a lot of the devastation from the train,' she said soberly. 'It's heart breaking what Hitler's doing to our city.'

'Not to mention all the poor people who've been killed.' Ellie-May shook her head sadly.

'Frank makes his bed in the Anderson shelter every night, but I can't abide being shut in that thing unless I have to. Me and Alice, we prefer to sleep in our own beds until the siren goes off.'

'How is Alice?' Penny asked as they boarded the bus and found seats near the front. She glanced out of the window at the dark shopfronts. It was beginning to snow, soft flurries of white tossed about by a bitter wind.

'She's doing all right. As I told you in my last letter, she's away for Christmas. The family who've taken Arnie in invited her to spend Christmas with them. Somewhere in Devon, they are. She left this morning and she's staying until the new year.'

Penny gazed out of the window. There were very few cars on the road, dimmed headlamps picking out the falling snow. The light from numerous torches bounced along the pavement. Though the blackout had been in force for well over a year, Penny still found it strange and eerie to see the city so dark and quiet.

They got off the bus in Northam Street and walked the short distance arm in arm past the empty shells that had once housed Goldstein's Tailors and Hanson's Drapers, huddled against the cold wind and swirling snow. Not a chink of light was visible from the windows. It was quite dark now. The moon was hidden behind dense cloud. A thin blanket of snow covered the street, drifting against the walls and it was a relief to climb the stairs to the warm flat above the shop.

'At least this weather might give us a reprieve from old Hitler,' Ellie-May said drily, inserting her key in the lock. She ushered Penny inside and followed her up the stairs.

'Penny,' Frank said as she stepped into the cosy parlour. He stirred in his chair, but didn't get up. 'You're looking well.'

'Thanks ... Frank.' Penny hesitated in the doorway, unsure as to whether to approach him for a kiss. She caught her mother's eye.

Ellie-May gave a slight shake of her head, saying cautiously,

'She looks very well indeed. The country air certainly agrees with her, don't you think, Frank, love?'

Frank grunted noncommittedly. He still hadn't completely forgiven Penny for, as he put it, running off to Dorset and leaving him in the lurch. Ellie-May motioned for Penny to follow her into the kitchen.

'Just to warn you,' she whispered once they were safely out of earshot. 'I haven't said anything to Frank about Jack, and I'm not going to.'

'But what about my letters?'

'He never reads them. He prefers me to just give him the summarized version.' Ellie-May placed her hands on her hips. 'Good grief, Penny, can you imagine what he'd be like if he knew? I feel as though I'm constantly walking on eggshells around him as it is.'

While Ellie-May made the tea, Penny unpacked her bag, laying a pat of butter and a dozen eggs and a ham on the kitchen table.

'Butter!' her mother exclaimed.

'Churned by my own fair hand,' Penny said, grinning at her mother's delight.

'I'll boil the ham tomorrow,' Ellie-May said, eyeing the joint of meat with relish. 'We can take it with us to your Uncle Arthur's tomorrow evening.' She looked up at Penny, who was taking the cups down from the cupboard. 'Did I mention we were spending Christmas at Arthur and Victoria's this year?'

'You did,' Penny confirmed. 'Why aren't we going to Grandpa's as usual?' Her brow furrowed in concern. 'He's all right, isn't he?' Her eyes narrowed. 'Things are all right between the two of you?'

'Grandpa's fine, love,' Ellie-May assured her, swilling the ceramic teapot with hot water to take the chill off it. 'And yes, like I told you, me and Grandpa sorted out our differences a good while ago. We just thought that this year we'd do things differently. Let's face it, there's no room to swing a cat at Grandpa's. And with the children growing up, they need space to stretch their legs. There's much more room at Uncle Arthur's, and the children will much prefer to stay at home and play with their new toys, such as they are.'

'I got them some comics,' Penny said, pulling out a chair and sitting down.

'Well, I hope they like the gloves and hats I've knitted them,' Ellie-May said, joining her daughter at the table and pouring the tea. 'Toys are so hard to come by now, and so terribly expensive.'

'The fact that we'll all be together is a blessing enough,' Penny assured her. 'Have you heard from the twins, or Nora?'

'Nora sent a Christmas card. She's doing well enough. She worries about us all, of course. Bea and Jess are spending Christmas together at Bea's. Jess was hoping our Tommy would get some leave over Christmas, but he hasn't been able to manage it, so that's that. Trevor's going along all right, no change but, of course, we don't expect any.' Ellie-May picked up her cup and blew the surface of her tea.

'I'm really glad Bea met Duncan,' Penny said. 'He's a good man.'

'They've been together for years now,' said Ellie-May. 'They seem happy enough.'

'Well, good for them, I say. Life's too short not to grab your chance of happiness where you find it.'

'Isn't that the truth,' Ellie-May said, setting her cup down with a sigh.

Later that night as Penny lay in her old bed, her mind drifted, as it so often had over the past couple of weeks, to thoughts of Caleb. Her disappointment at discovering he had left the dance without a word had been acute. They had been getting on so well, or so she'd thought, and she had been looking forward to them chatting more. She had felt a connection with him, and she had been convinced he had felt the same. His scars didn't bother her. Why should they? His disfigurement didn't define him. He was a warm, loving human being, which had made his desertion all the more hurtful.

She sighed and rolled onto her side. She had clearly misread the situation and imagined an attraction on his side where, clearly, there had been none. Just as well, really, she consoled herself philosophically. Caleb's life was on the line daily. It wouldn't be a good idea to get involved. And yet . . .

She sighed again, plumping up her feather pillow, and closed her eyes, determined to put Caleb Johnson out of her mind for the entire Christmas period.

Penny didn't get a chance to broach the subject of Jack again until late on Christmas Day. Frank had gone to park the car, leaving mother and daughter alone in the flat. Ellie-May stoked the fire while Penny made them both a warming mug of cocoa. She curled up on the sofa, hands wrapped around her steaming mug. 'Silent Night' was playing on the wireless.

'Mum,' she said hesitantly. Ellie-May looked up from her mending basket. 'You never ask after Jack in your letters anymore and when I mention something about him in mine, you seem to ignore it. Why?'

Ellie-May regarded Penny in silence for a moment. How could she explain to her that just thinking about Jack with Jennette was like cutting her heart with a knife. Oh, Penny was very careful never to mention Jennette in her letters and she was grateful for that but the only way she could deal with the heartache was to put him out of her mind completely which, as she had discovered over the past eight months, was much easier said than done.

'I'm a married woman, Penny, and Jack has his own life to lead. What is the point of pretending otherwise?'

'But . . .' Penny began but Ellie-May cut her off with a wave of her hand.

'Please, Penny, let me live my life as I see fit. Now.' She picked up the *Radio Times*. 'That play we fancy starts in a couple of minutes. Hopefully Frank will call in at the club on his way home and we can listen to it in peace.' She smiled brightly, and tried not to think about Jack and how he might be spending his Christmas Day evening.

*

Over forty miles away, Jack was pacing nervously in front of the fireplace. He poured himself a whisky, Dutch courage, and downed it quickly, chuckling softly. The way his heart was knocking against his ribcage, he felt like an anxious schoolboy about to embark on his first date.

It had been a good Christmas, all things considered. Deon had turned up on his doorstep late Christmas Eve, just as Jack had been about to drive Jennette home and they'd stayed up talking until the early hours of Christmas Day.

Now, listening to Ida and Jennette chatting companionably in the kitchen as they cleared away the detritus of their Christmas Day, Jack decided it had been one of the nicest Christmases he'd had for a long time. His only disappointment being that Penny hadn't been there. But he understood. She needed to be with her mother. He hoped her Christmas had been a pleasant one. He reached into his pocket, his fingers closing over the small, square box.

He had thought long and hard about what he was about to do. The advent of Penny in his life had thrown the way he contemplated his future into a whole new perspective. Whatever the years ahead held, she would always be a part of his life and, as such, he would always consider her when making plans.

But Ellie-May . . . He wandered over to the window, gazing out over the snow-covered hills, his mood turning melancholy. If he had even the slightest hope that he stood a chance with her, he wouldn't be taking this step but Ellie-May had made her feelings quite clear last spring. He had no place in her life.

He was forty-five years old. He couldn't afford to put his life on hold any longer for a dream that would never be realized.

A burst of laughter erupted from the kitchen, breaking into his despondency. Jennette appeared in the doorway, clutching a damp tea towel.

'Everything all right?' she asked, catching a glimpse of his ravaged expression as he turned from the window before he managed to rearranged his features into a smile.

'Just wool gathering.'

'I was just checking to see if there was anything else for washing,' she said jovially. Jack looked at her fondly, appreciating the way the soft lamplight caught the golden highlights of her hair. The steamy kitchen had lent a pretty flush to her cheeks.

'Jennette.' Jack cleared his throat, feeling ludicrously nervous.

'Yes?' Jennette leaned against the doorframe, gazing at him expectantly.

'Forget about the dishes for a minute.' He fixed his gaze on her face and put down his glass, quickly crossing the small space between them.

'I know I'm a bit old for all this,' he said, with a self-depreciating laugh. Clinging onto his stick for support, he got clumsily down on one knee as Jennette gasped, tears filling her eyes. One hand clutched at her throat.

'I'm an old cripple and a bit worse for wear,' Jack continued, the effort of bending his knee showing in his face. He grunted, his fingers tightening around his stick, knuckles whitening with the effort, and pulled the dainty black velvet box from his jacket pocket. 'Jennette du Randt, would you do me the honour of becoming my wife?'

Jennette flung her arms around his neck and burst into tears. 'Jack,' she cried, tears streaming down her cheeks. 'I can't believe it.'

'Well?' Jack said, his voice muffled by Jennette's bosom. 'Will you have me?'

'Yes. Oh, yes, Jack. I want to marry you more than anything.'

She watched him slip the ring onto her finger. It was a perfect fit. She turned her hand this way and that, admiring the way the modest diamond glittered and sparkled in the lamplight.

Jack struggled to his feet and took her in his arms. They were in the midst of a long and passionate kiss when Ida bustled in with the tea tray.

'Oh, don't mind me,' she muttered, hastily averting her eyes. Jack and Jennette broke apart, laughing through their tears.

'Ida,' Jennette trilled. 'Jack and I are getting married.'

'Well,' Ida cried in delight as she hugged first Jennette, then Jack. 'It's about time! I'm that pleased for you both,' she said, pink-faced with joy. 'This calls for a celebration.' She bustled from the room to return a second later with a bottle of Jack's homemade elderflower wine. 'Forget the tea. I'll get the glasses.' She hugged Jack again. 'Oh, lad,' she said,

'I'm that chuffed. You both deserve every happiness. Oh,' she continued to chatter on as she busied herself fetching glasses and pouring healthy tots of the pungent elderflower wine. 'You've made my Christmas, you have. You've made my Christmas.'

Deon was equally chuffed when he came in with Star a short while later. He grabbed Jack and slapped him heartily on the back. 'About time,' he beamed jovially, echoing Ida's sentiments. 'Congratulations Jack. Welcome to the family, my friend.'

CHAPTER THIRTY-EIGHT

1941

The new year started off wet and cold. Penny had returned to Willowbrook Farm the day after Boxing Day and Ellie-May was feeling her loss keenly so she was overjoyed to find a letter on the doormat when she opened the shop a week later.

She unsealed the envelope and unfolded the sheet of writing paper, smiling fondly at Penny's untidy scrawl. Leaning against the counter, she began to read.

> *Dear Mum,*
> *I know this will come as a bit of a shock to you, but Jack and Jennette got engaged on Christmas Day . . .*

Ellie-May frowned and reread Penny's opening sentence. Jack got engaged on Christmas Day? But, hadn't Jennette introduced herself as Jack's fiancée last spring? Her frown deepened. Had she been lying about being engaged to Jack?

The bell jangled and the door opened to admit a middle-aged woman in a damp fox fur. Ellie-May shoved Penny's letter in her pocket and plastered on a smile.

'Good morning, Mrs Bagshaw.'

'It's a dreadful day,' the woman grumbled, shivering as a sudden squall shook the window in their frames. She handed over her ration book. 'Did you have a good Christmas?'

'Thank you, yes,' Ellie-May replied. 'Our daughter was home for a few days.'

'How lovely for you. We spent the day with my brother over in Portsmouth.' Her eyes grew wide, and she leaned closer, lowering her voice and shaking her head sadly. 'It's heartrending to see the devastation the bombing has done to that city.'

'We haven't come off too lightly either, have we?' Frank remarked, emerging from the back, and rubbing his hands together in an effort to get the circulation going.

'You're not wrong there,' Mrs Bagshaw said, handing Ellie-May her shopping list. 'When is it going to end? That's what I'd like to know.'

'Well, if the Americans would stop all this neutrality nonsense and give us a hand,' Frank said, 'we'd soon give old Hitler what for.'

'You're probably right,' Mrs Bagshaw responded drily, rummaging in her handbag for her ration book. 'My husband says they're keeping well out of it and, personally, I can't say I blame them.'

As the day wore on the queue of customers seemed

never-ending. *If another customer asks me if I had a good Christmas, I'll scream,* Ellie-May fumed, accepting yet another ration book and tearing out the coupon. Her heart was a leaden lump, and all she wanted to do was curl up under the eiderdown and go to sleep. If only she hadn't let Jennette fob her off like she had. She should have insisted on waiting to see Jack instead of scurrying home with her tail between her legs.

Aware of Frank's scrutiny, she made something of an effort to pull herself together, but try as she might, she couldn't put thoughts of Jack out of her mind. She should have asked Penny if what Jennette had said was true but she'd behaved like a stubborn old mule, refusing to speak about him for fear of letting her emotions get the better of her. Well, she thought bitterly, he was well and truly lost to her now.

Somehow, she got through the day. She was bone-weary by the time she dragged herself upstairs later that evening.

'Are you all right, Ellie?' Alice was in the kitchen scrubbing potatoes. 'You've been out of sorts all day. You're not sickening for something, are you?'

Ellie-May shook her head and opened the pack of bacon she had brought up from the shop. 'I'm all right,' she replied, stifling a yawn. 'Just tired.' She had barely slept in days as seldom a night went by that the air raid sirens didn't get them out of bed at least twice.

'You go and sit down,' Alice told her firmly, dropping the potatoes into a pan. 'I'll bring you a nice cup of tea.' From far away came the strident clatter of anti-aircraft guns, followed a split second later by the air raid siren. 'Oh, Lordy, here we go again,' Alice said, wiping her hands on her apron. They gathered up hats and coats, and as they made their way down the stairs, Ellie-May's abiding thought was that if a bomb was to land on her right now, the oblivion would be truly welcome.

CHAPTER THIRTY-NINE

It was bitterly cold as Penny drove the small Ford van towards the village, milk churns clanging in the back. Snow was piled in high drifts on either side of the narrow lane. Snowflakes danced in front of the windscreen and the ancient wipers were having difficulty keeping the glass clear.

Her breath clouding in front of her face, she drove past the turn-off to Boyne Mead. She had only seen Jack briefly since her return from Southampton, ten days earlier. Lambing season had started with the new year and, always a busy time, it had been particularly so due to the continued bouts of bad weather.

Penny still wasn't sure how she felt about Jack's engagement. She liked Jennette, and she wanted Jack to be happy, of course, but . . . She wondered how her mother had reacted to the news. She worried about her mother, and not just because of the bombings. That Ellie-May was unhappy was plain, married to a man she could never love, and who grew more controlling with every passing year. At least her mother had Alice for company, and that gave Penny a modicum of comfort.

The village of Butt's Mead came into view, a dark smudge on the stark landscape and she eased off the accelerator, the van's wheels skidding on the snow-covered cobbles as she pulled up outside the post office. She jumped down into the snow, clapping her gloved hands together in an effort to get the blood flowing. It was bitterly cold and her breath billowed in front of her as she ducked under the low lintel and stepped into the warm post office. She joined the short queue at the counter, her heart skipping a beat when she realized she recognised the man in front of her.

'Caleb?'

With obvious reluctance, Caleb turned towards her. He had seen her arrive through the window and, in spite of his resolve, his spirits had lifted at the sight of her.

'Penny. Hi, how are you?'

'I'm well, thank you. Hello, Mark.' Penny noticed Caleb's friend further up the queue. Mark lifted his hand in brief acknowledgement as his turn came to be served.

'I had hoped to see you at the New Year's Eve dance,' Penny said, hoping her voice didn't betray just how disappointed she'd felt when Mark told her Caleb had elected to stay at the base instead of attending the party.

'Dances aren't really my thing,' Caleb replied. He clenched his fists, forcing himself to keep his tone neutral. Let her think he didn't care. It was for the best.

Deflated by the coldness of his manner, Penny felt herself

blush. 'Did you have a good Christmas?' she asked brightly, desperate to keep the contact going. She had missed him.

Caleb shrugged. 'It was all right.' She waited for him to ask after hers but, when no more conversation seemed to be forthcoming, she blurted out, 'Are you going to the Valentine Night dance?'

Again, Caleb shrugged. 'Like I said, dancing's not my thing.'

'Right.' Penny felt her cheeks flame with embarrassment. 'So you did. Sorry.' She cleared her throat, feigning nonchalance. 'Well, it was good to see you.' It took all her strength to keep her voice steady. To avoid making eye contact with anyone, she glanced up at the clock above the counter. 'Actually,' she said, a slight tremor to her voice. 'I'd better get going. I'm on the milk run and I don't want to miss the train. I'll call for the post on the way back.'

Burning with humiliation, she turned on her heel and yanked open the door, grateful for the cold air on her burning cheeks.

Well! She sank into the driver's seat, angrily blinking back the tears that threatened to spill down her frosty cheeks. 'Stupid, stupid girl!' she cursed herself crossly as she turned the key in the ignition. She had clearly been reading something into her friendship with Caleb that simply hadn't been there. At the Christmas dance he had seemed so sweet and kind that, even though they barely knew each other, she had felt a connection. Obviously, Caleb hadn't felt the same.

It took her shaking fingers three attempts to get the engine to splutter into life. She ground the gears and pulled off, sending a shower of snow into the air. She didn't see Caleb standing in the doorway of the post office, staring after her, his expression one of bleak despair.

'What the heck was wrong with you in there?' Mark demanded as he steered the Jeep up the steep track towards the air base. 'You were downright rude. That's not like you.'

Caleb stared out of the window, his eyes clouded with misery. He rubbed his face with a gloved hand, his head lolling sideways as the Jeep bounced over a particularly deep pothole encrusted with ice, and stared dismally out of the dirty window.

'Mate?' Mark cast him a sideways glance. 'Did you hear me? I said, what the . . .'

'I heard you,' Caleb grunted morosely.

'So? What's your problem? You choose to stay in on New Year's Eve, you're rude to one of the most attractive girls I've seen in a long time, who, I might add, is very obviously interested in you. She seemed really disappointed when you didn't show up.'

'I'm not looking for a relationship,' Caleb replied, his excuse sounding pathetic even to his own ears.

'So? We're at war, mate. Who knows if either of us will be around tomorrow, never mind next week. You've got to live for the moment. Grab every chance of happiness you can. I'm not saying marry the girl, just have some fun while you're here.'

Caleb shook his head. 'That's just it, Mark. I don't want to just have fun. I really like her.'

Mark turned his incredulous gaze on his friend. 'Then what the hell is your problem?'

'What woman would want to be saddled with this?' Caleb slapped his scarred cheek.

'Jeez, Caleb, will you get over yourself? Penny certainly doesn't seem to mind. Anyway, I'm no oil painting myself.'

'You don't look like Frankenstein's monster,' Caleb said drily.

'And neither do you, you idiot. You've got a few scars. Big deal! By the time this damn war's over there are going to be hundreds of blokes scarred and maimed. Your scars do not define you. Penny is obviously prepared to see beyond them to the bloke you are underneath. If you're keen on her, go for it, mate. Time may not be on our side.'

CHAPTER FORTY

The middle of February brought a welcome thaw and the lambing season was in full swing. It was Penny's first day off since the new year and she was standing beside Jack's crouched form, hands shoved deep in the pockets of her winter coat, collar turned up against the chill wind, watching him fix the fence on the chicken coop.

Jack took a nail from between his lips.

'Have you heard from El lately?' he asked, hammering the nail into the wood.

'I got a letter last week,' Penny replied, kicking at a clod of earth with her boot. The wind scoured her cheeks, bringing tears to her eyes.

'Is she well?' Jack glanced up, squinting into the sunlight.

'She seems to be.' In fact, Penny had been a little confused by her mother's letter. She seemed to be under the impression Jack and Jennette had been engaged for some time. Penny gave a slight shrug of her shoulders. She had no idea where her mother had got that idea from.

'I saw her once, you know?'

'What?'

Jack got slowly to his feet, leaning on his stick for support. 'Last spring. A few weeks after you first came to see me. I travelled to Southampton, stood across the street from Frank's shop.' He rubbed his brow, his gaze somewhere in the middle distance. 'They came out, the two of them, arm in arm. She looked ... happy.'

'*Happy?*' Penny said, incredulous. 'Jack, Frank makes Mum's life a flipping misery.'

Jack winced, each of Penny's words like a painful dart in his chest.

'She looked happy enough to me. It was the same day I received her letter, remember? I told you about it. She has no interest in rekindling our friendship.'

'Is that why you asked Jennette to marry you? Because you believe Mum and Frank are happy? Is it a rebound thing?'

Jack gave a harsh laugh. 'Jennette and I have known each other for two years, Penny. It's hardly a rebound, is it? I'm not getting any younger and, well, we live in uncertain times. Who knows what tomorrow will bring?'

He gave an exasperated sigh. 'Penny, I think about your mum every day. I don't think I will ever stop loving her, but I've got to let her go. She doesn't want to be in touch. We lost our chance a long time ago, Penny. Now I have to take what bit of happiness I can. Jennette makes me happy.' He shrugged. 'What more can I say?'

Penny sighed. The wind tugged at her untidy ponytail, making her eyes water. 'So,' she said in a conciliatory tone. 'When's the big day?'

'First Saturday in March,' Jack said. 'Blandford Registry Office. I'd like you to be there.'

'I wouldn't miss it.'

'Thanks, it would mean a lot.'

He gazed wistfully over the low drystone wall at the lambs gambolling in the field beyond, unable yet to find the words to tell Penny that, once the war was over, Jennette was keen for them to return to South Africa with Deon to run the family vineyard. He wasn't entirely sure he wanted to shoulder such responsibility, or that he was up to the challenge. What did he know about the cultivation of grapes? Still, the war seemed likely to drag on for years yet. There was no point worrying over the future. Not until he was sure he actually had one.

Penny caught the whiff of the rabbit casserole Jennette had simmering in the oven, Ida having taken a very rare day off to visit a sick relative in Fontmell Magna, and was thinking about her mother, and how she would feel about Jack's impending marriage, when the drone of approaching aircraft drew her gaze skywards. Her breath caught in the back of her throat and she clutched Jack's arm.

They both stared up in horror. The plane on the edge of the formation was clearly in desperate trouble. Flames leapt from one of its wings and it appeared to be struggling to maintain altitude. It was low enough for Penny to make out the faces of its stricken crew.

'Oh, God,' Jack whispered. 'I hope they make it to the base. Go on, lads,' he urged them, shielding his gaze against the sun's glare. It glinted off the wing of the other planes as they skimmed the surrounding trees.

'Go on,' Penny willed them on, her hands clenched. 'You can make it.'

Suddenly, the stricken plane seemed to dip. It lurched sideways, and then went into a dive, disappearing from view behind a bank of trees. Seconds later there was an almighty explosion. Plumes of black smoke billowed from behind the copse.

'What on earth was that?' Jennette appeared in the doorway, wiping her hands on her apron. Her gaze was instantly drawn to the billowing smoke and she groaned. 'Oh, no!'

Penny had already vaulted the fence and taken off, running across the paddock, Star close at heel, barking her alarm. Jack hobbled after them, the uneven ground impeding his progress and causing him to lean heavily on his stick.

Penny's eyes were streaming, the acrid smell of burning aviation fuel filling her nostrils and catching in her throat. She coughed and stumbled to a halt, her mouth falling agape at the carnage before her eyes. Star barked in agitation, rubbing her face on the grass as the fumes aggravated her senses.

She rubbed her eyes. The plane had broken in two. Squinting through the smoke, Penny could make out the bodies of several airmen strewn across the grass. Flames licked the cockpit, wherein was slumped the charred remains of the pilot and co-pilot. Bile rose in her throat and she vomited into the long grass. The sickly stench of burning flesh and rubber hung heavily in the air, the thick cloud of black smoke rising up like a pall over the crash site.

She sank to her knees beside the nearest casualty, a boyish youth with short-cropped fair hair, his sightless blue eyes staring heavenward. Sobbing quietly, Penny crawled from one lifeless young man to another.

Star barked as Jack rounded the trees and ran over to him, her ears flat. He put a reassuring hand on her head, stopping short at the sight of Penny hunched over a dead airman, tears rolling down her soot-blackened cheeks. Breathing heavily, and ignoring the throbbing ache in his damaged leg, he moved as swiftly as he could towards her.

'They're all dead,' she wailed, her expression stricken. Jack breathed in, his nostrils flaring, the stench of charred human flesh making him gag. Ash and soot swirled around the burning plane. The heat from the flames was almost unbearable.

'There's nothing you can do for them now,' he said softly, leaning over to help her up. Clinging to his hand, she allowed him to hoist her to her feet. She felt sick, and useless, her heart breaking for the eight young men who had lost their lives.

She turned at the sound of approaching engines. A convoy of military Jeeps was bouncing across the fields towards them. Within minutes the crash site was swarming with

military personnel, medics, MPs – and Flight Lieutenant
Caleb Johnson.

Grim-faced, he swung himself out of the Jeep and stopped
dead, staring at Penny across the devastation.

'They're not our boys,' one of the MPs told Jack, scratching his chin. 'Probably from the base over near Sturminster
Newton. It looks they took a hit in the fuselage.'

'The pilot was having a hell of a job maintaining altitude,'
Jack said.

'We've been in touch with our colleagues,' the MP said
gruffly. 'They'll be mounting a recovery operation ASAP.
Flight Lieutenants Johnson and Timmins will remain here
until they arrive.'

'Sir,' Caleb acknowledged the order. He couldn't take his
eyes off Penny. She stared back at him with reddened, tear-
filled eyes, shoulders slumped, her face a picture of abject
despair. Her hair was a tangled mess and her cheeks tear-
stained and streaked with soot. She was beautiful.

Not an hour had gone by since that day in the village post
office nigh on four weeks ago, in which he didn't cringe with
self-loathing at the obnoxious way he'd treated her

The look of devastation on Penny's face caused him actual
physical pain and he was filled with an overwhelming urge
to protect this woman for the rest of his life.

'They're all dead,' she muttered dully. Her eyes glazed over
and she began to shake violently.

'She's going into shock,' Jack shouted in panic, limping
towards Penny as quickly as he could.

'Keep her warm and get some brandy down her throat,' the medic advised, barely glancing at them.

Shrugging off his jacket, Caleb draped it across Penny's shaking shoulders. Her face was chalk-white and her eyes glassy as she stared unseeing into the distance.

'Penny, love, come, let's get you home.' Jack put his arm around Penny's shoulders, nodding at Caleb. 'Thank you, Flight Lieutenant.'

'Caleb . . .' Penny croaked, her voice hoarse from smoke inhalation.

Jack's brow rose in surprise. 'You know my daughter?'

'Yes, sir,' Caleb answered politely, painfully aware of his scarred face. 'We met for the first time at Wyke Hall.'

'Ah, I was a patient there myself, many years ago.' Jack thrust out his hand. 'Jack Pickup.' He nodded, looking pointedly at Caleb's scars, his own scar tightening as if in sympathy.

'I'm afraid my scars were not heroically gained, sir,' Caleb said. 'A car accident.'

'Nevertheless . . .' Jack's words trailed away as he caught sight of Penny's ashen face. Fearing she might faint, he gripped her arm tightly. 'I'm sorry. I must get Penny back to the house. She's had a nasty shock. Thank you for the loan of the jacket. I'll see it's returned to you.'

'Of course, sir. Not a problem.' Caleb stepped back as Jack made to lead Penny away. Some focus had come back into her eyes and they met his briefly before she turned away.

Caleb stood rooted to the spot, his chest heaving. If he didn't apologise now he would lose her for ever.

'Penny?'

Penny faltered and turned her head, ever so slightly.

'I'm sorry,' he said, the apology sounding lame even to his own ears.

Penny nodded. Slipping her hand through Jack's arm, she turned towards Wayside, carefully adjusting her steps to align with her father's awkward gait.

They reached the garden gate just as Ida was returning home. She and Jennette fussed over Penny like mother hens, insisting Jack call the doctor, and bringing her cups of steaming tea laced with brandy and sweetened with what Penny feared was Jack's entire sugar ration.

The doctor diagnosed mild shock and assured her she would be as right as rain by morning. Ida, still fretting, insisted she spend the night and a message was dispatched to Willowbrook Farm.

Penny climbed wearily into Jack's spare bed wearing one of Ida's voluminous nighties. Dark beams ran across the ceiling, and the window looked out over the rolling Dorset countryside. There came a gentle tap on the open bedroom door and Jack peered in, his brow furrowed in concern.

'How are you?' he asked softly, coming into the room, the floorboards creaking beneath his feet as he lurched towards the bed. Penny sat up against the crisp white pillows, her expression sober.

'I keep seeing those poor boys.'

'Me too,' Jack sighed. They were silent for a while, each lost in their own thoughts.

'That Caleb seems a nice man,' Jack said at length.

'He is,' Penny agreed. 'But he's made it very plain he isn't interested in me.' She looked down at her hands. They were callused and chapped from hard work and the elements.

Jack threw back his head and laughed. 'Oh, Penny, that young man is besotted with you.'

'*Really*?' Penny lifted her chin, cherishing the flicker of hope Jack's words gave her. 'You think so?'

'I don't think so, I know so. He couldn't keep his eyes off you. That fella is smitten.'

'But he was so rude to me, and even today he was very stand-offish, didn't you think?'

'It's probably his way of coping,' Jack said. 'It isn't easy, living with such a disfigurement.' He rubbed his own scar with his fingertip. 'He's obviously got a complex about his face so he finds it difficult to believe anyone can see past it, and love him, scars and all.'

'He's so wrong,' Penny whispered.

'Well, my love, I think you'll have to make the first move.' He placed his hand over hers. 'And don't wait too long. A life filled with regrets is no life at all.' His eyes clouded for a moment before he shook himself. 'Now,' his said, his voice taking on a more cheerful note. 'Try and get some sleep. Everything will seem clearer in the morning.'

He kissed Penny's cheek and got up to pull the blackout curtains, plunging the room into darkness, the only light being the slant of daylight coming in from the window on the landing. 'Sleep well.'

CHAPTER FORTY-ONE

After yet another restless night, Penny woke with a renewed sense of purpose. Her sleep had once again been haunted by dreams in which Caleb was one of the dead airmen from a week earlier, his sightless eyes staring up at her face, his scarred face a rictus of horror and terror, and worst of all, regret. She had to let him know how she felt about him, even at the risk of embarrassing herself. Whether he felt the same way or not, she knew without a shadow of a doubt that she couldn't let him fly off on another mission without having made her feelings clear. If, after that, he was still not interested, well, she would just have to learn to live with the rejection.

Breakfast was the usual hurried affair, and by half past six Penny and Daphne were loading the churns onto the van.

'Do you usually apply lipstick before you drive the milk to the station?' Daphne quipped drily as Penny swung herself up into the driving seat. 'You haven't got a crush on the stationmaster, have you? He must be seventy if he's a day.'

With a shake of her head, Penny grinned down at her

friend. 'I thought I'd come back past the airfield,' she said, feigning nonchalance, even though her heart was thumping with nerves. 'It's a pleasant drive on such a clear day.'

'Oh, yes?' Daphne's eyes narrowed. 'And would you be hoping to bump into a certain young flight lieutenant?'

'Oh, Daph,' Penny sighed. 'I have to tell him how I feel. Look what's just happened. If anything were to happen to him, and I never got the chance . . .'

Daphne's blue eyes clouded. 'Do what you need to do, Penny,' she whispered, her lower lip trembling. 'Before it's too late.'

Penny reached down and squeezed her friend's arm. Her Tony was stationed in France and it had been some weeks since she had heard from him.

'Go on,' Daphne urged Penny softly. Her constant worry over Tony was evident in her features. Her pretty face was marred by anxiety, and endless sleepless nights had left her looking drained with dark shadows beneath her eyes. 'I'll cover for you.'

'Thanks, Daph,' Penny said, her heart aching for her friend.

She coaxed the van to life and bounced out of the yard, chickens squawking and scattering before her. She drove along dark, muddy lanes. Her gaze was fixed firmly on the dimly lit road ahead but her mind was somewhere else entirely.

'Nice day for flying,' Mark said conversationally to Caleb. He removed his air force-blue cap to run a large hand through his short-cropped hair. 'I doubt I could ever tire of this view. It's like being at the top of the world.'

'It is the highest airfield in England,' Caleb reminded him, pausing in his inspection of his aircraft to gaze out over the rolling hills. In the distance the market town of Shaftesbury shimmered in the pale morning mist, the church towers of St Peter's and Trinity just visible through the haze.

He rubbed his face with a gloved hand. The recent plane crash had sobered them all. While they were all realistic enough to accept that they were none of them invincible, such an incident was always a forceful reminder of just how precarious the life of a fighter pilot was, and how easily a flying mission could end in tragedy. Caleb felt sorry for the families of the poor men. They would have received the news by now. Eight more families destroyed. He shook his head. It didn't bear thinking about. At least if anything happened to him, there wouldn't be many who would mourn. He couldn't imagine his brothers and sisters losing too much sleep over his demise. Circumstance had made them more strangers than family. His elder sister, Kitty, might shed a tear, he supposed, but she'd likely be the only one. He thought of Penny, wondering how she was doing as he crouched down to fasten his shoelace.

The truth was, he had fallen for Penny the moment he saw her in the library at Wyke Hall. Never imagining that he'd ever see her again, he'd allowed her into his dreams, even daring to imagine what life might be like with a woman like Penny. Of course, he hadn't known the severity of his scarring then. Even some of the older, more experienced nurses had struggled to conceal their shock the first time they saw him without the bandages. Only Matron had been brisk and cheerful, though she had refused his demands for a mirror. He'd waited until her back was turned before grimly making his way to the bathroom. At first his confused brain had refused to accept what his eyes were seeing. He had gripped the edge of the porcelain sink so hard his knuckle had turned white, unable to comprehend that the monster reflected in the mirror was none other than himself.

Matron had found him twenty minutes later, slumped on the cold tiles, his shoulders heaving, tears streaming down his ravaged cheeks, sobbing and blubbering like a baby. For the next few minutes she had just held him, letting his angry tears soak into her blouse. That had been the last time he'd cried, but there had been many times, too many to count, when he'd been flying over the Channel, that he had contemplated plunging his aircraft into the cold, grey water. It was only the lives of his crewmates that kept him from doing just that.

How could he expect any woman to love him, looking as he did? Especially one as lovely as Penny. She could have her pick of men. He shook his head again, desperate to expel her image from his tortured mind.

'You still playing stubborn as far as that Penny girl is concerned, are you, mate?' Mark said now, as if reading his friend's mind. 'You're an idiot. I saw the way she looked at you the other day. Why don't you swallow your pride and take her for a drink when you're next on leave?' He scratched a sun-reddened cheek. 'I've said it to you before, and I'll keep saying it. God knows none of us know how long we've got. Gotta grab every bit of happiness we can, mate.' Caleb got to his feet. Leaning against the fuselage, Mark took a tin of tobacco from the breast pocket of his flying jacket and nimbly rolled a cigarette.

'I don't want to put her on the spot,' Caleb said. He shoved his hands in his pocket, gazing wistfully over the verdant valley. 'If she wants to be friends, the first move is going to have to come from her.'

Mark exhaled a cloud of smoke, his full lips stretching into a broad grin. He slapped Caleb hard between the shoulder blades. 'Well, mate,' he said jovially, nodding in the direction of the mess hut. 'Looks like you're about to get your wish.'

Following his gaze, Caleb's eyes widened at the sight of a battered green van bouncing over the rough grass. 'Bloody hell! What ... ?' Stunned, he could only stare as Penny steered the van towards him, stopping midway between the bunkhouse and the hangers. Several wolf whistles rang out as the men broke off from their various activities to appreciate the pretty but anxious-looking woman who emerged from the driver's seat.

She stood beside the open door, her heart pounding so hard she was sure it could be heard across the entire airfield. Caleb swallowed hard, acutely aware that he was the focus of the attention of his entire squadron. They milled about, arms folded, grinning and nudging each other, enjoying the brief diversion from the daily monotony. Caleb licked his parched lips and walked slowly towards the van. 'Penny . . . what . . . What are you doing here?'

Penny flashed him a tentative smile, glancing nervously at the assembled men grinning at her good-naturedly. She drew in a lungful of air, drawing strength and courage from their silent encouragement. Caleb was a respected and well-liked member of the squadron. If, God love her, this girl was prepared to see beyond the man's scars and love him for the man he truly was, then they would applaud her every step of the way.

'I needed to see you,' she said, beseeching him with her eyes. She faltered, her gaze locked on Caleb's. 'The crash . . . I can't stop thinking about it and I . . . I need to tell you how I feel.' The words came out in a rush, tumbling over themselves in her haste to make him understand.

'So tell me,' Caleb whispered. 'Tell me how you feel.'

Penny looked him straight in the eye. In that moment they were the only two people on the airfield as Caleb closed the space between them, his hands coming to rest gently on her shoulders. 'How do you feel?' he asked again, softly, his warm breath caressing her face.

'I . . . I think I'm falling in love with you,' she whispered, holding her breath and hardly daring to hope he felt the same.

'I've been such a fool,' Caleb said. 'A bloody fool.' Unable to contain himself any longer, he brought his lips down to meet hers. A resounding cheer rang out around them.

They were both laughing when they pulled apart.

CHAPTER FORTY-TWO

Over the next few months Penny and Caleb saw as much of each other as their hectic schedules allowed. To Penny's immense joy, both Jack and Ida took an instant liking to him. From the tone of her letters, it was clear that Ellie-May was thrilled Penny had met someone nice and was looking forward to meeting him.

One damp Sunday afternoon Ellie-May caught the train to Salisbury. The historical city had thus far been spared, and her tall spire, the tallest in England, rose proud and majestic over the city that dull November afternoon as she made her way down Fisherton Street to the Georgina Rose café. She chose a table by the window with an unobstructed view of the shop-lined street and ordered a cup of tea, which she drank watching passers-by unfurl umbrellas and duck beneath awnings to escape the sudden downpour.

It had been a difficult year. There had been numerous bombing raids across Britain and hundreds of people had been killed. With so much suffering and devastation, Ellie-May knew she needed to put her regrets behind her.

Once she'd recovered from the pain of Jack and Jennette's engagement she had been determined to use every ounce of her willpower to forget about him, but, in her unguarded moments, she would remember.

She shook herself sternly. Jack was married now. Her pride had refused to allow her to ask Penny about the wedding, and her daughter had been less than forthcoming, saying only that it had been quick and informal.

Ellie-May could convince herself that she was happy for Jack, pleased that he had moved on, and, for a while the despondency was kept at bay, but only for a while.

She pushed all thoughts of Jack from her mind as Penny came around the corner, linking arms with a tall, sturdy-looking man in a blue greatcoat, a scarf pulled high up his face and holding a black umbrella. Her heart lifted as she watched them splash across the road, dodging traffic. Penny let go of her hat to point towards the café, and the wind almost took it, Penny only snatching it back in the nick of time. She threw back her head, laughing, and Ellie-May was struck again by how much her daughter resembled her father.

She sighed inwardly, her weary face lifting in a smile as the bell above the door jangled merrily and a squall of cold rain blew Penny and Caleb into the steam-filled café. Ellie-May got to her feet and the two women embraced warmly while Caleb shook out the umbrella and placed it in the stand.

'Mum, I'd like you to meet Caleb,' Penny said proudly, taking his hand.

'Hello, Caleb,' Ellie-May smiled. 'I've heard a lot about you.'

'I'm pleased to meet you, Mrs Cartwright.' Caleb held out a large, capable-looking hand. Ellie-May took it, looking into his eyes. Penny had warned her about his scars and though she had thought herself prepared, it still took a great deal of effort on her part to hide her shock as he self-consciously unwound his scarf to reveal the full extent of his disfigurement.

'It's very nice to meet you, too,' she said brightly, as Penny and Caleb shed their wet coats, draping them over the back of their chairs. 'Penny has told me so much about you that I feel I know you already,' she said, already warming to him. She picked up a menu. 'What do you fancy? Tea and a toasted teacake? Or a crumpet? They do look nice.'

The café owner, a large woman in a pink floral apron and iron grey hair scraped into a tidy bun, ambled over to take their order, carefully avoiding eye contact with Caleb all the while. Mortified on his behalf, Penny glowered at her furiously, but Caleb shrugged it off. He was slowly learning to ignore people's negative reactions. He was only grateful that Penny was prepared to look beyond his scars and love him for who he was.

They made small talk until their tea and teacakes arrived, each one glistening with a thin smear of melted butter.

'How's Frank?' Penny asked Ellie-May as she spread

raspberry jam over her teacake and took a bite, licking the stickiness from her fingers.

Ellie-May swallowed her mouthful before answering. 'Oh, you know Frank, he doesn't change.' She didn't add that the older he got, the more demanding and jealous he had become. She was just thankful he had no inkling Jack was alive. God alone knew how he'd react. She shuddered at the thought.

'Are you chilly, Mrs Cartwright?' Caleb asked. 'We can move closer to the heater if you'd like.'

'I'm fine, Caleb. Thank you.' Ellie-May smiled warmly. She knew she'd like this young man. He would be good for Penny. Perhaps once the war was over . . . but, well, what was the point of making plans? Live for the moment, that's what most young people were doing these days, and who could blame them. Who knew how long they had left on this earth, any of them?

'Alice and I went to Above Bar Street the other week,' she told Penny, picking up the dainty gilt-edged teacup and taking a sip. She set it back down in its saucer, her agonized gaze fixed on Penny's face. 'It fair breaks your heart to see what they've done to it,' she said. 'Building after building reduced to rubble on both sides. Heartbreaking it is, absolutely heartbreaking.'

'It's the same in all the big cities, Mrs Cartwright,' Caleb said. 'Hitler hopes to weaken our resolve, but all he's doing is making the British people more determined to beat him. We won't let him get the better of us, you'll see. We'll win this war, or my name isn't Caleb Johnson.'

'I hope you're right, Caleb, love,' Ellie-May replied. 'Sometimes it's hard to believe this war will ever end.'

'I feel the same,' Penny nodded in agreement. 'It feels like we've been at war for ever.'

The afternoon flew by all too quickly. Caleb and Penny needed to get the three-ten to Gillingham for Caleb to be back at base by four.

'You'll be all right on your own, Mum?' Penny fretted as they embraced on the draughty platform.

'Of course, my train will be here any minute,' Ellie-May said, adjusting her hat. 'It was lovely to meet you, Caleb,' she said, surprising him with a kiss on the cheek. 'Write soon,' she called after Penny, as she and Caleb boarded the train. 'I'll miss you.'

CHAPTER FORTY-THREE

1942

Snow had been falling steadily for the past three days, but the sky was crystal clear, that January morning, the wintery landscape dazzling in the sunlight. The whiteness of the snow almost hurt Penny's eyes as she trudged across the yard to the dairy, the cold air nipping at her pink cheeks, her breath clouding in front of her face.

She glanced up at the sound of approaching aircraft, shielding her eyes against the sun's glare. Eight planes flew overhead, sunlight glinting on their metalwork. The lead plane waggled its wings and Penny grinned.

Caleb.

She unwound her scarf and waved it in the air. She stood in the yard, sunlight glancing off the frozen mud, watching until the planes disappeared into the hazy distance, uttering the same silent prayer she prayed each time Caleb and his squadron set off on a mission. 'Please God keep them safe and bring them home.'

Later that afternoon she was cleaning out the cowshed when she heard the tell-tale drone of returning aircraft. Setting her broom aside, she hastened out into the yard, the familiar anxiety tying her stomach in knots as she gazed upwards, searching the darkening sky. She hadn't realized Daphne had followed her outside until she reached for Penny's hand.

'Oh, my God!' Penny gasped, her whole body gripped by panic, her frightened mind refusing to believe what her eyes were telling it. Out of the eight planes that had left the base that morning, just five now limped home. One was flying so low it seemed impossible it would crest the bank of trees at the far end of the field but, at the very last second, it gained sufficient altitude. A choke catching in the back of her throat, Penny scanned the darkening sky.

'Caleb,' she croaked hoarsely. 'One of them is Caleb's. I'm sure of it.' She slumped against Daphne. 'Oh, Daph,' she wailed. 'How will I bear it?'

'You don't know for sure that Caleb's plane is one of the missing.' Daphne shook her firmly by the shoulders. 'And even if it is, he could have bailed out, or crash-landed some-where. You mustn't think the worse.'

The farmhouse door flew open and Anne came running out.

'I saw the planes,' she began soberly, breaking off at the sight of Penny's anguish. 'Oh, Penny, is it Caleb? Oh, my love, I'm so sorry.' Penny crumpled into Anne's waiting arms.

'All right,' Daphne rebuked her brusquely. 'Let's not get

hysterical until we know there's something to get hysterical about.' She met Anne's gaze over Penny's head. 'Let's get her indoors and have a cup of tea. I'm sure Jim won't begrudge us a drop of his brandy. We've all had a bit of a shock.'

It was Mark who told them what had happened. He turned up at the farm early the following morning, his face grey and drawn, his eyes bloodshot from lack of sleep. He found Penny, sick with worry, sluicing down the cowshed. Her face was drawn and there were dark circles beneath her eyes. One look at Mark's expression caused her knees to buckle and she slumped against the wall with a groan of despair.

Mark held her while she cried.

'His plane was shot down over France,' he told her a short while later, seated at the kitchen table, mugs of tea untouched. Slumped in her chair, her eyes red and swollen from weeping, Penny had to bite her lip to keep herself from screaming. She didn't want to hear what he was about to tell her, but she knew she'd never rest unless she did.

'We were on reconnaissance. The bastards were waiting for us. We lost three planes, a lot of good men. Caleb's plane was the first to be hit. Flames were billowing from the fuselage ...' Mark paused, dragging his hands down his tired face. 'I was desperately trying to avoid being shot myself, but I think most of Caleb's crew managed to eject. I counted the open chutes and I'd swear on my life there were eight, so we can only pray they landed safely and they've been taken prisoner. It's the best we can hope for.'

He fell silent, his face ravaged by the horror of the previous night. 'One of the planes went down with all men on board. The poor buggers didn't stand a chance. A few managed to escape the third plane before it crashed. One of the lads ...' Mark's voice quivered. 'His chute caught on the tail of my plane.' He inhaled deeply, swallowing down the bile that rose in his throat, his stomach curdling at the memory. Fighting down the urge to retch, he forced himself to continue.

'He fell off somewhere over the Channel.' Penny heard the catch in his voice, and fresh tears welled. She knew from what Caleb had said that the men regarded each other as family. The loss of any member was a hard blow to bear. 'We heard late last night that he didn't make it.'

Penny nodded dumbly. At least there was a chance Caleb was alive. Rumours abounded about the treatment of prisoners of war. Some POW camps were all right, others were hellholes. She had heard talk of beatings and torture, routine executions and starvation rations. She exhaled slowly, trying to still her beating heart and force such images from her mind. She had to believe that Caleb was safe and that one day he would come home to her. He had to be alive, the alternative was unthinkable.

A sudden thaw had turned the yard into a quagmire. The snow had all but melted, just a few patches remained in places where the sun's rays had failed to reach. Penny was in the barn when Jim's shout brought her running to see the telegram boy pushing his bike through the mud. The past week had dragged, worry and anxiety had been Penny's constant companion, but now she felt strangely calm as she took the telegram from the boy.

Silently, her three friends gathered around her. Jim, his expression grim, laid a comforting hand on her shoulder. Even the dogs were subdued.

With shaking fingers, Penny slit the envelope, and would have collapsed, had her friends not had the presence of mind to hold her up.

'He's alive,' she breathed. 'Oh, thank God, he's alive!' Her relief was overwhelming. 'He has been taken as a prisoner of war, but he's all right.'

She felt weak with relief. The war was over for Caleb.

'It's the best news you could hope for, lass,' Jim said in his gruff way.

Penny nodded. 'At least I'll be able to write and send parcels through the Red Cross.' She gazed out over the drab landscape, forcing herself to breath evenly as her heartbeat slowly returned to normal. The coming months would be hard for them both, but they would survive and one day, when the war was over, they would be together again.

CHAPTER FORTY-FOUR

1944

Ellie-May had queued for almost two hours at the grocers, and she was gasping for a cup of tea as she made her way back along Northam Road, letting herself in through the back.

It was a sultry June day and the back room of the butcher's shop was chilly by comparison. The table had been scrubbed clean, yet the metallic scent of blood still lingered in the cool air. Her footsteps sounded loud on the stone floor as she crossed to the door and climbed the stairs.

'Where the hell have you been?'

The tone of Frank's question took her by surprise. 'Shopping,' she replied, moving past him to the kitchen. She set her basket on the table, eyes wary.

'You've been gone hours,' Frank snarled. 'It's half-closing, you should have been back an hour ago.' The corner of his lip lifting into a sneer that revealed yellowing teeth. At the age of fifty-one, Frank was going to seed. His blond hair had thinned and, like his father before him, his fondness for spirits had taken its toll on his looks and his health. He suffered regularly from gout, which did nothing to improve his temper.

'The queue was halfway down the street,' Ellie-May defended herself. 'Mr Atkinson stayed open longer to accommodate everyone. You know what it's like, Frank. You see it yourself here every day. It takes time to sort out everyone's rations.'

'Are you sure you were at the grocers?' he said with a mirthless laugh as he walked towards her, his expression so menacing, she was grateful for the table between them.

'Yes.' She sighed wearily. 'Where else would I be? Look, I'm sorry I was a long time.' She winced at the quiver in her voice, hating the pathetic creature she had become, always on the defensive. She took a deep breath, forcing herself to keep calm. 'There was nothing I could do. I'll just put these things away,' she said, opening the pantry door. 'Then I'll make us a nice cup of tea.'

She reached for the tea caddy just as Frank grabbed her arm, yelping in pain as it fell to the floor. Despite the searing pain that shot up her arm, she was more upset by the sight of her precious tea leaves scattered across the linoleum.

'Frank, what . . . ?' Tears welled in her eyes as his fingers dug deeper into the tender flesh of her upper arm.

'Tell me the truth,' he snapped, dragging her around to face him. 'Where were you?'

She looked at him in total bewilderment. 'I don't know what you're . . .'

The blow knocked her off her feet and she fell against the edge of the table, striking her cheek on the corner. Pain exploded across her face as she crumpled on the floor, clutching her throbbing cheek. She stared up at him, eyes clouded with confusion.

'Frank ...?' She grabbed hold of the chair and pulled herself to her feet. She felt dizzy, her left eye was weeping. 'I don't understand.' She had never seen him quite this angry before.

'Where were you?' he demanded, as she sank onto the chair, holding her cheek in her hand, the spilled tea now quite forgotten. He had a queer look on his face, almost triumphant.

Ellie-May frowned. 'I told you ...'

'Don't lie!' Frank screamed in her face. She flinched, waiting for the next blow. He thrust his face into hers. She could smell the tripe and onions on his breath.

'You were with *him*, weren't you?' he hissed. His fingers found her shoulders, digging into her flesh until she winced with pain. She shook her head.

'Who?' she squirmed beneath his grip but he only squeezed harder. Her eyes brimmed with tears. 'Frank, you're making no sense.'

He let go of her, grinning nastily as she massaged her sore shoulders. Her cheek throbbed.

'You were with Jack, weren't you?' he snarled.

'*Jack*?' Ellie-May stared at him with incredulity.

'Oh, don't play the innocent with me.' Frank glared at her.

'I bet the two of you have had a right laugh at my expense.'
He leaned against the dresser, arms folded across his chest.
'So, when did it start? How long after we were married were
you sneaking off to warm that gypsy's bed? You whore!' he
shouted, making her jump. 'You've been cuckolding me
for years.'

'That's not true!' Ellie-May stared at him aghast. How had
he found out about Jack? 'I've never been unfaithful to you,
Frank. Why would you even think that?'

'I found this in your bedside cabinet.' From the inside
pocket of his jacket he pulled out a folded sheet of paper.
Ellie-May knew what it was instantly, colour draining from
her cheeks.

'Ha, you recognise it, then?' he sneered. 'Dated a couple
of months after we were married. Bet you kicked yourself
for being so hasty. If you'd only waited but ... oops, too late!
You were saddled with me. Not that you let that stop you,
I'm sure. You've probably been at it with Gypo Jack like a
bitch on heat our entire marriage.'

'It's not what you think,' she whispered. 'I never knew
the letter existed until Mum died. Penny found it when she
was clearing out her things. I had no idea Jack was alive until
then, I swear.'

'Ah, yes, Penny. I might have known she'd be behind it.
She always was her father's daughter.'

'Frank, I haven't been in touch with Jack, I promise you.
Penny sees him, yes, but I haven't. Not since he went off to
France. He's married to someone else and ...'

'You know an awful lot about him. Keep tabs on him, do you? Penny keeps you updated no doubt.'

'It's not like that. Please, believe me. I'd never break my marriage vows.'

'I've always been second best, Ellie, always.' Frank glowered at her. 'Maybe you did believe Jack was dead, but that didn't stop him coming between us, did it? He was always there, like the proverbial spectre at the feast!' He swore loudly, running a hand through his thinning hair. Perspiration beaded his upper lip and glistened in the creases of his forehead. 'You never gave me a chance, Ellie. I loved you. I really loved you. All I ever wanted was for you to love me the way you loved him!' He smashed his fist on the table. Ellie-May flinched. 'I'm going to the pub,' he announced coldly, his eyes like flint.

She remained motionless until she heard the slam of the flat door, followed by the dull thud of footsteps descending the stairs. Then she put her head in her hands and cried.

When she could cry no more, she got wearily to her feet and splashed cold water on her swollen, blotchy face, before trying to rescue some of the precious tea leaves. Some had worked their way into the cracks in the lino and could never be salvaged, but she swept up what she could. She made herself a much-needed cuppa and turned on the wireless, trying not to think about what the future held for her and Frank as she listened to the news broadcast.

The past year and a half had brought significant victories for the Allied forces. In January 1943, British forces had captured Tripoli from the Nazis and in May of the same year, the capture of Tunis had ended the campaign in North Africa. In early September the Allies had invaded Italy and, closer to home, whole villages had been evacuated to make way for American troops training in preparation for the Normandy landings. Then, in October of last year, the Italian army had surrendered unconditionally to the Allies.

In spring the streets of Southampton had teemed with troops and, just last week, on June 6th, the greatly anticipated D-Day had finally arrived with 155,000 Allied troops landing on the beaches of Normandy. Along with the rest of the country, Ellie-May had echoed the words of General Dwight D. Eisenhower, 'Good luck, and let us all beseech the blessings of Almighty God upon this great and noble undertaking.' So far, the news from France remained promising.

She sighed, her thoughts turning to Caleb. A prisoner of war. Who knew how he was being treated. One heard such stories. Only a couple of months earlier, in April, two Slovakian Jews, Rudolf Vrba and Alfréd Wetzler, had escaped from the notorious concentration camp of Auschwitz and their reports of cruelty and the systematic extermination of Jewish men, women and children were so horrific as to be almost unbelievable. How anyone could treat their fellow human beings in such a way was beyond the comprehension of most right-thinking folk, thought Ellie-May now as she drank her weak tea, a cold compress pressed to her aching cheek. If Germany could treat their own countrymen in such a cruel manner, it was unlikely they would treat their enemy any better.

'Caleb will be fine,' Alice consoled her that evening as they made their way arm in arm to the bingo hall, having called in at the fish and chip shop on the way. 'The Germans have to abide by the Geneva Convention like everyone else.'

Ellie-May nodded. 'I hope you're right.'

To her relief, Frank had stayed at the pub the rest of the afternoon, which meant he'd be in a filthy mood when he came home later. To appease him she'd left his supper warming in the oven, along with a brief note letting him know where she'd gone.

Their footsteps echoed in the quiet street. The sunlight cast a golden glow over the buildings, the dark chimneys silhouetted against the still-blue sky, clouds tinged pink. Ellie-May took off her cardigan, enjoying the warm air on her bare skin.

'Archie's a proper country boy now,' Alice was saying, somewhat gloomily, as they strode towards Six Dials. 'I can't imagine him wanting to live in a city again, once the war's over. I expect your Penny will be the same.'

'She never liked working in the shop,' Ellie-May agreed. So engrossed were they in their conversation, in the normality of it that, for a moment Ellie-May didn't register the unfamiliar sound. She unclipped her handbag, intending to look for a handkerchief but instead glanced upwards, her ears becoming suddenly attuned to the strange noise.

'What is it?' Alice asked, as they came to a halt, both women staring up into the summer sky. 'It sounds like a very fast truck,' she glanced up and down the street. 'But there isn't any traffic . . .'

Ellie-May followed her gaze. The entire street seemed frozen, faces turned to the sky as the noise grew louder. Ellie-May caught the flash of sunlight on metal, way up high. She blinked, shielding her eyes against the glare. It looked like a tiny plane, and it was heading straight for them.

Anchored to the spot, Ellie-May could only stare as Hitler's latest deadly weapon, the V1 missile or 'Doodlebug', sailed over the rooftops of Northam. Wide-eyed with terror, her eyes followed the missile's path. Then the noise stopped, leaving a frightening, deathly silence in its wake. The explosion, when it came, shook the ground. Ellie-May screamed, grabbing Alice in terror. The air raid warning sounded and she was dimly aware of people running. Someone was shouting.

'Northam Street?' she whispered, shaking her head to clear the ringing in her ears. 'They said it hit Northam Street.'

Galvanized into action, she grabbed Alice by the arm. They joined the throng of white-faced men and women streaming along Six Dials towards Northam Street. In the distance she heard the wail of sirens. The air was thick with swirling dust. Seagulls circled overhead, screeching their alarm. Oblivious to the screams and shouts of those around her, Ellie-May ran as fast as she could, her throat raw, her chest heaving, Alice clinging to her hand as they stumbled over rubble and debris, hardly able to comprehend the devastation. Stumbling to a halt, Ellie-May could only stare in shock at the crater that, moments before, had been her home.

'Oh, God, no!' she wailed, sinking against Alice. All around them people were shouting for survivors but the two women could only stand in silence, paralysed by the sight of twisted metal and lumps of concrete. Blinking dust from her eyes, Ellie-May could pick out bits of shattered furniture. A shred of curtain still clinging to an upstairs curtain rail. A vase lying amidst the rubble, miraculously unscathed.

'Are you hurt?' A young auxiliary policewoman paused beside Ellie-May, her gaze taking in her swollen cheek. The skin around her left eye was turning a nice shade of aubergine. She shook her head.

'I'm all right,' she replied hoarsely. A thick layer of dust coated her throat, making speech difficult. She motioned towards the rubble. 'This was my home . . .'

'Mrs Cartwright! Mrs Cartwright!' The voice startled Ellie-May, and she frowned at the sight of the man stumbling towards her, his face streaked with dust. He gazed in mute horror at what remained of the butcher's shop. 'Frank?' he whispered, eyes registering his shock. 'Did he get out?'

'What?' Ellie-May swallowed. 'I thought Frank was at the pub . . .' Her gaze swept the ruined building.

'He left,' the man groaned. 'About ten minutes before . . .' His words trailed away.

'Frank,' whispered Ellie-May, nausea churning her

stomach. 'He wouldn't even have had a chance to get the shelter. There was no warning.'

'Don't give up hope,' the policewoman said, her eyes full of sympathy. 'We've pulled survivors from worse than this.' Ellie-May nodded, dumbly. 'They've got tea in the van over there,' the policewoman told Alice. 'Your friend could do with one.'

Alice nodded. 'Come on, Ellie-May. You've had a shock.'

Shaking violently, her cold fingers wrapped around a mug of steaming tea, Ellie-May sat on the kerb with Alice, watching as the search for survivors went on late into the night.

Five men, three women and four children – one a babe in arms – were killed on that beautiful, sunny summer evening. Frank's was the last body to be recovered. Ellie-May went to identify him the following morning. To her surprise, there wasn't a scratch on him. Lying in the makeshift morgue, his hair and skin covered with a fine white dust that clogged his nostrils and formed little snowdrifts at the corners of his shut-tight eyes, he looked like he was asleep. She held his cold, lifeless hand in hers, her vision blurred with tears as she kissed him goodbye.

Alice was waiting for her outside.

'Are you all right?' she asked, her eyes kind. Ellie-May nodded, stifling a yawn. They had spent the previous night in the school gymnasium, along with others who had been bombed out of their homes and neither woman had slept well.

'I don't feel grief as such,' she tried to explain as they

walked towards the train station. 'More regret, really. I know our marriage was difficult, but Frank didn't deserve to die like that.' She blew her nose. 'What time is your train?'

Alice glanced at her watch. 'Three quarters of an hour. I could walk with you to your dad's. I've got time.'

'Thanks, but you don't want to risk missing your train.' The women embraced quickly, blinking back tears. 'Keep in touch, and give that boy of yours my love.'

Ellie-May watched until Alice was swallowed up by the crowd, before turning in the direction of Church Street, all her worldly possessions crammed into a brown paper bag.

'She's here, Dad,' Ellie-May shouted to Sid in the kitchen two days later as Penny rounded the corner of Church Street. She had been watching from the parlour window for the past half an hour and she hurried out into the street, pulling her cardigan around her shoulders for the sun had yet to penetrate the narrow, cobbled street. 'Penny!'

'Mum!' Penny quickened her pace. 'Oh, Mum.' Penny hugged Ellie-May warmly. 'You look so tired.'

'I'm all right, love. It's so good to see you.'

'I came as soon as I could,' Penny said. 'I'm so sorry about Frank and your home.' Though shaken and shocked by the news of her stepfather's death, she had shed few tears.

Sid stood in the doorway. 'Ah, love. You're a sight for sore eyes and no mistake.'

'Hello, Grandpa. It's good to see you.' Penny hugged him. Rose was in the kitchen with two of her grandchildren.

She made them all a cup of tea which they carried outside into the yard.

'There are plenty of shifts available over at the munitions factory in Millbank Street,' Rose told Ellie-May as they soaked up the sun, watching the children playing some elaborate skipping game. 'Both my girls work there. I had to give it up on account of my bad back so I look after the grandkids now.'

'You don't need to work, Ellie-May,' Sid pointed out, leaning down to scratch his ankle. He was seventy-seven now, and frail, his pale skin seemed almost translucent in the bright daylight, his eyes rheumy.

'I'll go mad sitting around all day, Dad,' Ellie-May replied. 'How're your boys getting on, Rose? Have you heard from them?'

'I haven't had a letter from either of them in a while,' Rose said heavily, 'but I'm hoping no news is good news.'

'Our Tommy's been discharged from hospital,' Sid brought Penny up to date with the family news. 'Shot himself in the foot, apparently. He'll be rejoining his regiment in a day or so.' He inclined his head towards Ellie-May. 'There's a letter from Nora on the mantelpiece. It's taken ages to get to us. It's date-stamped February. I'll send her a telegram tomorrow, let her know about Frank.'

'Thanks, Dad.' Ellie-May got up to clear away the cups, and dropped a kiss on the top of his pink, liver-spotted head. 'Perhaps we can have a nice game of dominoes after tea,' she suggested.

'I'd like that.' Sid looked so pathetically grateful that Ellie-May had to turn away.

Carrying the cups into the dim kitchen, Ellie-May exhaled her guilt. She knew she hadn't spent as much time with Sid as she would have liked over the past year, but Frank had even become jealous of her spending time with anyone, as if he couldn't bear her to give her attention to anyone or anything that took it away from him. She took a deep breath, filling her lungs with the warm summer air wafting in through the kitchen window. She felt as though a heavy load had been lifted from her shoulders. Frank was gone, God rest his soul. She would never have wished him dead, but with his death she was finally free; free of his petty jealousy; free of his fists and cutting remarks.

Free.

'When do you go back to Dorset?' she asked Penny later that night as they prepared for bed by lamplight. It was still daylight outside but the blackout curtains let in not a chink of light.

'On Friday, after the funeral.'

Ellie-May climbed beneath the covers. She was wearing an old nightshirt of Sid's, her own clothes having been obliterated by the bomb. 'I was thinking about Caleb the day Frank died. Have you heard from him?'

Penny nodded, her eyes glistening with tears as she climbed in beside her mother. She missed him so much. She kept his letters under her pillow, the pages crumpled and tearstained from repeated reading. 'I got a letter last week. The first in over three months. He's all right, he says. He keeps his letters cheerful, and they're full of funny stories about his fellow prisoners, but it must be pretty grim.'

'I shouldn't think it can be very jolly.'

'He received the Red Cross parcel.' Penny smiled. 'He said thanks for the socks. They came in very useful.'

'He's on the prayer list at church,' Ellie-May assured her, as were dozens of others, sons, daughters, husbands, lovers.

Penny squeezed her mother's fingers with an appreciation she couldn't voice and reached over to turn out the lamp.

As she lay in the darkness, it was on the tip of Ellie-May's tongue to ask after Jack, but she bit back the words. Her husband was barely cold, and already she was thinking of another man.

'Jack sends his condolences, by the way,' Penny said, as if reading her mind.

After a moment's silence Ellie-May said, 'Tell him thank you.'

They fell silent, listening to the distant sound of the anti-aircraft guns, far away over towards Portsmouth. To their relief there were no raids that night and they both slept soundly until morning.

CHAPTER FORTY-FIVE

1945

On April 30th, Adolf Hitler and Eva Braun, his wife of less than forty hours, committed suicide and, consequently, on May 8th, Germany surrendered. After six difficult, heart-breaking years, the war in Europe was over.

A month later, exhausted from his twenty-four-hour journey, filthy and unshaven, Caleb stood in the doorway of the cowshed watching Penny as she went about her chores, totally oblivious to his presence. Her overall was streaked with cow muck, she had straw in her hair and a smear of something across her cheek, and he couldn't wait to take her in his arms.

Suddenly realizing she was being watched, Penny turned towards the figure silhouetted against the June sunshine. She took a step closer, her eyes widening in surprise and disbelief.

'*Caleb*? Oh, Caleb!' The broom clattered to the floor as she flew across the barn into his arms. He was skin and bone, and his eyes held that haunted look of someone who had endured the unendurable, but he was her Caleb, and he was home.

He covered her face with kisses, her eyes, her nose, her cheeks, both of them laughing and crying simultaneously, and then his lips found hers and they were kissing for the longest time.

'I've pictured this moment in my mind so many times,' he whispered when they finally broke apart, his voice hoarse with longing. 'The thought of seeing you again is the only thing that kept me going.' He shook his head in an attempt to erase the memories of his imprisonment from his mind, the cruelty of the guards, the way they had constantly made fun of his scars, the near-starvation diet and savage beatings meted out at random.

'Oh, Penny,' he groaned softly, pressing his lips to her forehead. 'Will you do me the honour of becoming my wife?' he asked, looking into her eyes. Penny grinned. It wasn't the most romantic proposal, standing in a smelly cowshed, ankle-deep in dirty straw and cow muck, but she couldn't care less. She entwined her arms around Caleb's neck and kissed him hard on the mouth.

'I would love to marry you, Flight Lieutenant Caleb Johnson,' she whispered softly. 'And the sooner the better.'

Penny's wedding day dawned fine and sunny. It was the middle of September and the war was finally over. Just weeks before, America had dropped two atomic bombs over the cities of Hiroshima and Nagasaki, bringing about Japan's surrender. Daphne's boyfriend had survived the horrors of a Japanese POW camp and was on his way home. Edie's John had made it home unscathed, as had Rose's sons and sons-in-law as well as Penny's cousin, Tommy.

Now, her eyes misting over, Ellie-May stared at Penny's reflection in the full-length mirror. She was wearing a powder-blue suit, a crown of late summer roses circling her cloud of dark curls.

'You're beautiful.'

'Thanks, Mum.' Their eyes met in the mirror. 'Just a few months ago I would never have believed it was possible to be so happy.' She turned, looking Ellie-May up and down admiringly. 'You look very nice yourself. Very elegant.'

'Do you think so?' Ellie-May bit her lip uncertainly, scrutinising her reflection with a critical eye, acutely aware that today she would come face to face with Jack for the first time in thirty years. She had barely slept for the past week.

'Mum, you're an attractive woman. That outfit really suits you.'

Ellie-May looked at the woman in the smart dove-grey suit staring sombrely back at her, taking in the milky-white complexion, the dove-grey hat with a short veil set at a slight angle on auburn hair. She was relieved that on the outside she appeared poised and in control. Hopefully no one would realize that inside she was a gibbering wreck.

The bedroom door burst open and Daphne and Edie twirled into the room wearing pink suits, their hair adorned with garlands of tiny pink roses.

'You both look exquisite,' Ellie-May told them admiringly.

'Thank you. It's such a shame Anne couldn't make it,' Daphne said, doing a twirl to show Ellie-May her dress to its best advantage.

'She sent a telegram with her warmest congratulations,' said Penny.

'I received a letter from her last week,' Edie said. 'She seems very happily settled in Wyoming with her GI husband.'

A car pulled into the yard and Ellie-May held her breath as Daphne leaned out of the window, her golden curls catching the light. 'Jack's here,' she said casually, pretending not to notice the sudden flush of colour in Ellie-May's cheeks. 'Hello, Mr Pickup,' she called down. 'You look very dashing, I must say.'

'Wow! Jack, you look great,' Penny laughed, leaning over the window ledge as Jack, wearing a dark suit and navy tie, emerged from a midnight-blue saloon. He grinned up at Penny.

'And you look radiant, my dear,' he said, ducking into the house and out of view.

Face flaming, Ellie-May busied herself gathering up discarded clothing, her insides turning to water.

'Oh, I'm nervous,' said Penny, flouncing away from the window and flopping on to the bed.

'Careful,' Ellie-May chided her, 'you'll crease your suit.'

'Your nerves will disappear the moment you see Caleb standing at the altar,' Edie assured Penny, taking the bouquet of late summer wildflowers from Ellie-May. Edie had gone out early that morning to pick them, tying the slender green stems together with pale blue ribbon. 'Come on, we'd better get going. Caleb will think you've changed your mind.'

Daphne grabbed her Box Brownie from her bunk and Ellie-May took a photograph of Penny with her two bridesmaids. She doubted it would be a very good picture, her hands were shaking so much.

'I'll see you downstairs, Penny.'

Ellie-May stood at the top of the stairs, trying to still her beating heart. For weeks she had experienced an upheaval of emotions. She was excited at the prospect of seeing Jack, yet at the same time filled with dread. She could hear him talking to Jim, the sound of his voice like an echo from years gone by. Her chest rose and fell in nervous anticipation. In a matter of seconds, she would come face to face with the man she had loved for thirty-five years.

And she was utterly terrified.

She could hear the girls' carefree laughter in the room behind her. Soon, Penny would be ready to make her grand entrance. Steeling herself, she took a tentative step downwards. She was shaking like a leaf yet her legs felt wooden and it was all she could do to get them to cooperate enough to bring her to the foot of the stairs.

Jack turned at the sound of her footsteps and the smile froze on his lips. His heart beat erratically as he stared at Ellie-May. She took his breath away, age and maturity only serving to enhance her beauty.

'El,' he rasped, his mouth bone dry.

'Hello, Jack.' she smiled, her serene expression belying the turmoil within. 'It's good to see you.'

'You, too, El,' Jack said softly. 'You too.'

Their eyes locked across the table, oblivious to everything but each other. Sensing the poignancy of the moment, Jim slipped quietly out the door, the dogs behind him.

'I feel like I'm fourteen again and just walked into Cartwrights',' Jack said, his voice hoarse. 'You look even lovelier than you did then.'

'You're pulling my leg,' Ellie-May said, blushing. She dropped her gaze, not wanting her face to betray how hard she was fighting the urge to run into his arms.

'I most certainly am not,' he contradicted her. The longing to sweep her into his arms and never let her go was almost overwhelming. He was about to speak when there was a commotion on the landing, followed by giggles and footsteps coming down the stairs and Penny stood in the doorway, smiling shyly.

'Mum, *Dad.*'

'Wow! Penny, you're beautiful,' Jack said gruffly, his eyes suspiciously bright.

'Thanks.' Penny kissed his cheek, inhaling the now-familiar scent of his aftershave. She shot Ellie-May an anxious look, but her mother was concentrating on the bridesmaids who had followed Penny into the kitchen.

Jim stood in the doorway, the dogs milling about his legs. 'Well, Penny,' he said in his usual gruff manner. 'You certainly scrub up well, and that's a fact.'

'We'd better start for the church,' Ellie-May said, careful not to meet Jack's gaze. 'Grandpa will be waiting for us.'

'Sid came?' Jack exclaimed, pleased. 'I'll look forward to speaking with him later.'

Jack set off with Penny and the bridesmaids in his car and Ellie-May heaved a sigh of relief. There, it was done. The awkwardness of the first meeting was over. Her shoulders sagged as she relaxed.

'Mrs Cartwright?' Jim said, looking as uncomfortable as he felt in his old suit. He held open the door of the van.

'Thank you,' Ellie-May said, settling herself in the passenger seat.

The bells were ringing as they pulled up behind Jack's car. The ancient stone church glowed butter-yellow in the warm sunshine, nestled amongst the weathered gravestones.

Avoiding Jack's gaze, Ellie-May got out of the van and walked over to where Penny and her bridesmaids were waiting by the gate. 'Be happy, Pen-Pen.' She kissed Penny on the cheek and hurried into the church, blinking back the tears.

'Ready?' Jack smiled at Penny, swallowing the lump in his throat. He was scarcely able to believe he was about to walk his daughter down the aisle.

'I'm ready,' Penny replied, slipping her hand through the crook of Jack's arm, her nerves calmed by his steady presence.

Before they had time to say anymore, the first strains of Wagner's 'Bridal March' reached their ears, and the vicar appeared to lead them down the aisle.

For Jack, the small congregation was a blur. His eyes

burned with unshed tears while his treacherous heart lamented the fact that it was with Jennette he would be sharing this momentous day and not Ellie-May. Gently, he took Penny's trembling hand and gave her to Caleb.

Ellie-May sat in the front pew, painfully aware of Jennette's presence directly behind her. She had caught the briefest glimpse of Jack's wife as she'd slipped into her seat, but it was enough. Dressed in shocking pink, she resembled an exotic bird, young and carefree, leaving Ellie-May feeling old and dowdy by comparison and feeling every one of her fifty years.

She felt rather than saw Jack slide into the pew beside Jennette, and it took all her willpower not to turn around. She pressed her feet firmly to the floor, feeling the heat of Jack's gaze on the back of her neck.

'Dearly beloved,' the vicar began, his benign gaze scanning the congregation. 'We are gathered here in the sight of God . . .'

Ellie-May surreptitiously wiped her eyes, the sight of Penny gazing adoringly at Caleb making her well up. Beside her, Jim, not given to displays of emotion, reached into his pocket for a handkerchief. Ida, seated on the other side of Jennette, wept unashamedly.

CHAPTER FORTY-SIX

'I love you, Mrs Johnson,' Caleb whispered as they emerged into the sunlight twenty minutes later.

Penny turned to face him, her eyes bright. 'I love you, too, Flight Lieutenant Johnson,' she whispered back, an attractive blush creeping up her cheeks.

In the hall across the way, Ellie-May and Ida were putting the finishing touches to the modest buffet. Sunlight slanted across the floorboards and a gentle breeze wafted in through the open doorway, stirring the coloured paperchains strung across the ceiling. A small arrangement of late summer roses, pink and white, adorned each white-clothed table.

'Your daughter is an absolute credit to you, Mrs Cartwright,' Ida said as she unwrapped a platter of sliced ham. 'I'm that fond of her. She's the granddaughter I never had.'

'Thank you, Ida.' Ellie-May paused in removing the covering from a plate of chicken, her gaze roaming the assembled guests to where Jack was leaning over Jennette, one hand resting casually on the back of her chair, the other on her slender shoulder. The stab of jealousy almost took her breath away and she looked away quick. Only then did she realize that Ida was still talking.

' . . . Jack a new lease of life. He loves her to bits. It'll be a terrible wrench for him when he sails off to Africa.' Her brow creased. 'Well, it's bound to be for both of them, and me an' all. I love him like my own son, and no mistake.'

'Africa?' Ellie-May murmured, her heart skipping a beat. 'Jack's going to Africa?'

'Going to run a vineyard, apparently.' Ida's eyes grew misty. 'I'll be lost without him, and that's the truth.' She forced a smile and patted Ellie-May's arm. 'But today isn't the day for melancholy thoughts, is it? Today is a celebration. That Caleb's a lovely lad, Mrs Cartwright. You couldn't have wished for a better son-in-law.'

'I know. I'm already very fond of him,' Ellie-May replied distractedly. The thought of Jack being halfway across the world filled her with dread. 'Does Penny know? About Jack leaving?'

Ida shook her head. 'He only told me a couple of days ago. I don't think he really wants to go but Jennette's parents are putting the pressure on, you see? They're not getting any younger and they want to hand the reins over to Jennette and her brother.'

'But Penny will be heartbroken.' *As will I*, the thought flashing unbidden into her head.

'I know,' Ida acknowledged. 'He's dreading breaking it to her.'

As if realizing her mother was speaking about her, Penny came over, radiating joy.

'Are you all right, Mum?' Penny asked, as Ida excused herself and bustled off. 'You know, with Jack and everything?'

'Yes,' Ellie-May said in an over-bright voice. 'Of course. Jack and I, we're ... Well, it's water under the bridge now, isn't it?' Ellie-May sat down and Penny squeezed her hand. She glanced over her mother's shoulder, smiling. Instinctively, Ellie-May turned to follow Penny's gaze, her smile faltering to see Jack approaching the table, his dark eyes fixed on her face.

'This is something, isn't it?' he said amiably, seeming not to notice how flustered Ellie-May had become. 'You and I meeting after all these years.'

Her reply caught in her throat as she found herself drawn by his dark, fathomless eyes. Her pulse quickened and she turned her face away, before her longing heart betrayed her.

'Jack?' Sid laid a trembling hand on Jack's shoulder.

'Mr Bramhall, sir.' Jack straightened up. 'How are you?' he asked, his voice full of warmth. He'd always had a lot of time for Ellie-May's father and the sight of his old neighbour, bent and ravaged by age, tugged at his heartstrings.

'Jack,' Sid said, his rheumy eyes wet with tears, as he led Jack away from the table where they wouldn't be overheard. 'I owe you an apology, son. Keeping that letter from our Ellie-May, well.' He shook his head sadly. 'We did what we thought was best at the time, and that's the truth.' He sighed deeply. 'That Frank led my Ellie-May a merry dance and there's many the time I wished we had told her the truth, let her get a divorce if she wanted it and be damned with the scandal. We could have put up with a bit of gossip if it meant our Ellie-May was happy.' He patted Jack's arm. 'I'm sorry, Jack. Eileen and me, we got it wrong, but it's you and our Ellie-May who've had to pay the price.'

'I appreciate your apology, sir,' Jack said, offering Sid his hand. 'Thank you.' The two men shook hands warmly. 'Now,' said Jack with a sheepish grin. 'I think it's time for my speech.'

Sid clapped him on the back. 'Good luck, son. Make it a good one.'

Sitting beside her new husband, Penny surveyed the hall. There was a pleasant buzz of conversation, punctuated by bursts of laughter. She couldn't believe she was Mrs Caleb Johnson at last, and that she had been able to celebrate with both of her parents. It was a memory she would treasure all her life.

A hush fell over the hall as Jack tapped his glass.

'Thank you, ladies and gentlemen.' His voice quivered and he paused to collect himself, clearing his throat before he continued, 'As you know, I have only known Penny for five years. I had no idea I even had a daughter and it was . . .' His voice cracked as he struggled to compose himself. 'A wonderful surprise.' He smiled at Penny. She had tears in her eyes as she clung to Caleb's hand. 'Ever since you came into my life, darling . . .' His voice shook with emotion. 'I have been the happiest man alive. You are a beautiful, kind-hearted, intelligent woman and I'm so proud to be your father. Caleb, you're an exceptional young man, and I wish you both all the joy and happiness in the world. You deserve it. Ladies and gentlemen, please raise your glasses to the bride and groom.'

Glasses were raised and the toast echoed around the hall.

'Thank you, sir.' Caleb half rose from his seat and nodded at Jack. 'I won't let you down.'

Mark got to his feet, nervously clearing his throat. His best man speech was witty and heartwarming and he had the guests in fits of laughter. He finished by toasting the bridesmaids and the bride's parents, before announcing that it was time for the buffet.

The ladies of the WI had done an amazing job with their limited rations, but, delicious as the food was, Ellie-May found she had no appetite. She sipped her cordial, the steady hum of conversation wafting around her, trying not to see Jack laughing at something Jennette had said. She still hadn't processed the fact that Jack would soon be gone. It was probably for the best, she told herself sternly. The more miles between her and Jack the better, though it would be difficult for Penny, to lose her father again so soon after finding him.

Someone began playing the accordion and a smattering of applause brought her out of her reverie to see Caleb lead Penny on to the dance floor. She was so focused on the waltzing couple that she failed to notice Jack approaching her until she felt him tap her gently on the shoulder.

'Might I have the pleasure?' he asked, his brown eyes boring into hers. He had shed his jacket and tie, and rolled up his sleeves, displaying taut forearms that were tanned a deep brown.

'You want to dance with me?' she croaked, her gaze darting over to where Jennette seemed to be in conversation with Ida. 'Won't your wife mind?' she asked, jealousy lending an icy edge to her voice.

'It's just a dance,' Jack smiled at her. 'For old times' sake?' He propped his stick against the table and extended his hand. After a brief moment's hesitation, Ellie-May took it and allowed him to lead her on to the dance floor.

'I may have to lean on you a little,' he said apologetically as he took her in his arms. 'But I'll try not to step on your toes.'

In spite of her misgivings, Ellie-May laughed. At first their steps were awkward and clumsy, but she soon adapted to Jack's ungainly gait. She laid her head on his shoulder and closed her eyes, lost in the sensation of being in Jack's arms once more.

'I still remember the last time I held you like this,' Jack whispered into her hair.

'I'm so sorry, Jack,' Ellie-May murmured. 'If I'd known . . .'

'Oh, El.' Jack drew in a ragged breath. Just the feel of her in his arms was driving him crazy.

Sensing they were on dangerous ground, she drew back her head. She could see the love, the passion, for her in the depth of his dark eyes. 'Ida says you're leaving England?' she said, steering their conversation to a safer topic. 'Penny will be upset.'

'I know,' Jack sighed. 'I'll tell her tomorrow. I don't want to spoil her wedding day.'

'It's all a bit sudden, isn't it? When do you leave?' she asked, dreading the answer but knowing it was for the best.

'In just under a month. Jennette's father has been in ill health for a while and Jennette's always been keen to return home.' He smiled wryly and shrugged his shoulders. 'I owe it to her to give it a go.'

'Of course, you do,' Ellie-May agreed heavily.

'I'm ceding Wayside to Penny and Caleb. They both love the place and, with him leaving the air force and Penny leaving Willowbrook, they need a home of their own. I think they'll make a success of it.'

'That's very generous of you.'

'Well, she is my daughter. It'd be hers one day, anyway.'

The song drew to a close amid a ripple of applause. Jack held Ellie-May just that moment longer before releasing her. His hand resting on the small of her back, he escorted her back to her seat, where Jennette was waiting, her smile brittle, two angry pink spots on either cheek.

She glared at Ellie-May. 'If you've quite finished monopolising my husband, I'd like to dance with him myself.'

'Oh, golly!' Feeling flustered and humiliated, Ellie-May waved her hand at them. 'I'm so sorry.'

'Jennette.' Jack looked at Jennette in surprise. 'There's no need for that. I was just seeing El back to her chair.'

'No, no, it's fine,' Ellie-May waved him away, hot with mortification.

Unable to bear the sight of Jack holding Jennette in his arms the way he had held her just moments before, she slipped out into the fading light. She leaned against the van, shadows creeping across the grass. A brilliant sunset set the sky aflame, yet she was oblivious to the surrounding beauty, her heart heavy with grief as, once again, she mourned for a man who could never be hers.

CHAPTER FORTY-SEVEN

Penny peered out of the window at the overturned cart with mounting dismay. Tears of despair and frustration pricked her eyes. Her journey had been plagued with trouble from the start. Her train had been delayed for over an hour. Consequently, she had missed her connection at Salisbury and been forced to wait an hour for the next train, arriving in Southampton two hours later than she had planned. The free shuttle service that ran from the bus terminal to the Town Quay was crowded, and she had been obliged to stand, one hand clutching the overhead rail, while trying to prevent her lilac hat from being crushed in the melee. She could smell her own body odour, aware of the unpleasant trickle of perspiration down her back.

The weather was unseasonably mild for October and, even with the windows open, the interior of the crowded bus was hot and stuffy. And now, as if matters weren't bad enough, her journey had been brought to an abrupt halt by the upturned cart, its wares strewn across the road. The air resonated with the impatient honking of car horns and the muttered grumblings of stranded passengers.

Frustratingly, Penny could see the RMMV *Capetown Castle* in the near distance, shimmering in the misty haze, its big red and black funnel belching smoke into a murky overcast sky. She choked back an angry sob. The ship was due to sail in under half an hour. Unless the obstruction was cleared very quickly, there was no way Penny would make it in time.

Drivers were getting out of their cars now and angry shouts reverberated up and down the street. A policeman attempted to appease the stationary drivers while the occupants of the cart did their best to clear the debris from the road. Penny watched them with growing impatience. She was contemplating getting off the bus and running the rest of the way when there came a triumphant shout from along the street. To her immense relief, the congestion slowly began to ease. The bus lurched forward and Penny held her breath, praying she would get there in time.

In the ship's luxurious library, Jack fiddled with his cufflinks and watched the big hand of the clock slowly reach the hour, his brows knitting with disappointment and concern. Penny had been due to meet him for tea before they sailed. He had expected her two hours ago, but now the time had come for all non-passengers to disembark. He straightened his tie, taking consolation in the fact that Penny and Caleb would be coming out to Cape Town in December for the party

Jennette's parents were throwing in their honour; a sort of belated wedding celebration.

Quelling the twinge of unease deep in the pit of his stomach, he stepped on to the deck. Seagulls wheeled overhead. The sky was a dull grey, broken by patches of blue, the horizon a dirty smudge in the distance. He looked down into the oily water. The air was filled with the shouts of dockworkers and stevedores, the groan and clang of machinery. He took a deep breath, inhaling the salty, ozone scent of the sea, overlaid with the smell of seaweed, damp and industry.

He was on the threshold of a new chapter in his life. A new venture, a new country lay before him. His future spread out before him like a blank page, yet he felt bereft.

He was missing Penny, of course, and Caleb, and Ida. He smiled in spite of himself. He and Ida had said their goodbyes two days ago when he and Jennette departed for Southampton and she had been as stoic and resolute as always. He'd asked her to come with him. After all, she was sixty-nine now, way past retirement age.

'You might be happy swanning off to some godforsaken country on the other side of the world,' she'd responded brusquely, putting him firmly in his place, 'but I've got your Penny to look after and when, God willing, the babies start coming along, she'll need me more than ever.'

He hoped Penny would be able to persuade her to come out in December as well. He hadn't been fooled by her lack of emotion, and he had been right. That night his old housekeeper had wept copiously into her pillow. As far as she was concerned, she had lost another son. She loved Jack like a mother and she would miss him until the day she drew her final breath.

Forcing his regrets aside, Jack made his way down below. Deep in the bowels of the ship, the engines rumbled, causing the carpeted corridor to vibrate gently. He reached the door to the cabin and went inside, calling a cheery hello.

'Did Penny make it?' Jennette was standing with her back to him in front of the dressing table. The slanting rays of sunlight streaming in through the open balcony doors picked out the golden highlights in her hair. Her trunk, half unpacked, sat abandoned in the middle of the floor. Again, Jack was struck by the opulence of the luxury first-class suite that, much to his chagrin, his in-laws had insisted on paying for.

'No,' he cleared his throat. 'Something must have happened. I'll go to the purser's office later and send a telegram.' He crossed the room, coming to stand behind her. 'We'll be sailing soon. It's time we went up on deck.'

Their eyes met in the mirror and Jack frowned in concern. 'Darling, what is it?'

He took hold of her shoulders, gently turning her towards him. A single tear worked its way down her pale cheek as she leaned back against the dressing table, her fingers clutching at the pale cream edging. Her back, reflected in the mirror, was ramrod straight as she inhaled deeply. She was looking up at him with huge, blue eyes filled with such sadness Jack's first thought was that she'd received bad news from home.

'What's happened? Your parents . . . ?'

'I don't want you to come with me,' Jennette whispered as a second tear followed the first. 'Please, you've got to leave the ship now, while you still can.'

Whatever he had been expecting, it wasn't this. He stared at her, incredulous. 'What? Jennette, what are you talking about? What do you mean, leave the ship? Has something happened to El?' He paled. 'Is that why Penny couldn't make it?'

'Of course, she'd be the first person you'd think of,' Jennette murmured, a strange smile on her face. 'It's always Ellie-May, isn't it, Jack? Your precious El.' She sighed, holding out her hands as if to ward him off. 'Please, Jack,' she said pleadingly. 'Don't make this harder for me than it is. I'm offering you a divorce.' The tears were coming thick and fast now and she bowed her head, letting them splash on to the tips of her pale green court shoes. 'Please,' she implored him. 'Just go.'

'Jennette.' Jack gripped her hands. 'I'm not going anywhere until you tell me what this is about. Why are you talking about divorce?'

With a deep, shuddering sigh that seemed to come from deep within her, Jennette met his puzzled gaze. The total devastation on her face took his breath away. She slowly shook her head. 'I've been fooling myself, Jack,' she said quietly. 'I saw the way you and Ellie-May looked at each other at Penny's wedding. You've never, ever looked at me that way.'

'Jennette, I . . .'

She shook her head, silencing him. 'I pretended to

myself that it would be all right; that once we left England everything would be different and you would forget her.' She gently pulled her hands from his grasp. 'Jack, you're always going to be in love with Ellie-May. Crossing an ocean isn't going to make a scrap of difference.' She lifted her chin in a gesture of determination. 'I don't want to be second best, Jack, and with you I always will be. You will never be able to love me the way you love her. She'll always come between us.'

Jack's hands fell helplessly to his side.

'You know I'm right.' Her eyes swimming with tears, Jennette took a deep, shuddering breath.

'I ...' Jack's voice trailed away, his shoulders slumping in defeat. 'I'm so sorry.' His lips brushed her forehead. 'I'm sorry, Jennette,' he whispered. 'Truly sorry.'

Jennette nodded. She managed a half-smile, blinking back tears.

'I'll be all right.' The blast of the ship's horn startled them both. 'You'd better go, Jack,' she said, turning away. She couldn't watch him walk out the door knowing he would never be coming back.

Jack hesitated. Deon stuck his head around the door, grinning. 'Hey, come on, you two. We'd better get up on deck. The ship's about to sail ...' He broke off, sensing the tension in the cabin, and caught sight of his sister's devastated reflection. He frowned. 'Hey, man, what's up?'

'Jack's leaving,' Jennette said in a choked voice. She leaned her forehead against the glass and closed her eyes.

'What?' Deon stared at his friend, stupefied, his eyes clouding with anger. 'Jack? What the hell are you playing at? We're about to sail, man.'

'Let him go, Deon,' Jennette said, biting her lip in an effort to hold her emotions at bay. 'It's for the best.'

Jack met his friend's gaze. 'I'm sorry, Deon. Jennette . . .' She held herself straight, determined to remain strong, dignified. She gave a slight shake of her head.

'Just go. My lawyer will be in touch.'

Jack bowed his head. He laid a conciliatory hand on Deon's arm but he shrugged him off. 'I'm disappointed in you, Jack,' he said, an angry edge to his voice. 'I expected better of you.'

Jack bowed his head. 'I know, and I'm sorry.' With that he wrenched open the cabin door and stepped out into the deserted corridor.

Penny ran as fast as she could, her chest heaving as she pushed her way through the throng of well-wishers lining the quayside, throwing apologies over her shoulder. She had lost her hat somewhere in the crush and broken a heel, her lopsided gait impeding her progress even further. The blast of the ship's horn shattered her ears, and she choked back a sob of despair as she fought her way to the edge of quay where the 27,000-ton ship sat low in the water, its masts rising up into the grey sky, flags snapping in the salty breeze.

She doubled over, gasping for breath, as seagulls screeched overhead.

She was too late. The realization caused her eyes to prick with tears of despair and self-pity as she watched the gangplanks being drawn away from the ship.

'Please,' she panted, catching the eye of a nearby steward. 'I have to get on board. My father . . .'

The steward shook his head, his expression not unkind as he said, 'Sorry, love. All non-passengers disembarked half an hour ago.' He pointed to the crowds thronging the upper deck. 'The best you can do now is hope he sees you.'

Penny shielded her eyes, gazing upwards, desperate to catch a glimpse of Jack amongst the horde of waving, cheering passengers.

The ship's horn sounded again and the tugboats moved into position. The huge, thick mooring ropes were removed and the anchor raised, the huge metal links clanging noisily as it rose from the seabed. Slowly the ship began to drift away from her birth, heading for open waters. Penny waved until her arms ached, hoping Jack had noticed her amidst the crowds. The decks were so crowded it was impossible to distinguish one person from another. She turned away, shoulders slumped in defeat. She would see him in December, she consoled herself. She would have to be content with that.

The crowd began to disperse. As she made her way despondently to the bus terminal, she whirled round at the sound of someone shouting her name.

'*Dad!*' Her mouth fell open in shock to see Jack pushing his way through the thinning crowd towards her.

'Dad!' She squealed, oblivious to passers-by as she flung

herself into his arms. 'What are you doing here?' she gasped. 'You're supposed to be ... Your ship ...' The ship's horn blared across the water and Penny frowned, glancing over Jack's shoulder. 'Where's Jennette?'

'Onboard with Deon.' He rubbed his hand across his face. 'It would never have worked.' He looked at the ground, and sighed. 'Jennette was more honest with herself than I was. She realized our marriage was a mistake and that she deserved better.'

He held Penny at arm's length, looking deep into her eyes, which were a mirror image of his own.

'The truth is, Penny, I'm still in love with your mum. I always will be.'

Ellie-May filled the kettle and set it on the hob.

'Will you have a cup of tea, Dad?' she asked Sid, who was seated in front of the fire, working on the crossword.

'I will, thank you.' He glanced up at the clock. 'Shouldn't our Penny be back by now? It's an hour since Jack sailed.'

Ellie-May nodded. She had been determined not to think about Jack going away and had spent the day tackling various household chores. She'd prepared a potato pie for their supper. It was cooling on the side. Penny would be staying the night and Ellie-May had already placed the flat iron in the bed. Once the sun went down, leeching the warmth out of the early autumn air, it would be chilly upstairs.

The clock on the mantelpiece in the parlour chimed the hour just as the kettle came to the boil, a cloud of steam forming droplets as it hit the window. She had just made the tea and set the pot on the table when she heard the front door.

'That'll be her now,' she said, wiping her hands on her apron and going through to the porch. 'Hello, love. Are you all right?'

Penny grinned. 'Hello, Mum. I lost my hat and broke my shoe,' she laughed, kicking off her shoes. 'I'll go in and say hello to Grandpa.' Her eyes twinkled with mischief. 'There's someone here to see you, by the way.'

'Who?' she asked, as Penny pushed passed her to the kitchen.

'Hello, El.' Jack stood in the doorway, leaning on his stick, his hair curling along the collar of his jacket, his broad smile crinkling the skin around his dark eyes.

'Jack!' Ellie-May pressed herself against the wall, suddenly afraid her knees might give way. 'I thought . . .' She swallowed. 'Why are you here?'

'Do you really need to ask me that?'

Ellie-May glanced over his shoulder, her gaze puzzled. 'Where's Jennette?'

Jack sighed, his eyes a dark pool of shame and regret. 'She's asked me for a divorce.'

'Oh, Jack, why?'

His eyes never leaving her face, he held out his arm.

'Take a walk with me?'

After the briefest hesitation, she stuck her head around the kitchen door.

'I'm popping out for a minute. I won't be long.'

456

Jack waited while she changed her shoes and put on her coat, fumbling with the buttons.

Arm in arm, they walked down Church Street, their footsteps echoing in the late afternoon quiet.

'This takes me back,' Jack said. 'Remember when we were kids? We knew these streets like the back of our hands.'

'They were good times, Jack,' Ellie-May said with a smile. They turned the corner and crossed the street, Jack leading the way, as he had always done. The smile on Ellie-May's face broadened as she realized where they were headed.

The tide was out and the mud glistened in the grey light. Gulls pecked at the flotsam and jetsam left behind by the tide, or wheeled overhead, their mournful cries echoing out over the oily grey waters. The docks had been hit hard during the bombing raids and evidence of the devastation was everywhere from the ruined warehouses to the half-submerged boats. Cameron's Shipyard, where Sid had worked, Baker's Wharf – they were nothing but empty shells.

Slipping her arm from Jack's, Ellie-May walked to the water's edge, staring out over the Channel. Jack came to stand beside her.

'Do you remember when we used to come down here?' she said. 'Scavenging for things to sell to the rag 'n' bone man? I was terrified of him.' She turned to smile at him. 'You were so brave.'

'Desperate, more like,' Jack said. 'I was petrified of him. I just didn't show it. If I couldn't persuade him to give me a decent price for our junk, Ma and I wouldn't eat.'

'Well, to me you were the bravest person on the planet. You were my best friend, Jack. My soulmate.'

'Oh, El.' Jack breathed. He took her by the shoulders, looking into her eyes so deeply, Ellie-May was sure he could see right down into her soul. 'I have loved you all my life. I don't think a day has gone by where I haven't thought of you. I tried, El, God knows I tried so hard to convince myself I could forget you; that I could move on. I truly believed Jennette and I could make a go of it, and if she'd wanted to stick it out then, by God, I would have done my damnedest to make our marriage work. I'm sorry for what happened between me and Jennette, I am. She deserves a man who truly loves her. It's you I want, El. It's always, only ever, been you. You're the woman I want to spend the rest of my life with.'

A cool wind blew in off the Channel, ruffling the grey waters.

'I never stopped loving you, either, Jack,' Ellie-May said, reaching up to stroke his cheek.

'My darling, El,' Jack said hoarsely. He got down clumsily on one knee, gripping his stick in an effort to keep his balance.

'Jack,' Ellie-May protested, laughing. 'Your trousers will be covered in mud.'

'They'll wash. My dearest El,' he said, smiling up at her. 'When I'm free, would you marry me?'

Her reply caught in her throat and all she could do was nod. Tears of joy sparkling on her lashes, she helped him up, and flung her arms around his neck. His hungry lips found hers and, in that moment, it was as if time stood still and they were fourteen again, life with all its hopes and dreams, stretching endlessly before them.

EPILOGUE

1953

Jack killed the engine and he and Ellie-May sat looking up at the imposing Victorian manor house. The many mullioned windows reflected the clouds scudding across the June sky.

'How are you feeling?' Ellie-May laid a reassuring hand on Jack's thigh.

'Nervous,' Jack laughed. 'Ridiculous, really, at my age.'

She smiled at him. After seven years of marriage, their love for each other had only grown stronger with each passing year.

'You don't have to see her, you know? We can just turn the car around and go home.'

'And have Penny give me merry hell?' Jack massaged his temples, his gaze taking in the ivy-clad walls and ornate balustrade of the building that had been his mother's home for over forty years. He raised her hand to his lips. 'All these years she let me believe she was dead. Why? That's what I

460

can't understand. Why would she do that?' He demanded angrily, throwing up his hand in disgust. 'Why would any mother do that?'

'I don't know, Jack,' Ellie-May replied softly. 'That's why Penny feels it's important you talk to Verity.'

'I don't know.' Jack grimaced, running his hand over his face. 'Sometimes I wish Penny had never seen that blessed article.'

Penny had come across the article quite by chance. Heavily pregnant with her third child, she had been at the clinic awaiting her antenatal appointment and just happened to pick up a copy of the *Echo* someone had left behind. The article had been tucked away on page three and she would have glossed right over it, had not the name Farquharson caught her eye. She had turned up at her parents' house, just down the lane from Wayside, breathless with excitement.

'Do you remember all that talk about Lord Farquharson being Jack's grandad?' she said, unfolding the torn-out article in her mother's sun-drenched kitchen. 'Read this.'

Ellie-May slipped her reading glasses from her apron pocket and took the piece of crumpled newspaper from Penny.

'LORD FARQUHARSON DIES IN HOUSE FIRE TRAGEDY,' she read aloud.

'"Lord Angus Farquharson, aged 99, has died following a fire at his stately home in Romsey, Hampshire. The tragedy happened on June 2 while the country was celebrating the coronation and is believed to have started in the kitchen.

'"Lord Farquharson, who has been bedridden for several

years, became trapped in an upstairs bedroom, having given his staff the day off to enjoy the festivities. By the time the fire brigade arrived the flames had taken a firm hold and it was some time before they were able to enter the building" – oh dear, how horrible.' Ellie-May peered over her glasses.

'Read on, Mum.' Penny said, flopping heavily into a chair and kicking off her shoes.

'"Lord Farquharson's body was discovered later that afternoon ..." Oh, poor man. "He leaves one daughter, Verity" ... *Oh my God!* "Miss Farquharson, age 77, and who goes by the name Pickup, suffers from severe nerves and is a long-term resident of the Malcomess Nursing Home." *Oh, my God,*' she said again, meeting Penny's gaze. 'Verity Pickup. Jack's mother, she's alive.'

Now, sitting in the car some three weeks later, she squeezed Jack's hand. He licked his dry lips and tried to swallow. He took a shuddering breath, feeling like a ten-year-old boy again, and unclipped his seatbelt. 'Let's get this over with.'

The crunch of their footsteps sounded loud in the tranquil stillness as they made their way up the steps and rang the bell. The broad oak door was opened a few minutes later by a tall, elegant-looking woman with neatly coiffed grey hair. Blue eyes smiled behind tortoiseshell glasses.

'Good morning. Miss Harper?' Jack cleared his throat. 'Jack Pickup, we spoke on the telephone last week?'

'Yes, good morning Mr Pickup, Mrs Pickup. Please, come this way, Verity is expecting you.'

Jack gripped Ellie-May's hand tightly as they followed her along a drab corridor, her heels clicking on the faded linoleum.

'Your mother preferred to see you in the privacy of her own room,' Miss Harper said as they passed a small sitting room where a few residents sat in disinterested silence, and up a flight of stairs. She paused outside a plain white door and, knocking softly, turned the knob, poking her head into the room. 'Verity, dear, your son and his wife are here.'

Ellie-May heard a muffled response and Miss Harper pushed the door open, standing aside to allow them to enter.

Verity had been sitting in a wingback chair, but now she got to her feet. She was slight, smaller than Ellie-May remembered, and her skin was like parchment, the lines on her face telling a story of heartache and loneliness. She wore a plaid skirt and dark green jumper. Her once-beautiful wheat-blonde hair was almost completely grey. Her black-framed glasses seemed too large for her face, yet her nervous smile was exactly as Ellie-May remembered.

'Ellie-May,' Verity said, her voice quivering. 'You haven't altered much.'

'It's good to see you, Verity.' Verity gave Ellie-May a perfunctory hug, her gaze darting nervously from Ellie-May to Jack.

'Mother,' Jack said hollowly. Verity breathed his name and held out her arms. After the briefest hesitation, Jack stepped into her embrace, tears running unashamedly down his cheeks as he wept.

'Oh, my boy, my precious boy,' Verity crooned, patting his shoulder. 'It's all right. Everything's all right.'

Her own eyes wet with tears, Ellie-May and Jack helped Verity into her chair, and settled themselves on the narrow bed.

'I don't understand,' Jack said, blowing his nose. 'Why did you let me think you were dead? Why would you be so cruel? I was ten years old, Ma, *ten*! Do you have any concept of what I went through?'

'Jack.' Verity reached for his hand. 'I'm so sorry. I didn't know. It was only years later that my father told me.' She shuddered. 'I told him that one day you'd come looking for me. The look on his face, the memory of it chills me even now. He laughed, Jack. He actually found it amusing when he said I shouldn't set my hopes on you, that as far as you were concerned, I was dead. Oh, Jack, I would never have left you there, I swear. I begged my father, begged him to take you too, but he wouldn't listen.' Tears wend their way along the creases of her face. Ellie-May wiped her eyes. 'In the end they had to drag me out screaming. I never wanted to leave you, Jack, never! You must believe me.'

'So why didn't you try and find me? Why didn't you come back for me?' Jack got to his feet, pacing the small room in agitation. The window overlooked the grounds, flowerbeds in bloom, leafy horse chestnuts and grand oaks.

'The day after he took me out of the workhouse,' Verity said earnestly, her red-rimmed eyes begging Jack to understand, 'my father brought me here. I've effectively been a prisoner here ever since.'

'But how is that possible?' demanded Jack. 'How has he managed to keep you here all these years? You're a grown woman, you could have walked out.'

'Jack, your grandfather was a manipulative, controlling man. He managed to persuade the doctors that I was suffering from my nerves and had me put away. I did manage to escape once, years ago, and I went to the workhouse, but it had closed down. I was going to find my way back to Church Street, I figured Eileen would know how to get hold of you.' She gave Ellie-May a wry smile. 'Thick as thieves, you two were. I reckoned that wherever you were, my Jack would be nearby.'

'So, what happened?' asked Jack brusquely. He had ceased his pacing and was standing with his back to the room, gazing out over the sun-dappled lawn.

'Matron reported me missing. My father was paying a lot of money to keep me hidden away. She couldn't risk antagonising him. The police were called. I was about two streets away when they picked me up.'

Jack exhaled and rubbed his eyes. He was struggling to keep his composure. Ellie-May reached across and took Verity's hand in hers.

'You've had a terrible time,' she said softly.

Verity nodded. Her gaze dropped to her lap. 'My mother died when I was two,' she said, her voice little more than a whisper. Jack had to strain his ears to hear. 'Whether it was grief that made my father such a cruel-hearted man or whether he'd always been that way, I don't know. But I received no love or affection growing up, not until I met my Seamus.'

'Seamus?' Ellie-May queried, seeing how Verity's eyes lit up at the mention of the name.

'Seamus Pickup. Your father, Jack.'

'Pickup?' Jack turned, scratching his head. 'So, it's not a made-up name? I really am Jack Pickup?'

Verity smiled and nodded, her eyes misty. 'For some reason my father allowed Seamus's family to camp on our land. I was eighteen, he was twenty. And so handsome. We fell in love. We planned to elope, but somehow my father discovered our plans and . . .' Verity's eyes clouded. 'He chased Seamus's family off his land. I heard rumours that Seamus was beaten up.' She shook her head sadly. 'Whatever, they left and I never saw him again. A week or so later, I found out I was expecting and my father threw me out and told me never to darken his door again.' She wiped a stray tear from her cheek. 'I got as far as Southampton, found a job.' She smiled. 'Thanks to Eileen. A godsend your mum was, Ellie-May. I made ends meet by taking in washing, stuff like that.' She shrugged. 'You know the rest.'

'I could have helped you, Ma,' Jack said, hobbling over to where she sat, his expression ravaged by indescribable grief. 'If only I'd known, I would have come for you.'

Verity nodded. 'I'm so sorry, Jack.' She held out her hand to him. 'I wasn't a very good mother, I know that. But I loved you, and there isn't a day gone by that I haven't longed for you, my dearest, darling boy.'

Unable to keep his composure a moment more, Jack fell awkwardly to his knees. He clutched her gnarled hands in his, and sobbed.

A week later, as a light drizzle fell from a cheerless sky, Ellie-May helped Verity into the front passenger seat of the car while Jack loaded her luggage into the boot.

'Penny and her husband, Caleb, are waiting at ours with the kiddies,' Ellie-May was saying. 'They're dying to meet you.'

'I'm looking forward to meeting them too,' Verity said with a sigh. 'I'm very blessed, Ellie-May,' she said, patting her daughter-in-law's hand. 'To have a lovely granddaughter and two adorable great-grandchildren, very blessed indeed.'

'All being well, this time next week, you'll have great-grandchild number three to bounce on your knee,' Jack reminded her with a grin, getting into the driving seat.

Verity gripped his wrist as he put the key in the ignition. 'Are you both sure you want this?' she asked, her lips quivering. 'To have me living with you? I don't want to be a nuisance.'

In the back seat, Ellie-May gave a light-hearted chuckle. 'Verity, you won't be a nuisance. You'll be company for my dad. Imagine all the memories you'll be able to share. And Penny and her family live just around the corner from us in Jack's old place.'

'And don't forget Ida,' Jack said, inserting the key and starting the engine. 'She's looking forward to meeting you.'

'As long as you're sure,' Verity said quietly.

Jack looked her straight in the eye. 'I'm as sure as I've been about anything,' he said. 'You're coming home, where you belong.' Jack caught Ellie-May's smile in the rear-view mirror, and his heart swelled. Penny and her family were waiting for him at home, he was married to the love of his life, and now, reunited with his mother, he finally felt he was where he belonged.

He squeezed Verity's hand and said: 'Right, Ma, let's go home.'

ACKNOWLEDGEMENTS

Firstly, huge thanks to my agent, Judith Murdoch, for taking me on. Thank you so much for all your support, encouragement and advice over the last three years. Secondly, thank you to the staff at Simon & Schuster UK Ltd, especially my editor, Rebecca Farrell. Your enthusiasm over Jack and Ellie-May's story has been overwhelming. Thank you for guiding and encouraging me to make their story the best it can be. Thanks, also, to Paul Simpson, for your brilliant copy-editing and for correcting my historical errors.

Thank you to my parents, Anne and Keith, my children, Warren, Melanie and Rob, my stepsons, Mark and Gareth, who converted my first draft from Open Office to Word, and their families. Your support has been heartwarming. To my husband, John. Thank you for your endless support, encouragement and patience, and for all the cups of tea. I love you.

Finally, thank you to my grandparents, William, May, Georgina and Gerald. Your memories of life during the first half of the twentieth century kept me enthralled for hours and fostered an enduring love of social history. I miss you all.